The Wapping Conspiracy

Tom Wareham

Copyright © 2014 Tom Wareham

All rights reserved.

ISBN: 1505819555
ISBN-978-1505819557

DEDICATION

With special thanks to Chris for all her support, suggestions and time.

Prologue

Under a blanket grey sky the dusk was settling slowly across the river, the waters slowing to a sluggish heave like a giant animal gasping its last as the flood-tide eased towards slack water. To the west the sky seemed darker, heavier, as the wind began to die and the thick cloying smoke of London's thousands of chimneys thickened over the rooftops. Across the wide breadth of the Thames opposite Greenwich the low flat marshes of the Isle of Dogs slowly turned from green to grey to purple. A light flickered briefly somewhere there in the darkness and then fluttered out like a lost moth.

To the north east, where the river turned at Blackwall, the tall masts of the East India Company's ships were still visible, the yards fore-shortening as the hulls began to swing away from the tide. There were lanterns moving there, perhaps as valuable silks and spices were secured for the night, ready for the barges that would come back for them at dawn.

Beside the river at Greenwich there were lights. Voices rang in the narrow passages that threaded between old houses down to the waters' edge. Lights in windows and the first bouts of shouting laughter in the town's taverns. Along the river's edge several dozen double ended peterboats were bobbing slowly as the last fishermen hauled in their nets or sculled themselves back to the shore. Timing was important. Within the hour the water would begin to ebb away leaving long stretches of stinking grey-black ooze to wade through. Now though, the water lapped in little ripples against timber wharves and revetments.

There was little time or attention for a small grey brig that drifted up on the last flush of the tide. It was just one of the hundreds of ships that had passed Greenwich that day, beating their way ponderously up against the prevailing south-westerly's on their way to the crowded mooring tiers below London Bridge. It had taken this ship an inordinately long time to get to Greenwich from Gravesend where she had arrived the night before, slipping in under cover of darkness.

Had he spared the time to linger by the river for a while to watch her carefully, a knowledgeable observer might have wondered about her. An observer might have noticed that this brig, with her two masts and stained canvas topsails, looked well-travelled. Her timbers were grey with wear and sparkled with long ingrained sea salt. Her ropes looked soft, well handled by men and storms until some of them looked wispy in places and suspiciously on the verge of fraying. There was no bright paintwork on her figurehead or stern galleries and even her name seemed to have faded to ghostly letters. A knowledgeable observer might have glanced curiously at the tanned men hung over the yards, packing the courses into tight rolls, while over their heads the topsails billowed gently to the roll of the ship.

River people were used to ships and men. They were used to merchantmen with their sparse crews, men worked hard by ship owners anxious to keep their costs down. But this ship had a tiny crew. It was hard to see more than twelve men on board, unless one added the two African boys who leant against the gunwales near the stern, close to a tall man with a hooked nose and fierce gaze. As they passed Greenwich the tall man barked a *sharp order and the two youths padded out of sight. A really knowledgeable observer, had he spent his time watching this ship, might have found himself wondering whether she really was intent on making it up the river. Her progress during the day had been surprisingly slow. Her sails not quite sheeted home and her yards not well set – at least not in a way that would give a seaman pride in the exhibition of his skills. That observer might well wonder on the professionalism of her crew, might puzzle about her Master and how serious he was about making the Pool before darkness settled on the river. At best, a river man might have said, she might pass Limehouse, but as to the Pool, it wasn't likely.*

But along the river no-one wondered about her. Eyes might have glanced briefly over her before settling to other business, but she was unremarkable and there were more important things. So, in the last light of the ending day, the brig ghosted her way up the river, silent but for the odd creak of timber and tightening rope, and soft slap of her topsails. Soon there was just darkness, peppered here and there by pinpricks of light, and the surprised calls of the gulls and terns as they wheeled up the river, circling and delaying as they waited for the river to slip back from the stinking mud, and for the turning tide to bring the first of the detritus of the City down-river once again.

Soon even the grey gulls had fallen silently and there was just the perpetual modest lap of ripples washing over the soft ooze, and the gentle sighing of a wind.

The cab was purring its way slowly forward in the semi-darkness. Its wheels rumbling in an alarming fashion over the ancient cobbles and paves of Wapping. There were few street lamps. Along the road the night seemed deeper and darker, as it threaded itself like a chasm between the tall, blackened brick walls of warehouses and docks. Such few street lamps as existed threw a weak yellow orb of light a few feet, but no further. Although there was no wind, those glowing balls created a strange illusion, seeming to hover slowly up and down fifteen feet above the ground. The light they emitted was sufficient to cast a faint glow on the blackened brickwork next to them, throwing deeper shadow behind the heavy barbed bars of the iron grilles over the blind windows of the old warehouses or glimmering slightly against the damp black paintwork of the ancient wooden loophole doors. But those brick walls rose ever higher, their tops vanishing in the darkness – but not total darkness. For just above the amber yellow glow of the lights a ghostly mistiness was forming in the air. The temperature was falling and with it one of London's infamous lung-wracking fogs was forming.

Nobody moved. There was no life, not a cat nor a rat. Even the river's flying scavengers had settled for the night, squatting like stones on acres and acres of soft mud, pecking and padding silently, selfishly for food. Only the river itself seemed to have any intent or purpose and it was going about its own business quietly, unconcerned with the affairs of men or ships or cautious London taxi cabs. For the cab that crept its way past the fortress-like wall of the London Dock was moving cautiously indeed. During the day it would have been difficult to move at all through this narrow labyrinth. Horses and carts, lorries, porters with barrows and trucks all loaded with sacks, crates, barrels and chests. All jostling and whistling and shouting and jockeying for room to move as they manhandled the immense quantity of the cargo of the busiest port in the world. Hundreds and thousands of dock and wharf-workers, carters and messengers, lightermen and stevedores, drivers and clerks laboured or pushed in the narrow riverside areas of Limehouse and Shadwell and Wapping. Many among them were transients. Casual unskilled men hoping for work, treading their way from the St Katherine Dock by the *brooding Tower, to the London Dock or West India Dock, hoping to be near the front of the crowd when labour was called on each day. Wind and rain made no difference to them. They needed money and they needed work, anything would do. But it was getting harder, for this was the 1930s and the country was in the deep vale of economic depression. And despite the enormous wealth represented by the cargoes safely locked in the vast warehouses of the port, there was unemployment, poverty and hardship, especially here in the old East End.*

But now it was night and all that had gone for a few hours. The streets of the Thames riverside turned into a different world. Over above Limehouse, there were pink lanterns in windows and men moved along the pavement softly, for this was Chinatown, with its exotic restaurants and gaming houses. Earlier these few streets had resounded sporadically to the pounding of feet as children ran down Pennyfields or Limehouse Causeway for a dare, laughing hysterically and thumping each other on the back as they reached the safety of Narrow Street or the West India Dock Road. But those boys had been called in to bedtime hours since. Now occasional cars creaked to a halt as the more adventurous young things from the affluent West End found their way to China Town in search of the exotic and risqué – a meal in a real Chinese restaurant or a drink in the infamous Charlie Brown's pub, where cocaine and marijuana came cheaper from ships newly arrived in the West India Dock.

But further west, here at Wapping, there was no such attraction. The warehouses were dark and silent and threatening and, as though sensing this, the cab moved forward reluctantly like a pet dog unwilling to face the cold night of its evening walk. In the glimmer of the headlights a round fat face under a flat cap could be seen peering through the windscreen, glancing anxiously to left and right and stopping every now and then to address a passenger in the back. For there was a passenger there. The glow of a cigarette flushed his face with orange light. A thin face glimpsed momentarily as though caught in the distant flash of a far thrown lighthouse. A long thin face with matching nose and neat, thin, black pencil moustache. After a while he too began casting impatient glances to either side. Dropping the window at his side he thrust a broad brimmed hat through the gap, and barked a single word, 'Here!'

The cab stopped. There was a lengthy exchange of words. Shaking of heads. Voices were raised, but then as though alarmed by the echo that bounced back at them within this cavern of commerce, the voices became quieter, calmer again. Sentences shrank to single words barked abruptly. After several moments there was a rustle of crisp paper and notes changed hands. The back door opened and the passenger unfolded himself from the cab. Tall and thin, the man spread limbs apparently cramped by their confinement, and stretched. He looked bizarrely out of place – garbed in a flamboyant white suit and cape, all matching the extravagant fedora. He gesticulated along the road with a cigarette holder and abruptly stepped back. There was a reluctant grunt from the cabby and with a clatter he put the taxi into reverse gear and executed a ragged three-point turn in the narrow thoroughfare until he was facing the opposite way. He glanced quickly at the man in the white suit, a glance filled with hatred, and turned off the engine.

The man nodded once and with a flurry of the cape, turned and began walking along the road. Around him the air thickened and he shuddered against the sudden chill. The fog became deeper and he was suddenly lost to the view of the cabby. His footsteps too suddenly stopped. The cabby watched him go and shrugged to himself. Then he shut the cab window and carefully rolled himself a cigarette.

Further down the road the man in the white coat was

feeling his way cautiously. His movements were wary and whenever an opening yawned in the wall beside him he stopped, listening before stepping forward quickly past the deep shadow. Every now and then he stopped, cocking his head in a curiously bird-like manner which the hat exaggerated slightly. But there was nothing in his movements to suggest fear. Indeed there was something eager, impatient about him. He continued along the road until he became aware of a muffled sound up ahead. His steps quickened. There was a faint glow beside the road ahead.

The fog had now thickened so that it felt like a cold velvet glove clutching at the throat and pushing thick fingers into the nostrils. Chill drops were collecting on the man's moustache and eyebrows. He wiped them quickly with a gloved hand and moisture trickled into his eyes. He glanced up suddenly and saw over the pavement a dark square of wood suspended from a bar. It was too dark to see clearly, but underneath it a window gave a rose glow to the mist. There was a sudden shout of laughter and noise as a door was roughly pushed open. Light fell into the mist and a thick shadowy figure stumbled through onto the pavement. He stood swaying noticeably while he pulled a scarf closer round his neck. Then he turned and saw the pale suited figure standing behind him.

'Jee-sus Christ! 'oo the fuck are you!'

Then without waiting for a reply he turned and staggered off into the mist leaving a waft of hops and tobacco behind him in the damp air. The man in the white suit paused briefly, put a hand on the brass lever of the door handle and pushed. The hubbub within withered into a falling silence, then there was a single peal of nervous feminine laughter, and a gruff voice.

'You Palmer?' He stepped inside.

1. **An Incident East of Greenwich.**

Joycey was wearing black. He always wore black. Once it had been fashionable, but now it was just habit, and like most old habits it was comfortable. And once it had been jet black too, but now it was just a smoky slate. The jeans, tee shirt and leather jacket were soft with age, and the deep pockets of the jacket sagged like an old man's eyes. One of them now, was stuffed with a rolled newspaper, evidencing the casual care which he applied to his possessions. All of them. Almost unconsciously he adjusted his small wire glasses and glanced sideways at his own reflection as he strode past the large plate window of the posh Chinese in Nelson Road. He liked what he saw. His collar length hair was still mainly black, though streaks of grey had recently thrust their way through the curls around the ears. At first this had disconcerted him, but by accident he had discovered that a liberal coating of wet-look gel disguised this weakness. In a strange way the gel gave him more of a Romany look than before, and this, with the addition of a single earring completed a look which he thought fulfilling.

It was 9.15 in the morning and the heavy flow of rush-hour traffic was still pouring westwards through the bottle neck of the Greenwich one-way system. Angry faces peered through windscreens, fingers pattering or clenching steering wheels, angry horns, he had seen it all before, every morning, for twenty years. It was all somehow reassuring, just like the heavy staleness of the air on the pavement. He strode on, crossing King William Walk, past the subterranean conveniences where the rent boys waited in the evening, and carried on eastwards, passing the long iron-railed stretch of road between the old Royal Naval College and the Maritime Museum. On the lampposts overhead gaudy new plastic banners floated reminding travellers of the borough's Royal status. It was the area's sole legacy from the London Olympics, and now served only to rankle those who bothered to think about it. Outside the maritime museum an expensive new sign was being mounted to the railings. He stopped to watch as the workmen finished and peeled away the protective film. Joycey snorted and muttered aloud,

'Fucking Hell.'

The maritime museum had also been promoted. It now read 'Royal Museums Greenwich'. The workmen had heard Joycey's outburst, and they turned to look at him, perplexed. He looked back at them, pointedly.

'What is it?' he asked. 'Everyone wants to be fucking royalty nowadays?'

The men grinned, shrugged, and bent to gather their tools.

Shaking his head, Joycey strode on. It was all a joke, he thought to himself. Greenwich was still Greenwich. It was no more royal now than it had been before the Olympics. And what had changed about the maritime museum? It was still the same place, still full of the same old stuff. It was all airs and graces. Waste of time.

Half way along what was now Romney Road, he crossed over to walk on the north side, passing the broad courtyard of the old Royal Naval College with its neo-classical colonnades and heavy hanging lanterns. The broad grassy lawn between the buildings was busy with men and equipment this morning, young women with clipboards, headphones. Rails were being laid. Another period film. One day, he thought to himself, one day people were going to get bored with seeing the same old location in every film that came out. Joycey was grumpy this morning. He needed his coffee.

Eastward of the Royal Naval College and the maritime museum, Greenwich changed abruptly. The hordes of tourists who strolled ambivalently along the narrow pavements around the one-way system, or who collected hesitantly around the *Cutty Sark* never ventured into East Greenwich.

Where Greenwich was affluent and oozed a holiday atmosphere, its eastern partner was poor and decayed, its shops offering a dusty range of cheaper wares. Its burger bars and fast food takeaways were unbranded imitations of those in Greenwich. Its residents were poorer, older, as depressed as the area in which they lived. Nobody monitored the atmospheric pollution along the Trafalgar Road or safeguarded the facades of the Georgian buildings that had long since been converted to shops. Nobody was employed to sweep the cluttered gutters, and the few litter bins were crumpled and scarred by closing-time fires.

Signs of demarcation were evident even within East Greenwich. Behind the south side of the Trafalgar Road, there were tidy roads of Edwardian terraces, neat little gardens and faultless paintwork, but even these were interspersed with the brutal concrete structures of 1960s council flats. To the north of the road, the terraces were older, lacking the breathing space of the little gardens. Paintwork was blistering and windows often blinded by smoke-stained curtains of grubby net. The council blocks here were also older; 1930's LCC red-brick structures, though they still wore the same tawdry despair as those south of the road. The balcony walkways were festooned with lines of washing, and overflowing paladins, surrounded by dogs, lurked menacingly on the oil stained tarmac at the foot of the stairways.

Joycey strode on, passing the cheap gift shops, the Caribbean restaurant and pizza house, and the plumbers discount supplies shop, past the corner shop with the poster plastered windows, which sold everything from cheap alcohol to wilting carrots and dodgy cigarettes. He crossed two side-roads and pushed open the door of Kazim's café.

Kazim's was another habit. Kazim did the best espresso in Greenwich and Joycey liked his coffee dark - with poke. Kazim was Turkish, and his coffee was a fusion of strong Americano and Turkish silt. For twenty years Joycey had relied on it for his morning boost, and this morning was no exception.

The café was busy, as it usually was. There were five tables topped with imitation pine formica down the right hand wall, and four more and a games machine down the left. At the back of the café stood the obligatory glass fronted counter full of suspicious looking gateau and made-up rolls in cling-film. Kazim, himself stood behind the counter, a greying grizzle haired man of middle-age in a fading Addicks teeshirt. He smiled at Joycey, made up the required coffee without being asked, and scooped up the coins which were placed onto the glass counter with a series of sharp clicks.

All of the tables were occupied and all by men wearing what was patently work clothing. There were empty chairs at two tables. At one of them sat a man who was gazing vacantly through the steamed window, hungrily stuffing a sausage baguette into his mouth. The other was dominated by an excessively overweight man dressed in a grubby shirt and jacket. He had forced himself uncomfortably into the limited space between the table and the fixed chairs. His belly hung over the table and one leg, clad in a baggy grey tracksuit was thrust out to one side. He was leaning over, peering at a copy of the *Sun* and sipping noisily at a large glass teacup. Joycey slid into the space on the other side of the table, recoiling slightly at the stale smell of sweat and unwashed clothes.

'Morning Dusty. How's things?'

Dusty pulled a face, grunted and shrugged.

Joycey laughed. 'Anything for me?'

The large man sighed and straightened up as much as he was able, cranking his head round as far as he could to silently order another tea from Kazim. His podgy fingers flexed on the table top and he turned back with a sigh.

'Dunno mate, maybe later.'

Joycey nodded and smiled encouragingly, but Dusty was already leaning towards his page three girl. Joycey fixed his smile and sipped at his coffee. He could ignore Dusty's manner, and indeed his rank odour, because Dusty was useful. In fact he was one of the numerous useful people one could find in Kazim's at different times of the day. People who might have something they wanted to sell. Something they wanted to sell quietly, or quickly. It was a useful place, anonymous and undisturbed. Dusty's business was house clearances. He and his equally large son stripped the houses of dead people for a fee, and they made a healthy living out of it, sorting what they found and dividing it between the local auction rooms, antique dealers, second hand junk-shops and local tip. Joycey suspected that some of Dusty's rejects even ended up dumped in untidy heaps around the Kidbrooke estate in the middle of the night, but he kept these suspicions to himself.

Joycey's business was books. Second-hand. Even some antiquarian stuff if he could get it cheap and it looked interesting. He had also extended his range to include old maps and manuscripts, mainly because such things had been offered to him more and more over the years, and it seemed too good an opportunity to pass up. Dusty got lots of books, though most of them were worthless paperbacks, Mills & Boon romances and the like, which just didn't sell. But every now and again Dusty and his son got to clear the house of a more discerning reader, and then the gleanings could be worthwhile.

Then there were other sellers who would come to Kazim's in the expectation of finding him. That was one of the good things about Kazim's. It was discrete. The regulars were careful, cautious. Someone who asked too many questions was likely to leave quickly, disappointed. But mostly they were people who had something to sell, people who also didn't want to have to answer too many questions. And Joycey didn't often ask questions. He could sense when it was useful to press for more information or not. Often there was a silent furtive exchange of cash and goods, a deal which concluded without eye contact and with a hurried parting, with no looking back.

Once he had wondered about the legality of it all, but morality had changed long ago. The Tories had seen to that long before he started in the trade. Now, those who lived on the lower rungs had to do what they could with what resources they had. Survival meant thriving in the environment in which you existed. And East Greenwich lay under the long unethical shadows of the banking towers just across the river at Canary Wharf.

Joycey finished his coffee and left Dusty to his own thoughts. Five minutes later he turned into a side road and walked towards a small shop with a hand painted sign over its door and single window. The sign said 'Eastside Books' –

Joycey's ambiguous reference to the building's location east of the Greenwich Meridian. He stopped for a few seconds to peer at the window, where a selection of books had been laid out on angled wooden shelves. The covers of some of them were beginning to fade and he made a mental note to change the selection. Then he pushed open the door.

2. Marik and Takk

Sitting behind the small counter just inside the door was a stocky man in his mid-thirties with short-cropped blonde hair. He looked up as Joycey entered and his open, rather boyish expression was transformed by a broad grin that expressed genuine pleasure.

' Morning boss.'

'OK Marik, everything ok?'

Marik's reply was shaped by a Polish accent. Although his English was not unreasonable, he had always had a habit of dropping words here and there, and those he did use were presented a little too precisely.

'Oh sure. I open a little early to clear boxes.'

Joycey peered into the shop, which was deceptively much deeper than its narrow frontage suggested. Beyond the rectangular space lined with bookshelves at the front of the shop, a long corridor led towards the back of the building through a large space filled with ranks of yet more book cases. A few cardboard boxes still sat at various places on the bare floorboards, but Marik had obviously been hard at work. Joycey was impressed and nodded appreciatively.

'Good Marik, that's good. I saw Dusty round at Kazim's. But I'm not sure if he will be in later or not.'

Marik looked solemn for a moment and nodded thoughtfully. Joycey found himself wondering, not for the first time, whether in some way the Pole disapproved of Dusty and his business arrangements. But he let the thought go. Marik was entitled to his views. He just never said anything about them.

'And how was Sunday?'

For the past year they had taken it in turns to open the shop over the weekend, especially during the summer when there was just a little more chance of a stray tourist losing their sense of direction and stumbling across the shop. For, despite its dowdy, unfashionable location, Joycey had a good eye for his material, and callers were rarely disappointed at the books that were on offer. One noted collector had even sought the shop out following a tip-off about its first editions of English authors from the 1920s and 1930s – the contents of a loft in Blackheath cleared by another customer of Kazim's – and had declared the lot 'mouth-watering'. Joycey still enjoyed savoring the accolade and wished such moments were more frequent. Sadly, they weren't.

'Yes, Sunday was good. The sun shined.'

Joycey nodded as Marik dug in the drawer under the till and pulled out a small, stiff-covered note book. He handed it to Joycey with a jubilant smile. Joycey turned to the last page and scanned the list of titles and sums inscribed there, noting the underlined figure at the bottom of the column.

'A hundred and thirty quid! That's not bad.'

Marik nodded. They had both already calculated the small profit for the day.

Pinned on the wall behind the till were several plastic wallets containing maps and hand-written manuscripts. Joycey knew that most of them were old legal documents of relatively little value. But tourists were quite often taken – or taken in – by the exquisitely neat handwriting, and these were among some of his best-selling stock. But even Joycey knew a little bit about the need to conserve hand-written material. Now he inspected the documents carefully and pulled four of them from their mounts.

'These have had enough sun, I think Marik. We'd better change them round.'

Marik rose, and crossing the shop, pulled open one of a series of long shallow drawers in a wooden cabinet which sat in the centre of the shop. Joycey dropped onto the stool and watched him as he shuffled though a series of documents and then pulled one out. He leant forward squinting at it.

'Heh boss, how about this one, it looks nice.'

The blonde man laid the document on the cluttered counter and Joycey bent over it. It was an early-19th century title deed, with immaculate secretary hand lining its way across a heavy but lightly folded parchment. Pinned to the front was a small hand-coloured plan of a building, set within a plot of land. Joycey lifted the plan and squinted at the writing.

'Dartford. Yeah, that's not far away. See if you can find any more like that one. Look for Kent.'

Marik beamed. 'Kent. County of Kent, yes?'

Joycey nodded, already pressing the heavy parchment carefully so that it would slide into the plastic holder. Local documents always sold well, and if they had a plan attached, even better. Then, pulling a pencil and a square-cut slip of paper from a drawer, he thought for a moment, and then wrote '£40' on the paper before slipping it inside the plastic sleeve.

Marik was still rustling through the drawer. He gave a little exclamation of pleasure and nodded at Joycey. Joycey nodded back as Marik selected another document, and then another, laying them carefully on the books on top of the chest. When he had found enough he brought them over to the counter and presented them with a big grin. Joycey was reminded of a happy Labrador with a stick.

The documents were all fine copies and Joycey was quietly pleased. Marik was quickly developing a nose for what would catch the eye of a casual visitor to the shop. He was learning fast.

'Good Marik. These are very good. Can you put them up on the wall? I need another coffee.'

There was a small cupboard-like room at the rear of the shop, next to the musty smelling toilet, where they kept the basics for making tea and coffee. Now, as Joycey rose from behind the counter, Marik suddenly frowned and looked sheepish.

'Oh boss, I forgot.' He shifted from foot to foot, glancing nervously into the gloomier spaces between the book shelves along the corridor. 'She is in again.'

Joycey looked perplexed for a moment and then exclaimed, 'Again?' His voice rose in half protest. 'I...she...' His mouth worked but he fell silent. What was there to be said that he hadn't said before.

Marik chuckled. 'Yes boss, I know, but she's not harm you know.'

Joycey shook his head and snorted. Then he walked slowly down the corridor passing stack after stack of bookcases, all crammed with books. As he neared the back of the shop he paused, treading softly, and peered round the corner of a row of bookcases to his left.

She was exactly where he had expected to see her, where she always was, squatting on the floor with her legs crossed at the ankles. Unnoticed, he took a moment to inspect her, checking her clothing choice of the day, for it was always bizarre. This morning she was wearing a short grey skirt, which, because of her position, had risen a long way up thighs cased in thick black and white striped tights. Over this she wore a baggy, virtually shapeless red jumper which looked like it had been used as a sleeping bag at some point in its very long life. A blue leather bag on a long thin strap had been looped over her head and shoulder. A long grey woolen hat had been pulled over her head, though several strands of long dark hair had slipped from one side and hung like a curtain across her face. She brushed at this half-heartedly as she pored over a large book spread across her knees. He guessed she was in her early twenties, but he had long since abandoned the attempt to accurately assess the age of younger people.

'Blimey,' he quipped, stepping suddenly round the corner of the book case. 'You here again?'

The young woman glanced up at him briefly before turned back to the pages in front of her. 'Maybe I'm a ghost.'

'I should charge you rent.'

She snorted. 'I suppose that would be overpriced too.'

Joycey laughed. 'Cheeky, aren't you.'

She scowled sideways up at him for a moment, with dark eyes. Then she turned back to her book and mumbled, 'I speak my mind, mostly.'

For a moment Joycey was silent. The woman was

engrossed in whatever it was she had found and he instinctively felt that he could just creep away and leave her, and that she would still be there, sitting just like that, an hour later. It had been the same now for weeks. Every two or three days she had appeared in the shop, sometimes entering so quietly that she was unnoticed, especially if there were other customers about. Then he or Marik would find her, just there, on the floor, engrossed in a book. On two occasions they had nearly locked her in when they came to lock up in the evening. Marik had even turned the lights off on one occasion, and her sudden appearance from the gloom had spooked him severely. The Pole thought she was weird, and was obviously a little uneasy about her - but then, thought Joycey, he was a Catholic. He had come to the conclusion that she was a student from the nearby university. Since she continued to ignore him, he decided to test his theory.

'Haven't you got a lecture to go to or something?'

'Eleven o'clock,' she replied without turning from the page.

It was Joycey's turn to snort, though he did so sportingly.

'Tuh. Students. I don't know.'

'You don't know what?' she snapped back at him, a note of irritation sharpening her tone.

Her question threw him for a moment. He was being rhetorical, she was being literal. Now he decided to play the part a little further, to see what he could draw from her.

'Don't start til eleven, then I suppose it's in the pub all evening. Surprised you find time to do any work. When I was a student…..'

He was shocked suddenly by a vicious glare.

'This is reading time. If you were once a student you should understand the need for preparation.' Her fierce glare slid back to the page in front of her before she finished with; 'And you are interrupting it.'

Joycey felt suddenly irritated. 'This is a bookshop, we sell books...'

'So I gather.'

'So haven't you got a library to go to?'

She snorted. 'It's full of arseholes at this time in the morning and besides, your shelves are better stocked.'

As she turned her glare back to the book again, he swallowed the retort that had been forming on his lips, for he couldn't help smiling to himself. He was secretly rather flattered and decided to leave her in peace. Perhaps, he thought, she might end up buying a book just to spite him.

'Do you want a tea, coffee?' he asked suddenly. 'I'm making coffee.'

'Herbal,' she said without looking up.

'What?'

Her gaze swiveled from the page and gave him a pitying look. 'I only drink herbal.'

'Oh,' He turned away, then turned back. 'Tea's herbal isn't it?'

There was an angry sigh from the far end of the book cases and he turned away, defeated.

Five minutes later he walked back up the corridor holding

a mug and saw Marik hovering impatiently in the daylight by the shop door. The girl was still where he had left her, hunched over her book. Feeling slightly foolish, he paused and sipped at the hot liquid.

'Good book then?' he asked.

She straightened up, pressing the palms of her hands into her back and eyed him sideways. 'It's a key text.'

'Oh, good.' He replied limply. Marik's voice came from the front of the shop, calling him, so he turned to go. 'Well if you're going to be my tenant I should at least know your name.'

She shrugged. 'It's Takk'.

'Takk?'

'Takk.'

'Isn't that a children's ....'

Her glare sent him stumbling quickly away to where Marik was waiting with a customer.

3. A café referral

Dusty had nothing. He didn't say that he had nothing, he just didn't say anything, and Joycey just had to assume. Several times during that week he had seen the overweight house-clearer wedged into his usual spot at Kazim's, but since he never looked up from his newspaper, Joycey took the news as read. On the Friday though, he entered Kazim's later than usual to find the café unexpectedly empty. Behind the counter a thin, tired-looking woman by the name of Cheryl was spreading a yellow greasy-looking paste across the inside of a bread roll. She nodded at Joycey, making the hooped earrings in her prominent ears dance under her tightly drawn-back hair.

'Late, init, for you?' Her voice was as thin as she was.

'Yeah, Cheryl. A few too many last night. You know.'

She laughed, already making his usual espresso. 'Oh, it was like that, was it?'

Steam billowed around her as she turned to slide a mug onto the counter. He dropped coins into her hand and nodded.

'Feller been asking for you.' She said, opening the till.

'Oh yeah? Not Dusty?'

'No, young chap. Scruffy looking. Said Dusty had given him your name.'

'Say what he wanted?'

Cheryl shook her head, making the silver hoops waggle violently.

'Nah. I told him where yer shop was. He said he might try it, but might come back today, 'bout three.'

There was a clunk and the door to the café opened. A nervous looking man entered, glancing about him. Joycey could spot a stray tourist instantly. So could Cheryl. When she spoke again, her voice had softened, purring from a broad, welcoming smile.

'Hello Dear, what can I get you.'

Marik was sorting books on the floor. Joycey kept a store of books in a garage lock-up in a back street behind Deptford Creek. It wasn't very secure. In fact it had been broken into three times. But whoever broke in was clearly disappointed to find that their potential haul was just boxes of old books. Burglars in Deptford weren't really literary types, so nothing was ever taken, but Joycey took the precaution of not keeping any of his more pricey stock there anyway. Even so, every now and again he needed to pull out a few books when the shelves in the shop began to look a little thin. So on this particular morning he had fired up his battered van and deposited half a dozen slightly damp cardboard boxes on the shop floor. An odour of mould had gradually pervaded the shop.

Fridays were always quiet, so while Marik addressed

himself to the task of finding homes for all the books, Joycey smoked cigarettes and read through the local newspaper. It didn't take him long. It contained the usual ingredients of photographs of depressed-looking council tenants pointing to mouldy wallpaper or mug shots of men who had failed to turn up in court, reviews of the latest amateur dramatic offering in the community theatres in Eltham, and advertisements. He read it through twice and then, rolling it tightly, he dropped it into the rusty tin wastepaper bin behind the counter. One of these days, he thought, they would give up on news stories altogether, and just print adverts.

At lunch time, Joycey ambled his way to Kazim's again. A cold October wind had swung round to the north-east, and the temperature had fallen noticeably. Dressed in his habitual leather jacket, Joycey made no concessions to changes in the weather, preferring to ignore the effect that it had on him, or others. Even so, as he approached he noticed how the windows of the café were thickly steamed up, obscuring the view of the interior. It discomforted him a little, not knowing who would be in there before he opened the door. It wasn't unusual for a couple of the local uniformed to grab a break in there on colder days. Not that that worried him, particularly, it was just that he liked to be a little forewarned. Scanning the café as he entered, the only surprise was Takk sitting hunched over a tablet in one corner, an empty plate and cup pushed to one side in front of her. She was staring at a book which lay open on the table and didn't look up. He ordered a hot sausage roll and squirted a generous helping of tomato sauce inside it before sitting down on the opposite side of the room.

He ate quickly, savouring his lunch and trying to stare through the misted glass at the vague shapes and colours of the passing traffic. Kazim entered, nodded, and passed through to the back of the shop after exchanging a few words with Cheryl.

Then a gang of builders arrived noisily. They were dressed in the inevitable uniform of shapeless jogging pants, yellow boots and paint spattered hoodies. Like Joycey, they paid little regard to the temperature, though for different reasons, and no sooner had they entered the café than the volume of noise began to rise. As they stood jostling each other boisterously in front of the counter they noticed Takk, and began pointedly prodding one another and sniggering. Finally one of the younger ones took a step towards her and called out:

'Fancy a hot sausage love?'

There was an outburst of laughter but there was no response from the young woman. Her finger nails tapped on the little screen of the tablet. The young man called out again.

'Oy, you.'

There was no response. He tried again.

'Oy.'

Takk's concentration didn't falter. Her eyes flicked between printed page and the screen. There was a moment's awkward silence and then the builder, unexpectedly ignored, suddenly lost confidence. His bravado collapsed and he turned hurriedly to hide amidst the group of men, who began teasing him with mock sympathy. It didn't help. His embarrassment turned to frustration, and he could be heard muttering.

'Fuckin weirdo.......Lezzie I reckon anyway.'

Takk seemed oblivious, though for the briefest of moments Joycey thought he detected a ghost of a smile flicker across her lips.

Feeling unaccountably irritable, Joycey rose after a few minutes and made his way back to the shop. He was still feeling irritable when he arrived there and found that Marik had turned on the battered single-barred electric heater they kept under the counter. Now an odour of burning dust mingled with the fragrance of mould. It was not a pleasant mixture, and as soon as Marik had disappeared to have his lunch, he turned off the heater and sat listening to it ticking to itself. As the shop cooled down, he found himself getting even more irritable, as though the temperature was having a corresponding effect on his mood. A sort of thermal sliding scale. Then he realised why. There had not been a single customer all day. That meant no takings, and the rent was due at the end of the week. Furthermore, they were heading into winter, which meant fewer tourists, and therefore even fewer sales. He was not happy. He turned the electric heater back on grumpily, found the old tobacco tin which he used as an ashtray in one of the drawers and rolled a cigarette.

When Marik returned thirty minutes later, it was to find Joycey hunched over the crossword in the newspaper. The dictionary with the missing front cover was open on the desk beside him. The Pole smiled to himself.

'Turned cold boss, isn't it.'

Joycey grunted.

'They say rain to come, much. Storms and rain. Like last year, but more.'

Joycey grunted again and shrugged.

The door shuddered open and a young man in a reefer jacket walked in. Joycey pointed him to a set of shelves part way back into the shop and the man strolled unconvinced into the gloom.

'Let us know if you can't find what you want,' Joycey called out into the back room. 'We've got more books in our store.'

Marik returned to unpacking books and Joycey pored over the newspaper once again. Half an hour later, the young man returned to the counter with an armful of books and a big grin. Joycey found himself smiling.

'Found something then?'

'Yeah, quite a few actually. Just what I needed for the course. You know.'

Without looking inside the covers Joycey knew that the books weren't going to be expensive. They weren't. Ten books. Less than fifteen pounds. But then, he thought to himself, these were fairly cheap editions of fairly common books. The sort of books which could be got for the same price on Amazon, if you were prepared to swallow the hefty additional postage.

He dropped the books into an old carrier bag, and the notes exchanged hands. The man pulled open the door and stepped out. Just as he went to pull the door to behind him, another figure shouldered his way in. Joycey glanced up to find himself looking at a thin young man in a dirty looking denim jacket. He had a narrow face with a whispy beard and eyes that looked strained within deep eye sockets. The skin over his cheek bones looked pallid and unhealthy. The man glanced nervously round the shop, hesitated and then cleared his throat.

'You Joycey?'

Joycey looked him up and down, non-committedly. 'I might be. It depends on whose asking.'

The man looked anxious. 'Dusty. From the caff. He said to speak to you.'

'Oh yeah? And why did he say that?' Joycey had a feeling

that perhaps he was being a little too scratchy and defensive. He hadn't meant to be. It was just that the exchange had started on a particular course, set like the dialogue in a crime drama and, with his existing irritable humour, he didn't feel a strong inclination to make the effort to change direction.

The man was looking uncomfortable. He glanced desperately from side to side, and then seemed to take some comfort from the sight of Marik staggering towards some shelves with an armful of books. He glanced quickly back at Joycey and then looked out through the door of the shop, ducking his head to peer past the stickers and notices that obscured part of the glass. 'I've got something,' he mumbled.

The words 'Well don't give it to me,' nearly slipped from Joycey's lips but he managed to restrain himself. The man's estuarine accent did not make him any more attractive.

'Might be worth something, I think. I don't know. I was going to take it to the museum. But Dusty said to show you. Said you might be interested, like?'

Joycey made a mental note that he might need to thank Dusty. He stubbed out his cigarette. 'Well that depends. What sort of thing are we talking about?'

The man glanced around again and then patted his left breast. 'I got it here. It's a letter. A map. Could be very old. Could be worth something.'

4. A Stray Paper

The young man's eyes were mobile, and he shuffled nervously as he tapped the breast of his jacket. Joycey knew a guilty conscience when he saw it, but he just smiled thinly.

'Well what is it? A letter or a map?'

The man's expression changed to one of anguish. 'It's both. Look…'

Thrusting grimy fingers into one of the breast pockets of the jacket he began to tug clumsily at something. For several seconds he struggled impatiently. There was a short tearing sound which made Joycey wince momentarily, and then the man was pressing something down on the desk. It was a brown envelope, very crumpled and dirty.

Joycey sighed, glancing up at the man to make it clear that he was already disappointed, and leaned forward to slide his fingers inside the open end. He slowly pulled out a thick, folded yellow document.

'Thing is,' the man licked his lips. 'Is it worth anything? That's what I wanted to know really.'

Joycey said nothing. The document was stiff, mottled, and crackled under his fingers. He carefully eased open the folds, feeling the resistance of age. It was a small letter, about eight inches by five and contained about a dozen lines written in a small hand. The letters slanted to the right, though it was immediately apparent that the writer back-looped the upright of the letter 'd' with a noticeable backward flourish. At the top of the letter was a date. 29th April 1701.

Joycey squinted and lifted the paper to peer closely at the handwriting. Then with some difficulty, he read the following.

'Cous

Since it must be I am condemned to dye, I have writ his ldship this day and told him of what is to be offered if he will secure what I wish I am assured he will bee honble to this but as I doubt not some trickery might befall from other honble gentlemen known to you Whereof do you beg our friend H remove that we bt from the Old Mrcht in the woes If he cavilles show him this He will know all as we spoke thereof Doe not trust ye Dowgat man The silks you may take to the mercer in Cheapside the value thereof to have unto yrslf Wm'

He turned the paper over. The reverse contained what looked like a very crudely drawn map of what appeared to be an island, shaped rather like a grinning mouth. In the bottom left a cross had been inked in at a diagonal. The line pointing up to the top right corner of the page was topped with the letter 'N.' Joycey had lived in Greenwich long enough to recognise this as a compass mark. In the centre of the island little upright lines had been drawn around the word 'marshes'. Below the bottom edge of the 'grin', the words 'moorings' appeared several times with little anchors. A dotted line ran along the southern shore. Along the southwest shore were the words 'well' and 'sugar loaf.'

The young man was leaning forward, anxiously. 'Well, what do you think? Is it worth something? It's old isn't it, it must be worth something?'

Joycey laid it down on the desk. 'Well,' he hesitated, 'I don't know.'

The man's gaze was scanning his face, expressions of anxiety and suspicion alternating across his features.

'Thing is,' Joycey started, 'there's no name or address on the letter. The map looks a bit old, but it doesn't show very much and don't say where it is. And, well the letter…' he winced. 'Well, letter or whatever it is…' He shook his head dismissively.

The man's face fell.

Joycey felt a stab of sympathy. 'See if we had more about it, that might make a difference.'

The young man's mouth opened, but no words came out.

Joycey allowed a long silence to settle, then he said, 'If we knew where it came from that might help.'

The man looked even more anxious. Joycey leaned across the desk.

'Look, the thing is, I don't know what it is, and nobody's going to buy something if they can't put a name or place to it. See. They like to know what it is, what it might be about. A little bit of mystery may be a good thing, but this, this.' He waved his hand dismissively over the document, which had already folded itself up again.

The man gave a barely audible moan and Joycey felt a

vague pang of conscience. When he spoke again his voice had moderated into a slightly more sympathetic tone.

'Well. Where did you get it, then?'

Sweat was glistening on the man's forehead now.

'We been doing a job in Catford…some time ago,' he added hastily. 'For an old lady. She was selling the place and wanted her loft cleared out, so we got sent down there … There was loads of old books and paper. But we were told to put all the stuff in a skip and burn it. I thought it looked old, but the boss said not to bother, just to get rid of it. I saw this bit and kept it. Thought it might be worth something… you know.'

Joycey avoided the man's eyes. He'd heard the old-lady's-loft story many times before and knew better than to ask any further, but he also guessed there was some truth in the story.

'Catford?'

The man nodded slowly. Joycey thought quickly. Someone might buy it for the map. This was Greenwich and there was something vaguely maritime about it after all.

'I don't know…' he murmured, shaking his head again. 'Couldn't offer you much for it.'

The man had become agitated. He was glancing all too frequently out through the smudgy glass of the door, and when a car door suddenly slammed a little further up the road, he jumped with alarm.

'I can't give you more than a tenner.' Joycey proclaimed at last.

'What?' the man wailed, clutching at the front of his jacket. His fingers were leaving slight smears on the fabric. 'It must be worth more than that.'

Joycey sat back, folding his arms and shaking his head resolutely. 'I'm sorry. I don't know that anyone would be interested in it even at that price, and I've got rent to pay, not to mention wages...' He let the sentence hang in the air. The young man looked close to tears.

'All right. A tenner.' His voice sounded tight, as though choked.

Joycey pulled open the drawer under the desk and rummaged there for a moment. Then he looked up and called out to Marik. 'Marik, you got a fiver?'

Marik came shuffling from the back of the shop and, digging into one of the pockets of his jeans, he pulled out a crumpled note and handed it to Joycey. It was a ruse. Marik knew that there were plenty of notes in the drawer, but Joycey liked customers to think that there was precious little cash in the shop. It suggested that takings were poor and provided an excuse for paying under the odds for something.

Joycey waved the two fivers at the man who hesitated for a moment as though about to change his mind, then he slowly took the notes and pushed them into the pocket of his jeans without looking at them.

'If...' said Joycey, leaning back nonchalantly in the chair, 'you find anything else like that, let me know. You never know, I might be able to give you a little more.'

Joycey's smile looked sincere, Marik was staring down at his toes. The young man shrugged unhappily and opened the door of the shop. Then, instead of stepping outside, he paused, almost cowering in the doorway as he took a careful look at the cars parked along the side road. Then after a long moment he stepped out quickly and hurried away.

For a moment there was silence. Neither Joycey nor Marik moved. Then Joycey rolled forward letting the front legs of his chair down onto the grubby floorboards with a soft thump.

'Well, what did you make of that?' he asked.

Marik pursed his lips and stared out of the window. 'I don't know, Boss. Him scared I think.'

'Hmm.' Joycey was turning over the document on the desk, gazing at it carefully. Marik came over to join him, standing behind to peer over his shoulder. He unfolded the letter again and slowly read through the faded brown handwriting. He shrugged and turned it over to look at the map. Then he blew air through his clenched teeth and shook his head.

'Well, I don't know. I suppose we might get a tenner for it if we put it in the window. At least it's a bit older than the stuff we usually get. 1701. Might attract someone.'

'What have you got?'

The voice made them both jump and Marik almost fell over the waste paper bin as he span round. In the doorway to the back of the shop stood Takk, a large book held in one hand.

There was silence for a moment. Marik looked at Joycey, uncertain. Joycey looked at Takk, his expression blank. For some reason he felt reluctant, slightly guilty in the light of the young woman's searching gaze. Finally he simply shrugged.

'Oh someone just brought in something.'

He knew his answer was limp, especially as the document was still clutched in his fingers. Takk walked slowly forwards and twisted her head round to look at it. She glanced at him and he nodded as she took the document from him and carefully unfolded it on the desk. Then she lifted it towards the light and peered at it closely before putting it back on the desk and inspecting the handwriting. Over her head Joycey and Marik exchanged glances. Then, unable to bear the silence any longer, Joycey spoke.

'It says 1701.'

Takk straightened up and gave him a pitying look. 'Yes. That is generally what is signified by the numbers one seven zero one in a date.'

Joycey flinched, but the young woman paid no attention.

'1701,' she murmured. 'I think it's genuine too.'

In spite of himself, Joycey grinned. It was as though he had passed a test.

'So. You're some sort of expert are you?'

She sniffed. 'No, but I've had to study a lot of papers from this period. I know what they look like.'

'What about the map on the back?' he asked.

Takk turned the paper over and gave a quiet exclamation. 'Interesting.'

Joycey grinned at Marik who was smiling and had moved forward to stand next to Takk.

'What do you make of it?' Joycey enquired again. 'It looks like a sea chart of an island.'

A curtain of dark hair suddenly flopped from Takk's shapeless woollen hat. She pushed it back with one hand and stared at the faded lines of the drawing. Then she nodded.

'Could be an island.' She traced the details with a black painted fingernail. 'This looks like a coastline and these…,' she pointed at the series of small drawn anchors. 'These indicate good ground for anchoring a ship.'

'Yeah? How do you know all that?' Joycey was conscious of a hard glare suddenly turned towards him.

'I've seen a few like this,' she said simply.

'Oh yeah, part of your course is it?'

'Yep,' she snapped. 'Mind if I take a shot of it?' She was already pulling a smartphone from a pocket.

'We-ell,' Joycey hesitated, 'I suppose…if it helps us find out more about it.'

Takk was already tapping the back of her phone, rotating it to get the best focus. 'I'll see what I can do,' she said without smiling.

5. The Break-in

On his walk home a few nights later Joycey found himself deviating from the busy Trafalgar Road to stroll along Park Row for a pint at The Plume of Feathers, the town's oldest and least spoilt pub. One pint became two, and then three. And after his lingering fourth, he ambled slowly back through the amber mist of the streets towards home.

It was nearly nine when he shambled along Straightsmouth and let himself in to find Mickey complaining stridently behind the door. He scraped some food into a bowl on the floor and then dropped some bread into a toaster for himself. He ate slowly and unenthusiastically in front of the television, searching hopelessly for anything entertaining before making his way to bed with a pounding headache. He didn't bother undressing. He just unrolled himself on the bed and pulled the duvet over. Seconds later, he felt the cat land on the bed, and then nothing more.

He was asleep. But the pounding in his head insisted on getting louder. There was almost a physical violence to it that shook the floor under the bed, and resonated up the stairs. He groaned angrily and then realised that there was actually someone banging loudly on his front door. Swearing, he dodged past the cat, who was standing, tail quivering at the top of the stairs, and stumbled down into the hallway. It was still dark, but a muddy orange light from the street flowed through the fanlight above the door, accentuating the cracks between the bare floorboards.

He pulled open the door and felt a cold wave sweep over him as he saw the black uniforms of two police officers standing on the door step. Something cold and clammy seemed to wrap itself across his forehead as he gaped, exchanging stares with the two men.

'Mr Joyce Becket?' The closest policemen was asking, his cap was pushed back on his head and his hands seemed to be tucked into the arms of his sleeveless jacket.

For a moment Joycey felt himself forming the response 'Who's asking?' but then, almost laughing at the stupidity of it, he nodded.

'Yeah?'

'Are you the proprietor of Eastside Books in Lassell Street?'

'Yeah. Why, is there a problem?'

'I'm afraid you've had a break-in sir. Perhaps you'd like us to take you there?'

Joycey had little time for the Old Bill, and he was deeply suspicious of what appeared to be their offer of kindness, but he accepted it nevertheless. Now, deeply disconcerted, he found himself being whisked through Greenwich at high speed. For a moment he wondered whether he was being kidnapped, but the car flew down the almost deserted Trafalgar Road and turned smoothly into Lassell Street. The narrow road was full of blue flashing lights from two cars already standing outside the shop. As soon as he opened the car door, Joycey could see that the large front window had been kicked in, leaving a gaping hole surrounded by savage glass teeth.

The sound of radio conversations buzzed and crackled and one of the cars drove away, almost silent in the night. An officer appeared in the shop window holding a torch. Joycey identified himself and the officer beckoned him, saying that it was safe to enter. Almost in a daze he entered the shop through the window and found himself in a mess of glass fragments, books and manuscripts. The officer swung the torch round quickly and Joycey saw immediately that the front of the shop had been trashed. In response to questions, he turned on the electricity and admitted that there was no alarm. More officers appeared, possibly looking for some form of forensic evidence. Another took a statement and one gave him the emergency number of a window repair man. Almost as a parting comment, one of the officers informed him that the neighbours had reported the sound of breaking glass at 1.15pm, but no-one had seen kids or anyone else in the vicinity. One woman said she heard a car drive off, but that was all.

At six Joycey phoned Marik, who arrived looking sleepy and dishevelled, and by seven a brusque almost silent man was boarding up the window.

When daylight eventually came, the shop was in semi-darkness. Marik had swept up the glass and was picking any undamaged books and papers from a heap on the floor, and Joycey was in the little kitchen making tea and swallowing painkillers. From the front of the shop he could hear Marik saying, 'Oh dear, oh dear' repeatedly, and he wished he would stop.

At 7.30 am Joycey went off to Kazim's for breakfast leaving Marik sitting like a provoked guard dog inside the shop. He made a mental note to stick up a 'Business As Usual' sign, before pushing open the door of the café. The place was heaving and noisy, with thick-set men packed into the tables shovelling up eggs, beans, sausages, and bacon as fast as they could. Behind the glass counter Kazim and Cheryl were both on duty. As he approached they eyed him sympathetically.

'Hear you got problems, Joycey?' Kazim nodded with a serious expression. Cheryl nodded at his side, the big ear-rings swinging wildly.

'Blimey, nothing's secret for long round here is it,' he grinned sourly.

'Someone seed the police outside, early like,' Cheryl added, looking sideways at Kazim. The Turk nodded in confirmation.

'That's right. First bloke in this morning mentioned it. Robbery is it?'

Joycey shrugged, raising his voice against the background din.

'Who knows, nothing much taken as far as I can see, so my guess is it was someone arsing about on their way home from the pub. Or kids. Who can tell, eh? Don't know what the place is coming to.'

Kazim and Cheryl both tutted and nodded in stern agreement. Then they turned to the more important task of organising food. Joycey ordered a strong coffee, then bacon rolls and more coffee to take back to the shop. He needed to check whether he had any insurance.

When he arrived back at the shop clutching a greasy paper bag and two Styrofoam cups, he found Marik in a state of agitation. The cause was all too soon made clear. As Joycey dropped the greasy bag on the desk, Marik jabbed a finger at the wall behind it. There, amidst the group of plastic folders pinned to the wall was a gap. The map brought in three days earlier had gone.

6. PC Roscoe

Out on the black depths of the river a launch was motoring easily down on the tide. It was 4am and there was little else moving. The superstructure of the launch was low in profile except where the wheel-house windows rose to give a better view on all sides. As the hull rocked slowly over the tide the engine's exhaust rose slightly from the water, emitting a little popping purr and a puff of blue smoke. The sound was soporific and it was not surprising that, with the snug warmth of the wheelhouse, two of the crew were dozing on the leatherette benches. The green lights of the instrument panel reflected against the windscreen and dimly lit the white shirt and face of the woman at the helm. PC Jane Roscoe was no longer so young, but she had a fine bone structure which defied the shallow ravages of age and preserved an attractive looking face. She had also retained the figure which had always made her popular with her male colleagues in the Metropolitan Police.

More than this, she was respected for her toughness and her ability on the water. Like the rest of the crew she had been a beat bobby before requesting a transfer to the river division. The fact that she came from a family of Thames watermen might have swung things a little in favour of her application. Not that her elder brothers had been too impressed when she had originally stated her intention of joining the police. Careers were not something that featured in the traditional lives of the Roscoe women, and joining the police especially savoured strongly of some form of betrayal. There had been bad tempers and arguments at the time, but she was wilful and could easily hold her own across the breakfast table. Living with a large and predominantly male family had taught her to use her voice to powerful effect to get heard, when necessary. And it had been necessary when they objected to her career choice. But in the end they had come round, and when several years later she had announced that she was applying for the river police, the family had suddenly rallied round to offer enthusiastic support and advice.

Most of the men who joined the Marine Police were put through an intensive two year training on the river before they were allowed to take charge of one of the division's powerful launches. That two years was still five years less than the apprenticeship of the river's traditional Watermen and Lightermen, who found every opportunity to scorn the river police and sneer behind their backs. But even they had a sneaking respect for PC Roscoe. She had benefited from family knowledge and this had given her something of an edge over most of her male colleagues when it came to knowing the river, its tides and wharves. She was also a natural when it came to boat handling.

Now as the launch chugged its way slowly down past Charlton, Jane Roscoe found herself rocking slightly on her toes to the gentle rise and fall of the deck beneath her. She glanced momentarily at the two men snoozing nearby. 'Hamish' Davis, four years her junior, was lying back with his mouth half open, making a quiet gurgling noise in his throat. On the starboard bench, Sergeant Charlie White was also lying motionless. There was a faint reflection under his eyelids and she smirked quietly to herself. As usual Charlie was pretending to be asleep, secretly watching her, mentally undressing her for the thousandth time.

'Probably got his hand in his pocket again', she thought to herself. 'Dirty bastard'. But she also felt sorry for him. Charlie's wife had died two years before and, where he had once been cheerful and cheeky, able to flirt and tease in a relatively harmless way, he was now hesitant and uncertain when it came to women. Still, apart from that he was harmless, and he was a good copper, and a good boat-handler, there was no doubt about that.

She eased the wheel slightly to starboard to set the launch on a course between the green navigation lights of the central turtle-backs of the Thames Barrier. And as she did so she arched her back to ease the stiffness, conscious that the movement would send a little thrill trembling through her observant colleague. But he gave no sign and she put her tongue between her lips and smiled to herself.

The river was quiet for the early hours of the morning. On either bank, street lights glimmered, and the lights of an occasional car slid past or sent sharp beams flashing out over the water as they turned. As the launch slid between the tall silver towers of the barrier, the sound of its engine was amplified for a moment, and there came the dark sluicing sound of the tide running against the vertical walls and drums of the barrier itself. Then they were through, and to the left the lights of a freighter lying at a wharf lit the north side of the river. Bright spotlights illuminated the decks and open hatches. As yet, there was no work going on, but in a few hours the cranes would begin working and the heavy clanking crash of falling scrap iron would fill the air. On the freighter itself lights blazed in open doorways and a tiny orange glow at the railing pinpointed a sleepless member of the crew. Such ships never really slept. They just dozed waiting for the dawn.

Once upon a time the river had been filled with ships, its wharves lined with battered and rust-smeared freighters unloading the cargoes of all corners of the world. The River Police had been much busier in those days. Smuggling and theft were commonplace and patrols were always watchful for small wherries lurking in the shadows beside a freighter as drugs, alcohol or even guns were lowered by crew members anxious to enhance the meagre seamen's wage. But that was long before Jane Roscoe's time. Her knowledge of those days came from the yarns of the occasional retired officer visiting the station at Wapping, keen to satiate old memories by exploring the eccentric collection in the river police museum, which was housed in the same building. Active officers didn't have much time for the museum – it only seemed important for the older men. And when they had spent several hours gazing over the dusty glass cases they inevitably made their way to the station's rest room in search of tea and a friendly ear. That was when the yarns started, how old Bill so-and-so had drowned, what really happened when the *Magdeburg* sank at Broadness Point, the old pea-soupers etc. It was polite to sit and listen for a while, smiling, and then eventually make a discrete get-away.

When it came to yarns, though, there was one thing that always left the active officers tight lipped with forced smiles. Death on the river. Nowadays, the river police spent a lot of their time trying to prevent suicide attempts or rescuing idiots from the swirling waters. The Thames had always attracted death. They said that in ancient times it had been used as a place for ritual sacrifice, and later it was the usual place for disposing of murder victims. The rolling brown waters still seemed to attract those seeking premature death. The river's numerous bridges offered easy launching platforms for those seeking escape from the misery of a city long gone bad. During the day-time, potential suicides were often spotted before they jumped, identifiable because they lingered unusually long, leaning over the parapet and staring fixatedly at the brown waters swirling below. Sometimes, by the time they had managed to get a leg up onto the parapet wall a passer-by had grabbed them. But not always. Londoners didn't really like to get involved. And at night, there were often few people to see, and the really desperate often just slid off into the water, unnoticed. There was little turning back, once in the cold depths. The tides ripped quickly through the bridges, and there were eddies which would spin you round and round, so that any last-minute eagerness to try and survive would be gradually beaten and choked out of you.

Then there were the river's pleasure craft which ploughed up and down at night, full of drunken revellers, pumping rhythmic music loudly out from bank to bank and pulsating with disco lightshows like demented light-houses. On summer evenings the men at the helm of those were often too intent on avoiding other craft and bridges to see anybody thrashing desperately in the water. Worst of all were the dozens of heavy iron lighters moored up in pairs along the river. These floating boxes of rusting iron were deadly. As the tide raced, the hulls rose at the front and a threshing vortex formed underneath. Anybody swept under them would stay there for hours turning over and over as the rushing waters span them down and smashed them up against the rough bottom of the hull. Jane Roscoe had once stood helplessly, weeping bitter tears of frustration as a young woman had been swept into one of those merciless death-traps. The corpse had been found a week later, far down-stream, bloated and battered beyond recognition so that the forensic team even had problems getting evidence for the dental records. It was a side of the job that they didn't laugh about.

Now, ahead, were the hazard lights on the Woolwich

Ferry terminals, though it would be hours yet before the ferries started up for the morning rush. She glanced at the clock on the panel and did a quick mental calculation. Down to Erith and then back to base for breakfast. And if she was lucky one of these daft sods would wake up before then and make some tea. But when she looked again, Charlie's eyes had closed properly and he seemed to be snoring between pursed lips. She sighed quietly and peered through the wind screen again.

Slack water in about half an hour and then they could motor back up on the first of the flood tide. Breakfast, fill in the watch log and then home and bed. It sounded good to her. They drifted down past Woolwich where the ornate buildings of the old arsenal had been converted to luxury flats, and then on past Thamesmead with its brightly lit tower blocks. Near Erith, she gently span the wheel and the launch heeled slightly across the tide as it began its gradual progress back up the river. The movement woke Charlie and he sat up grunting. He rubbed his eyes and peered through the windows at the sky.

'You shouldn't have let me kip for so long, you know. ' He said limply.

She knew right enough. There were always supposed to be two of them on watch. It was a simple safety regulation, but Jane had never worried about it. She knew that in the old days the Thames lightermen would manage their huge iron barges single handed with nothing more to control their movements than the tide and a long barge sweep. 'If you knew what you were doing, you were unlikely to get into trouble', was what they had always said to her. Sometimes she had wondered about that, especially hearing of those odd occasions when the corpse of a lighterman had been fished out of the water. There were collisions and strange tide-rips, and flotsam that could hole a vessel or bring you to a sudden jerking standstill, and rope hawsers that could tighten suddenly and catapult you over the side. It wasn't something that was always in your control. But that was life. That was life on the river.

Charlie rose to his feet jerkily and peered up at the sky through the windscreen. The he turned and opened the door at the back of the cabin, the purr of the engine suddenly turned to a growl and there was a gust of chill air. She heard him grunt again.

'Looks like rain.'

'Good-oh,' she replied, glancing over her shoulder. Past the silhouette of Charlie's body she could see streaks of light behind ragged tears in the cloud. The wind was from the east.

'I'll make some tea,' he said. 'Better wake up Noddy there!'

'I'd wait til you've got a mug for him, you know what he's like when he wakes up.'

'Too right.' Charlie was fussing with an electric kettle and mugs. Chipping lumps of sugar from a sticky paper bag. The mugs were the rigid plastic variety, the sort that bounced when they hit the deck, as they often did. He brought Jane her tea first, standing for a while a little closer to her than was really necessary, before sighing quietly to himself and shaking Hamish awake.

'Come on Sunshine, time to join the land of the living.'

Hamish sat up slowly, complaining about the hardness of the benches, despite their leatherette cushions.

'Didn't stop you from getting your head down though!' Charlie quipped

'Too bloody right.' Hamish took a slurp of tea. 'Whew,

that's good though. Needed this.' He stood up and staggered out of the cabin on to the deck, where he could be heard farting loudly.

Jane Roscoe was still at the wheel keeping her eyes on the river as the cabin gradually filled with a grey light. As the launch rocked its way gradually back up river, the city began to wake, and as though flexing its limbs and stretching life back into its extremities, there was an increase in activity and life along the river banks. Cars and lorries, and buses already filled with early morning workers. The first raft of barges carrying the City's waste appeared on the river moving heavily downstream behind a small powerful tug. As they passed, a man appeared in the door of the tug's wheel-house and waved cheerily. He cupped his hands and called out, but his words were whipped away by the river breeze.

'What'd he say?' Jane asked.

Charlie was hanging idly with his elbows over the cabin door. 'Don't know. Couldn't hear. Something cheeky though I 'spect.'

'You can put money on that,' Jane laughed. 'Is Hamish alright?'

'Yeh, he's having a quiet fag.'

'Tut, tut, naughty boy.'

Charlie nodded silently. Smoking on board was against the rules, but no-one was going to say anything about it. Colleagues didn't do that. Knowing where the important boundaries were was vital to good team working. There were little things that could be overlooked, like Charlie's little sexual quirks, and Hamish's surreptitious smoking. They were not important enough. There were far more important battles to be fought sometimes, more important stands to take than these. And, Jane thought to herself, everyone was entitled to a little bit of oddity. Where would we be if we were all identical, perfect and never did anything that stretched the rules a little? Besides, she thought, that was all good old East End tradition.

They had passed the Woolwich Ferries now, both actively thrashing their way sideways like startled crabs across the river. On the port side, were the newer blocks of flats, built in anticipation of Woolwich coming up in the world. Once a reasonable expectation, as the town had been retrospectively linked to the Light Railway and to Crossrail, giving locals speedy access to the City and Canary Wharf. Cheap rents and good salaries went well together. The tower blocks insinuated a feeling of quality, unlike the drab grey monoliths of Newham on the other side of the river. The towers on the south bank were twisted at an angle so that nearly every flat could claim a view of the river, and they had balconies, lots of them.

They purred powerfully on up Blackwall Reach, past the even newer developments of the Peninsula Village and the white dome of the O2 arena. Turning south the elegant facades of the Old Royal Naval College swam into view, catching the amber light of the early morning sun. As they drew level, Hamish's voice interrupted Jane's reverie.

'Something going on over there.'

Both Charlie and Jane turned to look. Over on the south bank, a group of people had gathered by the riverside walk – the path was popular with runners and at this time of day was used by many commuters making their way to Greenwich pier. As they watched, more people were being drawn from either side to join the group. Several of them appeared to be shouting and they were pointing down to the narrow strip of shingle at the river's edge.

'Powering up!' Jane warned, and she pushed the throttles forward on the control panel beside her. The big engines of the launch suddenly gave a deep throaty roar and the bows lifted. She turned the boat in a white spray of water. Charlie already had the binoculars clamped to his eyes. The pale faces of the crowd on the riverside walk came into focus first and then he scanned down and along.

'Someone in the water,' he said, his voice loud now with urgency. 'Could be a body at the waters' edge'.

The words set grim expressions on the faces of all three crew members. Hamish turned to a locker and began pulling out packs of rubber gloves.

7. A shock on the foreshore

Greenwich was closed. Or at least that was how it appeared the next morning. Joycey had not slept well. Something had been niggling him all night and he woke feeling irritable with eyelids that felt like sandpaper. Grey light was filtering through the curtains, giving a dull illumination to the general untidiness of the bedroom. Normally he didn't notice it, but perhaps because of his mood this morning, it got to him. Looking at the heaps of laundry perched unreliably on the chairs and chest of drawers, he felt depressed, and for a moment regretted that he was living alone again. It hadn't been his choice. Not really. He just seemed to be unlucky in his choice of partner. Sandra had been the last one, and he had really thought that she would make a go of it. But in the end, like all her predecessors, she had given him an ultimatum about his deficient domesticity. Then even she had given up the effort and stormed out, yelling over her shoulder to him not to bother calling.

He clambered from the bed and pushed the curtains aside, peering down into the road outside. Straightsmouth was narrow, with cars parked nose-to-tail along the southern pavement. Black rubbish bags had been gathered into heaps and he thought he could hear the bleep of a refuse vehicle reversing half way up the road. The road was so narrow that the bin-lorries often had problems negotiating it. Especially now. When Joycey had first moved in, the road had been part of Greenwich's poorer backwater. The little terraced houses cheap and poorly maintained. But then the area had come up quickly, the yuppies had moved in and the little workers' houses became bijou cottages. And with the yuppies came cars, and then bigger cars. Now, just beneath the cracked sill of his window, was the roof of an enormous four-by-four.

Joycey snorted and swore to himself. Who needed a fucking four-by-four in Greenwich Park? It was just a pose-mobile. He knew the owner. She worked in a bank in Canary Wharf, so the car stood outside the house all week, taking up space.

As he peered down, a sound behind him caught his attention, and Mickey strode stolidly into the room, stared at him for a moment, and then gave a hoarse wail.

'All right mate,' Joycey sighed. 'I know, you're hungry.'

It wasn't till he left the house that he noticed the quietness. Normally, at this time on a weekday morning, the air was pulsing with the throb of traffic. But this morning there was very little sound. As he walked along Straightsmouth, heading into the town centre, there was just the occasional whine of a car from the High Road to the south, and in the distance, the sharper whoop of a siren or two. He walked through the dank churchyard of St Alfege's, the church itself standing like a grey cliff amid its thin scatter of tombs and grass, and found himself staring at stationary traffic. It wasn't just slow, it was dead. Just looking at the drivers' faces, he could tell that it had been like this for some time. The one way system wasn't even breathing.

Turning into the bread shop by the churchyard, he bought a pasty and coffee in a Styrofoam cup and asked the puffy looking girl behind the counter how long the traffic had been like that. The girl was bored and therefore chatty. She smiled at him, leaned on her elbows on the counter and joined him staring through the shop window.

'For about an hour, I heard,' she confided 'they found something down by the river. Someone walking their dog found a body or something. Least that's what someone said when they came in just now. Police are all over the place. Cordoned off the road and everything. Course, once they get stuck on this bit of the road, they can't get off. Poor buggers. Glad I don't have to drive in, that's all I can say.'

Joycey scalded his tongue on the coffee and left the shop to walk towards the Cutty Sark, its masts towering unnaturally high over the rooftops. Inside the glass walls of the visitor centre, staff seemed to be pottering about as usual. A woman filling a rack of post cards nodded to him and he waved back. Strolling on towards the river, he turned right to take the riverside walk towards East Greenwich. On a nice summer morning, the narrow pathway beside the river could be a delight – especially before all the tourists arrived. Even he could enjoy the rippling sunlight on the Thames as it swept its way round towards the bulk of the O2 dome on Blackwall Point. He thought it was sad that there were no ships, but the days of the thriving old port of London had long gone. On this morning, however, there was no hint of joy in the walk. Clutching his Styrofoam cup he ambled on past the grandiose facades of the Royal Naval College, the soles of his shoes sucking softly on the worn grey paving slabs. A silver drizzle was falling, drawing across the drab grey river in slightly lighter curtains of mist.

Before he reached the broad lawns in the centre of the

Naval College, he could see unusual activity on the slick grey-green foreshore below the river wall. The Thames rose and fell twenty feet with every tide, so the gravel bank in front of the Naval College was only exposed for a limited period each day. In summer it was common to see families poking around in the mud and shingle, stirring up endless shards of pottery and glass that each tide exposed around the wooden stumps of the old Tudor jetty. But this morning there were no women and children scrabbling on the wet surface. A white tent had been erected near the bottom of the sea wall and figures in white protective suits were crawling along in a line, subjecting the foreshore to an intimate search. Other figures moved in and out of the tent flap, carrying small bags, cameras and other unidentifiable objects.

At the river gates to the Naval College he was stopped by a small crowd that had gathered to peer along the river wall towards the tent. He tried to push past, but then realised that they too had been stopped by a blue-and-white tape barrier. A thin, young police-support officer was holding the position with an anxious expression on his face. At the far end of the Naval College, the riverside path broadened suddenly and then did an abrupt right turn. Blue lights were flashing in the windows of the Trafalgar Tavern just beyond.

The young police officer was now trying to disperse the crowd, under the dark glare of a stocky, older officer. Joycey slipped quickly through the open gate and into the grounds of the Naval College itself, then strode briskly along the inside of the iron railings, thus by-passing the police cordon. A hundred yards further on his pace slowed and then stopped. Standing on an elevated position he could see over the riverside walk and down into the tent on the glistening foreshore, inside of which a forensic team were clearly busy at work on a dark shape which lay crumpled on the ground. But it was not so much the tent which caught his eye.

Just a few feet below him lay the grey stones of the riverside path with its paint-thickened old iron railing. But, nearly level with the tent, the stones were no longer grey. They still glistened with the sheen of drizzle that had been falling across them for some time, but the slabs were smeared with brown streams and blotches and soft coagulating lumps – and something that resembled a rotting string bag hung from the spikes of the railings. Joycey froze. Then, as realisation set in, he took a slow swig of his cooling coffee and hurriedly turned away, walking southwards into the Naval College and away from the riverside.

By the time he reached Kazim's, Joycey felt the urgent need for a stronger coffee – and for once he was glad that the café was empty of familiar faces. One of Kazim's sons was behind the counter, but it was the young sullen one who didn't speak, and Joycey left again without having to expose his sudden sensitivity. He was even more perturbed when he reached the shop and found it locked. He unlocked the door and entered.

There was no sign of Marik, and Joycey became aware of an unsettling feeling in the pit of his stomach. He was, therefore, hugely if quietly relieved when the young Pole arrived looking flustered and apologetic. Cross with himself for letting his imagination slip, Joycey simply grunted in response to Marik's explanations.

Once inside the shop Marik peeled off his coat and hung it on the back of an old wooden chair, and sat looking hurt. Feeling suddenly guilty, Joycey patted him on the shoulder and sent him off again to get more coffee and pastries from Kazim's, with strict instructions not to risk getting anything that had cream in it. Then he sat down on the stool, unrolled one of the free papers which he had picked up on his way to the shop and lit a cigarette.

He had only smoked half of it when the door was pushed

open and a tall, middle-aged woman stepped into the shop. She was dressed in old, but once fashionable, clothing and there was something a little disturbing about the way she kept avoiding meeting his glance. In a loud officious voice, she demanded books by a famous author of tawdry romances, and following Joycey's instructions she stomped noisily towards bookshelves in the back of the shop. A few minutes later Joycey heard her slapping books together irritably, and knew that he had one of the area's several eccentric customers on his hands.

He had smoked a second cigarette before it occurred to him that Marik had been gone an unusually long time. Once he realised this he became impatient, knowing that he was trapped in the shop with what he was in the habit of describing as 'a potential nutter'. Rising from the chair behind the desk he strolled along the front of the shop, peering out between the rows of paperbacks and comics that were displayed there. From where he stood he could see the corner of the road, and the traffic which was now flowing erratically in a westward direction towards the town centre. As he watched, Marik came loping round the corner, his body leaning forward over his long legs.

'There's a body, Boss,' he explained as soon as he entered the shop. 'They found a man down by the river. Dead. Killed. And there was a crash. Two crash, they think. Not together. Now they knock on every door. Stop people in the streets. It's like…like…' He stopped, waving a greasy paper bag in the air.

'Like a bloody police state is what it is.' Joycey grunted. 'Well at least you got the pastries.'

Marik smiled and presented the bag. Joycey opened it and peered inside. He was confronted with two dry-looking doughnuts, they were oozing a thick yellow substance. It was Kazim's infamous cream. He sighed.

'Well, never mind Marik. Let's have that coffee.'

Marik tiptoed through the shop and Joycey heard him talking to the mad woman for a moment. There was laughter. And then a loud series of thumps, as of a pile of books toppling to the floor. Joycey rolled his eyes towards the ceiling and then closed them as though offering up a prayer. In the back of the shop there was a sudden animated conversation. Then heavy footsteps came stomping towards him. When he opened his eyes, the woman was standing in front of him, her arms full of books and a wavering smile on her face. She dropped the books clumsily on the desk and then, peering out through the door, she said bossily; 'Right. I'll take all of these.'

Joycey sat up quickly and began checking the prices while the woman rustled deep in her handbag.

'That's twenty-five pounds,' he said, smiling at the side of her face. 'But make it twenty.'

She yelped a delighted laugh and pulled four grubby fivers and a crumpled plastic carrier from her bag. 'That's kind of you.'

Joycey produced one of his most ingratiating smiles. He knew the lot had only cost him a few pounds. One of Dusty's handy deliveries, two weeks earlier. As she banged her way awkwardly from the shop, Marik reappeared. He put two chipped mugs on the desk, and Joycey saw with dismay that Marik had made tea. The young Pole nodded towards the door. 'She gone boss?'

Joycey nodded, taking a sip of tea. It was too milky. Marik was peering after the woman.

'She good lady, that one. Pastor for her church. Method

typed, I think. Yes. Very good. Very…respectable.'

Joycey grinned quietly into his mug. He had clocked the two erotic novels tucked in the middle of the pile.

8. The Afternoon News.

It was Friday. Fridays were always good, for some reason. Joycey had once speculated that this might have something to do with the arrival of benefit cheques, student grants or any other form of payment. But then he had concluded cynically that people on benefits weren't really book buyers, and students would simply head for the nearest pub with their money. Nevertheless, Friday afternoons were usually good for sales.

The morning had dragged slightly, but then from 2pm onwards a steady trickle of potential punters had pushed open the door. A group of noisy teenagers had departed with an armful of old DC comics, and Takk had arrived, heaving a heavy looking canvas shoulder bag. If it had been anyone else, he might have been slightly suspicious as she disappeared into the back of the shop, but he had now grown used to her presence. She even extended the slight courtesy of a cool nod as she strode past the desk, leaving him smiling quietly to himself as he sat over his morning paper.

At 4pm Marik returned from a trip to the local newsagent, pushing the door open as Joycey was in the process of selling some heavily priced law books. Busy as he was, Joycey could see immediately that something was up. Marik's face was tense, his lips were tight and paler than usual, and he was bobbing up and down on his toes just inside the door. As soon as the customer had gone, Marik peered into the back of the shop and hissed, 'It was him boss. The body they found.'

Joycey looked at him blankly. 'Who Marik? What do you mean? What body?'

Marik was quivering with pent-up excitement, struggling to get his words out. 'That body in the river. It was him. The map man.'

Marik thrust an arm forward suddenly and gesticulated at the empty plastic document holder pinned to the wall behind the desk. It had contained the manuscript which the young man had brought in the week before. Joycey stared at it, frowning as the information sank in. Then Marik gasped, and pulled a rolled-up newspaper from under his arm. He flattened it in front of Joycey and slapped a hand on the front page. There, under a bold headline, was an artist's impression of what was unmistakeably the man in the grubby denim jacket.

Joycey felt his jaw muscles tighten uncomfortably and, slumping in his chair, read quickly.

Police in Greenwich are appealing to the public for information in connection with a suspicious death there on Monday night. The victim, identified as Gavin Douglas, 26, of Saville Road, Lewisham, was discovered near the River Thames in the early morning by a man walking his dog. The victim had suffered extensive injuries and police are anxious to speak to anyone who might have seen or heard anything suspicious at this location between 12pm and 2am. It is believed that Mr Douglas was employed on a casual basis and police officers are anxious to hear from anyone who had any connection with him in this way.

A spokeswoman from the Metropolitan police was unable to confirm whether the incident was connected to a fatal accident involving two vehicles in College Approach at the same time.

There followed a contact telephone number and brief interview with someone who had been in Greenwich the following morning, complaining about the traffic. Joycey scanned the page again, conscious of Marik's eyes upon him. He was trying to think, but just felt confused. But there could be no doubt, the face staring up at him from the front page of the local rag was that of the young man in the denim jacket.

'It's him isn't it boss?'

Joycey slumped back in the chair, making it creak with complaint. Then he nodded.

'Looks like him Marik.' He sighed heavily. 'That's weird, isn't it? He was only in here the other day. Standing where you are.'

Marik glanced down at his feet guiltily, as though expecting to see the space occupied by something else, and then took a step sideways.

'Someone killed him, after he came, sold map,' Marik persisted.

Joycey looked at him bleakly and after a lengthy silence, he nodded. 'It's a strange world Marik. It just goes to show you never know what's around the corner. Something like this…,' he tutted and tapped a finger on the paper. 'I guess you never know when your number is up, do you?'

Marik was frowning, trying to understand this. Then he gave up. 'You think because of ..?' He was pointing towards the empty document holder on the wall.

'No…no,' Joycey shook his head vigorously, then turned abruptly to stare at the little plastic folder as though it had suddenly turned into something unpleasant. 'No. How could it have anything to do with…' He stopped, thinking of the gore on the riverside path, and shuddered.

'What's that?'

Takk's voice made them both jump, and once again Joycey was startled by the young woman's ability to appear silently and unexpectedly. He now remembered her arrival an hour or so earlier. She was now without the heavy canvas bag, but she did have a book in her hand.

'It's none of your business,' Joycey snapped but Takk, ignoring him, had moved forward to stare at the newspaper.

'He was in here.' She leaned forward and turned the paper to quickly read through the report. Joycey and Marik exchanged uncomfortable glances over her head. When she had finished reading she gave Joycey a level, penetrating look.

'Fuck! It was him. He was actually in here.' She repeated with shocked emphasis.

Joycey nodded.

'And now he's dead.'

'So it seems,' Joycey sighed, fumbling in his jacket pocket for his tobacco tin.

'He sold you that manuscript.'

'Yeah, the one that got nicked.'

'What?' Takk's expression seemed to snap into deeper shock.

Joycey smirked, glad for some indescribable reason of

having disconcerted the young woman with the searching glare. 'Yeah. The other night. When we got done over. Whoever it was took the letter.'

Joycey pointed to the vacant plastic wallet on the wall.

'Gone, see.'

Takk's eyes were wide. 'He came in here and sold you the letter, and now he's dead. I heard you talking to him. He was nervous, wasn't he? Do you think he was afraid?'

'Nah,' Joycey snorted. 'Why would he be? He was just selling an old letter. People come in and do it all the time. There's nothing strange about that.'

Takk ignored this comment. 'Well it seemed to me he was afraid of something. Had he stolen it?'

Joycey's mouth opened but no sound came out. He glanced at Marik but the young Pole was staring at Takk with a worried expression.

'Do you think that I would…,' he began to protest but then his impetus faltered as Takk's head tilted to one side and she gave him a thin smile. 'No…' he asserted feebly at last.

'I did hear your conversation,' she stated flatly. 'He was definitely on edge.'

Joycey remembered how the young man had broken into a sweat, his nervous glances through the window, and he knew that Takk was right.

'So why else would he have been afraid?' She asked.

Joycey shrugged, reluctant to continue the line of thought.

'If it was stolen…'

'It's just a coincidence,' Joycey whined.

'Might be. Might not be. Shouldn't you tell the police he was in here, anyway?'

Joycey felt his face go cold. 'Whoa there, hold on a minute, let's not get ahead of ourselves. Why do we need to contact them? There's nothing we can say about his murder. All that we can tell them is that he came in here earlier that day to sell us an old letter.'

'Which may have been stolen.'

Joycey was beginning to feel out of his depth. 'We haven't got any reason for thinking that.'

'Then why was he afraid?'

'Who says he was afraid?'

'Are you saying he wasn't? He looked it to me.'

Takk was glaring at him and as his eyes met the blackness of hers, he felt unable to tear them away again. Unhelpfully, Marik was nodding behind the girl's back. For a moment there was an uneasy silence, broken only by the ticking of the electric heater as the thermostat kicked in.

'Ok, ok. He did seem nervous. But look, in this business you often get people dumping stuff they've found. Sometimes they're just uncomfortable about selling, you know? Worried about asking too much, that sort of thing.'

'And sometimes it's because it doesn't belong to them.'

'Well,' Joycey looked pained, 'yeah, sometimes people bring in old library books. This is a second-hand book shop. You can't always check inside every book when someone brings in a box-load. And then we get house clearance stuff, you can never tell where that's come from, and sometimes you got no right to ask, either.'

'And sometimes it might just be stolen.'

'Yeah, I suppose. Yeah, sometimes.'

The tension in the air seemed to break suddenly.

'Well, now that we've established that,' Takk said, looking at each of them in turn, 'the thing is this. If this guy stole that letter, it might have something to do with his death. And if it did, it seems to me that the murderer could be the person he stole it from.'

Joycey thought this through and eventually nodded. 'I suppose that's possible, if we think it was stolen?'

Takk held up a finger abruptly, and he fell silent. 'So the question is, why was it worth murdering for?'

9. The night tiding

Takk's question had left Joycey feeling disturbed and more than a little lost. Over the years he had bought plenty of stuff which lacked what was technically known as 'legal provenance'. Dusty and some of the other dealers were not beyond buying a few dodgy items now and then, and slipping them in amongst a crate load of legitimate house clearance. Everyone knew that's what they did, but provided you asked no questions you got told no lies and if Old Bill came asking you had nothing to tell them. It was as straightforward as that. But there had never been any consequences before.

Now Takk was staring him down with a piercing glare that he found difficult to meet. 'You have to phone the police,' she said with determined emphasis.

He had protested, prevaricated and eventually given in and it was under her strict gaze that he eventually and very reluctantly made the call. Having triumphed, Takk made sudden excuses and hurried off to keep some appointment; and for the last hour Marik had kept himself busy in the back of the shop. Joycey was in no mood to talk and avoided what he felt was the young Pole's air of accusation – unintentional though it may have been.

For, having made the call, Joycey's heart had sunk completely. The whole episode was getting too deep and he had this feeling that he was beginning to drown. He rolled another cigarette and as he was smoking it he remembered Takk's assessment. If Gavin Douglas had been murdered by the person he stole the letter from, then that person had probably now also broken into the shop and taken it back. Now every time he tried to recall the image of the letter and map, it was the image of the bloodied paving stones that kept focussing in his mind.

The police arrived within the hour. Their arrival caused some anxiety, as even in plain clothes, neither man offered the appearance of a police officer. One was young, casually dressed in jeans, hoody and black leather jacket. He reminded Joycey of someone from the drug squad. The other man, who turned out to be the senior of the two, was older, perhaps in his fifties, with grey hair and sagging lines around his mouth. He was wearing a navy blue suit and a light rain-coat, and he smelt strongly of stale cigarettes. He introduced himself as DI Walker, and the other as DS Martin. They produced their ID quickly without the glimmer of a smile, and while the older man began questioning Joycey, the other began a thorough nose around the shop while darting suspicious glances at Marik.

Marik found a stool from somewhere and offered it. DI Walker sat, sighing and gazing at the piles of books and magazines. Finally the policeman's eyes came to rest on Joycey and he gave a thin smile.

'So, Mr Becket, what's the story?'

Joycey gazed at him, frowned and blurted, 'Well as I said on the phone. The bloke you found on the beach the other morning. He was in here a couple of days before.'

'Oh yes,' DI Walker looked bored. 'And what would he

be wanting in here?'

Joycey hesitated, not sure how much to say, how much to reveal. He shook his head. 'Oh not a lot. Trying to sell something, that's all.'

'Sell something?'

'Yeah.'

There was a long silence. Joycey was conscious of the policeman's intense scrutiny.

'What sort of something would that have been then?'

Again Joycey hesitated. Marik, leaning against the wooden print chests in the middle of the shop stirred uncomfortably.

'Oh just an old letter he had, that's all.'

'A letter. When was this?'

'A week ago…'

'The day his body was found by the river?'

'The Friday day before.' This time he glanced at Marik, who nodded in confirmation.

'And what time did he leave here?'

Joycey told him.

'And when did you realise it was the same man?'

Joycey explained about the newspaper. This time DI Walker glanced at Marik, who nodded uncomfortably. The policeman nodded slowly for a moment.

'So what was this letter?'

Joycey explained, giving a vague description of both the letter and the map. The DI's face was expressionless. When Joycey had finished he nodded again.

'You say it was quite old?'

'Yeah, it was dated 1701. We reckoned it was genuine. Old, you know and a bit unusual.'

'Really? A bit unusual was it?' The face expressed surprise. 'In what way was it a bit unusual?'

Joycey felt his face getting warm. 'I...we don't get stuff like that very often. I mean.'

'I see. So you didn't know much about it?'

'No, just though it might be interesting. You know. Not worth much but ...well, you know.'

The policeman ignored Joycey's last comment. 'But you thought it was worth buying anyway?'

'Yeah. Well you never know, do you? And in this trade you have to take a chance sometimes. Take a risk on something. Might be junk might not be. You have to try it see.'

The policeman was silent for a long while. Eventually he straightened up and asked quietly, 'And what did it say, this letter?'

Joycey frowned, trying to recall the content. 'Dunno really, it was a bit garbled, and hard to read. Old hand-writing, and a bit faded. Something about a merchant and some stuff. Silk I think. In Cheapside. There was a map of an island on the back that was nice.'

'So, bit of an expert on maps then are you?'

Joycey laughed. 'Nah, no way. Not me.'

The policeman was nodding thoughtfully. Suddenly he turned towards Marik.

'What about you? You an expert?'

Marik jumped, looking like a petrified rabbit. He shook his head and squeaked in protest, but Walker had already turned back to Joycey.

'So, neither of you are experts.' There was a long pause, then he asked, 'So who was?'

Joycey felt his face flush quickly. 'What do you mean?'

'Well, you said, 'we reckoned it was genuine'. You've said you don't often get that sort of thing, and you clearly don't know much about it. So who thought it was worth buying?'

Joycey was thinking of Takk and felt flustered. There was no point involving her in this.

'Well I just sort of guessed,' he blustered. 'We get a few maps every now and again.' He waved at the wall of plastic envelopes behind him. 'So you get a nose for things after a while…I can kind of feel if they're worth anything.'

The policeman was silent, gazing intently. Then he sighed and sat more upright on the stool. 'Ok. Ok. So you bought it. How valuable was it? What did you think you could get for it?'

Joycey shrugged. 'Not much. A few quid, probably. Some people like that sort of thing. Get it framed and hang it in the living room. Look nice in the house in Blackheath. You know.'

'Hmm, if you say so.' The policeman was gazing at the other documents. 'How often do you get people bringing old documents to you?'

'Not very…'

'So this didn't strike you in any way as odd then?'

Joycey suddenly saw the trap he had walked into and felt a cold mist swathe his neck. 'Well, you know, you get all sorts…'

The policeman gave him a long look and then pulled a sheet of paper from inside his jacket. He flattened it on the desk and tapped it with his forefinger. Joycey glanced down and saw that it was the sketch of the face of the young man, Gavin Douglas, the same image that had appeared in the newspaper.

'You recognise him? It may not be completely accurate. Only we had to use this one.' He pushed his hand back inside his jacket and extracted another sheet of paper before continuing. 'Because it wouldn't have been fair to show this, would it?'

He slid the paper under Joycey's nose. The paper was the print out of a photograph. It was Gavin Douglas again. But this time the face was not shown full on. In fact, the head lay sideways on weed stained stones and mud, but the face was grotesque. The mouth, stretched open, was too wide, revealing fragments of white bone and teeth, the left cheek was gone and an eyeball hung down over the upper lip. Joycey looked away quickly, swallowing thickly as bitter fluid burnt his throat.

'Nasty business, isn't it?' the policeman leaned forward, speaking softly, 'So, why don't you tell me the truth. Tell me what you know about this document.'

Joycey shook his head and gave an outraged squawk. 'Jes-us! I've told you all I know, for Christ's sake.'

Across the room the younger policeman was standing still, watching intently. Joycey wanted to look at Marik, but something told him this might be a bad idea. He licked his lips and took a deep breath, trying to steady and deepen his voice. He never felt comfortable in the company of Old Bill and now he felt on very thin ice indeed.

The policeman's face suddenly turned dark. He rose to his feet, planted his hands flat on the table and pushed his face close to Joycey's and bellowed angrily,

'Gavin Douglas had a criminal record longer than your dick, sunshine. He had a severe drug habit and fed it by nicking stuff at every available fucking opportunity. He broke into more houses in south east London than I care to count, and mixed with some very nasty people. So, don't fuck me off Mr Becket. You saw that guy's face. His head was literally kicked in. Whoever did that wasn't in the fucking Girl Guides.'

The policeman's voice quietened. 'So. Let's stop fucking about here, ok? What was this letter about? What was the map? And how much was it worth?'

Joycey was shaking. He slipped his hands under the desk to hide them. 'It wasn't worth much, that's all I can tell you.'

'But you bought it. How much for?'

Joycey told him.

'And what did this letter say?'

'I've already told you,' Joycey protested. 'It was this garbled stuff about some silks and a merchant. We didn't understand it. And the map was some sort of island. But it didn't say where or anything. Could have been anything. I don't know!'

The Policeman slowly stood upright, staring down his nose at Joycey.

'And where did he say he got it?'

'He said he got it...' Joycey hesitated for a moment,

realising how unlikely it was going to sound. 'He got it clearing an old lady's loft.'

'Oh yes. And where did this old lady live?'

'Catford, but he didn't say where. It was a long time ago, he said.'

There was a long silence.

'So did anyone else see the letter after Gavin sold it to you?'

'No.' Joycey lied.

The policeman stared at him for several long moments then looked away. Joycey knew that he didn't believe him, and he didn't dare look at Marik.

'I don't suppose you have a photograph of the letter?' DI Walker sighed wearily.

'No, sorry.' This time he wasn't lying but he felt the older man's gaze on his face all the same.

'So, this break-in. Anything else taken.'

Joycey looked at Marik for confirmation. The young Pole shook his head and shrugged slightly.

'Doesn't look like it. No.'

'No money, stamps, nothing at all?'

'No. Though I guess whoever it was might have helped themselves to a book or two. We wouldn't really be able to tell,' he explained.

'No, quite. So whoever broke in here may have been after the letter and nothing else.'

Joycey was quiet.

'Well, we'll leave it there for now, shall we? If you do think of anything else to tell me, you will get in touch straight away this time won't you.' From the tone of his voice it was clear he expected nothing of the sort. He turned towards the door. 'Only, there does seem to be some sort of connection, doesn't there? Between the murder of Gavin Douglas and the theft of the letter? It's a bit too much of a coincidence for my liking.'

Joycey nodded unhappily. 'So you do think that whoever killed him came for the letter too?'

'Well, that would seem to be a very strong possibility, wouldn't you think?'

'Yeah. Suppose.'

'So I would get yourself a stronger window, Mr Becket. Next time, whoever these people are, as I said, they won't be asking for bob-a-job.' The old fashioned reference made Joycey want to smile suddenly.

The younger policeman appeared beside his older colleague suddenly and gave him an indecipherable look. Then they were gone.

10. The revelation of Takk

It was nearly lunchtime and Joycey was hungry. He was huddled in his jacket at the desk, watching rods of thick rain falling heavily past the gaping aperture that was the front of the shop. The rain had brought a cold wind blowing in from the east, and the temperature in the shop was distinctly uncomfortable. Two men, who looked like they were more used to smashing glass than installing it, were manhandling a large pane on the pavement. Joycey watched them grumpily, still agonising over the cost involved, when Takk appeared. She surveyed the exterior of the shop for a moment and then walked in and sat herself down on the same stool which DI Walker had used the previous evening. Joycey eyed her with dismay.

'If you've come to tell me 'I told you so' I'm not in the mood.'

'I'm not surprised,' she said drily. 'I heard about your visitors'.

'Oh did you.'

'Sure. Sit in Kazim's long enough and you hear more news than on the telly.'

Joycey snorted. 'Nothing's private round here is it. Anyway, unless you've come round to buy something we're closed.'

Takk didn't move, so he tried glaring at her, but her expression made his wilt, slowly. 'We need to talk about the letter that guy brought in'.

'It's too late. We ain't got it any more'

'I know that.' She gazed at him, her slightly aggressive mask softened and she looked sombre. 'We still need to talk. I think the letter's important.'

'Obviously,' he snorted. 'Pity it's gone.'

'That doesn't matter,' she muttered and then leaning closer she hissed, 'Don't forget I took photos of it. I've had a good look at them. Got some things to tell you.'

Joycey leaned back frowning to focus on her earnest face. 'Ok, but not here. I need to eat, let's go somewhere else.'

Summoning a surprised Marik from the back of the shop, to keep an eye on things, he half-led the young student down the side street and turned into a road beside a railway line. At the end, a short narrow flight of stairs led up between two houses and here Joycey paused, looking cautiously behind them. Then he led the way up the steps to emerge near the bottom of Greenwich Park. Takk followed this behaviour with a slightly amused expression on her face but she offered no comment and followed him in sturdy silence.

Crossing the road, Joycey led the way quickly to the Plume of Feathers. Stepping down into the old pub he led the way to a quiet table near the back of the bar, in an area which also served as a restaurant. Although he offered her lunch, Takk would accept only a beer. So he ordered two of these and a salt beef sandwich, and re-joined her at their isolated table. Takk was sitting with her tablet in front of her, and as Joycey sat down she turned it so that he could see the screen.

'These are the images.'

Joycey glanced at them and snorted. 'Yeah, I remember what they looked like.'

'But did you have a good look at them? A really good look at them? And did you read the letter, I mean, read it properly?'

Joycey took a swig of beer and rolled it round his mouth for a moment before swallowing. 'You said you thought it was important. The police seem to think this Gavin Douglas was murdered because he took it, and then the same person broke into the shop to get it back.'

'Isn't that what I was telling you yesterday?'

'Yeah,' said Joycey thoughtfully, 'though he could have been killed because he took the letter, not because of the letter itself.'

'Except that the letter's now been taken too. If your burglar was also the murderer, he - or they - were taking a big risk in breaking in to your shop too. Was anything else taken?'

'No,' Joycey shook his head, 'not as far as I can tell'.

'So he ...or they,' she added with emphasis, 'came for the letter alone. So it must have been important.'

Joycey gazed at her earnest expression then nodded reluctantly.

'So,' she asked, 'What could it be about an old letter that is so important?'

Joycey exhaled noisily through pursed lips and shook his head again. 'I don't know. You tell me.'

Takk tapped on the screen again and the tablet flickered back into life. There was the map of the island which they had seen before. 'What do you make of this?'

'It's a map of an island?'

With a deft flick, she enlarged the pasty-shaped image. The brown lines expanded, becoming smudged and the surface of the paper looked pitted and abraded. She began to scroll back and forth until the southern edge of the map filled the screen. There was definitely a clearly marked coastline with carefully inked-in lines to represent water against the shore, and the little drawings of anchors. In several places the word 'moorings' had been neatly drawn in in a tiny hand. The southern shore of the island swept round like a large grin and in several places other words, now much faded had been inked in. From left to right they read 'Ye Woes', 'Hermitage', 'well', 'Sugar Loaf', and further round towards the eastern end of the island, the word 'Pelicans' appeared. Inland the centre of the island seemed to be criss-crossed with streams and marshy land, and there didn't seem to be any sign of hills or high ground. There were some lines running parallel to the south coast, as if in indication of paths or tracks, and several ran off of this towards the north, into the swampy area, but the northern part of the map seemed to lack any detail. In fact the north coast of the island was indicated by two smooth parallel lines that ran in an unbroken arc from east to west, though they broke up ambiguously at the extremities. There was one feature however which stood out clearly. One track seemed to wend its way from the southern shore to the northern tip of the island, and where it ended a small square had been drawn in and in very faded lettering, they could make out the words 'Old Redout'.

Takk extended a finger and tapped the screen with a black painted nail. 'That's curious, and so's that!' She tapped several of the words and Joycey craned his neck to look.

'Pelicans. Where do pelicans live?'

'Well not in the cold polar regions. I checked.'

'Well that may be some help.' He muttered without conviction.

'Not really. All it tells us is that this island is likely to be in a warmer part of the world. Pelicans are pretty widespread.'

'And Hermitage?'

'I don't know. In the 18th century, wealthy aristocrats often built hermitages as romantic features in the grounds of their country houses. But this letter's a bit early for that. Unless it's a place where a real hermit lived? What about the map, doesn't it remind you of something?'

Joycey shrugged and looked blank. 'No, not really.'

Takk was chewing a thumb nail and frowning at the screen. 'I can't remember what it is, but I will. Now what about this?' She swiped the screen and the image slid sideways to reveal the buff colour of the paper again, now lined with the dark brown, rust colour of the hand writing. Once again Takk enlarged it and quietly began reading it through.

'*Cous*

Since it must be I am condemned to dye, I have writ his ldship this day and told him of what is to be offered if he will secure what I wish I am assured he will bee honble to this but as I doubt not some trickery might befall from other honble gentlemen known to you Whereof do you beg our friend H remove that we bt from the Old Mrcht in the woes If he cavilles show him this He will know all as we spoke thereof Doe not trust ye Dowgat man The silks you may take to the mercer in Cheapside the value thereof to have unto yrslf Wm

April 29th 1701

When she had finished, she sat hunched forward, tapping her teeth with her nails. Joycey had glanced round several times, but no-one seemed to be taking any notice of them, and Takk's voice had been too quiet to carry through the growing hub-bub of the front bar. He peered at the screen again, but after a few seconds he gave up. Although he could read the hand, the contents just seemed to make no sense.

'What do you reckon then?' he asked at last.

'It's a puzzle, that's for sure.' She skimmed the page again and then took a long, impressive swig of beer, wiping her lips with the back of her hand. 'Perhaps more of an intrigue than a puzzle though.' Then she laughed suddenly.

'What do you mean?'

'Ok,' she sat forward looking very thoughtful. 'There are some things we can work out here. Or at least, I think we can. The writer's name is William. Wm was the standard abbreviation for the name. And, whoever this William is, he is writing to someone he knows, because the term 'cous' is again an abbreviation, for cousin. And the term 'cousin' was used often for family members or close friends.'

She glanced at him and he nodded.

'Now,' she tapped with her finger nail again. 'What's the first thing that strikes you about what he says?'

Feeling a little like a school boy out of his depth, he scanned the letter again quickly, and shrugged helplessly.

'Look at the first line,' she hissed.

He read it through, then she lost patience. 'Jesus! The man's been condemned to death!'

The significance slowly dawned on Joycey and he took a slow sip of his beer. 'Is that what he means? *Since it must be I am condemned to dye.*'

'Yes! And this William has spoken to someone in authority, the judge or perhaps an actual Lord. And I think he was trying to do some sort of deal or make a purchase perhaps? The sense is often difficult to make out when they don't bother with punctuation like this. But it looks as though this William was trying to obtain something or to make sure that something happened, and he thought that whoever this Lord was, he would stick to the deal.'

She looked at Joycey and when she saw his blank expression, she read through the first part of the letter to illustrate her point. When he nodded, she carried on.

'This next bit seems to indicate that he was worried that some other people might interfere with the deal. Hence the word 'trickery.' He suspects them. He refers to them as 'honourable gentlemen' which might mean they are also people in a powerful position. Or may be he meant it ironically.'

'Meaning they might be dishonourable?'

'Yes. But I think, because he uses the phrase 'other honourable gentlemen' he is talking about peers of this first lord.'

'The one he is trying to do the deal with.'

'Yep. And whoever they are, the recipient of the letter

knows them because he says…'

'Known to you.'

Takk smiled and Joycey felt strangely as though a light had been turned on him. He had never seen her smile warmly before. Even so, he was feeling a little awed by her analysis of the letter.

'Now,' she pressed on. 'The second part of the letter refers to another party, someone called 'H'. He is clearly an associate of both the writer, William, and the recipient of the letter.'

'Because he calls him 'our friend'.'

'Yes, I don't think he means it ironically. William is asking the recipient to ask this 'H' to remove something they bought from an old merchant.' She frowned. 'I'm not sure what he means by 'in the woes', though. My guess is that the merchant was depressed. Or perhaps it was something William bought when he was depressed…'

Joycey laughed roughly. 'Hah, we've all made purchases like that. Buy in haste and live to regret it.'

'But then the phrase also appears on the map.' She tapped the screen until the image of the map reappeared and she pointed to the tiny faded lettering next to the south-west shore of the island.

Joycey craned his neck to peer at the screen, and grunted. 'That's odd isn't it.' There was a moment of silence and then he asked abruptly, 'And what does 'cavilles' mean?'

'It's an old word. Isn't often used nowadays, but it usually means to prevaricate, or grumble. I think he, William, thought that H might be reluctant to remove whatever it was they had bought from the merchant, and the letter was meant to be used in some way to give authority to the recipient.'

'Ok.'

'Anyway, William says that H knows all about it because they 'spoke thereof'. So it must be part of a plan. The next bit is really useful.' Takk's dark eyes were shining and she was looking really pleased with herself. She quickly finished her beer. Joycey read through the last two lines of the letter and waited for her to speak.

'So, William says not to trust the Dowgat Man.' She beamed.

'Ok, so who or what is the Dowgat man?'

'I'll come to that in a minute. Read the next bit.'

Joycey read it through quietly. 'The silks you may take to the mercer in Chepeside, the value thereof to have unto yourself.' Well, there's a Cheapside in the City.'

Takk nodded enthusiastically. 'Absolutely. The mercers were City merchants who specialised in the trade in imported luxury fabrics, especially from the East Indies. Silk was one of the most valuable. And they were concentrated around Cheapside in the seventeenth century.'

'You seem to know a lot about it.'

She pulled one of her sour expressions. 'What do you think I'm doing my PhD on?'

'I didn't know you were doing a PhD'. He didn't like to admit that he had assumed from her appearance that she was an undergraduate.

'You never asked.' She snorted, her face resuming its

normal impassive expression.

'No, I'm sorry. Get you another?' he rose tapping her glass with his own.

'A small one.'

When he returned, she hunched forward and continued her analysis.

'So. This may have something to do with trade. But silk seems to be involved in some way, and I think it has something to do with the East India Company.'

'The East India Company?'

'Yes, you have heard of them?'

'Of course' he exclaimed. 'Who hasn't? They were hugely corrupt and ruled India for years.'

She nodded. 'It's a bit more complicated than that, but I am sure it has something to do with them, and, even more importantly, I think there was some sort of conspiracy going on.'

'Oh, how can you tell that?'

'The Dowgat man. In the 1690s the East India Company got into serious difficulty and a rival company was set up. The men at the centre of this rival company were commonly known as 'The Dowgate Men' because they met in a building in Dowgate Hill in the City.'

Joycey sat back and took several long, slow mouthfuls of beer. 'I still don't get it.'

'No, I can't say I fully understand it either. But there is another clue. The date.'

'Go on'.

'Well this is written in 1701. The government were trying to suppress the import of silks from the East Indies around this time, because it was undermining the domestic silk weaving trade in London. The East India Company became hugely unpopular and the silk weavers rioted in the streets in 1697, sacking the company's offices. In 1700 the government acted and prohibited the import of silk from the Indies.'

'So what do you think?'

'Could be this has something to do with smuggling. And perhaps this William had been condemned to death for it in some way.'

Joycey smiled. 'Nice story. Pity we don't have the letter any more. It could have increased the price.'

'Yes but even so there's still a problem. It doesn't make it valuable enough to kill for.'

11. Marik finds a book

The shop smelt damp. The faintly bitter tang in the air mingled with mustiness and an even more rank air of decay to create an altogether unwholesome atmosphere. Even Joycey noticed it and it made his humour even thinner.

He had woken to a dark Monday morning of low clouds and gloomy air, as though the sky had sagged over east London, weighted down with a voluminous baggage of water. By the time he left the house it was raining hard and the drops looked sulphurous as they splashed on the pavements and roadways.

Typically, Joycey lacked an ability to alter his dress according to the requirements of the weather, and although the battered leather jacket gave some protection, his suede boots didn't. Before he had reached the yard of St Alfege's Church, his toes were running with water, his feet making little squelching sounds as he walked. Stepping out from under the even darker shadow of the church's bulky grey stone, he pulled his collar up against the lashing rain drops, as though this might in some way offer protection to his feet. It didn't help. Furthermore, his hair was overdue for cutting and the dark, rat-tails directed the water down inside his collar with horrible efficiency.

The window of Kazim's was obscured by condensation, emphasising that the temperature outside was falling rapidly – as though Joycey really needed reminding. His fingers, where he clasped the inadequately buttoned front of his jacket together, were aching with cold, and rain collected in annoying drips on the end of his nose. He pushed open the door and stepped into the noisy fug, welcoming the familiar smell of bacon and coffee. A mountainous figure was making its way towards the door and they met in the narrow corridor between the tables. It was Dusty. He wore a faded hoody which was chronically inadequate for his bulging middle so that it exposed a grubby checked shirt spattered with drips of egg yolk. He stopped and raising his head, squinted at Joycey between puffy eyelids. It was almost like Goliath assessing David on the verge of battle.

'Yer,' Dusty groaned. 'Got yer stuff. Got it on Saturday in Lee Green. It's in the van. Bring it down later. Busy first thing. Bloody rain.' He pulled the hood over his head and thrust pudgy hands into the pockets of the hoody so that it immediately stretched and pulled up, revealing his shirt tucked into the elastic of the inevitable grey jogging pants. He squeezed past in a miasma of stale sweat and tobacco reek, so that even Joycey felt obliged to hold his breath for a moment. Then the fat man pulled open the door and wobbled out slowly, his body wheezing along in its usual swinging gait.

Joycey shrugged to himself and turned to the counter, where Kazim and one of his sons were arguing in sharp, Turkish exclamations, as though stabbing one another verbally. Kazim turned and greeted Joycey with an angry shake of the head.

'He wants a car,' he growled, emphasising the first word. 'Just for the girls. He think I don't know what it's all about. But I tell him I wasn't born yesterday, you know.'

Kazim's son scowled over his shoulder as he worked the

Espresso machine and gave Joycey a dark look.

'They cost money to run, insurance, all that.' Kazim started again. 'That's right isn't it', he appealed.

Joycey laughed. 'Don't involve me, Kazim. I can only afford the old van. And that wouldn't pull anyone.'

Kazim laughed. Joycey's battered old Ford transit was well known. He had bought it years before from a local heavy metal band whose fifteen year career had never taken them anywhere more exotic than Southend. When they finally realised their career was never going to take off, the drummer had absconded with most of their equipment and only the van was ever recovered. Since the other members found it a bitter reminder of their failure, they sold it off for a song, and Joycey sang well. Even so, the van had seen some hard use in its time. It had been hand painted black and white, like a zebra, except that years of rust attack had led to red patches in various places, and there were even holes in the lower bodywork. Fortunately, a friendly little garage under the railway arches near New Cross, kept it moving and just about legal.

Dusty and his equally overweight boy arrived at the shop at about 11.30, their open truck loaded with soggy cardboard boxes and soft shapeless bundles in black plastic. While Dusty stood in the door of the shop smoking a cigarette between podgy yellow-stained fingers, the boy staggered in time and again with the sagging boxes. Joycey watched with a degree of dismay before opening the first of the boxes and rummaging with little enthusiasm. There were a lot of battered paperbacks which were fit only for the recycle bin, and which sent him into a fit of tutting and sighing, while Dusty looked on without the slightest trace of concern. But then, buried deeper in the second box, he turned up several nice looking 1950s novels with near mint condition covers, and his mood lightened.

Watching from the inner doorway, Marik recognised the signs, and smiled to himself. The way Joycey became quieter, his fingers turning volumes over quickly, scarcely pausing as he found something he liked the look of, before covering it with something trashy and worthless. There were eight boxes in all, several of them dark and collapsing from the soaking in the back of the truck.

When he had trawled through them, Joycey stood back, leaning against the desk and rolled himself a cigarette. Dusty was looking out of the door, ignoring him, as though watching for something at the end of the road.

'Blimey, where'd you get that lot, Dusty? Old folks home? Ain't much there today.'

Dusty turned, blocking the light from the doorway, rain splashing on the wet stains on his shoulders. He shrugged and growled, 'If you don't want it mate I won't bring it no more. Simple as that.'

'Well, if I give you fifteen I'll be robbing meself, but since you're a regular.' Joycey's language had a habit of slipping deeper into the vernacular when talking to Dusty. He was already pulling three fivers from his wallet when Dusty glanced casually over his shoulder and grunted.

'Yer, alright, mate, save me a trip to the tip anyway.'

The notes changed hands and Joycey watched from the doorway as Dusty lumbered across the pavement to where the boy was waiting in the front of the truck. The vehicle rocked violently as he climbed up behind the driver's wheel and peered ahead across a jumble of discarded coffee cups, old papers and empty cigarette packets. Then he drove off without looking back, while the boy gave Joycey an intense and hostile stare.

The Rain was hammering loudly on the windows before Dusty's truck had turned into the Trafalgar Road and Joycey shut the door, cursing as it ground against the door frame.

When he attempted to move one of the boxes, the cardboard parted like a rotten sponge, and books slithered out onto the floor. He called Marik back out from the rear of the shop, his voice breathless with temper. The young Pole responded to this situation in the usual way by smiling and nodding, meeting Joycey's grumpiness with his own good nature, so that the older man gradually felt embarrassed and awkward.

Then, while Marik began to sort the books, Joycey made coffee and smoked another cigarette before going through the piles that were growing around the desk. He pointed out the slightly more valuable ones and urged Marik to take care with the covers. Then he sat and began marking prices on the inside of the covers in light pencil. After years in the business, he had a good nose for value. But even so, there were some that he wasn't sure about and he put them to one side until he could check their value.

After an hour or more, they had sorted the books, leaving an untidy heap of rejects on the floor. Many of these were children's books which, in Joycey's experience, were hard to sell unless they were in excellent condition and well-illustrated, or unless they were significantly old enough to attract a collector. Marik began piling them into one of the sounder cardboard boxes.

Rain was still driving against the windows, and the light had faded so much that the shop was filled with gloom despite the fluorescent strips. Then, Joycey heard Marik give a chuckle.

'Hey Boss,' his beaming face appeared over the pile of books on the desk. 'I found your map again see!' Then, laughing gleefully he held open a large picture book. There, on the glossy page, was a drawing of a map not dissimilar to that on the missing letter.

Joycey snorted and held out his hand. The book was handed over and he glanced quickly at the page. There, drawn on old parchment was a chart of an island, roughly square in shape, with indentations, coves, hills and trees. The surrounding sea was embellished with two small drawings of sailing ships, and the bottom right hand corner was dominated by a compass rose with straight lines radiating out from it. Handwritten annotations marked the island in several places. He peered closely and read out several of them.

'Skeleton Island, Spyglass Hill, Swamp.' Along the bottom of the map in red ink, a hand had written: 'Treasure Island. Aug. 1750. Given by above JF to Mr W Bones Mate of ye Walrus Savannah this twenty July 1754. WB'. He laughed and flicked the book over to glance at the cover. It was *The Treasure Island* by Robert Louis Stevenson. He turned back to the map and gazed at it with some amusement.

'Hey Boss, perhaps we should put it up there for sale'.

Joycey considered for a moment. The book was tatty. The spine was loose and many of the pages just hanging in place by the binding threads. It was unlikely it would sell. Then he carefully tore the page from the book, pulling it gently from its thread so that the damage to the page was minimal. 'There.'

Then, folding the page deftly, he slid it into the empty plastic folder on the wall. From a distance, and obscured by the light reflecting off the plastic, the page could have been mistaken for a real document.

Marik grinned as Joycey took a post-it note, wrote '£35' on it, and slapped it on the folder.

'Now', Joycey grinned, 'let's see who's the first to enquire about that!'

12. At the Warrington

At the end of a week made long by incessant rain and poor trade, Joycey pushed open the doors and stepped inside the comfort zone of the Warrington Arms. Outside it was raining again, and against the grey light, the bright lamps of the pub, with its battered red flock, wallpaper embraced all comers with an almost maternal welcome. Inside, a hubbub of chatter and laughter swelled into the air like the welcome of the tropical jungle at dawn, and Joycey shouldered his way through a good humoured crowd to the bar and ordered a pint.

The Warrington Arms was a dinosaur of a venue. A battered old Victorian pub with a cavernous, high-ceilinged interior, and a central bar of stained old mahogany and ebony beer-pumps. Behind the bar, bottles stood in neat rows in front of old etched mirrors advertising a long since forgotten brewery. Around the walls, benches, chairs and tables were cluttered in profusion, and everything conveyed an air of shabbiness and informality. Upholstery, where it still existed, was torn and stained with years of food and beer, and the tables exuded an air of ancient vinegar that no amount of spraying could eliminate.

But despite this care-worn air, the pub was hugely popular

and attracted a loyal following of students and men of Joycey's age. For, not only were the prices markedly lower than London's usual wallet-stripping average, the pub was one of the few in East London that still provided a venue for live bands. And it was for this reason that Joycey regularly ventured from his home territory south of the river on a Sunday lunchtime. For the Warrington Arms lay hidden in a narrow back street in Whitechapel, north of the river.

There was an atmosphere of rarity about the pub itself, for it had remained relatively true to its origins while most of the other pubs in the area had suffered the indignity of gentrification. A wave of reproduction was sweeping east of the Tower leaving a trail of trendy bars or strip-pine eateries. The Warrington, as it was usually known, had survived two world wars and the holocaust of regeneration, and only a few of its neighbouring houses remained, clinging on either side of it like decrepit geriatrics, while the rest of the street was lined with the concrete facades of blocks of flats.

It was here, every other weekend, that Joycey met up with that select band of people whose status hovered somewhere between friends and acquaintances. For, truth be told, Joycey was not the sort of man who really had close friends. His life of wheeling and dealing had required both a fleetness of foot and an unreadability that attracted little moss. So now, on his regular Sundays, he met up with a small group of men and women for an intermittent catch-up on gossip, to share a few beers and memories, before they returned to their everyday ordinariness of life. And of course, there was the band. The Warrington was best known for showcasing young bands who were trying to establish themselves, and for this reason on most nights of the week, the place was heaving. But Sunday lunchtimes were a more sedate affair. The bands were noticeably older, and this was matched by most of the clientele.

Today's offering was a three-piece who went by the name of Wicky and the Wheelers – and who specialised in romping cover versions of classic rock songs. Wicky, whose real name was Philip, was the only one of the three with hair on his scalp, and his Stratocaster was hung ridiculously on an ample belly held in place by a belt and suitably faded jeans. The drummer, sporting a ZZ Top beard, banged his drums several times from his position between the monumental amplifier stacks and they tore into their opening number with zestful enthusiasm. Groundbreaking it might not have been, but it was well played and comfortable, and soon everyone was stomping their feet, shaking their heads and shouting at the tops of their voices.

As the first hour passed, the band roared through one familiar old favourite after another, each one receiving whoops of recognition and approval, and sealed with loud applause and the thunderous stamp of feet on the bare boards.

After five pints, Joycey had mellowed enough to be slightly uncertain of where he ended and the rest of the world began. He wasn't drunk, but he was well into affability, that state when all the world can be your friend and even your enemies can get a reprieve for the asking. Furthermore, as far as he could tell, the rest of the pub felt the same way. And that was one of the nice things about these Sunday sessions. All very friendly. Never any aggro. Never any hassle.

Outside it grew dark. Stopped raining, and then started again. People came and went, but not many, and the band played on. Joycey and his associates clung proprietorially to their corner of the bar, parting occasionally to allow passage to the bar itself, but always reasserting their right of possession. Every now and again, someone would join them and then leave again. There were quick trips outside to smoke in the rain, or rapid dives into the evil smelling lavatories. But Joycey and company were always there for the duration.

It must have been at about 3pm that Joycey felt a tug at his sleeve and turned to find a stocky young man with a cropped haircut standing beside him. Not recognising him, he smiled amiably and nodded. The man pulled a twisted grin then cupped his hand to his mouth to shout up at Joycey.

'You Joycey Becket?'

Joycey nodded, wondering vaguely who it was that knew his name.

'You the bloke what got his shop done in, yeah?'

Somewhere in Joycey's slightly wandering brain, some unknown keys suddenly snapped into place and, a warning signal was partially registered in a dim corner of his consciousness. He stared at the man again, bringing his features into sharper focus for a moment.

'Who are you then?'

The man gave another twisted grin and seemed about to laugh. But even as Joycey stared, the man shrank in size and backed away quickly. Before Joycey could speak again or move, the man was threading his way quickly through the crowded bar. Over the tops of heads, Joycey saw the door swing open and close. He frowned and turned to speak to the others but there was a sudden crescendo of drums and guitar chords and the band finished their current number. A loud howl of approval filled the room

Unsettled, Joycey peered around the room, but no-one met his gaze. He glanced quickly round at his associates who were all still chattering and laughing – but there was not the remotest sign that any of them had registered the presence of the stranger. It was as though the man had never been there and, as the moments passed and the band launched into yet another Stones song, Joycey himself began to wonder. But he was also aware of an odd feeling that had pierced the cosiness of his afternoon, as though a door had been left open and a chill wind had entered and sought him out. He was no longer comfortable and in his sudden isolation, he felt vulnerable. He looked round again, to see if anyone was looking at him, but all eyes were on the band, and he felt even more alienated.

It was perhaps this disturbance which encouraged him to slip beyond his normal limits and down three more pints before the band hammered to the end of their afternoon set. As the crowd gradually dispersed, Joycey was swaying uncontrollably and grinning stupidly, much to the amusement of his associates. On the far side of the room a pair of eyes had been monitoring his progress with, initially, disapproval and finally with concern. As Joycey pulled himself upright and gritted his teeth in an attempt to control the random spinning of his vision and the unwelcome nausea, his observer prepared to leave.

13. On Wapping Wall

It struck Joycey that the pavement under his feet felt firmer than usual, as though it was resisting his weight, pushing back up against him in protest. In reaction his knees seemed to buckle all too easily and he made a slow, unsteady progress through streets that were murky with mist and bursts of rain. The air smelt cold and the sweat on his brow felt strangely warm. It seemed to be taking a long time to get anywhere and his blood seemed to be pulsating unhealthily in time to his movements. After a while, the drumming in his ears resolved itself into the sound of the Stones' 'Paint it Black' and Joycey began to mumble the words, jerking his elbows and shrugging in what he believed was a passable imitation of Mick Jagger. Not everyone was impressed. A cat stared at him in alarm from under a car and an approaching young couple veered suddenly across to the far side of the road.

The Whitechapel Underground Station found him some time later, having caused confusion by drifting further along the Whitechapel Road than it had any right to. By the time he reached it, though, the rain was again falling in shimmering curtains that all but blotted out buildings on the far side of the road. He ducked inside and finding his oyster card after some searching, stumbled uneasily down the long flight of steps, obeying an instinctive feeling that this might be less problematic than the confined space of the lift. There was a long wait for the train and by the time he had seated himself inside the rattling carriage he was beginning to wish that he had stopped somewhere to relieve the pressure in his bladder. It didn't take long for the train to get to Shadwell where, as he waited for the train to depart again, he crossed his legs firmly, determined not to surrender to the discomfort. By the time the train had reached Wapping station the sweat on his forehead had become hot and his resolution dissolved. As they screeched to a halt deep in the station's noisy crypt, he leapt to his feet and sprinted heavily for the stairs.

Bursting through the gates at street level he turned left in the semi -darkness and darted for the nearest dark doorway. There he urinated copiously, leaning with his head pressed against the rough surface of cold stonework. No-one passed and he was glad. When he had finished, he looked quickly up and down the empty road and began walking. He knew he was walking along Wapping High Street, but after about ten minutes it dawned on him that he might have walked past the station without paying attention. He stopped, turned about and about again, and then became totally confused. Looking one way and then another, the high vertical walls of the old converted warehouses and the new heritage apartment blocks all seemed similar. There were lights in some of the windows, a few parked cars, but the rain had driven most people off the streets and now, this close to the Thames, a bitter wind was beginning to bluster its way between the buildings.

Joycey paused several times to look around. In the distance he glimpsed one or two dark figures moving along the pavements but too far away to speak to. He walked on anyway, not quite trusting himself to articulate an enquiry in any intelligible manner. As the chill seemed to deepen he turned the collar of the leather jacket up, grateful now for the soft heaviness of its antiquity. But as he walked on, his head spinning slightly, he became aware of a return of the unease that he had felt earlier. And this gradually resolved into the feeling that he was being watched. Several times he stopped, looked around and saw nothing – or paused to listen, hearing only the buffeting of the wind on the building facades and the thin spattering of the rain above his hoarse breathing.

After several hundred yards the road suddenly submerged into a length of darkness. Whether it was a power cut or a sequence of failed street lights he didn't know, but he was conscious that he was moving from the relative comfort of the amber light into deeper shadow. He walked on, numbed fingers clutching at the front of his jacket, until he reached a small cross roads. To his right, behind a low wire fence, there was a patch of derelict land filled with what looked like the dying remnants of summer vegetation. To his left a dark alleyway leading down towards the river. Just as he went to pass this, he heard his name being called quietly. He turned and as he did so something hit him from the right hand side, spinning him into the entrance of the alleyway. His left arm flailed out to find support and his knuckles rasped on rough brickwork.

'Fuckin 'ell,' he shouted in outrage, but before he could react in any other way a stocky dark figure rose before him, and something hard hit him under the ribs. He doubled up and dropped to his knees, and another blow banged into his left cheek, splitting the skin across his cheek bone. Something came up from below and connected with his lips, his mouth flooded with the taste of iron.

'Shit!' he yelled.

Fists grasped the front of his jacket, lifting him from his

knees and then thrusting him down onto the pavement again, the violence of the movement making his knee caps scream with pain. Joycey suddenly vomited profusely, like a human fountain, and the figure backed away slightly, swearing.

At that moment there was a loud shriek in the distance. It came again and there was a flash of light, then another. An angry voice grew louder, closer. There was a stampede of footsteps and Joycey's assailant melted away somewhere. On his hands and knees, spitting bile and blood, Joycey wretched and shook his head. Someone was kneeling beside him, a pale face in the darkness. Then he heard a woman's voice.

'Are you all right?'

He shook his head, trying to clear the ringing muzziness, and a small hand inserted itself under his armpit and began to haul him upwards. He put a hand to the wall to steady himself and blinked to focus on that pale face just above him.

'Who was that?' she asked.

'Christ knows.' Joycey wiped his mouth with the back of a hand, leaving a smear of blood.

'Look, there's a pub just along there, we'll go and get help.'

He resisted but his saviour was insistent, and he was still a little shaky. Together they tottered along the road another hundred yards and came to a riverside pub with green windows behind the brick arched gateway of an old warehouse. As they stepped into the light of its floodlights, Joycey found himself looking down at the anxious face of Takk.

Their entry into the fairly crowded pub caused something

of a stir. Alarmed faces turned in their direction and, at the stern shake of the head from a man in a suit, a barman rushed towards them, arms outspread to block their way.

Takk stood her ground, shouting loudly.

'This poor man's just been mugged outside. He needs help.'

The agitation in the pub changed flavour rapidly. The bar manager rushed forward with a stool, several of the drinkers rose quickly to assist and Joycey was rapidly seated and dabbed with wet paper towels until a first-aid kit was located. He refused an ambulance and Takk acted the role of an unconnected bystander, thus eliciting more sympathy. A police car arrived and Joycey was led to a quiet corner to make a statement, while Takk stood at the bar looking as though, without too much provocation, she might just bite. When her turn came to be interviewed, Joycey watched intrigued as her demeanour changed from that of a scratchy cat to one of calm and mature confidence.

Within an hour, it seemed, the event had virtually been forgotten by all except Joycey and Takk. The police had gone, having taken details and notes; many of the clientele had gone to be replaced by new arrivals who glanced briefly at the couple seated at a low table in the corner but then moved on with only slight curiosity; and the bar staff changed shifts after a brief exchange of information that also involved surreptitious glances towards Joycey's battered visage.

Joycey's battered jacket had been dabbed with the wet paper towels, so most of the blood had gone leaving just a few distasteful smears here and there. His face, though, was badly swollen and he mumbled through swollen lips. It seemed hardly possible for Joycey to look more disreputable, and it was therefore no surprise that they were surrounded by a discreet zone of privacy.

'I saw you, earlier.' Takk volunteered, 'At the Warrington.'

'Oh'.

She gazed at him for several long moments, then said disapprovingly. 'Drink at lot don't you.'

He shrugged. 'Not usually. Not this much anyway.'

Takk's face was impassive.

'Why were you there anyway?' he asked. 'Never seen you there before.'

'Not likely to either. Not my sort of place. It was a mate's birthday. He lives close by with some others from Uni and he thought it would be fun.'

He looked at her closely. 'And was it? Fun, I mean?'

'No. As I said, that's not my sort of music and I don't drink that much.'

'Oh. What sort of music do you like then?'

She stared at him. 'Stuff you'd never've heard of.'

Joycey felt like he'd been smacked again, though not quite as hard as before.

'Well, I suppose it was lucky you were here,' he observed after a while, then he frowned suspiciously. 'Why were you about anyway, were you following me?'

Takk looked away abruptly.

'You were following me, weren't you?' He laughed, feeling vaguely pleased.

She snorted. 'You were pissed.'

'So?'

'I was curious. That's all.' Her eyes fixed on his for a moment, black pupils unwavering, giving nothing away. She was clearly going to offer no explanation.

'I don't need a minder.' He grunted eventually.

'Yeah, right.'

He looked away, defeated. Takk sat immobile, her gaze gradually softening.

'How are you feeling, anyway,' she asked after a long pause.

Joycey shrugged again and said nothing.

'Who was that who attacked you?'

'No idea.'

'I suppose he was after your wallet then.'

Joycey dabbed at his mouth with the back of his hand and took a sip of well-iced water. He had wanted something stronger but Takk had overruled him, to the approval of the bar staff.

'I don't think so. He knew who I was.'

Takk's dark eyes were fixed on him for a long moment. 'How do you know?'

'I heard him call my name, just before he hit me.'

Takk's eyes widened. 'Friend of yours then.'

Joycey laughed shortly and shook his head. Then he told her about the stranger who had approached him in the pub. She hadn't seen the man.

'But he knew about the break in,' she observed.

'Seems so.'

'Did he mention the letter, the map?'

'No.'

'But he may have known about it?'

Joycey shrugged. 'Suppose so'.

There was another long pause while Takk ferreted in the deep canvas bag she had slung across he shoulders.

'I'm going to get some water,' she explained, 'do you want some more?'

He nodded, downing the dregs and ice cubes, and thanked her. His face was throbbing as he watched her stride in a determined fashion towards the bar. She seemed to diminish in height as she reached the bar itself but her gestures and posture defiantly contradicted any suspicion of vulnerability. She had played down the courage with which she had intervened to help him, and using the phone camera had been a clever idea - though the images captured had been too blurred to be of any help. Not for the first time he found himself viewing her with unusual respect.

She lifted the glasses from the bar and began walking back towards him. But after several paces she stopped suddenly, her eyes fixed on something he could not see on the wall to his right. Whatever it was she took several steps towards it and stood stock still for an unnaturally long time. Then she turned abruptly and walked quickly towards him.

'I think,' she said with quiet excitement, 'I have an idea.'

14. Making a connection

Takk had extracted her tablet from her bag and was busy tapping away at the screen. From where he sat, Joycey could make out very little of what appeared on the screen, so quickly was she swiping away images and documents. Then at last she nodded to herself and turned the screen towards him.

'You recognise this.' She hissed quietly

Joycey squinted, remembering once again that it he was long overdue for some new glasses. Screwing up his eyes he managed to get the image into near focus and recognised the colour and handwriting of the stolen letter. He glanced at Takk and nodded.

'Yeah.'

'The date on this is 29th April 1701, right? And what did we agree the name of the author was?'

Once again Joycey felt like he was being set a test, like a school boy, but the quiet and insistent urgency of Takk's voice prevented any protest. He thought for a moment, scanning the letter for the clue he needed.

'Um, didn't you say it was William?'

'Yes', she hissed, 'and the letter indicated that he was about to die, right?'

He nodded solemnly. His ribs were beginning to ache badly.

'Well I know a William who died a few days after this letter was written.' There was a glow of triumph in her face. 'In fact, this William was executed, and if it is the same person, I think I may have an idea what the map is too.'

Joycey refocused on Takk's face. She was leaning towards him, her eyes searching his face for a response. He shrugged.

'Go on.'

'Where are we now?'

'In the pub.'

'Which pub? What's the name of this pub?'

'The er, Prospect of Whitby.'

Takk groaned in exasperation. 'No it's not The Prospect of Whitby. I know the Prospect and it's a lot further back towards Limehouse.'

'Oh come on, give us a break' he moaned weakly. 'This hasn't been the best day I've ever had.'

'This is the Captain Kidd. We are sat in the Captain Kidd.'

He looked at her for a long moment, slowly digesting this information. 'The Captain Kidd.'

'Yes' she hissed excitedly. 'And what was Captain

Kidd's first name?'

'Johnny.'

She snorted. 'It was William. William. He was William Kidd. Do you get it?'

'So you think our letter was written by Captain Kidd?'

'Could be. And what was Captain Kidd?'

He thought for a moment, trying to pull together shreds of intelligence from a brain that was now trying to focus on pains growing in various parts of his body.

'Wasn't he a pirate?'

'Yes.' Her voice rose in excitement. 'And he was executed on the riverside here at Wapping, just days after your letter was written.'

'Hang on, let me get this straight.' He repeated her words, allowing the meaning to force its way into his brain. When it had, he stared at her. 'How do you make that out?'

'Look, we have a letter written by someone called William…'

'Not any more we don't,' he interjected, but she ignored him.

'…who had been condemned to death just a few days before the letter was written. Someone who seemed to be connected with a plot or conspiracy of some sort.'

He forced his eyes to scan the letter again, reading slowly, forming the words with his lips. Then he nodded at her. She gave him a long look, as if assessing him. Then she turned the tablet round and rapidly tapped the screen with her long black nails. Finally, she gave a snort and turned the screen towards him again.

There was the Wikipedia page for Captain William Kidd. She tapped it significantly.

'Captain Kidd was executed on the river bank here at Wapping on 23rd May, 1701. According to this, he was framed or set up, and died proclaiming his innocence. Don't you see, the circumstances fit with your letter. And it says here that he plundered East India Company ships which were carrying silks, gold, silver and other valuables. And see...' she tapped the screen again so that the letter flicked back into view. '...the letter refers to silks which could be taken to the mercer in Cheapside.'

Joycey's brain was still muzzy. The soft light of the pub, and the long lasting effects of alcohol, were making him drowsy. He gazed round the bar and then a thought struck him.

'So he was executed here, outside the pub?'

'Well, that's what the pub reckon anyway. There are some display panels on the wall beside the bar.' She looked pointedly in their direction.

'Bloody hell,' he murmured eventually. 'So we had a letter written by a famous pirate. It was probably worth money. No wonder someone wanted to steal it.'

'Steal it, or get it back?'

He shrugged. 'Either way, we haven't got it now.'

'No, not exactly. But we do have photos of it, which is nearly as good. Anyway, the thing is that something about this letter is important. So important that someone was prepared to kill for it.'

'You said that before.' He observed ruefully.

'Yes. And I think they've now tried to warn you off too. The thing is that now we also know more about the letter.

Whatever it is that makes it important…'

'Or valuable.'

'Yes…whatever it is, it has to have something to do with Captain Kidd.'

Joycey shrugged unhappily. His face was throbbing and there was a dull ache in his abdomen. The alcohol had served as a temporary anaesthetic, but as that effect began to wear off, his body was becoming increasingly aware of the damage it had received.

Takk was looking at him with some concern. 'I think we'd better get you home.'

Joycey stared at her bleakly. He didn't really want to move and he was secretly extremely grateful when she suggested they get a cab.

It was mid-day when Joycey finally made his way to the little shop in East Greenwich. He wasn't worried about being late – he never was; for it was Monday, and trade was never enthusiastic on a Monday morning. Besides which, he knew that Marik would be there to open up, as he did most mornings. It wasn't the first time that he found himself being grateful for the young man's Eastern European sense of responsibility. Joycey put it down to the legacy of the Communist era, when everyone had a clear understanding of their sense of duty and had to work.

On this Monday morning, however, a change had taken place within the shop. Although the sign on the door said the shop was open, the door itself resisted when he pushed it. It was locked, and he had to rap with his knuckles to get Marik's attention. The young man came hurrying out with a slightly sheepish expression on his face.

'Sorry Boss, it was her idea. She said so.'

He walked into the shop and then turned in surprise as Marik locked the door again. Just inside the back area of the shop, a small trestle table had been set up with a battered looking desk lamp, which Joycey recognised from the old cupboard in the kitchen. Several books were piled on the table, and Takk was sat there with an expensive looking laptop. She looked up as Joycey entered and nodded curtly.

'Feeling better?'

'Course!' he winced and Takk frowned at him briefly.

'Busy?'

She nodded, her eyes rapidly scanning the page of a book propped open against several others. For a moment, he a considered a quip about her finding a university to work in, but then reconsidered it.

'So,' he asked at last, 'what's going on?'

'She said better to lock, boss.' Marik explained

'Yes of course.' Joycey nodded, not really understanding.

Takk looked up and glared at him for several moments. 'I'm going to find out what this is all about,' she said with determination. 'And this seems the best place to start.' She waved a hand over the books scattered on the table.

'Don't tell me, we've got books on Captain Kidd.'

Takk snorted. 'Sometimes I wonder how you make a living at this. You don't seem to have any idea about your own stock.'

'I buy books, I sell them for more than I pay, and I make a profit,' he shrugged, then added as an after-thought; 'Usually.'

Takk's eyes fixed him with a bleak glare and he wondered what had happened to the caring woman he had seen the previous evening.

'Well, you've got some useful books here on Kidd. In fact your stock on piracy and the East India Company is very good. My guess is that these have come from a previous student from the Maritime Institute. Someone who was doing a PhD.'

'You could well be right.' Joycey was thinking about a strong coffee. He turned away, but then hesitated. 'So why have we got the door locked?'

Takk spoke without looking up. 'Because we don't want anybody to know that we are looking into this. After all, you were probably being warned to keep out of it. If anyone comes in, I'll simply hide the books until they've gone and pretend to be just another customer.'

Joycey nodded and went to make a coffee without commenting further. When he returned Takk was deep in concentration and Marik was standing in the doorway, casting wistful expressions in her direction. Joycey grinned to himself, recognising the signs.

The afternoon passed slowly. After an hour, Joycey sent Marik for coffee and bacon rolls from Kazim's – though Takk refused anything but herbal tea. A slightly doubtful Marik departed with a specific request for Fennel. While he was gone, Joycey cast several glances into the back room, from whence came the continuous sound of Takk's nails clattering in the keys of her laptop, but she was bent over the books, the shapeless woollen hat pulled down over her ears as though to keep out a draught. Every now and then there was a quiet thump as she cast a book aside. Once she uttered a quiet exclamation and but this was followed by a prolonged silence.

When Marik returned, the two men ate silently at the desk, as though afraid to break a spell that had been cast over them. Takk sipped her tea, but said nothing, hardly even looking up from her work. As the hours passed, Joycey found himself getting more and more curious, and it became something of a struggle to conceal his impatience. He wanted to ask questions, to get at least some idea what she knew. Finally he started to get irritated and wondered whether to ask her if she didn't have a lecture to go to.

This state was disturbed abruptly, once, when someone tried the front door and then rattled it in frustration. Marik opened it to reveal a thin woman in a barbour jacket with a small white dog on a lead. Joycey looked at it with some distaste, but it transpired that she was looking for another book shop entirely, and she was soon sent on her way in a non-too courteous fashion.

It was dark before Takk appeared in the doorway looking tired but triumphant. She gave a rare smile at both men and nodded.

'Well, I think I've got some idea, about Captain Kidd anyway. Which may explain the letter.'

'Yeah?' Joycey grinned at her expectantly.

'It's a long story, but I'll try and keep it short. Thing is…'

'What?'

'I need to eat.'

15. Captain Kidd

After some discussion it was agreed that they would make their way separately to the Plume once again. Takk thought that it was possible that if anyone was watching them, they might be getting more suspicious about the fact that the three of them had locked themselves in the bookshop for so long. So Joycey left first in order that he could bag an isolated table in the pub's restaurant area. Marik and Takk deferred to his insistence that he was more likely to recognise a stranger there than they – and Joycey was confident in Marik's ability to secure the shop and make his way discretely. Besides, it was unlikely that the two of them would attract much undue attention walking through Greenwich together.

It was raining persistently as Joycey plodded his way through the back streets, more conscious of this various aches and pains than anything else around him. He entered the pub, ordered a pint and sat down in the semi-gloom at the back of the bar. It was a good position, beyond the door to the Gents toilet, so no customers would be likely to wander past. He sat sipping his pint and looking, as casually as he could, at the other customers. Several he recognised, and those he didn't looked innocent enough. Five minutes later, Takk and Marik arrived. They were laughing at something and it seemed to Joycey, with the slightest hint of jealousy, that she seemed more relaxed in the young Pole's company. They ordered their drinks and made their way to the corner. Takk's shoulder bag looked heavy, a fact which was confirmed by the quiet thump as she dropped it on the table. She gave him a brief smile and then took the stool at the narrow end of the table so that she was sitting with her back to the wall.

'Ok, so...' Joycey began expectantly.

Takk gave him an exasperated look. 'Food first, we need to order. That's why we came here, after all.'

Joycey conceded the point, even though he was customarily satisfied with a couple of pints. He grabbed a menu from the bar and then placed their order, selecting a light snack for himself, just to be sociable.

When he got back to the table, Takk had pulled her laptop from her bag, along with two hard-backed books which she had carefully laid on the table face down. Marik was gazing at her with what looked like a confusion of adoration and respect, which she seemed to be ignoring.

'Ok,' she began at last, speaking softly after a careful look round the bar. 'I'm going to assume that neither of you know anything about Captain Kidd. Ok?'

They nodded solemnly.

'I knew a little about him before this, because my research has been about the East India Company, but this is just amazing.' She realized that the two men were gazing at her blankly, so she cleared her throat and carried on in a more serious voice.

'This Captain Kidd thing is incredible. And what I've already gathered is that there are two schools of thought about him and what he did. One side thinks he was an innocent man who was framed and ended up being executed to cover up a major scam. The other side argues that he really was a pirate who mishandled things completely and paid the price for it with his life. These two books...' she tapped finger nails on the backs of each of the books laid in front of them, '...these take the opposing views. So it was really useful that you had them both in the shop.'

She gave Joycey a sweet smile. He found it disturbing.

'No-body knows much about Kidd's early life. He was born in Scotland around 1650, and by the late 1680s he was in command of a privateer in the Caribbean.' She stopped, seeing their puzzled expressions. 'A privateer was a private warship. In time of war they were given a licence to go and attack enemy shipping, usually merchantmen. It was a form of legal piracy, especially as they got to keep most of any plunder they captured.'

Seeing them nod, she carried on with her narrative.

'So, Captain Kidd was in command of one of these ships and he was recruited by the Royal Navy to help fight the French. According to both of these books he was good at his job, but wasn't very good at controlling his crew because they eventually mutinied and sailed off with his ship.'

Joycey grinned.

'Anyway,' Takk continued, 'he made his way to New York where, for about six or seven years he lived as a very successful merchant. Now the thing is this. New York was a British colony and its merchants were very prosperous. And just like the more affluent people in London, they wanted to be able to purchase luxury items like fashionable silks and spices from the East Indies. The problem was that the East India Company had the complete monopoly on trade with India and China, so all goods from the East Indies had to be imported from London, which meant the New York merchants had to pay higher prices to get them. And then on top of that they were subjected to additional and - they argued - unfair taxation. So to get round this they resorted to the simplest solution. Smuggling. But since this was illegal, the only way to get the items they wanted was from people who had acquired them illegally. In other words, pirates.

By the time Kidd settled in New York the whole thing had become well organised, with a trading base on Madagascar. That's off the south east coast of Africa,' she added seeing Joycey's vague expression. 'The pirates took their stolen plunder there, and traded East India produce for the stuff that they needed, guns, gunpowder, new sails, equipment for their ships...'

'Rum,' Marik interjected with a big grin.

'Yes, Rum too. The Americans were able to get rum from the Caribbean, and take it to Madagascar. The trade was highly lucrative, but of course, it was taking profit away from the East India Company, and the government were losing revenue from taxation.'

'Can't imagine they were too happy about that,' Joycey said wryly.

'No. The East India Company began to demand the government do something to reign in the New Yorkers and to put a stop to piracy. The problem was that New York had a corrupt government which was taking its own cut from the smuggling trade, and the Admiralty was too busy fighting the French to spare any ships to suppress piracy in the Indian Ocean.'

At this point a waitress approached carrying plates, and Takk fell silent and cleared the books from the table. When the waitress had gone, she resumed her narrative.

'Kidd was almost certainly involved with the smuggling trade, because as it later turns out, he knew a lot about the pirates and navigating in the Indian Ocean.'

'That doesn't make him a pirate though, does it?' Joycey asked, looking enviously at Marik's steak and chips.

Takk thought for a moment and then said, 'No, perhaps not on its own. But it's what happens next that is most revealing. In 1695 he suddenly turned up in London. And within months he had been given a royal commission to go and hunt for pirates in the Indian Ocean, and to do this he was given a heavily armed ship called the *Adventure Galley*. According to one view, he had come to London on a legitimate trading venture and fell in with a syndicate which coerced him into taking on the mission. Kidd himself always claimed that he was unwilling to do it. However, the opposing view is that Kidd came to London deliberately to find people with money to back the expedition.' Takk concentrated on her food for a minute, allowing this information to sink in.

'So,' Joycey observed, 'someone was willing to back the idea?'

'Yes and this is where it becomes really interesting. The return on the investment was going to come from the illicit sale of the pirates' plunder in New York. And the people who invested in the expedition were some of the most powerful politicians in the Whig government in Westminster.'

Joycey laughed. 'Bugger me, corruption at Westminster, nothing changes does it.'

Takk ignored him and continued her narrative.

'So Kidd was given a ship and a crew, and was made to sign a contract which set a very strict timetable for the completion of the project. Then he set off from Deptford. But he only got as far as Sheerness before he was stopped and most of his crew were pressed into the Royal Navy. In fact his ship was seized too, initially, but one of the investors in the project was the First Lord of the Admiralty and he intervened to get Kidd and some of his crew released.'

'Hang on,' Joycey was picking his teeth with a match. 'I don't get it. If he wasn't a pirate, why'd they stop him and seize his ship?'

Takk grinned. 'Because as they passed the navy ships anchored off Sheerness, the *Adventure Galley* was supposed to lower her flag as a mark of respect. Instead, Kidd's crew all swarmed up the rigging and mooned at them.'

Marik was looking lost, so Joycey explained. 'They dropped their pants and waved their bare arses.' Marik looked a little embarrassed.

'Well,' Takk observed slowly, 'I suppose if they were all pirates that wouldn't be too surprising would it.'

Joycey shook his head and grinned. 'Nah. Typical pirate thing that.'

'Anyway, it meant that Kidd had to go and get another crew, and the only place he knew where he could get the sort of men he needed was New York.'

'That's the wrong way for Madagascar then.'

'Yes. It put him badly behind schedule. Anyway, to cut the story short, Kidd recruited a new crew in New York. Somebody there saw what was going on and claimed they were nothing but a gang of pirates and that Kidd wouldn't be able to control them. Then they sailed for the Indian Ocean.'

'Hang on,' Joycey was scratching his head. 'He was supposed to be hunting down pirates to take their treasure from them. So why'd he recruit a gang of pirates into his crew?'

'Probably because they would be happy to act like pirates? Anyway Kidd obviously knew about the pirate trading bases on Madagascar because he headed there first. The problem was that there were no pirates. He hunted the area for months but, for whatever reason, there were no pirate ships around. Or at least, that is what Kidd claimed.'

She finished forking food into her mouth and wiped her lips with a napkin. 'Now this is where the controversy really begins. According to Kidd…and to historians who claim that he was innocent of piracy…he decided to sail to the Malabar Coast – that's on the west coast of India. He didn't find any pirates there, but he did find two French merchantmen, and since Britain was at war with the French and he was a privateer, he attacked and captured them both. According to Kidd, the captains of both the ships presented him with French papers or passes, and this was all the proof that he needed that they were legitimate prizes, and one of the ships, the *Quedah Merchant* carried a hugely valuable cargo.

According to Kidd and his modern supporters, it was at this point that things started to go wrong. The *Adventure Galley* literally started to fall apart. She had been built close to here at Deptford and wasn't particularly well built. The syndicate who put up the money were in a hurry, so she may not have been properly inspected before they bought her. So, by the time, Kidd had taken his two prizes, she was in pretty poor condition. In fact, she was in danger of sinking. So Kidd decided to sail to Madagascar, presumably in the hope of being able to carry out repairs. But when he got there his crew promptly mutinied and joined a pirate ship which was already there.'

'Wait a minute,' Joycey frowned, 'why did he go to Madagascar then? If he'd already got what he wanted, why did he sail somewhere where he knew there were likely to be pirates? That don't make sense.'

'I agree. It didn't sound like the *Adventure Galley* was in any fit state to fight them off and, on top of that, he had his two prizes with him. When you think about it, the last thing he should have wanted was to run into a well-armed pirate who might take his prizes from him. On the other hand, it is possible, as Kidd claimed, that his ship was in danger of sinking and there was nowhere else he could go to either carry out repairs.'

'Hmm, but if the other ship the *Qued,,,Qued..*'

'*Quedah Merchant.*'

'Yeah, that one. If she was in good condition, why didn't he simply transfer everything to that and abandon the *Adventure Galley*?'

'Well that could have been his intention, because that is what he did in the end. But at the time, when he got to Madagascar he couldn't do anything because his crew abandoned him.'

'He lose crew twice.' Marik observed quietly.

Takk gazed at him for a moment. 'Yes Marik, you're right. It was the second time one of his crews had mutinied. This time though, they may have had good cause. While they were off the coast of India, the crew became impatient with their lack of success, and when the ship's gunner, challenged him about it, Kidd killed him on the spot.'

'Sounds like a pirate.' Joycey commented. 'Blackbeard shot someone didn't he?'

'Kidd didn't shoot him. He hit him over the head with an iron-bound bucket and fractured his skull.'

'Nice.' Joycey drained his glass.

'There's a lot of things about Kidd which are slightly odd,' Takk observed quietly. 'Anyway, somehow he managed to save the *Quedah Merchant* and all the plunder from the two ships, but it took about a year before he could sail it away from Madagascar.'

Both of the men were frowning and Takk could see that Joycey was trying to find the words to ask a question, so she asked the question for him. 'I know, why did it take so long?'

'Yeah and how did he keep all his plunder if his crew turned pirate. Surely they would have simply taken it off of him, told him to piss off?'

'Seems more likely doesn't it. But Kidd's story – and he stuck to it - was that he abandoned the *Adventure Galley* and managed to defend the *Quedah Merchant* against the pirates until he could scratch a small crew together to help him sail away.'

Joycey looked unconvinced.

'It is pretty lame,' Takk agreed. 'But that was his story. There is an alternative view which I will tell you about in a minute. Kidd's orders were to sail to New York or Boston where he was to deliver the plunder to one of the syndicate – actually the colony's new Governor, the Earl of Bellomont. However, according to those who think Kidd was innocent, the syndicate had panicked, and Kidd had been declared a pirate, with a price on his head. When he turned up at Boston, the Governor had him arrested and shipped back to England in chains.'

Joycey rose to his feet abruptly. 'Who need's a top-up?'

16. Kidd betrayed

In response to Joycey's question, Marik hesitated and then nodded, and Takk asked for a lime and soda. When Joycey returned Takk resumed her narrative.

'Kidd was brought back to London, and put in Newgate prison for nearly a year. Then he was put on trial by the High Court of the Admiralty. He thought he was going to be charged with piracy, but as he had kept the French passes from the two ships he captured, he thought these would prove his innocence. However, before he was charged with piracy he was charged with the murder of his gunner. Since there were several witnesses to this event…'

'What, from his crew?'

'Yes, some had deserted earlier and they turned King's evidence. They gave quite damning statements to the Admiralty Court. In those days the accused had no right to a defence lawyer, and Kidd was either ill or incompetent. He more or less admitted to the charge, claiming that his gunner was a mutinous dog and deserved to die – or words to that effect. Perhaps a more sympathetic court might have agreed with this, but in fact it's clear they wanted to get Kidd. So he was found guilty, and the sentence carried a mandatory punishment. Death.'

Takk let the word fall onto the table, and it sat there in a strange silence while the hubbub from the rest of the bar seemed to recede into a distance. The two men were looking thoughtful. Finally, Joycey leant forward.

'So he wasn't charged with piracy?'

'Yes he was. Immediately after they had convicted him of murder they charged him with piracy. Kidd called for the two French passes to be shown to the court, but they had disappeared. And what was worse, some of the witnesses denied that the passes had ever existed.'

'So he was found guilty of piracy too?'

'Yes.'

Joycey sighed. 'Well I suppose I can see why some people may have thought he was innocent. I mean, if the evidence he relied on to clear his name had been 'lost'. That is, if it ever existed, I suppose.'

Takk gave one of her cynical snorts. 'Oh they existed. They were discovered by a researcher in the Public Records Office just before the First World War. They are in the National Archive now. Here…' she thumbed through one of the books and turned it to show a black and white photograph of a battered looking document. 'This is the pass for the *Quedah Merchant*.'

There was a silence. Finally Joycey asked, 'So, if he was set up, why? Who wanted him out of the way? Presumably, it was the syndicate.'

Takk nodded. 'I said they were some of the most powerful and important men in the land. In fact they were all senior members of the government. In addition to the First Lord of the

Admiralty, the group also included the Lord Chancellor and the Secretary of State. Some historians even argue that King William himself was involved, though care was taken to keep his involvement a secret.'

'Blimey.'

'And they were all members of the Whig party who were in government at the time. The problem was that the Whigs were losing their grip on power, and when the Tories started to hear rumours that senior members of the government were involved in a dodgy privateering expedition, they went on the attack in the hope of bringing the whole government down.'

Joycey was frowning. 'But these French passes. If they really did exist…what does that mean?'

Takk leaned forward over the table. 'Well, this is where it gets complicated. Because I said there were two versions of events. I gave you the story as told by Kidd and his modern supporters. There is another radically different version of events.'

'Go on'.

'According to a range of other sources, Kidd left out half of the story because it was even more damning. And there is clear evidence that supports this alternative story. According to – let's call it the real version of events – when Kidd failed to find any pirates on his first visit to Madagascar, he panicked and decided that he had to get some plunder in any way he could. So he decided to do what other pirates had already done – he attacked the Moslem pilgrim fleet in the Red Sea. Basically he decided to turn pirate.'

Marik gave a quiet whistle, but Takk pressed on with her story.

'Problem was that the pilgrim fleet was protected by an East India Company ship and Kidd was driven off. The Company's merchants in India immediately started sending reports back to London about Kidd's activities, and the East India Company alerted their supporters in the Tory Party.'

'Why were the East India Company so het up about it then?'

'Piracy was upsetting the Mogul Emperor. He thought all the pirates were English, and he was threatening to expel the company from India because of it.'

'I thought the East India Company more or less ruled India.'

'Yes they did, about a century later. But in the 1690s, they were in a very uncertain position. Their profits were collapsing and they were under attack at home and in India. They realised that the Kidd episode had the potential to bring down the Government.

And there's another twist to this. You remember what I told you about the Dowgate men? They were the ones trying to set up a rival to the old East India Company. Well Kidd's syndicate were involved with them too. So the old East India Company had yet another reason for wanting to link them with an infamous pirate. It would not only bring down the government but undermine their rivals in the New East India Company. And on top of that if Kidd was brought to justice at their insistence, it might also appease the Mogul. They had a lot to gain from it.'

'So let me get this straight. Kidd turned pirate and attacked the pilgrim fleet.'

'Yes. The fleet carried lots of merchants bringing valuables back from Mecca and the Mogul was a devout Muslim, so it was seen as a particularly outrageous act.'

'But Kidd didn't get anything. He was driven off.'

'True, but Kidd wasn't the first English pirate to attack the pilgrim fleet. A few years earlier a flotilla of pirates led by Captain Henry Every had captured several pilgrim ships carrying valuable cargoes. Worse still, the pirates went on the rampage and, according to several claims, raped the women who happened to be on board. It turned out the cargoes and the women were closely connected to the Mogul court.

Then when Kidd was driven off, he retaliated by allowing his crew to go ashore and go on the rampage. So news of his atrocities quickly spread along the coast of India.'

'And he didn't admit to any of this?'

Takk shook her head. 'No. Would you have done? And there's more. Kidd claimed he only captured two ships. Whereas, both the East India Company and members of his own crew indicated that he captured five or six in total. And he also robbed merchant traders along the coast. So he certainly appeared to have been more of a pirate than he was willing to admit. When he was brought to trial in London, he was actually charged with five counts of piracy in addition to murder.'

'Right.' Joycey looked thoughtful. 'I can see why those Whigs were worried.'

'Yes. It looks like the whole project was dodgy to start with, but when Kidd actually turned pirate, the syndicate realised the danger and began distancing themselves from it as much as possible.'

Joycey was looking puzzled. He was now chewing on the end of his matchstick again. 'What I don't understand….what I don't get is why he still made his way to Boston. After all, if he had turned pirate, surely he would have known that the deal was off. Why didn't he just disappear with the loot...I suppose there was actually treasure after all that?'

Takk shrugged. 'As I said, there are a lot of unanswered questions about Captain Kidd. Those historians who defend him claim that he was innocent and only ever captured the two vessels with French papers. They say that because Kidd was innocent – or believed he was innocent, there was no reason not to follow his orders and deliver the plunder to the Earl of Bellomont in Boston.'

'They deny he captured other vessels then?'

Takk nodded. 'They claim the East India Company invented that story so that the Tories could embarrass the Whig government. Their argument is that someone had to pay the price for the activities of the English pirates like Henry Every. And since Every had completely vanished with his plunder, Kidd made a very convenient scapegoat.'

It was Joycey's turn to nod.

'Which...,' Takk began digging in her bag, 'takes us back to this.' She extracted her laptop and then, after a careful look round the pub, opened it and tapped the keys. The two men leaned forward and saw the image of the stolen letter appear on the screen.

'We may not have the letter, but at least we have a copy.' She smiled. 'And now, I think we can understand more about what it means.'

Joycey craned his neck and began to read quietly.

'*Cous*

Since it must be I am condemned to dye, I have writ his

ldship this day and told him of what is to be offered if he will secure what I wish I am assured he will bee honble to this but as I doubt not some trickery might befall from other honble gentlemen known to you Whereof do you beg our friend H remove that we bt from the Old Mrcht in the woes If he cavilles show him this He will know all as we spoke thereof Doe not trust ye Dowgat man The silks you may take to the mercer in Cheapside the value thereof to have unto yrslf Wm

Joycey repeated the final word. 'William'.

It was as though a shadow had been cast over the three of them as they sat huddled over the low table. Because now, the significance of the letter was clearer. Eventually Joycey spoke.

'So who do you think he was writing to?

'A friend or relative I guess. Though it would be interesting to know the identity of the lord he refers to. And he has obviously written making some sort of offer to someone. It would be interesting to know who or what that was all about.'

'What about 'our friend H'?'

'Oh, I have an idea about that. One of the syndicate was a London merchant by the name of Edmund Harrison. By all accounts he lent most of the money for the project, and more or less managed it, drawing up the contracts etc.' She sighed. 'However, I'm not sure what he meant by 'that which we bought from the old merchant in the woes'. Though the name does appear on the map. So maybe it's a place where they purchased some silks. But I also think that silks might have been part of the plunder.' She shrugged again. 'I really don't know. I need to do more work on this.'

There was a long silence. Joycey was focussing on the end of the matchstick which he was slowly shredding with a long fingernail and Marik was slumped with his chin resting on one hand. He kept giving wistful glances sideways at Takk, but she seemed to be ignoring him.

Finally Joycey sighed and dropped the matchstick onto his plate.

'Well it's a great story. And if we still had the letter…well it might all be useful. But we don't. So I'm not sure that there's any point in pursuing it any further is there? After all, we have kind of been asked to drop the matter.' He grinned and gingerly pressed his fingers to his ribcage.

Takk's eyes were black, fixed on Joycey's face. She glanced quickly at Marik and licked her lips before speaking. 'But don't you see. That's exactly why we have to find out more. Whoever attacked you knows you no longer have the letter. It's not the letter that is important. It's what the letter says. And what the letter says is apparently valuable to someone and…,' she hesitated, lowering her voice further, '…and is worth killing for. That's why we have to find out.'

'But what does the letter mean?' Joycey's voice was almost peevish. 'We don't know that.'

'No,' snapped Takk. 'But I will.'

17. At the British Library

On Tuesday it rained. Takk took her breakfast late and with little enthusiasm in one of the student canteens on the Greenwich campus. Initially she sat with a small group of students who, although they belonged to her year were sitting a different course. They were not really friends, though she was friendly enough with them, for Takk had that ability to present herself socially when it either suited her or was required, without committing herself in any way. In turn her fellow students thought she was studious without being noticeably offish – and this permitted her both a certain amount of space and social inclusion.

When they had departed, she took out her diary and scanned her lecture program for the week. Then she took out her tablet and checked several online sites. When she had scanned these for some time, she sat thoughtfully picking at a loose strand of wool which she had pulled from the side of her hat, twisting it round and round her finger.

Tuesday was a busy day for lectures, but the lecturer for the last session was infamously dull. His talk could easily be read up later. So she made a snap decision to leave at 3pm. There was other work to do.

The previous night in her room in the hall of residence she had pored over the bibliographies of the books on Captain Kidd, paying particular attention to the locations of primary source material. Then she had read through the final chapters of the books again until a significant statement began to stand out in her mind. Most of the books she had 'borrowed' from Joycey's shop – at least those which seemed to be more reliable in a scholarly sense – included the same reference. And the more Takk read and re-read it, the more its significance seemed to grow. By the time she had turned off her desk light and settled down to sleep, an idea had embedded itself so deeply in her mind that it would not rest – and she ended up lying awake until the early hours, watching as streaks of rain glistened like pearls against the window.

Later that afternoon Takk took the train to London Bridge and then the Northern Line to the bustling tunnels of King's Cross station. Like most of London's terminus stations, there was rarely a time during the day when they weren't busy, and Takk made her way unobtrusively through groups of lost-looking overseas tourists, joining the thin stream of pedestrians along the pavement heading in the direction of the British Library. For this visit, Takk had abandoned her usual canvas bag and had stuffed her tablet and sheaf of notes inside a cheap supermarket carrier bag, knowing that it would save time inside the library. Once inside the marble hall of the foyer she simply changed her carrier for one of the library's transparent plastic bags, then took the lift up to the Reading Room where she was greeted with a cheerful but hushed welcome from the duty archivist – a young man who was used to Takk's sporadic attendance. Already armed with the references gleaned from her borrowed books, she logged into one of the terminals and submitted her request for several documents.

To her surprise and slight dismay she found that one of the volumes she wanted was already in use. For a moment she sat gazing round the reading room trying to see if she could identify who might be researching the same material. But she quickly realised this was a waste of time. It could be any of the fifty or more people sat along the long lines of tables. Instead she decided to take a more direct approach and asked the duty archivist if he knew who might be using the volume in question. He flicked through the receipt folder behind the desk and frowned.

'It's a Doctor Bootham.'

But when asked if he could point the man out, the archivist shook his head slowly and explained that he hadn't been on duty very long and the volume had been delivered some time earlier in the day. However, he promised to let her know as soon as the volume was handed in at the returns desk. Feeling slightly disconcerted, Takk made her way to her own desk and waited.

Scattered at intervals along the rows of tables in the library, people were bent in study, faces turned down, brows knitted, eyes flickering as they scanned and read. She peered at them, assessing them surreptitiously, and saw only the usual polyglot of researchers. The young, eager students, the greying writers and academics and the obligatory retired enthusiast, usually identifiable by their untidy heap of jumbled notes and scattered papers – signs of a retirement project long since beyond control. She herself had been warned about this – in fact all post-graduates were. Don't let the research get out of control, don't get overwhelmed by the data – don't lose sight of the object of your thesis. There were anecdotes about people who had started their research and who lost control, and who were still plodding on decades later, lurking like ghosts in the corridors of the Institute for Historical Research. Getting deeper and deeper into the research process without a hope in hell of ever regaining the perspective necessary to be able to write up their findings. Takk thought it was sad, and assured herself that she knew life was too short to get like that.

Nearly half an hour after her arrival, a man in a grey overall made his way towards her, pushing a trolley with slow, deliberate steps. On arrival he asked her name, scanned her desk for any offending objects like cameras or pens, and then deposited two large leather-bound volumes in front of her. They landed with a heavy thump that wafted up the fragrance of antiquity blended with a background of mustiness and some sort of conservation fluid. She took a deep breath and smiled. There was, she thought, nothing like the smell of old documents. They exhaled an air of the past, of authenticity and mystery.

She thanked the man and began leafing through the first of the volumes. It consisted of a series of manuscript letters which had been mounted on a standard sized paper frame and pasted into the volume. Each sheet bore its own individual folio reference, rather like the page numbers of a book. She knew the pages that she wanted to read, but she allowed herself the indulgence of scanning each page, enjoying the changing flow and colour of the hand writing, recognising names here and there. Then she turned to the second volume and a sense of anticipation grew, as though she was on the scent of a quarry upon whom she was closing. For the folios contained the correspondence sent to Robert Harley, the leader of the House of Commons at the time of Captain Kidd's trial. Most of the letters related to political activity and there were hardly any that related to the Captain Kidd affair, but then she turned a page and the name on the reverse stopped her dead. For there at the bottom of a letter was a signature – and she recognised the abbreviated first name as the first name on Joycey's stolen letter. And the surname confirmed everything. For the signature on the letter was Wm Kidd. She turned the page over again, reading from the beginning and barely conscious that she was holding her breath. For, under her finger tips, was a letter written by the imprisoned pirate himself.

Then she read it again, slowly digesting each statement. Finally she turned on her tablet and began to type:

Kidd to Harley. ? April 1701. Kidd refers to his long imprisonment and impending trial, and states "I hope I have not offended against the Law, but if I have, it was the fault of others who knew better, and made me the tool of their Ambition and Avarice, and who now perhaps think it their interest that I should be removed out of the world". Kidd claims Bellomont and another New York merchant by the name of Robert Livingston, were the organisers of the project, and that he himself was 'cajoled' into the job. That he only took two ships and that Bellomont has taken the French passes together with "my cargo". Finishes by saying that he cannot defend himself without the passes and denying any connection with some ? papers ? pamphlets which have been produced and may be offensive to Harley.

She sat back, unconsciously chewing the end of her thumb and gazed thoughtfully at the letter again. Then she continued typing:

This sounds like Kidd trying to reinforce his own story before his trial and deflect the blame onto others. He seems determined to direct blame at the Earl of Bellomont. Why doesn't he name any of the others in the syndicate? Where does Robert Livingstone come into the picture. [No more recent book seems to think he is so important]. And why no mention of Edmund Harrison? The books indicate that he was a major organiser of the expedition.

Again Takk sat back thinking. People moving near the

entrance to the reading room distracted her for a few moments, and a man walked behind her slowly, probably invigilating, she thought. Then she tapped the screen with black painted nails again. In the quietness of the reading room she was suddenly conscious of the little clatter they made on the glass.

From what we appear to know, Kidd is trying to stick to his story to strengthen his own version of events. So why doesn't he name the 'others' who he blames for his situation. And if, as he claims, his activities were so legitimate, why does he feel the need to claim that he was a reluctant participant.

For several minutes she sat gazing at the letter, and then had the strangest feeling that she could see through the eyes of the Admiralty Judge. What had he made of all this? Kidd pleading innocence, clear evidence of piracy, and the unspoken presence of some sort of conspiracy. Then she shook her head and began leafing through the folio once again. Several irrelevant pages turned over, and then she found herself staring at the letter she had really come to see. It was another letter written by the pirate to Robert Harley. But this one was shorter, the hand writing was thinner, shakier, and the spelling was more random. Then Takk remembered that the gaoler of Newgate had reported that Kidd was ill. This letter was also dated, May 12, 1701. Just days before his execution on the riverside at Wapping.

She leant forward, breathing lightly again as though her breath might blow the very words from the surface of the paper.

"Sir

The Sence of my present Condition (being under Condemnation) and the thoughts of having bene imposed on by such as seek't my destruction thrby to fulfil their ambitious desieres makes me uncapable of Expressing myselfe in those terms as I ought, therefore do most humbly pray that you will be pleased to represent to the Hon'ble house of Commons that in my late proceedings in the Indies I have lodged goods and Tresure to the value of one hundred thousand pounds...."

Takk felt her heart skip a beat. She read the sentence again, drinking in the meaning of the words, and then she continued.

"...which I desiere the Government may have the benefitt of, in order thereto I shall desiere no manner of liberty but to be kept prisoner on board such shipp as may be appointed for that purpose, and only give the necessary directions, and in case I faile therein I desiere no favour but to be forthwith Executed according to my sentence.'

Takk slumped back in the chair, her heart pounding. Her face felt warm and she glanced round wishing that there was someone there that she could talk to about this. Researchers were still scattered around the room heads down to their work. Some new ones had arrived unnoticed, including a ginger haired man in his thirties or forties, who now sat almost opposite, partly hidden by the desks' central partitions. He looked up suddenly and their eyes met, as though he had sensed her gaze. Takk looked down abruptly, suddenly afraid of contact, and began tapping on the tablet.

Almost at the last hour, Kidd tries to bargain for his life.

She stopped, leafing through the notes she had taken the previous evening. Then, finding what she wanted, she began tapping again.

In a written statement to Bellomont in July 1699, Kidd suggested that he had left some of 'the cargo' somewhere in the Caribbean. Bellomont himself reported to the Board of Trade that Kidd had boasted that the cargo was hidden and nobody would find it without his help. Some of Kidd's crew had mentioned the island of Hispaniola.

Now Kidd tries to buy his liberty with the plunder. One hundred thousand pounds worth in 1701 – surely more than the plunder of just two ships? Kidd always claimed that their cargo was relatively small. If it was really valuable, why didn't the pirates take it from him when he was at Madagascar?

Now Takk's thoughts were racing ahead - faster than she could type. She had arrived at a deduction which was almost too exciting to contain. In his final letter, in his desperate last minute gamble, Kidd had blown his own story and confirmed the accusations against him. Rather than taking just two legitimate prizes – he had taken five or six ships as claimed, and in the process he had 'acquired' a hugely valuable collection of plunder, which he had hidden in the Caribbean.

Absorbed, she swiped the screen again until the photograph of Joycey's letter appeared and she read it through again.

'*Since it must be I am condemned to dye, I have writ his ldship this day and told him of what is to be offered if he will secure what I wish I am assured he will bee honble to this but as I doubt not some trickery might befall from other honble gentlemen known to you Whereof do you beg our friend H remove that we bt from the Old Mrcht in the woes If he cavilles show him this He will know all as we spoke thereof Doe not trust ye Dowgat man The silks you may take to the mercer in Cheapside the value thereof to have unto yrslf Wm April 29*[th] *1701*'

Now, she understood. For suddenly, Kidd's letter made sense. It had obviously been written to someone after the final letter to Harley. The second sentence was a clear reference to the very same letter to Robert Harley that lay open before her on the desk. And clearly, Kidd still feared some form of betrayal. The second part of the letter seemed to be referring obscurely to some form of precaution against trickery by others – probably members of the syndicate. Perhaps there was a clue in the reference to the 'Dowgat man'. But the important thing was that the letter seemed to confirm the existence of the pirate's hidden treasure. And now, Takk allowed herself the indulgence of a further idea. Joycey's letter had included the map of an island. Perhaps it had been intended to give an accomplice an idea of where Kidd's plunder had been hidden. Perhaps it revealed where the treasure was in the Caribbean. Perhaps it was still there. Perhaps… it was the reason why someone had been willing to commit murder.

With scarcely controlled excitement Takk collected up the folios and carried them to the Returns desk. The archivist rifled through a card holders and handed her two receipts. Then, with an exclamation, he remembered her request for the missing volume.

'Oh! I am so sorry. I totally forgot. It was returned about thirty minutes ago. It may have been returned to the store by now, but let me check.'

As the archivist scurried off into a back room Takk turned round, and as she did so she caught a movement towards the back of the reading room, where she had been sitting. Surely, the ginger haired man in the grey suit that had been sitting opposite her was now standing at her desk? She turned and strode forward quickly heading for her desk. The man, did not look up but he began to move smoothly, walking away to reach the far side of the reading room, keeping the ranks of tables between them. Before Takk could reach her desk, the man was heading at some speed towards the exit.

Scanning the desk, she felt sure that her papers had been disordered. Her plastic bag was open and the tablet, which she had previously pushed fully inside, lay half upon the desk. Whoever he was, he may have taken some of her notes and had obviously intended to take her tablet. Scraping her papers together she trotted briskly towards the exit of the reading room, seething quietly as the elderly man on duty there slowly inspected her bag and papers.

Outside she looked around quickly. There was no sign of the man in the grey suit, but the sound of a bell made her turn quickly, just in time to see the lift doors closing – and before the view was blocked completely, she glimpsed grey fabric. Darting across the mezzanine, she began running down the marble stairs, taking dangerous leaps, the soles of her pumps skidding on the smooth surface. She stopped at the ground floor and hid behind the staircase, panting loudly, eyes on the lift doors. The doors opened. Two women came out, chatting casually. Then the doors closed. Takk turned and ran down the remaining stairs to the basement, arriving in time to see a young man leave the lift before its doors closed again. But there was no sign of a grey suit. Perplexed, she raced up the stairs again, nearly demolishing an elderly woman who was tottering unsteadily down. Gasping apologies, Takk came to a halt in front of the lifts – but the lift had risen again to the upper floors. She whirled round. The foyer was dotted with people, but as hard as she looked, there was no sign of the man in the grey suit. Feeling strangely angry with herself, she made her way slowly to the exit and out into the rain soaked forecourt of the library.

The Northern Line platform at Kings Cross was crowded. There had been a signalling problem earlier, and now the station was crammed with bad-tempered commuters and confused foreign tourists. Takk had to queue to get through the barriers, and then she was eventually permitted to join the dense crowd gathered at the platform level. Even then there were several long, frustrating waits, as trains slid in to the station, filled themselves and then departed again with a screech of wheel on rail. Each time, the crowd pulsed forward, shuffling and muttering until finally Takk found herself standing close to the platform edge with a press of people behind and beside. Clutching her carrier bag, she stood and stared down at the little black mice scuttling furtively along the track bed, wondering whether anyone else ever noticed them. Every few seconds she glanced sideways along the tracks in the direction of the tunnel, involuntarily willing on the next train. A rush of air finally heralded its approach, together with a gathering roar and clatter from the tunnel. Swift as a tsunami, the long snake of the train slid from the tunnel, rushing along the platform.

Suddenly, Takk felt a pressure on her right shoulder. For an instant, she gathered an angry breath, ready to unleash a furious comment to whoever was behind her – then her mood turned to panic as the pressure turned to a definite shove. A hand on her shoulder was pushing her inexorably forwards towards the platform edge and the screech of the oncoming train. Her pumps slid on the platform surface and her heart leapt into her mouth. The train driver's face had turned into a mask of horror, he seemed to be bracing himself back against the wall of his cabin. She screamed – a full, terror-wrought shriek such as she had thought impossible, and twisted violently to the left. The pressure on her shoulder suddenly vanished and her left arm was wrenched painfully backwards. The handles of the carrier bag snapped, and she was falling uncontrollably back among the legs of the crowd around her.

There were exclamations and cries and then willing hands helped her to her feet. Takk peered round, her vision blurred by hot tears of anger, but her assailant had gone, and so had her bag with its collection of notes and the tablet.

18. An Inspector calls.

Joycey had just got in. It was nearly 8pm and he had been detained as he usually was at the Plume on his way home. Then he called at the mini-market to make a selection from their limited range of microwave meals and purchase some cat food, before cutting through the alley into Straightsmouth. The cat welcomed his arrival, arching his back and tiptoing with anticipation to his empty food bowl. Joycey fed him first, put the kettle on, and then pushed the meal container into the microwave. He was still checking the cooking instructions when there was a loud knock at the door.

At the front door he hesitated, his hand hovering over the broken security chain – another of those domestic jobs he'd never got round to. He put his cheek to the door and called out.

'Hello?'

'Mr Becket?' a voice growled.

'Who wants him?'

'This is Detective Inspector Walker'.

As the door opened the light from the hall fell across the

face of the police officer who had questioned him several days previously.

'Mind if I come in?'

Joycey's unease grew. The policeman just pushed his way in confidently and made his way into the kitchen where the cat glanced at him with little interest before carrying on with his meal.

'So, feeling cautious, are we?' The policeman smiled.

'What d'you mean?'

The policeman ignored the question and positioned himself with his back leaning against the kitchen counter. 'I think you should be careful, Mr Becket. You never know who might come knocking on your door one of these nights, do you.'

The policeman's smile had a sickly tinge to it, which somehow mirrored the way that Joycey was feeling.

'I don't know what you mean.' Joycey was trying to sound innocent, pleasant, but he had watched enough detective dramas on the television to know that he just appeared pathetically guilty. The policeman simply smiled.

'Well,' he said at last, 'I thought I might just drop in to let you know how we are making progress with our enquiries.'

'Oh. What enquiries?'

The smile didn't waver. 'Those would be our enquiries about the murder of Mr Gavin Douglas, Mr Becket. The very brutal murder of Mr Douglas, that is. Because we now know that that young man met a very nasty end. Very nasty indeed.'

'Oh'.

'Mmm. Doesn't that worry you Mr Becket?'

'Why should it. What's it got to do with me anyway?'

'Aren't you curious about the way Mr Douglas met his end? In my experience Mr and Mrs Joe Public are always interested in the gory stuff, really. The stuff that gets in the Sun, you know what I mean.'

The policeman offered his sickly smile again. Joycey shook his head. 'No not really.'

'Of course, perhaps you already know how Mr Douglas met his end. Eh?'

Joycey screwed up his face. There was a sudden loud 'ping' from the microwave and Joycey remembered that he hadn't bothered to check the cooking time of his meal.

'What are you saying? I don't know anything about the murder. You know that.'

'Do I? It seems to me that you must know something Mr Becket.'

'No I don't.'

'Well I think you do.'

The accusation took the wind from Joycey's sails suddenly. He sat down on one of the kitchen chairs and began fumbling in his jacket pocket for his tobacco. The policeman watched him, a look of sympathy softening his features. Joycey glanced up and distrusted what he saw.

DI Walker clasped his hands together and let his arms hang limply in front of him. 'Tell you what I will do, Mr Becket, and I really shouldn't be doing this. But I will share some information with you. We now know a little bit more about Mr Gavin Douglas.'

'Yeah, well that's good, isn't it?' Joycey, now rolling a cigarette, gave the policeman a quick sideways glance.

'It is progress, as we like to say. Yes. Mind if I sit down?'

The policeman didn't wait for a response. He dragged one of the wooden kitchen chairs away from the table and slumped in it, looking immediately very comfortable and relaxed. Joycey began to feel exactly the opposite. The policeman crossed his legs and pushed his hands into the pockets of his raincoat. Then he gave Joycey another deceptive smile.

'Tell me, Mr Becket. Have you ever heard of Christopher Keeley.'

Joycey's brows knotted suddenly. He knew that name, but he couldn't quite recall how. The policeman waited, watching for a reaction.

'You must know of Mr Keeley, surely? After all, I gather you have lived in this area for some considerable time.'

'I suppose I may have done. Somewhere.' He puffed smoke.

'Does the Keeley Corporation mean anything to you, then?'

In truth, Joycey was beginning to feel a little concerned. Before he could respond, the policeman continued, his eyes fixed on the cat who was now sitting washing his fore paws.

'Christopher Keeley is the son of Derek Keeley, who used to be known round here in the old days as 'Copper Keeley'. Does that ring any bells now?'

It did. It certainly did. A cold feeling was beginning to spread through Joycey's lower limbs, but he said nothing and avoided the policeman's gaze. The latter continued as though he hadn't expected Joycey to speak.

'Copper Keeley was one of the biggest villains in southeast London in the fifties. Mate of the Richardsons and the Stones – though I don't think he had any connection with the Krays. Made his money out of scrap metal – or at least that was the legal side of his business. That's how they came to call him 'Copper'. Scrap copper. Had a series of scrap yards along the river and made an absolute fortune. When I joined the force the old boys still talked about 'Copper Keeley' like he was an old mate. Mind you,' the policeman gave a wry chuckle, 'in those days he probably was. Things being as they were then. Yes, very big round here. Had half the Labour Council in his pocket, or so I've been told. Yes, well, that was until he disappeared anyway.'

Joycey sucked on his roll-up. He knew this story. Copper Keeley had gone on a boating trip to France one beautiful summer's night, but he never came back. The boat disappeared without trace.

'Anyway,' the policeman sighed, 'Old Copper had three children. The eldest boy died of cancer in his teens. Then there was Christopher, and the youngest daughter, Kathy. She's out in Spain somewhere, I understand. Christopher inherited the family business.'

Joycey's eyes slid up to meet the policeman's gaze. It was inscrutable and his voice continued with its casual and dangerous amicability.

'Well, Copper Keeley wasn't daft. He sent Christopher to one of the top schools, made sure he got a good education and all that went with it. Then he paid for him to go out to Harvard, to get a business qualification. So when Copper disappeared, Christopher took over.' The policeman chuckled. 'You sure you haven't heard of him?'

Joycey shrugged grumpily. 'Don't know what it's got to do with me.'

'Ah well, we'll get to that. Chris Keeley, he's a very wealthy man now. And when I mean wealthy, I mean rolling in the stuff. You know that hotel at Blackwall, the one that has the blue lights on it at night? Well he owns that. And a lot of other stuff along the river too. You got to hand it to the guy. When Mrs Thatcher came along, he was exactly the sort of entrepreneur she wanted for the Tory party. He hung on to his riverside scrap yards just long enough, until the Tories provoked that massive rise in property values in the eighties. You remember? Set up the Docklands Development Corporation and then everything went mad. Local people sold their little slum cottages for hundreds of thousands to yuppies who thought they were bijou town houses.' He stopped abruptly, staring about him as though he had just noticed his surroundings.

Joycey grunted. 'Yeah, tell me about it. Places like this.'

DI Walker was silent for a moment. He nodded, perhaps momentarily feeling some genuine empathy for his host. 'Well, Christopher Keeley timed it right, and started selling his land at the height of the boom. Then he saw the crash coming and held on to the rest of the land until about fifteen years ago. Harvard taught him something, that's for sure. He waited until Old Maggie had gone and New Labour was in power, then he snuggled up to that Blair bloke, got himself an MBE or something, and set up his own development corporation. As I said. He's rolling in it.'

Joycey stubbed out his cigarette by folding it slowly and neatly into an old, badly cracked saucer. 'Like I said. I don't know what this has got to do with me.'

'Well, the thing is this, Mr Becket – and this is where

you might feel there is a bit of a connection – it turns out that Christopher Keeley is a bit of a... a 'collector'. I think that's the term is, isn't it?'

Joycey gave a casual shrug. 'S'pose it depends what he's collecting doesn't it.'

DI Walker was silent for a moment. Then he nodded. 'Yes, I suppose it does. Well it turns out that Mr Keeley has this thing about pirates, you see.'

Joycey felt his body stiffen. It felt as though a mild electric shock had jolted him upright in his chair, but he hoped that this was not the case. He tried to freeze his expression, not show any reaction. But whether he did or not, the policeman gave no sign that he had seen anything. Instead he carried on in a calm, level voice. Almost as though he was chatting to a friend.

'Odd isn't it. Pirates. Yes, he collects all sorts of things, apparently. Costumes and props from pirate films, original weapons, and there was even a rumour that he was donating a substantial sum to the building of a replica ship down at Chatham Dockyard.' He sniffed. 'Of course, it is only a rumour. I've not heard anything more substantial.'

The policeman gave his oily smile again.

'And he also collects old manuscripts and maps. I'm told that what he's got is as good as anything along at the Maritime Museum. That would be some collection, don't you think?'

Joycey was thinking hard. Unconsciously his fingers had found his tobacco tin and was working on another roll-up. 'I wouldn't know,' he said at length.

The policeman smiled again. Joycey was finding that these smiles were beginning to make him feel queasy.

'Hmmm, well, the thing is this. It turns out that Mr Keeley had decided it was time to get his collection insured. Not unreasonable given the circumstances. So he hired an expert to look at it all and give him a valuation. A man by the name of Bootham. Some sort of University chap I gather. Anyway,' the policemen leant forward, resting his elbows on the table, and continued in a more confidential tone. '…one evening this Mr Bootham decided to take some of the documents home with him so that he could carry on working on them. Unfortunately, he made the mistake of leaving his car unattended for a while and when he came back, some of them had gone.'

Joycey snorted. 'Can't trust anyone, can you.'

The policeman ignored this comment.

'Fortunately, Mr Bootham lives on the Cator Estate.'

Joycey grunted. He knew the Cator Estate. Despite its unpromising name, the Cator Estate was an exclusive area behind Blackheath village on the plateau to the south of Greenwich. But unlike Greenwich with its narrow streets of early 19th century brick-built terraced houses, the Cator Estate exuded an aura of opulence and privacy. Its roads were wide and lined with ancient trees. The houses ranged between Regency villas and large rambling Victorian gothic piles with, here and there, a few extravagantly glazed modern boxes erected by someone in the past with a taste for the architectural avant garde. Visitors to the area were made to feel just that. White painted gates stood at the entrance roads like eastern European border crossings, and signs everywhere warned hawkers and door-step vendors to stay away. And any non-resident quickly became overwhelmed with the feeling of being watched, because there were security cameras everywhere.

'Lucky him,' Joycey snorted again.

'Yes indeed. Very lucky as it turned out because when we checked the theft had been caught on cctv. And guess who the culprit was?

'I know you're going to tell me.'

DI Walker smiled. 'It was Gavin Douglas, Mr Becket. Luckily we had him on record. Turns out he had a string of convictions for petty theft and a rather nasty drug habit. He just happened to be passing as Bootham was unloading the car and seized the opportunity.'

There was a lengthy silence and then the policeman spoke again. 'I don't suppose he had any idea what he was taking or who he was stealing from, otherwise he might have stayed well clear.' There was another long silence. 'So, you see Mr Becket, I'm afraid technically speaking, you were in receipt of stolen goods, weren't you.

This time Joycey did sit upright in his chair.

'Hang on, I didn't know that.'

The policeman smirked.

'Anyway,' Joycey persisted. 'I thought this was a murder investigation?'

The oily smile returned to the policeman's face. 'You've gone awfully pale, are you feeling all right?' '

Even Joycey thought this might be true. All too vividly he was recalling the conversation he had had with young Gavin Douglas when he came into the shop. When he had claimed that the document had been found in an old lady's house in Catford.

The policeman sat back tucking his hands into his coat pockets again. 'Yes, well, we won't worry about pursuing the receipt of stolen goods just yet. As you say, our first priority is the murder of Mr Douglas. And it would help us if we knew why the document was so important. It might, shall we say, help us understand any motive.'

Joycey groaned. 'Can't this Bootham chap tell you?'

The policeman was silent, smiling.

'Look,' Joycey groaned. ' I don't know any more than I told you before. He said he found the letter when he was working in Catford. That's all. He didn't really say when.'

The policeman gazed at him for several long moments, and then he slowly nodded. 'And you don't know what this letter was about?'

Joycey shook his head. 'No, not really. It didn't make much sense. It was old and there was a map on the back. That's all, really.'

'And you don't have a copy of it anywhere?'

'No.'

The policeman sighed and slapped his knees. 'Well, ok. We'll leave it there for now shall we?'

He rose to his feet and made his way towards the front door, opening it himself. Then he turned back to face Joycey. 'I don't believe you are telling me everything Mr Becket. Which I think is unwise. It seems to me there is a clear connection between Mr Douglas's murder, the letter he sold you and the break-in at your shop. We can't say anything officially, you do understand, but some of the people who seem to be associated with Christopher Keeley are very unpleasant characters. Hangers on from the old days. You know what I mean.' He shrugged, turned away and then turned back, adding as though as an afterthought. 'Poor Mr Douglas was disembowelled, you know.

On the railings on the river path, then they dropped him over onto the foreshore and dropped rocks on his face. Like I said. They're not nice people. It would be best not to get involved with them, or to cross them. That would be my advice.' He smiled and nodded. 'Enjoy your lasagne. Hope it's not spoiled.'

19. Of Pirate Maps

The noise was deafening. They were sitting in a pub which had lately been taken over as the students' union bar in the centre of Greenwich, a building that Joycey had never entered before, and the place was crowded with noisy young students in various stages of inebriation. It was Wednesday night. Joycey felt highly conspicuous and slightly uncomfortable among the younger clientele, but Takk had explained that this was the intention. Anyone else would also stand out like a sore thumb. Marik was smiling, sipping slowly but with considerable satisfaction on a rare European beer which he explained had always been hard to find in England.

She then outlined the proceedings of the previous day. She described her suspicion about the ginger haired man and told Joycey and Marik how her bag had been snatched on the underground. She gave a detailed, slightly self-deprecating account of how she had been questioned by the Transport Police, how her details had been taken and how, eventually, she had just been dismissed without further comment. Handbag snatches were all too common and the police had little helpful to contribute to the situation, other than a vague commitment to get in touch if the bag was recovered.

She said nothing about the attempt to push her under a train, and now they huddled closely together, their voices lost amidst the cacophony that rolled around them. And in spite of the nature of her story Takk was grinning.

'Yesterday may have been a disaster in some ways, but at least by the time my tablet was snatched, I had already done the research. Your letter was definitely written by Captain Kidd after he had written to Robert Harley, offering to reveal the whereabouts of his treasure. So it has to refer to the treasure.'

Joycey was looking thoughtful. 'And the treasure was never found?'

Takk shook her head. 'No. Kidd had a small amount of it with him when he was arrested, but most of it was hidden away somewhere. I think it was like an insurance policy. '

'Why would he need that?'

'Well in spite of the fact he protested his innocence all along, he must have realised that having turned pirate he was going to be in trouble. The treasure was his bargaining chip. If the syndicate abandoned him…'

'Which they did…'

'…then he could try and use it to bargain for his life. Which is what he tried to do.'

Joycey nodded. 'So how much was it worth then?'

'Well he claimed it was worth a hundred thousand pounds, and that was in 1701. Put it this way, the sample of the treasure that Bellomont seized when he arrested Kidd in Boston, was enough to enable to Admiralty to buy the site of the Royal Naval College here in Greenwich, and to start building it.'

'A lot then.'

'Many millions of pounds. Yes.'

Joycey gave a low, barely discernible whistle.

'And,' Takk continued, her dark eyes burning, 'you have a map showing its location.'

'Had a map.' Joycey corrected.

'Well we still have a copy.' Takk lifted her bag to the table and rummaged sufficiently for them to see a corner of a photocopy of Gavin Douglas's map.

'But you have not the tablet.' Marik exclaimed.

'No but I always make copies, back-ups and things.' She shrugged. 'It's a habit.'

'So we still have the treasure map.' Joycey laughed. 'I wonder if the stuff's still there.'

'Well someone seems to think it might be,' Takk frowned. 'They murdered in that belief anyway. But there is another problem.' Once again she rummaged in her bag, and then struggled to free a bulky, hard-backed book in a faded pink cloth binding.

'Don't tell me, more of my stock has gone for a walk.'

Takk shook her head seriously. 'Not this time. This is a bit of a rarity. From the University library.' She snorted. 'Like you, they haven't a clue what they've got on their shelves.' She picked the book up and gazed almost fondly at the gold lettering on the spine. 'This is *Captain Kidd and his Skeleton Island*. It was written in 1935 by a man called Harold Wilkins. Wilkins was a bit mad. He went on to write a number of early books about aliens and UFO's long before they became really popular. Anyway, in this book he tells the story of two very eccentric brothers by the name of Palmer, who lived on the south coast of

England in the 1920s. Hubert and Guy Palmer. They had inherited quite a lot of money and they were both interested in maritime history and antiques. Hubert was the most interesting. He used to swan around wearing a white suit with a large wide-brimmed white fedora hat...'

Marik looked puzzled and looked appealingly at Joycey, who shook his head knowingly.

'...now Hubert was really interested in pirates. So much so that he decided to set up his own pirate museum. But he needed stuff to display in it. So, he decided to advertise in the newspapers for pirate relics. And before long people began contacting him to say they had got genuine pirate material, so Palmer began buying the stuff.'

'But how did he know it was genuine?'

'It wasn't, and that was the problem really. Judging by some of the descriptions and photographs of the objects that he bought, he was badly conned. But he was so intent on getting pirate material that he believed everything he was told. That's the problem with collectors, they are often so obsessed they don't worry about the authenticity. Anyway Palmer ended up buying various bits of furniture which people told him had belonged to Captain Kidd.'

'And he believed them all.'

'Yes. I mean it looks ridiculous now, but one of the things he bought was a sea chest with Kidd's name and a skull and crossbones carved onto the lid.'

Joycey frowned. 'But Kidd claimed he wasn't a pirate so why would he have a chest with a pirate thing carved on the top?'

'Exactly. It doesn't make sense. There were other things wrong too. Then there was a desk. The thing is Palmer claimed that when he inspected the desk closely he discovered that it had a secret compartment, which contained…' Takk paused, opening the book. 'This.'

Takk turned the book and there on the page was a simple drawing of the map of an island, similar to the one that had been on Gavin Douglas's letter.

'Well blow me!' Joycey exclaimed.

Marik took the book gently from Takk's fingers and turned it so that he could examine the line drawing closely.

'Then,' Takk continued, 'he looked at Kidd's sea chest and found another compartment.'

She took the book firmly from Marik, who looked disappointed. Then she opened it at another page and revealed another drawing, very much like the first.

'S'truth,' Joycey muttered, 'another of them.'

'Yes. And that's the problem. Altogether Palmer bought about five bits of furniture which were supposed to belong to Captain Kidd, and all of them had maps hidden in them, like this.'

Joycey looked thoughtful for a while. 'So you think ours is a fake?'

Takk sat back, taking a drink from her glass, and allowing her eyes to wander slowly around the room before answering. 'Well I can't say for sure. But if you look at these drawings, they are very crude and don't contain anywhere near as much information as yours. Besides, none of them had a letter associated with it. And as far as I can tell, the letter is genuine. It's the same handwriting as those in the British Library and, while it may be a bit of a puzzle, I think we are beginning to understand what the letter means.'

'So it could be genuine?'

'Could be. And what we do know is that someone else thinks it is. There's something else too. If you look on the internet you'll find quite a few websites about Captain Kidd's treasure. There are people out there spending a lot of time and money trying to find it and there are hotels and holiday resorts where you can pay to stay while you take a spade and dig for the treasure. There's a lot of money in Kidd, no matter how you look at it.'

'What happened to all Palmer's stuff?' Joycey asked.

'Oh, it disappeared for a while after he died. Then, just a couple of years ago, a private museum in America announced it had bought some of it.'

Marik suddenly cleared his throat. 'Why so many maps?' He asked quietly. Takk and Joycey looked at him in surprise. He reddened under their stare. 'I think too many maps.'

'Yeah, but they're fakes.' Joycey explained.

The young Pole shook his head. 'No, …yes they are fakes. So why this map so important?'

'Now there's a good question,' commented Takk quietly.

It was time, Joycey felt, to explain about Christopher Keeley

20. A broken door

Rain made the streets soft underfoot as Joycey said goodbye to Takk and Marik. She had informed them that she was tired and had an early morning lecture, and Joycey knew better now than to offer any sarcasm. Marik had offered to accompany her part of the way, and Joycey made his way alone through Greenwich, passing the dimly lit Georgian houses in Royal Hill and the modern monstrosity of the police station.

Walking home, Joycey found himself reflecting on their discussion about Christopher Keeley. Takk had reacted strongly to the news that Keeley had employed a researcher to value his documents, especially when she learned that his name was Bootham, the same as the man she had encountered in the British Library and who had, possibly stolen her tablet. Partly she was cross that Joycey hadn't shared the information straight away, but as they had talked about the role of Gavin Douglas, all three of them had become more circumspect. In the end though, Takk had pointed out that everything seemed to emphasise the authenticity and potential value of the Kidd letter. The real worry was that Bootham – or even Keeley – now knew for certain that they too were investigating it. And, though they hadn't really discussed it, what worried Joycey was the fact that if Gavin had been killed for stealing the letter, the situation was potentially much more dangerous than they had acknowledged.

It was with these thoughts in mind that Joycey made his way home. A cool breeze was flurrying up the road, rolling scuds of light rain into his face, so he pulled the collar of his leather jacket up round his throat and strode on into the night. Reaching the main road, which was oddly quiet at this hour, he crossed and cut through the dark alleyway to Straightsmouth. Walking along the pavement with his elbow almost brushing the front walls of the houses, he sensed the presence of occupants behind the lit curtains of their front rooms, heard the faint murmur of television, and once, a shrill conversation taking place. Half way along the road, a large black car purred slowly past him, its windows darkened and mysterious. It seemed to slow as it drew level, and Joycey immediately felt uneasy. Refusing to look in its direction, he let out a sigh of relief when it abruptly accelerated and drove off. Seconds later, the sound of tyres screeching on the wet surface came back to him as it took the distant corner into the main road.

Before he got to the front of his house he felt that something was wrong. The feeling was confirmed when he saw that his front door was ajar, a splinter of wood hanging from the frame like a white knife. He paused outside and pushed the door with his foot. It opened slowly to darkness, a still, heavy darkness. His throat suddenly felt dry. He glanced to left and right along the pavement, but there was no-one else in sight.

'Hello?' he called, listening carefully. There was no sound. He extended an arm, not really wanting to step across the threshold, and found the light switch just inside the door.

The light revealed more splinters of wood on the floor inside the door, and he could see through to the kitchen where the table appeared to be on its side. The back of a chair protruded through the doorway into the hall. Swallowing thickly, he stepped into the hall and called out again. There was no sound. Very slowly he walked along the hallway and looked through the door of the front room, on his right. When he switched the light on, a scene of chaos appeared in deep colour. His sofa had been scored with deep slashes from which foam extruded like infected wounds. The television lay in a pool of glass, his collection of vinyl LP's had been crunched under foot so that they existed now only in shards of black plastic and brightly colours shreds of card. A box full of old prints which he had been waiting to take to the shop had been tipped on to the floor and were now imprinted with the mark of wet shoes. On the wall a picture hung drunkenly behind broken glass, books littered the floor, glasses and bottles had been smashed in the fireplace and there was a smell of expensive malt whisky in the air.

He turned quickly to the kitchen, stepping over the fallen chair, to find all the cupboard doors open and the contents cascading out onto the work surface and floor. Drawers had been pulled open, cutlery and cloths, plastic bottles, plates, mugs, all strewn in a frantic profusion, many broken. Sugar, flour and ketchup had been smeared on the surfaces and walls like congealing blood. Blood. He suddenly thought of the cat and peered around quickly. Surely they wouldn't….

'Mickey, old mate. Where are you?' Joycey's voice sounded thin, tremulous.

There was no sound. No reply. No sign. He stumbled back into the hall and scrambled up the narrow stairs, his feet slipping on the worn carpet. The spare bedroom seemed untouched, but there was precious little in it anyway. The bathroom was a mess, toiletries scattered everywhere, but this didn't matter. He threw open his bedroom door, and found yet more chaos starkly illuminated by the shredded paper globe that had been his lampshade. His bed was thrown over, sheets and pillows tangled on the floor. Drawers pulled from chests and their contents dumped in a heap beside the bed. Some paperback books had been eviscerated, pages scattered everywhere. He stepped into the room and stopped. A furry tail was protruding from behind the end of the bed.

'Mickey?' His voice cracked. He called the cat's name again.

The tail was slowly withdrawn from view and a cross face appeared round the end of the bed. Then the cat came strutting slowly into view, his tail whisking angrily from side to side.

'Thank you, God! Are you all right mate?' Joycey knelt down slowly and ran his hands over the cat's smooth fur. Mickey began to purr and Joycey scooped him up and carried him from the room. 'What a fuckin' mess eh. Did you see who it was?'

Back in the kitchen he found and ripped open a packet of cat food and, finding an unbroken plate, squeezed the contents out for the cat. Mickey hunched hungrily over the food and began to eat noisily. Joycey watched him for a minute and then pulled his mobile phone from inside his jacket.

He half expected DI Walker with an 'I told you so' leer. But the officer who turned up was the younger Detective Sergeant, Martin. He wore the same black leather jacket and hoody as before and Joycey wondered momentarily if it was some sort of unofficial uniform for the plain clothes branch.

Martin was accompanied by a young WPC in uniform. Every three or four minutes the radio on her jacket buzzed quietly and she turned away to speak to it, covering her mouth with a hand. There seemed to be a lot of activity on the airwaves.

Martin listened to Joycey's explanation and asked whether he had seen anything. Joycey shook his head. Rain dripped from his hair onto his shirt. He was asked whether anything had been taken. He shrugged. As far as he knew there was nothing really worth taking. He had never kept cash at home and the only valuable things he had were either on his person or in his wallet. Martin gazed at Joycey's ringed fingers for a moment and asked casually whether he had any idea who might have broken in. Joycey shook his head again, but when his eyes met Martin's he knew that they were both thinking the same thing.

Finally, Martin asked whether he could have a look round while the young WPC, whose name turned out to be Patel, took a statement. Joycey shrugged and the young woman gave him a nervous smile. Joycey had already picked up the table and chairs, so they sat down while she scribbled hastily on a pad. Footsteps could be heard moving overhead as DS Martin moved slowly from room to room. There was the occasional inexplicable thump, but Joycey had little interest in what was going on. His mind was already racing towards other issues. He guessed that somebody connected with Keeley must have broken in, after all he hadn't crossed anyone else. But he couldn't figure out why they would turn his house over. Was it another warning, or were they searching for something. And if so, what could it be? The letter had already gone and he didn't have any copies.

At that moment there were heavy steps on the stairs and Martin appeared in the doorway.

'Well Mr Becket, you're lucky in one way, whatever they were looking for, they didn't find this.' He smiled sourly and held up a thin black object. It was a tablet in a tartan cover. Joycey recognised it immediately. It was Takk's.

Joycey decided quickly to show no reaction to this

discovery, even though his mind was suddenly racing. 'Oh thanks. Where did you find it?' he asked after a slight pause.

'Must have been on the bed when they turned it over.'

Joycey nodded to cover his confusion. His mind was whirling. Surely Takk couldn't have turned his house over or been involved in it in any way. But how had her tablet ended up there. The policeman was watching him curiously. So he said nothing. He smiled, offered his thanks and tucked the machine under his arm.

The policeman's expression turned briefly to one of suspicion. Then he muttered casually. 'Well, perhaps you did have something worth nicking after all?'

'Yeah, suppose so. Hadn't really thought about that.'

There was an awkward silence and then the two police officers departed to a fanfare of radio crackle. Joycey waited until he heard their car drive off and then he phoned Marik.

Marik arrived looking concerned and pink in the face. Joycey showed him from room to room and the young Pole tutted and sighed. Finally, having scooped up the reluctant cat for a few moments, Marik nodded.

'Is no problem Boss. I soon get this right again.'

'Thanks Marik, there's just one more thing. When DS Martin was looking round he found this.' He pulled Takk's tablet from under a newspaper where he had partly hidden it.

Marik's eyes widened and he stared at it for a moment, and then at Joycey. 'This hers,' he exclaimed. 'How did you get this?' His eyes narrowed for a moment as though in accusation.

'I don't know how it got here. They found it in the bedroom.'

There was a long silence. Both men were thinking so hard that even Mickey paused at his plate to look over his shoulder at them in curiosity.

'Someone must have planted it.' Joycey concluded. 'May have been DS Martin. May have been whoever broke in.'

'Could have been same person Boss.'

'What, you mean…?'

'Policeman. Yes.'

'I hadn't thought of that Marik. Why would they do that, though?' He hoped it was not anything like an attempt to frame him for the murder of Gavin Douglas. The thought worried him, but the possibility was just too complex for him to untangle. It remained as a nagging feeling that left him uncomfortable and feeling vaguely vulnerable.

'Shall I phone her Boss?'

Joycey looked at Marik in surprise. 'You've got her telephone number?'

Marik suddenly flushed a bright red and Joycey laughed.

'Yeah, you'd better. See if she wants to come round'.

The two men busied themselves righting furniture. Then while Marik began cleaning up the walls and surfaces in the kitchen, Joycey half-heartedly sorted through the wreckage of his record collection. Most of the collection was totally unrecoverable and he dropped the fragments dismally into a large black bin liner. When Marik had finished in the kitchen he appeared in the door of the living room with two mugs of coffee. While Joycey sipped his, he scooped up the muddied prints and piled them on the table and then he righted the remaining armchair and sat watching Joycey who had placed Takk's tablet on a small table in front of him.

At that moment there was a loud rap at the door, and Marik leapt up to answer it. Takk arrived, swathed in a thick scarf, with her habitual shapeless woollen beret and a long jumper that covered most of her thighs. She entered the front room, glancing about her with some curiosity and smiled at Joycey.

'Doesn't look too bad.' She commented shortly.

'You should have seen it an hour ago.'

Marik nodded. 'It was bad. Bad, bad.'

Takk sat down, her eyes on the tablet. 'So, what's the story?'

Joycey outlined the events of the evening. He wasn't feeling much like explanations, but he was curious about the tablet.

Takk listened with her brows drawn together, he lips pursed. When he had finished she sighed and shrugged. 'It doesn't make any sense to me. Why would someone go to the trouble of stealing it and then leaving it here?'

'Well I suppose it proves that whoever grabbed it from you at King's Cross and whoever broke in here tonight are connected in some way.'

She nodded, giving him a rare look of approval. He felt encouraged.

'We wondered...' he hesitated and glanced at Marik. 'We wondered whether that police officer, Martin, whether he planted it.'

Takk thought about this for a moment. 'I don't see what that would prove. Unless you really stole it from me on the underground?' She gave him a sudden glare.

'No, No of course I didn't. Jes-us!'

She laughed and he felt stupid.

'Didn't think so. No. Anyway, why would you?'

He shrugged unhappily. 'To get the copy of the map?'

'Hmm,' Takk hummed thoughtfully. 'Now there's a thought. I wonder if they erased it.'

She sat next to Joycey and began tapping at the screen. A file opened and the map appeared.

'There,' said Joycey. 'It's still there.'

Takk was staring at the screen. She swiped her finger over the glass, wiping her way through several images, then went back to the map. 'No it isn't!' she exclaimed. 'This isn't your map. This is one of Palmer's fakes. Yours has been wiped.'

21. Discovery

The discussion had gone on into the early hours. It was, unsurprisingly, Takk who came up with the most plausible explanation. The image of the real map, she decided, had been erased and substituted with one of Palmer's fakes because someone wanted to put them off the scent. For some reason, they – the murderer or Keeley or whoever was behind it all - didn't want anyone else to pay too much attention to the real map. Therefore, she concluded, it had to be genuine. A real treasure map. A real pirate treasure map.

Joycey listened to this explanation with a mixture of depression and delight. He felt pleased that they were in the process of solving a puzzle, and that they had some connection with a real treasure map. But at the same time he was conscious of the fact that they no longer actually had either the map or the letter. Furthermore, he was beginning to appreciate just how dangerous and determined their opponent was – whoever it was.

'First the shop gets broken into,' he commented. 'Then I get jumped on my way back from the Warrington. You get your bag snatched on the underground, and then the house gets turned over. Keeley, or whoever it is, really doesn't want us to get any closer to this than we are already. Next time, things could get really nasty.'

Takk looked sombre and sat in silence. It was Marik who spoke.

'Why bring it here. The Tablet. What for do this?'

Takk gave him a sympathetic smile.

'I think they wanted to make sure we got the wrong lead. So they gave us a false trail.' She gave a cynical laugh. 'They didn't think we'd know about Palmer and his fake maps. Luckily I kept copies of the real map on my laptop.'

'They didn't realise they were up against such an academic.'

Takk gave him an uncertain look. And then snapped angrily. 'I never describe myself like that. I'm just a student. That's all.'

Joycey held up his hands quickly in supplication. 'Sorry, sorry, sorry. I only meant that you knew about this stuff. That's all. Probably more than they do.'

Takk scowled.

'Well you do!' he protested.

Takk shrugged sulkily and Joycey looked at Marik appealingly.

'She knows lots of stuff Boss.' Marik nodded admiringly. 'Lots.'

Takk looked from one to the other and then spoke grumpily. 'Well fat lot of good it's done us anyway.'

There was a silence as the two men pondered this.

'Well we know about a real treasure map.' Joycey offered limply.

'And the Captain Kidd.' Marik beamed.

'Yeah, so what!' she snapped. 'If the map is real how does that get us anywhere. You gonna pay for us to go to the Caribbean to dig it up?'

'Sure. I just need to sell a few more comics and we're there.'

She smiled despite herself. Then she looked thoughtful. 'Hang on a minute. Since we can't afford to go the Caribbean to search for Kidd's treasure, why is Keeley so keen to stop us looking at the map.'

'I don't follow you.''

'Well. Keeley must know a lot about you by now. He knows about the shop and he knows where you live. Unless you really have got a hidden fortune, he must know we can't afford to go chasing the treasure.'

Joycey shrugged. 'Perhaps he thinks we'll go to the papers or something. Create some publicity. Make it harder for anyone to get the treasure on the quiet – I mean, I'm guessing that's what they want to do. Not share it with the tax man or anyone.'

'Yes it could be that, I suppose.' Takk looked unconvinced. 'But surely if Keeley is such a high flyer, he would have people who could squirrel all the proceeds away in some offshore account anyway. No, it seems to me he is going to a lot of effort to put us off the scent. There has to be another reason.'

Joycey thought, and then he thought again. Finally he came to a conclusion.

'I'm tired.' He said. 'And I can't see how we are going to get anywhere further with this anyhow.'

Takk nodded and rose to her feet. Marik hastily headed for the kitchen in search of his jacket. While she waited Takk began idly shuffling the pile of muddied prints on the table. Suddenly she gave a sharp exclamation.

'What's this?'

Joycey leaned over her shoulder. She was holding one of the prints, turning it to get a better view from the overhead light.

'Oh those,' he muttered. 'Got a pile of those. Can't remember where they came from. Spare stock waiting to go to the shop. Maybe I'll get Marik to take them with him.'

Takk moved into a brighter patch of light, shepherding Joycey backwards in front of her. She peered closely and held it out for him to see.

The print, which he thought rather dull, showed a topographical scene. On the left hand side was part of what appeared to be a new square fronted building with lots of windows. The right hand side of the image was dominated by the high vertical wall of a cliff, before which a group of sight-seers appeared to be standing in admiration. In the right background was a tall neo-classical church which stood proud of the existing surroundings and in the distance, filling the background from left to right, were the masts of hundreds of ships.

'Look,' she insisted again, her voice sharp with urgency.

Joycey squinted at the thin printed text underneath the image. It read, *A View of Wapping.* 1758. And underneath in faint writing someone had identified the features. The new building was marked 'The new London Hospital'; the distant church was 'St George's-In-the-East' . But it was the cliff to the right that Takk was pointing to. Underneath this feature, someone had scrawled 'The Old Redoubt'.

Joycey looked at her blankly.

'I need to get my laptop.'

'Now?' he moaned.

'Yes' she snapped. 'And do you have any old maps of the East End in the shop.

He screwed up his eyes and shook his head. 'No, yes…I mean possibly. There's a stock of old maps and repro's in the drawers. There may be something there.'

'We need to look at them as soon as possible.'

'Not now,' he groaned. 'I need to sleep.'

'This is important.'

Then Joycey had some inspiration. 'And I got to get the door frame fixed before I can go anywhere.'

Marik, standing in the doorway, looked into the hallway, where the front door was still propped closed in its broken frame. He nodded grimly from Joycey to Takk.

'That's right. Can't leave it like that Boss.'

Takk conceded the point, though she was seething with frustration. And after the briefest of discussions, she managed to wring one concession from the reluctant book dealer – that they meet at the shop at 8am the following morning.

22. Roque's Map

None of them were on time. Joycey had managed to contact a local chippy who owed him a favour, but the man was held up and arrived half an hour late. Takk overslept, and Marik, having arrived at the shop first, found he had left his keys at home and had to go back to get them. It was 9.30 before they were all assembled and Takk was the last to arrive, charging into the shop like an energetic tigress, spitting frustration and pent up energy.

She accepted a sharp black coffee without comment and insisted on being shown Joycey's stock of maps. Marik drew open several of the shallow drawers in the old wooden plan chest in the front of the shop and smiled. Takk ignored him and began to pull out the contents one at a time. Many of the maps were coloured and relatively modern, having been cut from old atlases in which much of the globe was still tinted by Empire. There were some even older, nineteenth century maps with elaborate cartouches featuring generally dubious depictions of peoples from different parts of the world, all gathered under the dominant figure of a Britannia triumphant. There were shipping maps with intense red tracks, all of which concentrated on the river Thames and Port of London. But there were some older, more fragile maps too. Several of Kent, which indicated that at one time Greenwich itself had been part of that county rather than London. Joycey moaned when he saw one of these. 'Forgot I had that. Had some chap in here two weeks ago looking for one of those. Find a plastic folder Marik. That one can go on display.'

Marik began rifling through the desk in search of a suitable holder.

Takk's search continued. When she had completed the first drawer, she carefully slid everything back and began on the next drawer. Almost immediately she gave an excited yelp.

'Here. This is the one.'

She was holding a large folded sheet of buff coloured paper. Marik quickly cleared clutter from the surface of the desk and she laid it down, opening it carefully.

'I'm amazed that you've got this. It's a copy of Rocque's map of Wapping from about 1745.'

Suddenly she was gone, dashing into the back of the shop. They heard her feet thudding to the far bookshelves, then padding backward and forwards in an agitated fashion before returning clutching a book. She put it face down on the desk. Then she grinned at them with satisfaction and pulled her laptop from her shoulder bag.

'Ok.'

She opened the lid of the machine, switched it on and quickly located the file she was looking for. Then she turned it so that Joycey and Marik could see the screen. It was the map on the back of Gavin Douglas's letter.

'I told you I kept multiple copies. So, this is the map of Kidd's treasure island. Yes?'

They nodded solemnly.

'And down here we have the words 'Hermitage' and 'Pelicans'.' She traced a finger nail along the southern shore of the island. 'Now,' she turned to the old map laid out on the desk. 'This is a map of the Wapping area from 1745 – that's just forty-four years after Kidd's execution. He was executed at Execution Dock, which is here.' She tapped a spot on the north bank of the river Thames, where the name of the Dock could be seen in small letters.

Marik gave a whistle. 'This real place then? Real Pirates of Caribbean Johnny Depp place.'

Takk smiled. 'It was a real place Marik, but as far as I know it was never actually a dock. I think the name was meant ironically. It was the traditional execution place of pirates. Whereas a dock is a safe place that you return to. See?'

Marik nodded without conviction..

'Now,' she ran a finger nail westwards along the curved seashore. 'What does this say, just here?'

Joycey leant forward. 'Hermitage Stairs.'

'And here?' She ran the nail back to the east, past the location of Execution Dock at the southernmost tip of Wapping.

'Pelican Stairs.'

She beamed at them. 'Yep! See. On Kidd's map it also says Hermitage and Pelican. I think Kidd's map isn't a map of an island in the Caribbean or anywhere else for that matter. It's a map of Wapping.'

Joycey stared at her in astonishment for a long time, while the strip light above them gave an intermittent buzz. Then he slowly shook his head.

'But you can't be sure, surely?'

'Oh yes I think I can.' She pointed a nail at the Kidd map again, this time tracing the outline of the southern shore. 'See. This matches the line of the Thames here. We thought it was the southern shore of an island. But that's only because it doesn't show the south bank of the river. And this line here which we took to be the north shore of the island, it's really the line of Ratcliffe Highway, which runs along the north edge of Wapping itself. It's a really old road, so it was certainly there in Kidd's day. And there's another thing which clinches it.'

She pointed to the single small feature on what they had taken to be the northernmost point of the island – the small square marked 'Old Redout'.

'This old Redout is the cliff which appears in your old print of Wapping.'

'The cliff?'

'Yes, except it's not a cliff.' She opened the book she had brought from the back of the shop. 'This is about the Civil War.'

Then, flicking through to the centre of the book where a group of plates were collected, she opened the book wide at another image of a buff coloured map.

'And this is a plan of London at the time of the Civil War, showing how it was fortified in 1642.'

They looked to see an almost unrecognisable map of the City of London, its houses clustered together between Westminster and the Tower of London, with just a small urban spread south of the river. A thicker line had been drawn round the whole city, marked here and there with rectangular or star-shaped features.

'Parliament had the whole of London protected against the King's army by a defensive wall, and it was strengthened at intervals by forts. Now here,' she pointed to the eastern end of the line, where it turned south through Stepney to reach the river about a mile east of the Tower of London. 'This is where the defensive line ran through Wapping. And here,' she tapped on the page, 'is where it crossed the Whitechapel Road. See, there is a redoubt here and another on the Ratcliffe Highway. The cliff in your print is what remained of one of these by the 1740s. So it had to be there in Kidd's time.' She snapped the book closed with a look of triumph.

Joycey was staring at Kidd's map, drinking in everything she said. Even Marik was staring hard, his brows knitted together.

'So,' said Joycey after a long silence. 'It's not a treasure map at all.'

Takk looked please with herself. 'I don't know whether it is or not. But the area was quite well developed in Kidd's time. It was the old port area of London, so there were lots of taverns and lodging houses and chandlers' shops. There were also merchants and sea captains living in the area. If you look at the detail on Rocque's map, most of the roads that were there then are still there – apart from a huge area in the centre that was demolished to make way for the London Docks in 1805. By Hermitage Stairs was Hermitage Dock and that was used to make the entrance to the docks from the river. It's where Pierhead now is.'

She enlarged the image of the Kidd letter on her laptop. 'Now look closely at this.' She enlarged the image so that the letters blew up enormously, the lines increasing into broad brown scratches and blurs. 'In the letter Kidd says that he is afraid of some trickery. So he instructs the recipient *'remove that we bt from the Old Mercht in the woes.'*

The two men nodded.

'Now although I managed to work out most of the letter, I couldn't figure out that bit. But if you look at Rocques' map - see what this part of Wapping was called in those days?'

Joycey peered, his lips moving. 'It says Wapping-in the-Woze'.

'Yes, Wapping-in-the-Woze. It was actually the name for the area round the old Hermitage Dock. And look really closely at these two words here.' She drew a line under two of the highly enlarged words on the screen. 'They don't actually say Old Merchant. It's just that the letter has faded more in some parts than others. The letters aren't O-L-D, they are Q-D. I misread the downstroke of the Q as a badly written L. So it isn't Old Merchant. QD is the abbreviation for Quedah. It's *Queda Merchant*.'

'The ship Kidd captured!' Joycey exclaimed.

'So the sentence isn't about removing stuff that was purchased from a miserable old merchant. It's actually about moving the stuff they brought from the *Quedah Merchant*. Exactly. And so where does Kidd say the stuff is?'

Joycey hesitated. 'In the Woze?'

'Yes.' Takk's voice had risen with excitement. 'It was in Wapping! And then look at the last line of the letter.'

They peered and Joycey read it out. '*The silks you may take to the mercer in Cheapside the value thereof to have unto yourself.*'

Takk's eyes were shining. She stared intently at each of them in turn. 'Don't you see what that means?'

'Um no, I don't really.' Joycey confessed feeling that he

missed something momentous.

'The Silks!' she hissed at them. 'The silks. It implies that the silks are at hand and could be sold in the City.'

They looked at her blankly.

'The silks were part of Kidd's plunder!'

They stared even more dumbfounded.

'It confirms it. The treasure must have been in Wapping. He must have brought in back and hidden it secretly. Don't you see?' Takk's words came tumbling out almost as fast as she could conceive them. 'Kidd anticipated trouble. He didn't hide the treasure in the Caribbean. He must have brought it back and hidden it closer to home, so that he could use it much easier as insurance. It was in Wapping and the map must have given a clue as to its whereabouts. It really is Kidd's treasure map.'

'Fuck me. I need a coffee.' Joycey threw himself back and scratched his head. 'Marik, could you do the honours. Three of Kazim's best strong black ones. And get some pastries too!'

23. Resolution

Over a belated breakfast, Takk and Joycey had tested her hypothesis while Marik munched silently. Takk believed that her interpretation gave a satisfactory explanation of the cryptic content of Kidd's last letter. It also explained, she added with glee, the mystery of Kidd's prolonged stay on the island of Madagascar.

According to all accounts he had lingered there a year, despite attacks from hostile pirates; and the fact that he had been unable to explain this long delay before setting sail for Boston, had helped incriminate him. But, Takk pointed out, if what he really did was to use this time to sail back to London in secret and hide his treasure, it really wasn't something he was going to be keen to reveal, since it would mean surrendering his insurance against betrayal.

While this revelation brought some satisfaction, it also added a more worrying element. And it was Marik who chewed over the issue for some time before sharing it.

'Keeley knows it too then Boss.' He commented quietly.

Takk and Joycey exchanged sudden glances.

'What do you mean Marik,' Joycey asked.

'Why he want to stop you. Change maps and frighten you off.'

Joycey looked at Takk again and she gave an unhappy shrug.

'Marik has a point. It would also explain why Keeley has been so keen to put us off the scent. If he thinks Kidd's treasure really is still in Wapping, we could be an even bigger threat than we realised.'

'And I suppose Gavin Douglas was probably killed because Keeley thought he might have helped someone to find the treasure.' Said Joycey quietly. 'When all he could really think of doing was selling it for a few quid. Poor bastard.' Joycey sighed. 'Shows how ruthless Keeley is then.'

Takk looked solemn – and her mood was infectious. 'We should go to the police.' She said at last.

Joycey looked aghast. 'Go to the filth! You've got to be joking. Why?'

'Because we may have evidence as to why Gavin was killed. We can help them identify his killer. And… because this is getting dangerous.'

There was a long silence. Looking from one to the other, Takk saw conflicted expressions and for a moment she wondered whether to tell them what had really happened on the underground. But the more she thought about it, the more she began to feel angry. She was still in two minds when a sly look came across Joycey's face.

'Pity,' he sighed. 'Think how it would have been if you had discovered Kidd's treasure.'

Takk looked at him suspiciously. 'What do you mean?'

'Well, think how interesting it would have been to find it. All that treasure stuff and who knows what else. Publicity, and you could probably write a book about it too.'

He smiled at Marik, avoiding her gaze, and pressed on. 'And then there's the money. It might be treasure trove or there might be some reward on top of everything else.'

Takk's lips worked as though she was trying to think of a suitable retort.

'We could at least find out where it is. Couldn't we?' He suggested.

In the end, it was Takk's academic curiosity that won over. Whilst protesting venomously that the money meant nothing, she could not deny that the prospect of searching for and finding a pirate's long hidden treasure was a tempting prospect. Once she had admitted this, her enthusiasm took over and, to Joycey's obvious delight, the conversation shifted to another area. What to do next. Surprisingly it was Joycey who summed up the situation.

'So assuming he hid the stuff in Wapping, where could he have put it? And how do we go about finding out?'

Takk was staring at the screen of her laptop, though it was clear her thoughts were elsewhere. Deep lines furrowed down between her eyebrows. Marik gave a non-committal shrug and cupped his chin in one hand looking expectantly from Takk to Joycey. Finally Takk puffed out her cheeks and blew.

'Well, we have a map which shows us the area in Kidd's time, so that might give us a starting point. Unless he buried the treasure in the cultivated vegetable gardens up near the Ratcliffe Highway, we are probably looking for one of the buildings that existed in 1701 – or the site of it.'

Joycey nodded. 'Ok.'

'The treasure which was taken by the Earl of Bellomont when Kidd was captured, consisted of bales of fabrics and chests. My guess is that Kidd's main treasure would be similar. So it could be quite big. I mean heavy, bulky. So assuming he arrived by ship, they would have to bring it ashore. But moving it far could be conspicuous. The obvious thing to do would be to hide it somewhere close to the river."

Joycey looked impressed. "That sounds a good start.'

'Hmm, it might be. There is something else. Kidd had other contacts in London.

'You mean the syndicate.'

She shook her head, already clicking her nails on the keyboard of the laptop,

'No. I seem to remember something about distant relatives living in London.'

She was now reading through her notes and muttering silently to herself.

'Yes, here it is. While he was in Newgate after his trial, he was visited by a Matthew Hawkins and his wife.'

'Ye-es?' Joycey looked blank.

'Well, they appear to be the only unofficial visitors he had. His wife and children were still in America. And for some reason, these two were allowed to visit him. We don't know who they were but their names don't crop up anywhere else in connection with the expedition, the syndicate or anything else. So unless they had been paid to bring food to him or do his washing, the only other likely explanation is that they were friends or relatives.'

'Ok.'

'So one line of research we could follow is to try and trace if there was a Matthew Hawkins living in Wapping in 1701. The other thing is to see if the Hermitage, Pelican or the Redoubt have any relevance, because they weren't marked on the map without reason. They may be locations we should check as a priority.'

'This is brilliant,' Joycey beamed, looking like a cheery version of his former self. 'How can we find this stuff out?'

'My best bet would be at the Tower Hamlets Local History Archive.'

Joycey shook his head. 'Never heard of it.'

'It's just off the Mile End Road.'

'Nope. Not me. Didn't even know it existed. Anyway,' he rubbed his hands together. 'How soon can you go?'

Takk gave him a bleak state.

'I can't.' She said bluntly. 'I have an essay to write. You'll have to go.'

24. Off the Mile End Road

Joycey had argued hard. He had pointed out that he had never done anything like it in his life. That he had left school prematurely. And when that failed to impress he admitted that he had been expelled at the age of fifteen and could barely read or write. Takk had given him a look of fierce disbelief and he had confessed to lying about that bit, but that he wasn't much of a reader really and didn't know the first thing about research. Then he didn't have tablet or a laptop, wouldn't know where to start.

Finally Takk exploded in anger and frustration. She had to produce some work by the following evening or she would be in deep shit. There was no alternative. Either Joycey or Marik would have to go and there could be no excuses unless they wanted to abandon the whole thing. This threat shut Joycey up for a moment. He looked at Marik hopefully, but the young Pole quite reasonably shook his head. It had to be Joycey.

'For Christ's sake you're not being asked to write an essay,' Takk stormed. 'Take a pencil and notepad and ask the archivist for any records relating to residents of Wapping around 1701. There are probably books on local history that contain most of the information. If needs be, ask the archivist for help.'

She gave a deep sigh. 'You'll just have to do your best.'

So that same afternoon a very uncomfortable Joycey made his way back across the river by the light railway, and then took the underground to Mile End. It had been a long time since he had felt quite much so out of his depth, but Takk had tried to reassure him that what he was doing was a bit like private detective work and that he should think of himself as an investigator looking for clues, clues about a missing person or place. This made Joycey brighten up, since much of the little reading that he did nowadays was crime fiction, which frequently involved private detectives. The idea made his task a little less daunting, and helped him to see himself in a less conspicuous and alien role.

Takk had also done some quick research to give him a start. They knew about the Hermitage Dock and Pelican Stairs. The other phrase that featured along the river bank in the map, was 'Sugar Loaf'. This had perplexed them until Takk found the Wikipedia entry which explained that in the 17th century sugar was imported from the Caribbean in heavy cakes known as loaves. Since Wapping was also the centre of the early sugar refining industry, sugar loaves would have been familiar to those living in the area. It didn't explain why Kidd might have put it on the map, but it was another clue.

The local history library was tucked down a side road off the Mile End Road. Few of the people sitting in the cars that congested that road every day had any idea that the library existed. It was tucked at the back of a modern university building, which stretched over the side road obscuring all that lay behind.

The library itself was like a quaint architectural throwback, marooned in the midst of the glass and concrete of the modern university complex. Its façade was of dressed Portland stone with rows of tall arched windows, though the paintwork was stained with the dust of London's inevitable pollution. The ground floor of the building housed the local lending library, but the first floor contained the search room for the historic archive for the whole borough. The interior of the building was something of a revelation as the architect had clearly allowed his grandiose aspirations to blossom on the first floor. The walls of the long rectangular hall may now have been lined with case after case of files and books, but the ceiling was still a feast of elaborate plaster mouldings, coffers and painted foliage that hinted at former glory. More importantly, the archive, hidden away in its basement was surprisingly rich - especially astonishing because the East End borough of Tower Hamlets was widely acknowledged to be one of the poorest in the country. Yet despite this, its boundaries had contained an area of enormous historical interest and vitality, and an amazing array of documents had survived to chronicle this pageant of events and personalities.

Joycey made his way cautiously to the reading room, where a man at an enquiry desk was busy with an elderly couple who were clearly very enthusiastic about something and were keen to talk about it in great detail. Joycey waited nervously for quite a while until the archivist had settled the couple at a nearby table and extricated himself from their attention. Now, with the enquiry desk clear, Joycey explained that he was looking for anything that might give him information about people and locations in Wapping in around 1701. The archivist listened patiently, his head cocked slightly to one side and a doubtful expression knitting his brows. In a sudden panic that he would simply be sent away empty handed for daring to enter with such a vague and hopeless task, Joycey added that he was interested in someone called Hawkins, and a location called 'Sugar Loaf'. The archivist directed Joycey to a shelf full of small booklets and pamphlets about the history of Wapping and suggested he start there. He himself would check the archive catalogue to see if they contained any useful references.

Glancing about the room, Joycey realised that the archive wasn't full of young academic types, but mainly elderly men and women who looked very ordinary indeed. He guessed that most of them were retired, and those who weren't had that familiar, slightly crumpled look of the long-term unemployed. Almost unconsciously Joycey began to feel more at home. And he was reassured by the fact that no-one seemed to have taken any notice of him or even to glance in his direction.

As directed he collected the books from the shelf and carried them to a table in the far corner of the room. The books looked familiar and he began to wonder whether he hadn't handled some of them in the shop at some point. Most dated back to the early 20th century and had been written by local amateur historians. Following advice from Takk, he checked which books had indexes, with a view to starting with those. But none were indexed. So he picked up a book at random and started leafing through it. It consisted of a series of short chapters about local buildings or personalities. He picked up another, and found that the contents were very similar. Both seemed to start with a brief and vague account of the arrival of the Romans, and of the possibility of their being a Roman port near Shadwell. They then followed up with virtually the same series of anecdotes.

After a while he warmed to the task and amused himself by noting that most of the books told the same story about Henry VIII chasing a stag all the way to Wapping from Epping Forest before killing it, with much relish, and then stopping at a local alehouse for refreshment. Putting the books themselves in chronological order he read each of the accounts in turn and noticed how the story got more and detailed with each retelling.

He also found himself reading through the account of the building of the London Dock. Although he had lived in London virtually all his life, he had never really understood that the 'London Docks' really consisted of about ten different, privately owned docks scattered along the river, and that they had only really become one in 1909. The first had been the West India Docks on the Isle of Dogs, which opened in 1802. And this had been followed in 1805 by the opening of the London Dock at Wapping. The fact that the creation of the latter had resulted in the demolition of much of the oldest part of Wapping and the excavation of two massive dock basins, triggered an alarm in Joycey's mind. It struck him that Kidd's treasure might have been found then or buried even deeper. Then he remembered Takk's suggestion that if it had been buried it would have to be close to the river and, looking at the plans of the London Dock, he could see that, apart from its two entrance locks, its basins were situated some way back from the river. It had been built leaving much of the 18th century riverside intact. Nevertheless, it was also clear that much of that riverside had been rebuilt in the 19th century, or bombed or redeveloped in the 20th. Little of the original cityscape remained.

He had almost given up with the local histories when he came to a thin pamphlet, which he had initially discarded as being unpromising. It was a cheap looking publication with a reproduction of a poorly executed line drawing on its pink paper cover. It looked like the sort of pamphlet he threw into the bargain box at the shop and sold for 10p if he could. The title was obviously hand-printed: *Curiosities of Wapping. Compiled by Cordelia Wainwright.* Inside there were about forty pages of rather smudged printing, which included several illustrations which he guessed had been drawn by Cordelia Wainwright herself. If the older books had been rather amateur, this had no pretensions of scholarship at all. It amounted to a random collection of nuggets and tales which had appeared of some interest to the author. Joycey flicked through the pages quickly and was about to cast it aside once again when his eye caught a heavily underlined sub-title. *'Unusual tales from the Coroners Court.'* It was followed by a few lines explaining that these were curious cases that had appeared before the Middlesex Coroners Court Sessions. His eye scanned quickly down a collection of single line entries:

July 27 1701. William Otto of Wapping threw himself from the house top while a lunatic.

July 29 Peter Trattles of St John's Wapping. Accidentally drowned. Fell from a ship into the Thames.

July 30 John Barwick, of St John's Wapping. Aged about 7 years. Accidentally drowned. Fell from a lighter into the Thames.

August 7 New born female child. St John's Wapping. Found drowned in the Thames. Supposed wilful murder by persons unknown.

August 15th. John Williams of Wapping. Casually drowned. Fell into Thames from Boat.

August 18th. Sarah Hubbard. St John's Wapping. Fell into Thames when barge overturned wherry she was in.

But it was the next entry that almost made him yell with excitement.

August 27th. Sarah Hawkins, of the Sugar Loaf, Wapping Old Stairs. Supposed drowned by falling into Thames.

And there underneath the entry, the author had inserted a note whose casual tone conveyed nothing whatsoever of its significance. It read, quite simply. *'This Sarah Hawkins kept a well-known alehouse and was said to be the cousin of the infamous pirate Captain Kidd.'*

Almost disbelieving the words in front of him Joycey read it again. He read the next line: *1st November. Thomas Hay, Wapping. Accidentally drowned. Fell from boat into the Thames.* Then he read from the beginning once again. He checked the next few pages, but the author of this modest little pamphlet had nothing more to say on the matter. There were no references, no explanatory notes. There was nothing else but this seemingly innocent statement, which carried as much charge as a bolt of lightning.

Joycey sat back as if in a dream. Gavin Douglas's letter had referred to somebody called 'H'. It had to be either Sarah or Matthew Hawkins, and the Sugar Loaf on Kidd's map had to be their alehouse. He quickly copied the entries down onto his pad and then, as an afterthought, made a note of the title of the booklet and its author.

Joycey was excited and pleased. He sat projecting a beaming smile around the room, half-wishing that someone would ask him what he had discovered. But no-one looked up from their own task. He was still simmering when the archivist eventually returned from his search of the catalogue. From the man's slightly downcast expression Joycey guessed that his search had not been fruitful. However the man brightened when Joycey showed him the entry in the pamphlet.

'Oh, yes, Cordelia Wainwright. She was something of a local character in the sixties. Very eccentric, but they used to say that what she didn't know about the East End wasn't worth knowing.'

He was scrutinising the page that Joycey offered to him and nodded again.

'Hm, Middlesex Court Sessions papers. You'll find them at the London Metropolitan Archive, if you want more detail. But, depending on what you are looking for, you might do better somewhere else.'

'What do you mean?' Joycey asked, baffled by the cryptic comment.

'Well, if you want to find out about properties near Wapping Old Stairs, you should check the London Dock Company archive at the Museum of London Docklands. They have a lot of the old title deeds for the buildings in that area. That will probably give you a lot more information. Plans even'. He nodded, blinking happily behind his bi-focal glasses.

Joycey thanked him and hurriedly carried the books back to the shelf. Takk was going to be so pleased about this. And he was so impressed with himself that he almost skipped from the building, pausing only briefly outside to roll himself a thin cigarette. The winter dusk had fallen and the temperature had plummeted. Overhead, the last traces of a dirty yellow sky was beginning to reflect back the murky light from the street lamps.

He was halfway between the library and the main road when a voice at his right shoulder startled him.

25. Taken

He span round but all he was aware of was a large black shape that seemed to hit him like a wall and the bright end of his cigarette arcing away in the darkness. There was no blow, but more the application of strength. A force which moved into him, lifting him from his feet and carrying him in the air with it as it moved. His lungs seemed to have collapsed and his vision blurred as if under a shallow pool. He was conscious of a car seat against his back and of banging his head against a glass window. Then he was in a fast moving car. His face seemed to be pressed against expensive smelling leather and, as his senses came back to him, his first thought was how comfortable the seat was. He turned his head to see street lights flashing past in rapid succession. The car was accelerating and weaving swiftly through traffic. Turning his head further he could make out the shapes of two large men in the front seats. He slid round into a slumped, semi-upright position.

'Who are you? What is this?'

The questions that seemed to croak from his throat weren't the result of any serious enquiry. They just seemed to be the first thoughts that came to mind, as though covering up a vacuum. There was no response from the men in the front of the car.

'Where are you taking me? What's this all about?' No response. 'You've got the wrong person,' he almost whined at last in desperation. Joycey saw the driver's eyes study him for a moment in the rear-view mirror and thought he detected amusement in the twitch of the eyebrows. But he couldn't be sure. The men said nothing, and the car simply sped faster as the dual carriageway cleared ahead of it.

They were heading east. Joycey recognised that at least. To their right he could see the lights of a plane descending towards the City Airport. They left docklands and Joycey could see that they were heading out towards the M25 and the Dartford Bridge, but after some time the car swung abruptly to the right and descended down a less-well-lit road. Joycey breathed a quiet sigh of relief. At least they weren't taking him out to Epping Forest – that would have meant an almost certain one-way trip. He guessed they were heading in the direction of the old Rainham marshes, several miles of desolate and undeveloped land by the river. There was a bird sanctuary somewhere there but not a lot else. The area was isolated between the river and the new high-speed railway lines. Apart from birds and night creatures, there was nothing and no-one for miles.

The car jolted suddenly and they were moving through almost total darkness with pin pricks of light receding into the distance. For ten minutes Joycey had become aware of a feeling of unreality, as though all of this was happening to someone else, as in a film which he was watching from the safety of a cinema seat. But as the car began to jolt down what was obviously an unmade track, into darkness, that sense of distance evaporated. Sitting in the back of the car he was confronted with a sense of smallness and vulnerability.

'What is this all about?' He tried again, but his mouth was dry and his shaking voice sounded like the squeak of a frightened kitten.

In truth he knew what this was about. There had never been any doubt. The face of DI Walker kept appearing in his mind, his lips moving as he warned about Christopher Keeley; then he heard Marik's voice telling him to be careful, and saw Takk sitting at a table clattering away at her laptop, oblivious to his peril .

The car crunched to a halt. The car rocked as the two men got out. One of them, grunting with exertion, stepped to the side of the car, opened the door and dragged Joycey out with rough strength. A bitterly cold chill ran across the upper half of his body and face, and he realised that he had been sweating profusely, and was shaking. His knees felt weak and uncertain, and he longed to sink down to the ground and just lie there and sleep. His arms were pulled behind his back and the old leather jacket was tugged roughly from his shoulders and thrown into the back of the car. The cold wrapped round his body like a claw. Then a large hand, gripping his upper arm, began to pull him away from the car and into the darkness. The ground felt hard and crisp under his feet, each tread making little crunching noises. Then they stopped. They were in almost complete darkness. Several miles away in almost every direction were lights, but here there was nothing but a blackness relieved only by the amber glow of London bouncing back from the low cloud base. Somewhere in the distance a duck quacked angrily and another replied with equal irritation. They stood there for several minutes and as Joycey's eyes adjusted to the darkness he could make out the bulky black forms of the two men now standing several yards away. The breath of all three was like silver steam, jetting in short rapid puffs into the coldness. The air smelt of snow.

'Right.'

Joycey heard the voice muffled, as though his ears had been stuffed with cotton wool. One of the men moved towards, him. He took a step backwards but his feet wouldn't move. There was no strength in his legs, they had just turned to rubber and he felt the world swaying about him. A hand grabbed his shoulder. Another hand started going through his pockets. He thought it was pretty pointless. His phone, keys and even the notebook were in his jacket in the car. A hand patted his arse and found his wallet, tucked tightly into the back pocket of his jeans.

'Give,' the voice said. Joycey fumbled and pulled out the wallet, almost dropping it in his haste.

'Now drop your trousers.'

Joycey went cold. There was a heavy feeling in his stomach and he felt sick.

'You what?' he said.

In the darkness in front of him there was a heavy sigh.

'Drop your fucking trousers mate! I'm not telling you again.' There was a pause and then the voice continued in a slightly tired tone. 'Just your trousers mate, I ain't fucking queer.'

Joycey fumbled with the button and zip on his jeans and pushed them down to his ankles. The man moved away from him and there came the sound on a few indistinct words. The coldness swept up Joycey's legs, chilling his testicles and making them contract. He wasn't sure that he hadn't pissed himself, but then, oddly, he reasoned that his urine would have felt warm. There was a small flash of light over where the men were standing. For a moment he thought it might have been a match but then he heard the sound of the keypad of a mobile phone. A few seconds later the man approached him again and held up

Joycey's mobile.

'It's for you,' the man said and stepped away again.

Hesitatingly, Joycey put the mobile to his ear.

'Mr Becket.' The voice at his ear was muffled but thin, a distortion which was strangely accentuated by the speaker on the phone. 'Mr Becket can you hear me?'

Joycey nodded in the darkness, realised what he was doing and responded.

'Hello? Yes.'

'Good. Now listen to me very carefully because I'm not in the habit of giving second chances.' The voice spoke slowly with a chillingly clipped precision. 'Do you know who this is Mr Becket?'

Joycey nodded again. His legs were feeling awfully cold and his teeth were beginning to chatter. 'I think so, yes.'

'Good, then perhaps you are not completely stupid after all.' There was a heavy pause and then the voice resumed in a questioning, waspish tone. 'I can take that as fact then, can I?'

'Y-yes.' Joycey's voice was still croaking and his throat felt hot and dry.

'I am going to be completely frank with you Mr Becket. I am going to do so because I am getting a little tired of you and your two young friends crossing my path, and I want to make it perfectly clear to you where we stand. Do you understand me?'

'Yes.'

There was a silence for several long seconds and then the voice continued.

'For some reason you have been taking an interest in a matter which does not concern you. I am a busy man Mr Becket. I have much to do and expect people who work with me to do as they are told. Most of those who work for me are trustworthy. Unfortunately some turn out to be less... honest.'

Joycey thought he heard a sigh and there was a pause again.

'This is the way of business in Europe today. We have to work with everyone and not everyone can be relied upon. I like to play fair Mr Becket, but some people always want more than there is on offer. Do you get my drift, Mr Becket? It's a sad fact that in this day and age business is just driven by greed. But then, it was the same in Captain Kidd's day, was it not?'

The unexpected mention of the pirate, jolted Joycey back to the present. The voice on the phone had been having some form of hypnotic effect, lulling Joycey into another place for a while. But at the sound of the old pirate's name, Joycey was suddenly crisply aware of where he was and the situation he was in. His mind felt sharper.

'Who?'

The voice on the phone snapped back at him waspishly. 'Don't waste my time Mr Becket! I know exactly what you know, and you know what I am looking for. Captain's Kidd's treasure. You know where it is by now.'

Joycey thought momentarily about denying this but then said limply, 'I might do.'

'Yes, indeed you might. And I am going to get it, quietly and without any fuss. Do you understand what I am saying?' Joycey nodded and grunted his affirmation of this statement. But the grunt did not satisfy. The voice suddenly barked angrily.

'Do you? Do you understand?'

'Yes.'

'I will do this quickly and efficiently because this is the 21st century and I am a responsible businessman. I want to complete the job with the minimum of fuss and possible interference. And I want to do this without anyone getting hurt. Casualties are so bad for marketing, you understand?'

Again Joycey nodded in the darkness. His teeth were clattering noisily now. The waspish voice continued.

'I have told my …associates that there is no need for anyone to get hurt. But this situation will need to be reviewed if I find that you or your friends have somehow wandered into view again. So I expect to neither see you, nor hear that you have been anywhere near anything to do with Wapping or Captain Kidd for the next six months. Do you understand?'

'Yes.' Joycey's mind was whirring despite his trembling knees and the chattering of his front teeth. Had something vital just been let slip. Why had Christopher Keeley indicated a period of six months.? What did that signify?'

The waspish voice was continuing. 'After that you can go back to doing whatever it is you normally do. You can dig up Captain Kidd himself for all I care.' There was a short burst of laughter. 'But if I do see you or hear of you, that nice little girlfriend of yours may get an experience you wouldn't like, either of you.'

Joycey's heart seemed to miss a beat as he thought of Takk, and his parched throat contracted so that he felt as though a huge fist was squeezing under his jaw.

'You do understand what I am saying to you, Mr Becket?' the voice was almost an electronic hiss in his ear. Joycey could only hum this time but this seemed to be accepted. 'Good, now tell my friends that we have finished our little discussion.'

Joycey waved the phone limply in the darkness, but the two men seemed to be engaged in quiet conversation. He glanced around him wondering whether he might make a run for it, he lifted a foot as though to take a step and then realised that he couldn't. His jeans had encumbered his ankles as effectively as any iron fetters. As he was pondering this the phone was wrenched from his hand and he was pulled roughly forward. The men now took up a position on either side of him and forced him to hobble forwards. Brambles tore at his legs and tough fibrous undergrowth clutched at his feet so that, tangled in the legs of his jeans, he stumbled continuously. But the men held him, squeezing his upper arms until they seemed to go numb and his elbows ached. They were moving downhill. The ground felt crunchy and there was the glistening reflection of water in front of them. Pools and patches that glinted back distant lights from what must have been the far side of the river. They stopped and one of the men held up Joycey's phone. Then with a violent twist of his wrist he sent it spinning away into darkness. There was a distant splash and the alarmed squawking of a bird.

The blow came unexpectedly out of nowhere. A huge fist sank into his diaphragm, driving breath from his body and a stream of water from his eyes. He doubled up and another blow hit him in the face, just off centre so that his right cheek took the full impact. Hands grabbed his elbows hurled him violently backwards and then forwards with a neck-jolting whiplash that made him cry out -but this time the hands were gone. He was falling forward at speed. He expected an impact with the ground but there was nothing and then he entered freezing cold water. Foul tasting liquid poured into his nose and as he gasped a slimy torrent rushed into his mouth making him gag. Then he was retching and choking and everything was going black.

26. The last bus from Dagenham

He was wrapped in a warm cocoon, a soft fleece that clung to his body and hugged him with a warmth he had never known before. He curled into it and knew instinctively that this was the position adopted by his ancestors and it was how they still lay when their bones were at long last exposed, uncovered to the world. There was something just a little disturbing about this thought and he couldn't quite put his finger on why this was. In his mind there were brown and purple visions of bones and people with dark hair and heavy brows all looking down at him. But then he thought this might have been an illustration from a book that he'd once glanced at, or perhaps it was that time he'd made a fool of himself at the Black Sabbath concert. He tried to think about it more clearly, but the effort seemed to be bringing on a headache and his ears were hurting. No, not so much his ears as the tips of his ears. And his nose hurt, but just the tip of his nose and his legs, well they felt numb; and his ribs hurt and breathing was painful like inhaling shards of glass.

Joycey opened his eyes and his mouth worked like a fish, filling half full of water that just tasted of cold. In the distance white lights staggered backwards and forwards, and around him a white mist seemed to be gathering. He started shivering, and once it started it took over his body and became uncontrollable. His teeth clattered like castanets and he wondered how long it would be until his teeth just shattered.

Slowly he rolled over onto his knees, conscious now that he was kneeling in about a foot of water. His feet were cold, and he tried curling his toes but nothing seemed to be happening. With a shock he realised that his legs were still bare. Like a drunk he staggered to his feet, lurching forward on rubber limbs until he sloshed, like some primeval monster, onto firm ground. He bent down to pull up his jeans but a sharp pain in his abdomen made him cry out. He pressed one hand to his stomach and with the other reached slowly down and pulled his jeans up over his knees. It seemed to take an age, but at last his numbed fingers were struggling with the zip, then he twisted the belt through the buckle and pulled it tight. The legs of the jeans felt cold, stiff and frozen and gave no comfort. He stood breathing heavily and looked about him, his head tilted forward as though trying to see out from under the hammer in his head.

A long way off in the distance was a low row of bright lights. He screwed up his eyes and peered through blurred vision. It looked like a lorry park or transport depot. Rows of white floodlights illuminated several dozen lorries and rusted looking containers. He began to stagger towards it, keeping his eyes fixed on the lights, but his feet kept snagging on old brambles and short stunted foliage that crackled under his feet, and several times he stumbled into water-filled pools and ditches, falling with a jerk that sent pain lashing through his body. It hurt less if he clutched his hands to his ribs, but then the backs of his hands froze. His breath came now in great hissing clouds, like a badly linked steam valve and he was sure he sounded like one too.

About ten minutes after he started he found himself teetering on the steep bank of a dike. Old dry reeds rattled around him, hissing and whistling in the wind, rattling brittle leaves at him like the spirits of angry medicine men. He stood, uncertain what to do. Further to his right he thought he could make out a wire fence crossing the dike itself. He stumbled and slipped along the slope towards it thinking that perhaps he might be able to clamber across it. But the wire, which was barbed, just sagged under the weight of his feet. He had no option but to step into the cold black water and wade, thigh deep, through a slurry of water and silt to the other side. He clambered out reeking like a sewer but, glad to have crossed this barrier, he nearly wept when he encountered another a hundred years further on, and then another. But each time he clambered up the opposite bank the lights of the transport depot were closer, and he clung desperately to that morsel of comfort.

Gradually, as he approached the transport depot, the ground around him became clearer, with frost-rimed bracken strands and glistening fingers of ice crystals. But he also saw as the depot came closer, that it was surrounded by a high perimeter fence topped with strands of barbed-wire. Beyond it nothing moved. Nothing moved at all. When at last he reached it, he stood for several moments with his fingers entangled in the wire, clinging heavily. There appeared to be no-one there. There was just stillness, and a heavy background hum that seemed to permeate the frost-hung air. After a while, he became conscious of another very faint sound off to his right, and realised that somewhere out of sight over a rise in the ground there had to be a road.

It occurred to him that if there was a gate to this depot there might be a night watchman, and if there was a night watchman there might be a telephone. He began to follow the fence, his left hand clutching at it with every other step. Gradually, his movements became smoother as though the activity was making his muscles massage blood back into circulation. He thought that perhaps he was beginning to feel just a little less cold, and wondered if this might be the effect of the arc lights of the yard to his left. He couldn't tell how long he walked like this, but he plodded slowly around the long perimeter of the depot until the fence began a great sweep round to the left. Finally he saw, ahead of him, the lines of curb stones beside a road. They led to a gate made of wire mesh and angle-iron. About fifty feet inside it was a small, square, flat-roofed brick structure with glass windows on three sides. As he approached he could see a faintly flickering blue light, which he took to be a television screen. Almost sobbing with relief he tottered forward to the gate, grabbed it with both hands and began to shake it frantically. The gate clanked and squealed under the movement and the wire sent hissing waves off to the left and right. The blue light flickered like a blinking eye. But inside the building, nothing moved.

'Hey! Hey!' Joycey shouted, his voice cracking with the strain. But there was just the ghostly flicker in the darkness. 'Help! I need Help! I've been…' he paused not sure what to say and then shrieked '…mugged.'

Nothing moved. Straining his eyes at the dark interior, Joycey thought he could see a still, immobile face gazing at him from under a peaked cap. But after another bout of yelling and gate shaking, he began to think that this was really just an imaginative illusion conjured up by wishful thinking. There were cameras on high poles though, he could make them out in the arc lights, their little red lights glowing mockingly down at him. He even thought that one of them moved slowly to look at him, but even this was uncertain. Finally, after nearly ten minutes of shouting and clawing at the gate, he threw himself back against it and sank onto his heels with his back leaning into the soft wire. The coldness pressed into his skin through the wetness of his shirt, and he thought mournfully about his old jacket. The wire hissed as a breeze swept up from the river.

Ahead of him a dark road stretched away towards the top of a ridge. Un-set curb stones lay untidily on either side, and the pavements themselves were just trenches of crushed brick and rubble and rags of old newspaper. An unfinished development.

There was nothing to do but to start walking. As he lurched to his feet, fluttering feather-like shadows drifting through the arc lights caught his eye, and as he raised his head to look, his face was coated in soft cold flakes of snow. Suddenly a wall of floating whiteness swept down upon him and the road disappeared from view behind a thick pale veil. The surrounding marshland disappeared. Wrapping his arms around his body, Joycey kept walking. After a while a ragged hedge joined the road from the right hand side, and as it seemed to offer some slim protection from the driving snow, Joycey walked as close to it as possible. But the uneven surface made him stumble so frequently that he soon gave this up and trudged slowly along in the road itself.

Gradually the glow from the arc lights began to fade behind him and as he climbed towards the top of the ridge, another glow appeared ahead. Soon the tall lights of road lamps appeared and as he reached the top of the ridge he found himself looking down onto a dual carriageway. The snow was now very thick and the lights beside the road had turned into mushrooms of light, each throwing a soft glowing cone of feathers onto an oval of ground below. The road's surface and the crash barriers were now fuzzy with a layer of snow, and Joycey noticed that his shoes had turned into soft white muffs and he could no longer feel his toes.

Reaching the junction with the road he instinctively turned left towards London. Conjuring up a mental map, he guessed he must be about four or five miles east of Barking. If he could get there it would be another couple of miles south to reach the Thames at North Woolwich where he could use the foot tunnel to get back across the river, or possibly the first ferry of the morning, though he didn't know what time they started running. He looked at his wrist but his watch was no longer there. He had no idea what time it was. His assailants had picked him up about half past five, and it couldn't have taken more than half an hour to drive out to Rainham marshes. It ought to be about 8pm, but something made him think it was much later than this. Perhaps he'd been lying in the pool for hours.

Walking on the road was becoming difficult. The snow was beginning to pitch into a soft velvet carpet. It felt like walking in huge carpet slippers, but underneath it was freezing fast and his uneven walk made his feet skid every now and again, leaving searing scars in the surface of the snow. The wind was driving the flakes into his back which was one advantage, as this seemed to take some of the chill out of it. It occurred to him that the thick cloud cover was acting as a blanket, raising the temperature slightly, for his cheeks, nose and ear tips felt ever so slightly less painful. But at the same time he realised that he was beginning to bend double and the idea came to him that there was a small flame inside his body which was gradually dwindling as he grew colder. It made him want to bend in on himself to protect it, to prevent that vital energy force being extinguished. It was as though he was wrapping himself around himself. He imagined that he could see this flame as a twisting column of green light that shifted like the aurora borealis within his chest, keeping him alive, but gradually, so gradually dying.

He had been walking for nearly half an hour when he heard the sound of a slow revving engine behind him. He turned unsteadily, and saw in the distance, the headlights of a car coming towards him. The beams probing forwards seemed to be made of spinning white flakes. Joycey stopped in the road, bent almost double, one hand clutching the collar of his shirt together, his eyes screwed against the snow, his mouth open. The car came on towards him, moving slowly, cautiously. Twenty feet away, it made a slight veer to the right as though the driver had jumped in surprise at the sight of him, and the engine gave a sudden, short roar of surprise. He glimpsed the scared face of a woman staring at him for a few moments, and then as he raised a hand, the engine roared again, the back of the car slewed wildly and it sped away, sending waves of snow up on either side. Within moments its red lights were lost to view. Shocked, Joycey stood gazing after it.

'Bitch!' he shouted after it.

Then grumbling loudly to himself he trudged on, cursing the uncaring nature of people in general and scared women drivers in particular. Misery clamped itself around his head and the aching started again, and for the first time, it occurred to him that he might die. He turned the thought over in his mind and imagined a newspaper headline about a man dying of exposure near Barking. Near Barking! He snorted at the absurdity and felt the shudder hurt his ribs. Then he thought of the likely reaction of his cronies, imagined Dusty's contemptuous fart of dismissal, and felt a glow of inner anger at the unfairness of things. Without realising it he was stumbling on, hunched against the snow once more. His back, was cold and clammy, and cold water dripped from the curled fringe of his hair.

Help came unexpectedly. He had drifted into a reverie which enabled him to plod on without thinking, his knees flexing while his calves seemed to be stiffening in the cold. In this state he became aware, rather abruptly of a large presence behind him. He turned, slowly, his whole body now moving stiffly like a cold statue and saw a few yards away, a single decker bus. Its engine was purring softly and it was moving gently forwards, its big tyres rolling with catlike surety through the snow. A bright orb of light preceded it only by a short distance and as it reached Joycey, the vehicle gently stopped with a soft whistle of air brakes. He found himself looking into the bright interior and the face of the driver, an older Punjabi man in a turban, with a thick grey streaked beard. The man sat staring at him for a moment and then with a startling hiss, the doors opened. The man pushed open his protective screen.

'You alright there?' The voice was melodic, like a song.

Joycey took a step forwards and hovered, his knees against the step.

'I've... been... mugged.' The words struggled from his lips. His throat was dry and he found to his dismay that his mouth didn't seem to want to work properly. 'I haven't got any money, and I need to get....home.'

'Get in, out of the cold now. Why aren't you wearing a jacket? This is no time to be wandering along the road here.'

Joycey stepped into the bus. He looked to his right, expecting to see rows of disapproving faces, but the bus was completely empty. The door hissed behind him. The driver looked him up and down slowly.

'You're in a bit of a state, my friend. What happened to you? You'd better sit down now.' He nodded to a single seat beside the door and Joycey sank gratefully back onto it, though he decided against leaning back in his wet clothes. The driver engaged a gear and the bus jolted like a horse and began to roll forward. The driver cast him several sideways glances.

'Where are you going, now? You can't go walking far in this, that's for sure? It's a bad night to be out. Where are you going?'

Joycey was shaking. 'I need to get to Greenwich. I was going to walk to North Woolwich.'

'Greenwich.' The man was shaking his head. 'North Woolwich now, that's a different thing. I can take you to Poplar. That's where I can take you.'

'Oh man, I'd really appreciate that. Thanks.' Joycey gasped, feeling uncomfortably short of breath. 'But I don't have any money, my wallet was taken …and my phone.'

The driver frowned. 'That's bad. Who did this thing?'

But when Joycey shrugged and shook his head he sighed. 'Well don't worry my friend, I am sure the bus company can afford to help you out. And I won't be tellin' them if you don't.'

He gave a solemn smile and nodded meaningfully at Joycey. After a few moments, the man gave him another sidelong glance.

'So you got mugged.' His face turned serious and he shook his head slowly. 'What a world, what a world. But this is a strange place to be mugged, man. What are you doing all the way out here?'

Joycey sighed. 'Two men grabbed me in Mile End. They pushed me in a car and drove me out here. They took my wallet and my phone.' His explanation tailed away. The driver gave him a long serious look.

'That all. Are you sure you ok man? I can get an ambulance if…?'

Joycey shook his head vigorously. 'No, it's ok. I'm just…just bloody freezing.'

'Here, I can turn the heating up, and here …take this.' He fumbled down out of sight and produced a thermos flask. 'Here.

C'mon have some of this.'

Joycey hesitated for a moment and then gratefully took the proffered flask. Unscrewing the top, his face was enveloped in the aromatic steam of strong, black coffee. He sipped it noisily and the driver's face split into a pleased grin.

As the caffeine seeped into his bloodstream, Joycey began to feel as though he had returned to a familiar world. The gentle roaring of the bus engine and its rocking motion lulled him into a reverie that was free from the violent redolence of the Rainham Marshes. He was conscious though of a pool of water that had gathered around his feet and little black rivulets that ran backwards and forwards along the floor of the bus. And as his clothing gradually warmed be became increasingly conscious of a strong sickly smell that clung about him. He found himself praying that the bus wouldn't fill up with passengers and, to his relief, the only other person who appeared to be out on this bitter night was an elderly man in a long brown coat who clambered aboard the bus like a zombie, reeking so strongly of beer that he could have smelt nothing else. Blind to anything but the driver, the man staggered to the back of the bus and collapsed across the rear seat. A short while later, loud snoring could be heard in the intervals between the gear changes of the engine.

The driver watched the old man briefly in his rear view mirror then, shaking his head, he said to Joycey, 'One of my regulars. I'll have to wake him up when we get to Silvertown.'

Joycey returned the grin and sank back into his dreams. As his body thawed out, it started to hurt and he began to wonder whether he would be able to walk down through the Isle of Dogs to the Greenwich foot tunnel. He wanted time to slow down so that he could sit in the warmth for longer, but the more he longed for it, the quicker the time sped past and in what seemed very little time the driver pulled the bus to a slow halt.

'Have to drop you here now.' He frowned as Joycey rose unsteadily to his feet. 'Can I call anyone for you?'

The man pushed open the barrier to his compartment and waved a mobile phone. Joycey felt a wave of relief flush over him, and resisted the impulse to kiss the man. When he finally heard Marik's sleepy voice on the mobile, he felt like kissing him too.

27. Dreaming

He was lying on a hard bed, an unspeakably hard bed and his body was itching. He thought it might be the damp clothes. He wasn't certain. His head ached and the room smelt dank. Hard, bare stone walls surrounded him. He wasn't sure how long he had lain there, but for some reason the day seemed important. It was Friday 23rd. He knew that. There had been food earlier but he hadn't been able to eat. He lay, aching and heavy and the hours dragged.

Eventually, the background rumble of sound, voices, shouts, screams, swearing were overwhelmed by a rhythmic chanting. The clatter of irons being rattled against stone. The door opened noisily and four men stood there. They were armed. His arms were seized and he was dragged through corridors, down steps into a courtyard. Overhead the sky was coloured by grey late-afternoon clouds. In the centre of the courtyard was a cart. It was lined with deep straw and he was pushed up onto it and thrust against the chest-high wooden rails of its side. Two men were thrown in beside him. They eyed him sullenly and said nothing. There was a jolt and the cart lurched forward through an arch into a larger courtyard. Waiting for them was a procession of soldiers led by an official-looking man sitting on a grey horse, carrying a long silver mace shaped like an oar. With a jolt and clatter of hooves, the procession passed under an arch with heavy, iron-barred doors, and began the climb up what he recognised to be Ludgate Hill in the City, passing the huge stone walls and scaffolding of the new cathedral. Men were gathered all over the wooden staging, their tools idle in their hands as the procession passed. The streets were lined with jeering crowds. It was all a blur.

He knew that he had been waiting for someone to come to him. For a message to arrive. He knew he was being carried to his own execution. Someone was supposed to bring his reprieve. And now it was getting late. As he struggled to keep his feet in the lurching cart, feeling the others bump against him, his temper grew foul. Men and women darted from the sides of the roadway, dodging the outstretched arms of the soldiers, to thrust tankards and horn cups of wine and ale towards him. At first he refused, but when one pretty young woman pursed her lips at him seductively he took her cup and drank the contents in one long gulp. He threw the cup back to her and she danced around laughing with her arms held high as the procession shouldered her aside and back into the crowd. There were other outstretched arms and beakers, tankards, he began to drink, laughing and swearing. Where was the messenger? Where was Harley's message? They would soon see.

They passed the grey walls of the Tower of London, where a sea of faces had gathered on the hill beside the road, he staggered and waved and there were cheers and shouts. Becoming more intoxicated by the attention and befuddled by the cheers and laughter, he began to play up to the crowd. Down towards the river, the rank smell of mud and weed and rotting timber grew stronger. Beside him one of the men was vomiting copiously on the side of the cart. One of the soldiers swore and dabbed ineffectually at his shoulder, to the amusement of his colleagues. He joined in the laughter.

The way was narrower now, with meaner houses and the people lining the streets looked hungrier, rougher, less willing to laugh. To the right, the river could be glimpsed between the houses and warehouses. The smell of tar and rope from chandleries and rope-works. Scent of wood shavings. A long muddy track. Through narrowed eyes, he recognised Wapping High Street with its houses crowding in ever closer on either side. Then abruptly there was an opening on the right, a long gravel bank down to mud and filth and there, a huge crowd of people were gathered in a heavy, terrible silence. Across the river stood the tower of St Mary's Church at Rotherhithe, and there, black against the silver water of the Thames, the wooden posts of the gibbet. The cart lurched suddenly so that Kidd and the other occupants of the cart had to hang on. The violence which had thrown Kidd against the wooden rail at the side of the cart had shocked him and suddenly he let out a great roar of rough laughter which rang across to echo from the distant water. Why, should he care now?

28. At Marik's

When he woke he was lying in a strange bed. He felt warm, cosy, but the instant he moved his body was wracked with pain and something like a cannon ball began thudding against the insides of his skull. He gave a deep groan and sensed movement. Opening his eyes he saw Marik's face hovering a few feet away. He looked worried.

'Boss, you ok?'

Joycey rolled his eyes round at the pale walls, the neat, plain furniture. Even in his discomfort he recognised it.

'Bloody Ikea .' He felt Marik's grin. 'Where am I then? Prison?'

'Mine,' Marik crooned soothingly. 'She said it was better this way. Safer.'

Joycey glanced around, expecting Takk's black glare, but she didn't appear to be present. 'She running things now is she?' He ran his tongue across his lips. They felt swollen and tasted salty.

Marik shrugged. 'She said was safer here.'

Joycey groaned and rolled his eyes. A movement at the periphery of his vision caught his eye. He looked again, and saw Mickey gazing at him from his perch on the seat of a chair. His green-gold eyes stared fixedly for several long moments then he casually stretched out a back leg, and began to lick it with an exaggeratedly nonchalant air.

'She thinks of everything, doesn't she?'

Marik smiled across at the cat and shrugged again with a happy grin. 'Clever. Yes. Bright girl.'

'How long have I been asleep?'

'Three, four hours. She said you should rest and she would see you when she get back.'

'Oh! Oh, did she now?' Joycey pushed himself up on an elbow, but he winced and fell back against the pillows with a groan. 'Marik, can you get me some Paracetamol or something. I'm dying here!' he whined self-indulgently.

Marik leant over him and lifted a glass from beside the bed. 'Soluble. Already mixed. Boss. She says you will want this soon.'

The young Pole's face was a mixture of concern and wry amusement as he helped Joycey drink the slightly salty and gritty contents. Then he stood up with a nod.

'Sleep Boss. Sleep some more and I cook dinner. And she be back soon I think.'

Joycey was formulating a response, but his mind kept slipping away from the words he was trying to marshal into a line.

When he opened his eyes again Takk was sitting in the chair across the room, typing quietly on a laptop. The room was darker and he was aware of a warm weight against his thighs. Moving his hand he felt the soft fur of Mickey lying there and for a moment he felt content. Then it occurred to him that the headache he had been suffering before, had evacuated the room, so he gave an exaggerated moan anyway. When he looked again, Takk's eyes were gazing at him, much as Mickey's had been earlier. It was at this point it occurred to him that under the sheets he was naked.

'Where are my clothes?' he demanded suddenly.

'They were ruined, and stank. Marik went to your house and got you some clean ones.' Her eyes flickered with dark amusement. 'And don't worry. He put you to bed, not me.'

For a moment he lay there silently. 'I need a doctor.'

'You had one. While you were out of it.' She sighed. 'We thought it was the best thing to do, considering.' Takk's face was impassive across the room.

'What did he say?'

'SHE said that there was nothing broken, but that the bruises were quite bad and you would hurt for a while. She seemed more concerned about how you got into such a state.

'Yeh, I bet. What did you tell her?'

'I told her you got pissed and fell down some concrete steps.'

'Oh, very nice.'

Takk's eyes were black dots. 'What did you expect us to tell her? All you could tell us when we got you back was that you'd been wandering in snowland – wherever that is. We realised that someone had attacked you, obviously.'

'Snow,' he muttered vaguely.

Takk rose and crossed to the window, lifted the curtain and peered out for a moment. 'It's stopped now. But it was quite heavy for a while. We thought it would stay but it seems to be melting. It's still cold out though,'

Joycey felt an involuntary shiver run through his body, and a pain shot through his ribs.

'We thought it safer to bring you here…both of you. Until we knew what had happened, anyway.'

He nodded, closing his eyes for a moment. There was the sound of a door opening and Marik ambled slowly into the room. He crossed to stand next to Takk, leaning back against the wall, his thumbs hooked into the pockets of his jeans.

'Do you feel like telling us what happened now?' She asked.

'Sure, always enjoy talking about myself.' He snorted, and proceeded to tell them how he had been forced into the car and taken to Rainham Marshes. As he outlined the telephone conversation with Keeley, he noticed the two of them exchanging meaningful glances. When he had finished, Takk thought for a moment. He thought she was going to comment on what he had just told them. Instead she gave a short, barked laugh.

'Some researcher you turn out to be. Send you on a simple job and this is what happens.'

Joycey's lips twisted into something resembling a smile.

'Anyway,' she continued. 'I don't suppose you found anything out at the local history library?'

Joycey made to sit up suddenly, but once again sudden pain jerked him back into line.

'Christ, yeah. I had forgotten. I found this book. Cheap little paperback by this Cordelia something or other. There was something in it about Magistrates Court records about deaths in the area in 1701. There was an entry for someone called Sarah Hawkins who they thought had drowned in the river. It said she kept an alehouse called the Sugar Loaf at Wapping Old Stairs.'

'Sugar Loaf!' Takk blurted out suddenly.

'Yeah,' Joycey continued, suddenly enjoying himself. 'And guess what. It said that this Sarah Hawkins was reputed to be a relative of Captain Kidd.'

He relaxed back against the pillows, smiling to himself and watching the emotions transforming Takk's stern features.

'Shit!' she cried out suddenly. 'Of course, that's it. Kidd was visited in prison by Matthew Hawkins and his wife. That must have been Sarah. And one of them must have been the H referred to in the letter. I thought H was Harrison, the one who lent the syndicate the money. But the letter makes more sense if it was written to Hawkins. It was addressed to his Cousin after all.'

She was tapping away at the lap top. Marik was watching intently over her shoulder.

'Yes,' she cried after a few minutes, her eyes burning. 'It fits. Kidd addresses the letter to his Cousin, and then refers to 'H' who is a man. The letter has to have been written to Sarah Hawkins. She was supposed to arrange for something to be moved by her husband. She runs an alehouse called the Sugar Loaf which was at Wapping Stairs, so it was easily accessible from the river – and I bet it had a cellar. '

Takk paused, her face glowing slightly in the dim light. 'Kidd hid the treasure in the Hawkins's alehouse in Wapping. We know he was going to use it as a bargaining ploy, and we know his plan failed, because he was executed.' She looked from Joycey to Marik and back again. 'The treasure was never found. So what if it's still there?'

Joycey was shaking his head slowly. 'No pub called the Sugar Loaf there now. And the librarian at Mile End said that a lot of the area was destroyed when the docks were built. '

'Maybe not a cellar though. And the thing is this,' she rose from her chair and crossed to the window, peering out as though anxious about something outside. '…the thing is this. Christopher Keeley thinks it is there. And so long as he has reason to think it's there, so have we.'

Joycey gave another low groan. 'I suppose he has even more reason now. His thugs must have got my notebook. It was in my leather jacket.'

'No, you left it in the library. The librarian left a message on your answerphone. Honestly, it's just as well you are useless.'

Takk was laughing suddenly, her face transformed into something startling. Marik beamed at them both and mainly at Takk. She gave him a playful punch on the upper arm and he yelped ruefully.

'Sorry'. She grinned at him. He looked ecstatic.

'This is all very well,' Joycey grumbled from the bed. 'But I've been beaten up by thugs twice in the last few days, had the house turned over and the shop broken into. And nearly froze to death on top of all that. This isn't a game we are playing here. Keeley's serious trouble, and his men aren't the sweetest I've ever come across. We ain't in a happy place here.'

Takk sat on the edge of the bed and darted solemn looks between the two men, the laughter stilled.

There was a long silence and Takk spoke quietly. 'Marik has an interesting question for you.'

Marik's face dissolved into uncertainty and for a moment he resembled the boy he had seemed not so long before. Takk was looking at him sternly.

'Go on,' she urged. 'Say it. What you said to me earlier.'

Marik looked from one to the other, almost panic stricken.

'Marik!' Takk's voice rose in sharpness.

'Boss…' he began, licking his lips. 'Boss, thing is this….' He stopped again, swallowed and blinked. Then he took a deep breath. 'Why they let you go Boss?'

Joycey felt Takk's eyes on him. Marik tried to explain.

'They have you and they let you go. Why they not kill you?'

Joycey was staring at him in disbelief.

'Christ! Thanks!' He wailed. 'That's a nice thing to say. Jesus!'

'No, no, don't take it the wrong way.' Takk said soothingly. 'Marik has a very good point.'

Joycey turned his stare on her.

'Think about it. Keeley had killed Gavin because he had taken the Kidd letter. Presumably they killed him partly as punishment, but probably also to stop him saying anything about either the letter or the map.'

'Yeah, so?' Joycey said cautiously.

'Well think about it. Not only did you have the map, but you were obviously trying to find out more about it. Even where Kidd's treasure might be.'

Joycey grunted.

'So they were prepared to kill Gavin, who probably had no idea what it was he was dealing with; but you know much more, so why didn't they just kill you while they had you.'

Joycey thought about it.

'They did rip me clothes off and throw me in the river. It was fucking cold you know!'

'I'm sure. But they could just have held your head under water and left you there for someone to find eventually. Instead of finishing you off, they let you go.'

Joycey grumbled to himself. He sensed that she was right about something. If they had wanted him to die of hypothermia, they could have tied him up and left him somewhere in Epping Forest. That was where the estuary gangs usually left their victims, and they weren't usually discovered for years. He looked from Takk to Marik. They were both gazing at him intently.

'Ok', he nodded. 'You got a point. So if they could have killed me, why didn't they?'

It was Takk's turn to look unhappy. 'I don't know.'

'Right. Well that's helpful.'

Joycey suddenly collapsed before the venomous assault of one of Takk's darkest glares. He closed his eyes and decided that it was time to sleep again.

Takk's sharp voice pierced his momentary reverie.

'And don't you think that after all that it would be better

if we stopped him getting his hands on Kidd's treasure?'

He opened his eyes reluctantly and sighed. 'Well, yeah, I suppose. But it might not be there anyway.' His voice had turned into a whine. 'After all, we don't know, do we? And Sarah Hawkins disappeared in the river a few months after Kidd's death, remember. Seems to me we could be in danger of following her if we are not careful.'

There was a long silence. Marik was looking grim.

'Tell you what.' Takk said at last. 'Let me see what I can find out about the Wapping Old Stairs. If I can find out anything useful that might give us a clue as to where the Sugar Loaf was, or its cellar, we'll think again. If I can't find anything out about it. We'll tell the police what we know …'

'Don't know about that.' Joycey grunted

'…and drop the whole thing.' She finished.

Joycey looked across the room at Marik. It struck him that something had changed about the young Pole. He looked somehow more stocky, more determined and athletic. But he also looked less baby faced. It was as though something had changed about him both physically and mentally.

29. About the Docks

When Joycey opened his eyes again it was dark, but an amber glow was seeping through the curtains, and from the road outside came the swish of cars running on wet tarmac. He sat up, feeling more mobility than before, though a sharp ache reminded him that it was not yet time to start leaping around. A quiet whistling sound came from near the bottom of the bed, and as his eyes adjusted he could make out the form of Marik slumped in a chair which had been pulled close so that his feet could rest on the bottom of the bed. Joycey gazed at him for a moment.

'Oy!' he yelled hoarsely. 'Who said you could out your bloody hooves on the bed.'

Marik jerked into life, and jumped to his feet muttering apologies intermingled with something in what Joycey took to be Polish. A light-switch clicked and a soft lamplight flooded the room.

'You better Boss?'

Joycey scowled and putting up a hand, rubbed the side of his face. It felt stiff and uncomfortable with what he took to be several days stubble. He rubbed sticky eyes and yawned.

'How long have I been here now?'

Marik looked distant for a moment. 'Two days Boss.'

'Two days! What about the shop?'

Marik nodded, smiling. 'It's ok. She put sign in door. On holiday. Back next week.'

Joycey's mouth worked silently, because he could think of nothing to say. He grunted angrily to himself and then snapped, 'Where are my clothes then?'

While he dressed, Marik explained that Takk had gone to the Docklands Museum to see what she could find out about the London Docks, Wapping Old Stairs and the site of the Sugar Loaf alehouse. Joycey received this news impassively and then demanded coffee.

Joycey was sitting in Marik's small, neat living room listening to some very loud music when Takk let herself into the flat. Smiling to himself, Joycey noted the fact that she had been given a key.

'What the hell's that?' She demanded in an outraged tone.

'AC/DC. Highway to Hell. One of the greatest rock tracks of all time.'

She shook her head in dismay and disappeared towards the kitchen where Marik was preparing something with vegetables. Sometime later, they both appeared carrying trays of food which, even Joycey had to admit, smelt good. Mickey followed them, keeping close to Marik's feet, tail erect and pink tongue actively searching his lips. Marik unfolded a table and they sat to eat. After several minutes, Joycey said, without looking up from his plate.

'So you want to go on with this. After all that's happened?'

Takk gave him a sharp look and he blundered on.

'I just wondered, you know. What with everything.'

She spoke without looking up again. 'If Kidd's treasure is there, it may be worth millions of pounds.'

'Sure, if it is still there.'

'And there may be historically valuable material there too, something which could help us solve the mystery of Captain Kidd's expedition.'

Joycey gave a little laugh. 'Well it may help you. It doesn't make much odds to me.'

'Fair enough. Anyway, we have an advantage over Keeley and his gang.'

Joycey was tempted to smile, an image of the Keeley Gang as a Wild West outfit flitted briefly into his imagination.

'Oh and what's that.'

'I think we are closer to the treasure than he is.'

'How's that then.'

'Well if Keeley knew where it was, why hasn't he already got it? He probably had all the opportunities. He seems to have known the significance of the map – though don't ask me how. But he certainly seems to have known how potentially valuable it could be. Otherwise he wouldn't have killed for it. So, why hasn't he got to it already?'

Takk's voice had the steady, even tone of an academic who knows he or she is on firm ground.

Joycey scooped food into his mouth and shrugged. 'Dunno, you tell me.'

'I don't think he knows where it is.'

'You reckon.'

'Yes. I think that is why they let you go. They hope you are going to lead them to it.'

'X marks the spot.' Joycey grinned.

It was Takk's turn to shrug. 'And there's another thing too. It may be more difficult for him to get it.'

'How do you make that out?

'Because he has the police watching him already and that's to our advantage. Because while he is trying to watch what we are up to he is also having to keep an eye over his shoulder for them. He must know by now that they are onto him in some way. So if we are clever and act quickly, we can get there first.'

'If we knew where 'there' is.'

'Well I have some interesting news, and after today, I am more than ever convinced he doesn't know what we do.'

Joycey stared at her for a moment. Marik had a dreamy look on his face.

'You remember the local history librarian told you that the London Dock records were at the Docklands museum.'

Joycey nodded and, after a tiny hesitation, Marik nodded too.

'Well I went there today and met their archivist. Her name's Vicky. She's really helpful.'

The two men nodded appreciatively. So Takk continued.

'I didn't tell her exactly why we were looking but I told her about the Sugar Loaf, and she was really interested. She told me straight away that nobody had looked at those records for years.'

She looked from one to the other. 'You understand what that means?'

They looked blank.

'It means Keeley hasn't seen them yet.'

They nodded, though she wasn't sure that they got the significance. After a thoughtful pause, Joycey asked,

'So what did you find out?'

'Vicky found me the early minute books of the dock company. They were really revealing. It seems the dock company wanted to build their dock as close to the City as they could. That's why they chose Wapping. And the area they selected to build the entrance to the dock was near Wapping Old Stairs. The problem was that the area was already quite well built up, with homes, tenements, lodging houses and commercial places too - and of course, more than a few ale houses. The dock company had to buy out all of these. They even had to pay off the old Shadwell Water Works Company because they had a conduit running across the area. In fact the dock company planned ahead for expansion and acquired a huge swathe of the old East End, and demolished the lot."

Takk paused and was gratified to see that the two men were listening intently.

'Anyway, many of the archive documents were destroyed during the war, but Vicky managed to find some early title deeds.'

In the soft light of the room, Takk's memory went back to her afternoon in the archive. And as she spoke, she was suddenly back there, in the cool blue light of the reading room.

She had opened the first deed box gingerly feeling rather like an Egyptologist breaching a newly discovered tomb for the first time, uncertain as to what lay there, and filled simultaneously with excitement and trepidation. The box had been filled to the brim with bundles of thick yellow parchment documents, each package bound together with faded magenta cotton tape. The documents themselves were folded, and thick and soft to the touch. Each bundle had an old card label tied to it covered notes written in a thin spidery hand in brown ink Deeds, Assignments, Conveyances all bound together in what were obviously meant to be meaningful relationships. After a while she realised that each bundle seemed to relate to an individual property or site. Each one purchased by the new Dock Company as it pursued its relentless acquisition of land in the old part of Wapping.

She had ploughed her way carefully with enormous patience through each bundle, poring over the crabbed brown handwriting, and peering at scratchy notices and amendments. Unfolding each crackling piece in turn, then folding it back up and retying each bundle, her gloved fingers becoming black with the soot of centuries that encrusted the surfaces of each document.

Takk tapped on the screen of her laptop.

'And there it was. At the bottom of the pile, a deed of sale of the Sugar Loaf alehouse by Wapping Old Stairs, lately belonging to Sarah Hawkins, to Josiah Hanbury.'

She beamed. 'And then there were deeds of sale from

Hanbury to another man, then another, and so on until it was sold to the London Dock Company. And,' she said triumphantly, 'There's even more. Vicky told me that documents turn up every now and again from all sorts of different places. And, listen to this. Four years ago a guy went into the museum with what looked like an old exercise book he'd bought in a car boot sale, and it turned out to be the rough notes of the engineers who were employed constructing the dock.'

The two men were silent, carried forward on her growing excitement. She scrolled through several pages on the screen until she found the notes she wanted.

'On 5th August 1804 there was a meeting at London Dock House to discuss the installation of a steam engine to drain water from the entrance lock and top-up the basin itself when required. Several engineers were there, including James Watt Junior who had been recruited as a consultant.'

'Didn't he do something with a kettle once?'

Takk ignored him.

'According to the notes, they had to discuss the foundations for the engine house, and someone had to draw a diagram of what was required. There's even a little sketch of it in the book, showing where the well would need to be, and the beam and boiler house. And in particular how they were going to build the brick conduits to carry the water from the lock and basin, to and from the river itself.'

'I hope this is going somewhere?' Joycey groaned suddenly with impatience.

'Just listen, will you, for Christ's sake! What's important is that according to the notes they had encountered a problem. They needed to build underground conduits alongside the new entrance lock. The problem was, there were tunnels there already – these were the deep cuts carrying water for the Shadwell Water Company and these lay adjacent to older underground structures. One of which was on the site of the old Sugar Loaf Inn.'

Joycey was staring at her silently.

'Anyway, they knew that the construction costs were running way over budget, so instead of removing the old structures, they decided to cut new conduits alongside the old ones, using the existing structures to reinforce the new conduits. Apparently, they saw no point in going to extra expense. So, unless things changed later, the foundations of the Sugar Loaf may still be there.'

30. In Wapping

The three of them sat there for a moment, digesting this information. Joycey looked unusually serious. Finally he spoke.

'Hang on a minute. Does that mean you think the cellars of the Sugar Loaf are still there?'

Takk nodded. 'Could be. Vicky checked for me, and there were no surviving records of any later work that might have disturbed the underground structures. Of course, they may have been destroyed later during the blitz. But they have to lie somewhere underground near the buildings on Pierhead – and those buildings are still standing from 1805 when the entrance lock was built. '

And the treasure might still be there?'

Takk shrugged. 'Could be.'

Joycey thought about this.

'How come nobody's found it before, then?'

'Because nobody's been looking for it,' she replied simply. 'At least, they've not been looking there for it. Hundreds of people have been looking in the Caribbean and America for it.

Even in the Indian Ocean.'

Joycey snorted. 'And it may have been here under our noses all this time.'

Again Takk shrugged.

Joycey's solemn expression gradually changed to one of sly delight. 'So we could really be on the trail of real pirate gold.'

Takk shrugged. 'Well, pirate plunder, anyway.'

Joycey became thoughtful. For some time he had had the feeling that things were just a little beyond his control and he didn't normally like that. His life was not accustomed to abrupt change or sudden unexpectedness. He was a cautious plodder, though he himself would never have described himself in those terms. But, he played it safe and now he felt conflicted. He was being carried along by something over which he seemed to have little influence. Furthermore, he had always kept out of the way of serious villains and his instinctive feeling was that that was the better path to take. He had never bothered them, so they didn't bother with him. But now he seemed to have fallen over something big-time. Something which he would have run away from at the first warning, in the past. But the current situation seemed so unreal. Pirate gold, treasure maps, Wapping. And, reassuringly, Marik was just as solid and reliable as ever. Even Takk, strange girl that she was, seemed to have become stronger and more sensible as the days had passed. In truth he knew nothing about her, but then in reality he knew little about Marik either. They were just their like the gateposts at the entrance to Greenwich Park. A solid, ever present part of life.

And behind it all, of course, was this lure of pirate treasure. It would have value, maybe not as much as Takk thought, but value nonetheless. And in Joycey's world you pursued anything which left you with more than you started with.

That was the first rule of successful business. And this pirate treasure could be a big gain with very little initial outlay. Like being given a pile of valuable books, rather than having to pay a few quid for them. There was attraction in that. And sure there had been a few knocks along the way, he had been beaten up twice and the house and shop turned over. But these things seemed a little unreal. Unreal unless he made a sudden move, that is.

'So,' he said at last. 'What do we do now?'

Takk gave a slight smile. 'Why don't we go and look for it?'

Marik's grin seemed to light the room.

The next morning was cold and grey, with a sharp easterly wind blowing up the river from the North Sea. Like the weather, the excitement of the previous evening had cooled a little. A brief discussion about what they were searching for and how they were going to go about it had given them a more realistic idea of what they were doing. It amounted to little more than a casual stroll around Pierhead and Wapping High Street. Nothing more than that. But when Takk had pointed out they would need to check the river wall as well as the buildings near Old Wapping Stairs, Marik had sensibly asked when low tide was. That had to be looked up. Fortunately, they quickly discovered that low tide was at 10.30am the following morning. Takk, who had seen some of the plans attached to the old title deeds, thought it was particularly important to look at the old dock entrance, which lay adjacent to Wapping Old Stairs.

So, in the morning, Joycey was determined to get going, and he even tolerated Marik's insistence that they all borrow waterproof jackets and fleeces or jumpers, of which he seemed to have an extraordinary number. When Joycey questioned this he was surprised when it was Takk who provided the explanation.

'Marik is a keen walker. He used to do a lot of out-door stuff before he came to London.'

Joycey gave them both a vacant stare - beginning to realise just how little he did know about the young Pole.

'Well I suppose there's a lot more I don't know.' He muttered at last.

Finally, with Takk enshrouded in a sharp looking black wax-cotton smock that looked as though it was in the process of swallowing her alive, they made their way to Joycey's van which was parked in a nearby street. They had already discussed the use of the van. Since it was highly individual and well known, it had seemed a risk to use it. So in the end they decided to drive to New Cross on the south side of the river, park the van and take the South London line under the river to Wapping itself.

It took them half an hour to get through Greenwich, and then another half hour to negotiate the crawling traffic through Deptford. Finally Joycey directed Marik to one of the garages under the railway arches, where he had liberty to park at any time. They then caught the train, and sat in silence as it rattled through Brunel's old tunnel under the river and stopped at Wapping. They emerged from the station just as rain started to fall.

From the station they turned left and began walking through the deep canyon between the converted wharves and warehouses. Occasionally a car flapped past on the cobbles, the tyres pattering and leaving greasy lines along the wet road. Joycey thought the air was filled with the smell of coffee and croissants from a block of luxury apartments, and he instantly felt hunger digging under his sore ribs.

They walked past the closed green wooden doors of the Captain Kidd pub, and Takk and Joycey exchanged significant glances but said nothing. A few yards further on they came to the red-bricked façade of the Wapping police station, the Headquarters of the Met police's Marine Division. Joycey glanced at it once, nervously, and then hurried past, leading the others at a faster pace. On their right a line of old iron railings marked the perimeter of an old churchyard which had been converted to a park. A few box tombs stood sombre and grey amidst the fading frost on the grass, and dead leaves lay heaped in sodden mounds of yellow and brown, barely stirring to the touch of the brisk wind. Apart from a couple of Asian teenagers gripped in an intimate clinch on one of the benches, the park was deserted. Takk turned into the park and headed for one of the gravestones propped against a brick wall. They followed.

Stooping, she attempted to read the weathered inscription on the stone, a blackened square slab with scrollwork corners. But the surface had spalled leaving ugly white patches on the sooty surface. She moved on to inspect one of the few isolated table tombs, and they followed her in obedient silence.

'Pretty much all eighteenth century,' she murmured.

'This was the graveyard of St John's Wapping,' said Joycey, suddenly. 'It was badly bombed during the war so they moved the stones and turned it into a park. That tower over there is all that's left of it.' He nodded towards a tall structure on the far side of an adjoining road.

Takk and Marik were gazing at him in astonishment.

'What?' he grinned, pleased with himself.

'Nothing.' Takk frowned.

'Well you sent me to do some research didn't you?'

'What else do you know?' she asked.

Joycey wracked his brains for a moment. 'There was a church here in Kidd's time. But it was demolished when this one was built.' He sighed. 'And that's all I can remember.'

Takk smiled. 'Well I'm impressed.'

Marik too was looking at Joycey with admiration.

For a few moments they stood in silence, and then Marik shivered. Takk looked at him.

'It's getting colder,' she agreed. Then added, 'And have you noticed how quiet it is around here?'

And it was true. The breeze was rustling the bony fingers of the trees and scuffling old scraps of paper along the paths, but apart from this the park was suspended in a bubble of tranquillity. There was no trace of the perpetual roar of London's traffic. They stood listening to the wind. Then, as they made their way back to the road, Takk stopped suddenly beside one of the box tombs. On the north side, the carved lettering was much sharper and she traced the words with a finger before reciting them out loud.

'In memory of John Simpson, Master Mariner of Alnmouth, who departed this life May 30th 1810 aged 53 years.'

'Where this Alnmouth?' Marik asked.

'Northumberland,' Takk replied. 'He was probably in the coal trade.' Then seeing Marik's perplexed expression she added. 'Bringing coal down to London from the north east of England. Lots of sailors in those days learned their skills in the coal trade. They think that was how Kidd started – working as a deck hand on a ship from Scotland.'

Marik nodded.

The light seemed to dim suddenly and another gust of cold wind whipped round the corner of the churchyard. Rain drops spattered noisily on their waterproofs.

'We better get on with it,' Joycey groaned.

They followed him back to the park gate and they continued westward along the road until they came, on their left, to a small private garden, lined on either side with short cobbled roads and terraces of elegant four-storey Georgian town houses. Inside the park were several neat flower beds, banks of shrubbery and mature plane trees. The park was guarded by tall iron railings, which stretched to the riverside itself several hundred feet away. Neatly painted signs hung on the railings stating that the park was a private area and that barbecues were not permitted.

'This was the old entrance lock,' Takk explained. 'They filled it in when the dock closed.'

Joycey ignored the signs and wandered along the front of the town houses, scowling up at the windows as he did so. Takk and Marik followed along the short road until they reached more iron railings which ran along the top of the river wall. The river itself lay much lower, and about sixty feet beyond a greasy stretch of mud and shingle. The air smelt of salt and weed and something slightly chemical. Takk was gazing at the houses on the eastern side of the little park.

'The cellars of the Sugar Loaf were somewhere under here.'

Joycey grunted non-committedly and led them back the way they had come. Fifty yards back along Wapping High Street was an attractive looking pub, its lead glazed windows set amidst a façade of cream and maroon tiles. Its name, 'Town of Ramsgate' was painted on a large red sign over the door. Joycey hesitated outside it, but Takk pushed past him into a narrow alley that slipped between the pub and the tall warehouse which loomed over it. Suddenly, they found themselves standing at the top of a set of steep steps leading down to the foreshore. To the left an iron hand rail gave protection from a deep drop onto a scattering of boulders and river-worn rubble. To the right a wall appeared to descend to the foreshore. At the bottom, a short causeway of uneven and wet looking stone blocks led out towards the swirling water of the river itself, twenty or thirty feet away.

'This has to be Wapping Old Stairs,' said Takk.

Gingerly descending the treacherous looking steps, they found themselves in a deep green chasm with tall buildings looming over them on three sides. There was a powerful smell of ammonia and salt. Looking back they could see that what they had taken for a high wall was in fact the remains of an older, steeper set of steps which had been left in situ. Joycey led the way forward along the causeway, but Takk stepped off this onto the surface of worn boulders and shingle, to explore the crunching surface beneath her feet. The area was littered with pieces of ancient bottle glass, fragments of clay pipes, driftwood, polystyrene and plastic water bottles. Marik followed.

As they moved forward the rounded green bulwark of the river wall to their right fell back in an elegant curled bastion to reveal Tower Bridge. Much closer than they had imagined and impressively tall when seen from the level of the river at low tide. To their left, in the other direction, the foreshore became finer, a mixture of brown sand and shingle, with the remains of blackened wooden stakes sticking up through it like rotten teeth. Further along, a precarious looking set of wooden stairs descended to the river and, beyond that again, a jetty led to a pontoon with blue painted sheds. A police launch was nosing its way alongside and they stopped to watch as one of the crew, a woman, sprang agilely from the boat to the pontoon with a mooring line.

'See where that boat is?' Takk called out above the wind. They turned to look at the police launch. 'According to the maps, Execution Dock was just the other side of that.'

They nodded in silence. And looked at her again.

'It's where Kidd was executed,' she explained.

They turned to look eastwards again and Joycey gave a sigh. The low grey skies, and the gusts scudding up the river, added to the gloomy aura of the place and made the deathly ceremony all too easy to imagine. Takk was the first to move. She had turned to look at Tower Bridge and was surveying the high green wall behind them. It sloped inwards as it rose, giving the area behind greater protection against the erosion of the river.

'My guess is that this was built as part of the docks,' she said. Twenty or thirty foot above them they could see the iron railings of the gardens of the town houses. They began to walk along the wall, conscious that the river itself seemed to close in as they did so.

'If this for ship,' Marik observed, 'river must be deep here.'

Takk was leading the way, her right hand held up against the wall.

'Makes sense,' she said. 'Just along here was the entrance to the lock itself, so I suppose they would have cut a deep channel so that ships could get in and out.'

And sure enough they soon became aware that there was a huge curving break in the wall ahead. And beyond that, the wall reappeared. As they made their way towards it, Takk gave a sudden cry and stumbled forward quickly. There in the wall ahead of them, about four foot in height and slightly less in width, was the arched entrance to a tunnel partly buried in sand and shingle. Joycey and Marik scurried forward to look and the three of them stood there silently. An ancient and jagged looking iron grille covered the entrance, but peering through it, the tunnel continued back for about fifteen feet and then curved away to the left, its green-coated stone blocks disappearing into darkness.

'What do you think this was?' Takk asked.

Joycey shook his head, peering at the grille with interest. 'Dunno. Didn't you say something about them building something to pump water in and out of the dock?'

Marik too was inspecting the iron-work closely, running his hands over the bars and digging at the stonework with his fingers. Then he squatted on his heels and looked at the lower bars thoughtfully.

'Here,' he said pointing a finger, 'these are rusted bad, I think....' As he spoke, he gave an experimental yank on one of the bars and it bent upwards as though it was made of plasticine. He turned a big grin on the others.

'Oh dear Marik,' Joycey said in mock admonition, 'you've vandalised it.'

Takk stooped quickly. 'I can get in under this.'

The two men looked doubtful suddenly.

'You might,' Joycey retorted, 'but I don't fancy crawling on my stomach on this stuff.' He dug his toes into the softer mud at the entrance to the tunnel. As though in response, a sour, pungent aroma rose from the ground.

'Now not good time,' Marik interjected. As though in explanation they heard the low rumble of an engine and a police launch slid by, nosing against the tide. One of the crew was gazing at them intently as they passed.

'Nah, now isn't a good time.' Joycey agreed quickly. 'We need to come back after dark.'

'When?' Takk asked, suddenly disappointed.

'Low tide is next,' Marik mumbled , 'soon before midnight.'

'And after that?'

He shook his head. 'Same time, eleven.' He waved an arm at the river.

'So, if we are going to do this,' Joycey said slowly, 'later tonight is going to be our best opportunity.'

'It may be nothing,' Takk cautioned. 'Probably just the remains of a tunnel that's been blocked off.'

'Yeah but why isn't it filled in then?' Joycey asked. 'There's loads of old entrances like this along the river. They all lead to something. So why shouldn't this?'

Takk didn't look convinced.

'We go tonight.' Marik said with unusual decisiveness. They both looked at him and then at each other.

'Ok,' Takk nodded. 'Let's do it.'

31. Preparations

Back at Marik's flat, Joycey and Takk were taken aback when the young Pole suddenly started insisting that they needed what he referred to obliquely as 'equipment'. His insistence was so abrupt and revolutionary that they found themselves in the small kitchen sheltering behind the pretence of making a meal – something neither of them were particularly adept at. And while they struggled to understand some of the contents of Marik's kitchen cupboards, he was busy on the telephone, speaking Polish in a low, urgent tone.

After they had eaten a hurried meal, he disappeared with the keys to the van and a promise to be back later. By 5pm they were sitting in the flat looking at a heap of objects in the middle of the living room carpet. There were three new safety helmets, still in their plastic wrapping. There were strap-on head lamps, face masks and goggles. A coil of manila rope, four water-proof torches. A hacksaw with half a dozen spare blades, a claw hammer and a heavy duty chisel. A folding spade and two crowbars.

Takk and Joycey had poked through this collection with some amusement. But they were perplexed by an object in a toughened fibre glass case which was held closed with strong clips. After Joycey had poked and pulled at it without effect for several moments, Marik took it from him and opened it.

'For the gas,' he explained.

'You what?' Joycey yelped.

'Hmmm,' the young Pole thought for a moment. 'Yes, underground, sewer gas.'

'Oh!' Takk caught on suddenly. 'It's a gas detector.'

'Yes, yes,' Marik was beaming at her and nodding enthusiastically.

'For Hydrogen Sulphide,' she explained.

When Joycey's blank expression failed to change, she offered more detail.

'Sewer gas. We don't know what's in this tunnel, and if we do find a hidden chamber, the chances are that it may be full of gas. It's the same sort of thing you get in sewers, hence 'Sewer' gas. You wouldn't get any underground workers going down a manhole without using one of these.'

'It's dangerous then, Sewer Gas?' Joycey asked, feeling that he already knew the answer.

'Yes it is. You know you hear occasionally of men collapsing and dying in drains and sewers – well Hydrogen Sulphide is why. It can be fatal before you're aware it's there.'

'Well I wouldn't have thought of that one,' Joycey scratched his head. 'But I suppose it has to make sense.'

'Sure,' Takk nodded at Marik. 'We don't know what's down there. If we find anything at all, that is. It must have been hard to get though Marik?' Takk looked at the young Pole.

He smiled. 'I know man. Good friend from past.'

Joycey was about to ask more when a question from Takk broke his train of thought.

'We can't get on the train with all this stuff.'

'We'll have to take the van.'

She looked unhappy.

'It'll be after dark, the van'll be less noticeable,' he reasoned.

'You reckon?'

'Sure. And look at the weather. There ain't gonna be that many people about on a night like this.'

He was right. The early morning rain had turned into torrential downpours, and the wind had been buffeting the windows of the flat for hours.

'Well we may have to be extra careful.'

Joycey thought for a moment. 'Marik, if we drive through the Rotherhithe Tunnel, take the long way round, we can do several loops to make sure no-one is following us.'

Marik agreed. 'Sure, good plan.' He nodded reassuringly at Takk.

'And what about while we are on the foreshore, when we get into the tunnel?'

Joycey sighed. 'Listen, it'll be alright,' he said soothingly. 'We'll be very careful and keep a good look out. Besides, it'll be dark by the river and we'll see anyone coming with a torch miles off.'

She snorted. 'If they're daft enough to use torches.'

'Well....'

'We won't.' she interrupted. 'We don't need to use torches until we get inside the tunnel. We know the way and we know where we are going. We can feel our way in the dark.'

'Well, there we are then.' Joycey beamed as though making his point.

Takk scowled, but let the matter drop.

Later that evening, Takk checked the tide-tables again. Joycey watched her with curiosity.

'What you lookin for?' he asked at last.

'I was just checking,' she said. 'It has to be tonight. Low tide gets earlier every day by about thirty minutes and I think the earlier we try the more chance there is of us being spotted by someone.'

'And that is the only time we can get in – to the tunnel.'

'Yes. Unless you fancy diving under twenty foot of water.'

Joycey gave a grin. 'Well I wouldn't want to get trapped in the tunnel by a rising tide. The Thames is supposed to be a pretty dangerous place at the best of times. The old lightermen used to say there were these deadly currents that appeared in different parts of the river at different times.' He stopped, looking thoughtful. 'I suppose that was why those people in the Court Records drowned like they did.'

'And Sarah Hawkins, perhaps.'

'Suppose, yeah.'

At 10 pm, they packed the gear as quietly as possible into Joycey's van, carrying it all in black bin-bags down the fire escape stairs at the back of the building. The previous two hours had been spent in an atmosphere of increasingly suppressed excitement. Takk had masked her feelings by digging out her research notes. It had occurred to her that it might be useful to remind herself exactly what Kidd's treasure had consisted of. After all, if they did find anything it would be useful to know what they might be dealing with – though she was increasingly and secretly doubtful that their search would come to much. Joycey and Marik had become irritatingly boisterous as she had tried to concentrate and, in the end, she had ordered them to go out and walk off their excess energies. Giggling guiltily, they had submissively gone for a quick walk along the river. While they were gone, she found her notes on the original inventory of Kidd's treasure, the one drawn up by the Earl of Bellomont in Boston. Unconsciously, she began reading it aloud.

'Fifty three silver bars, seventy nine bars and pieces of silver, seventy four bars ditto; one, two three, four....seven bags of gold, two silver candlesticks, two silver porringers; one, two three, four...bags of dust gold, one bag of silver and in it coined gold; one bag of three silver rings and sundry precious stones, one bag of unpolished stones; one, two three, four bags of gold bars.'

Then there were the bales of silk – though these may have been sold by Sarah Hawkins before Kidd's execution. And all this was just a fragment of what Kidd was supposed to have hidden.

The two men returned unexpectedly early, blowing on their fingers and huffing noisily about the weather. Joycey looked at Takk as she sat wedged in one of Marik's chairs and asked her what she had been doing. She sighed and decided to own up.

'Just checking what the treasure was.'

'Lots of lovely gold, I hope.' Grinned Joycey, rubbing his hands together.

'Yes there was some gold, and silver, and precious stones. But there were silks too. But the bad news is that some it was stored in bags. They may have rotted away by now.'

Joycey gave a chortle. 'We'd better take some carrier bags then.'

And that was how they had prepared.

32. The Tunnel

They were driving in relative silence, listening to the occasional clunk of heavy iron tools in the back of the van every time it jolted over a bump. Marik sat at the wheel, with Takk sandwiched in the middle. Joycey was gazing absently through the windows as they rolled through Deptford and Rotherhithe before sweeping round the large roundabout to dip into the old, narrow bore of the Rotherhithe Tunnel. Although the dirty, tiled walls were dimly lit, the night seemed even darker when they emerged on the north side of the river and turned for Wapping.

After some time, Takk thought of a question. 'Is anyone checking to see if we are being followed?'

There was a guilty and shifty silence for a few moments and then Marik, having given a long and rather theatrical look in the offside wing mirror, said that it was ok.

Takk gave him a sideways look that spoke scepticism, but it was lost on the Pole who pursed his lips and began glancing in the mirror rather more often than was necessary. But certainly, as they turned down the little hill that led down towards the river, the road behind them was vacant. Indeed Wapping seemed to have been abandoned as their wheels clappered their way onto

Wapping High Street.

Joycey suggested they park a little closer to the 'Town of Ramsgate' this time, as it might look suspicious if they began unloading the bags outside the Wapping police station, especially as there were surveillance cameras operating there. So they parked near the pub, climbing out and closing the van doors with careful stealth. Warm light streamed from the pub windows, sending elongated patches of glistening orange across the pavement and cobbles, for it had been raining lightly and steadily since they had left Greenwich.

From the pub itself came the gentle buzz of conversation, and the occasional outburst of loud laughter. Joycey stood gazing wistfully for a moment, wishing he could suggest they go there instead. But at the sound of a heavy clinking bag being lowered to the ground, he brushed the thought aside. Above their heads the drizzle was creating cones of misty light beneath the occasional street lamps. Marik locked the van doors and they stood there looking cautiously up and down the street, and up at the windows of the converted warehouses. Then Marik picked up the heaviest bags and they hastily followed him towards the pub.

Takk had been wondering how they were going to slip down the side alley without being noticed. But the curtains in the side windows had been slightly drawn, so they nipped past them at a crouch, carefully holding the bags off of the ground.

At the end of the alley Marik stopped and the others bumped into him, so that they all stood swaying in a nervous bunch at the top of Wapping Old Stairs. Some forty feet away and below them, the river slid past in a dark surge, its surface sparkling with multi-coloured diamonds from the lights of Rotherhithe and Bermondsey. A disco boat was pushing itself against the tide, lights flashing and a rhythmic thumping pulsating across the water towards them, though there seemed little evidence of anybody dancing.

Washes of drizzle swept across them like net curtains cast away in a breeze, as little scudding gusts blew their way towards the City. Gingerly they crept down the steps, feeling the handrail cold but reassuring under their left hands, and becoming increasingly aware of the dampness rising up from below them. As they reached the uneven boulders and rubble of the foreshore itself, they noticed the insistent plashing sound of the river, with its gently lapping waves. As the wash of the disco boat came ashore, the lapping increased in volume and speed, like a heartbeat suddenly racing with fear.

'Come on,' Takk hissed impatiently, and turning she began to stumble her way along the base of the old riverside wall, which now loomed high above them like a black citadel.

As Marik and Joycey followed, Tower Bridge appeared ahead of them. Its towers and platforms brightly lit and, with each light reflected in the river below, it seemed like a strangely dismembered gothic cathedral floating on a cloud of light. They crept forward keeping to the dark shadow of the old river wall. For a few moments, glancing up, Takk could see lights in the windows of the houses above them on Pier Head, but as they advanced, these disappeared. They were alone on the foreshore.

In what seemed only a few seconds they reached the ominous dark mouth of the tunnel. Little streaks of light seemed to be glinting from strands of weed on the grille. Takk leant forward pushing her face between the rough bars of the grille. A dank mist seemed to settle on her cheeks and a strong smell of seaweed, river mud and something far less pleasant entered her nostrils. From the darkness came the faint 'plok,' 'plok' of dripping water. She closed her eyes for a moment and shuddered.

Crouching beside her Marik began unpacking the gas

detector. It was a small device, little larger than a shoe-box. As he turned it on, an LCD screen illuminated, a green light flashed once and then began to pulsate steadily accompanied by a quiet beeping. Joycey and Takk found themselves peering over his shoulders to look.

'I test?' the young Pole warned, and there was suddenly a piercing sound from the machine, which he switched off quickly.

As the echoes of this noise faded away, their came the splashing and calling of startled ducks from somewhere nearby in the darkness. They glanced round nervously. The sound would have carried a long distance, and they now felt slightly more wary. But across the river only the lights wavered in the drifting rain.

Marik knelt down carefully, finding a comfortable spot for his knees between the stones and rubble. Thin streams of water dribbled from the tunnel and in a very short time there were dark patches on the knees of his jeans, but he paid little attention to this, concentrating instead on the iron bars of the grille. Joycey and Takk watched in silence as he located the vertical bar they had bent earlier. Already softened, he pushed and pulled it several times until it suddenly snapped in his hands. He then turned to the next one. This proved more difficult and so he pulled one of the crowbars from a rucksack and pushing it in behind the grille, hooked one end in front of the bar and then began pulling it out towards him. It didn't move, so he put his feet against the grille and pulled back with all the strength he could muster. The bar gave with a sudden bang and he fell backwards, grinning and gasping slightly in the glimmering light.

Joycey tapped him on the shoulder and took the crow bar.

'Here, let me,' he offered.

Again the bar was inserted, and Joycey leaned backwards

against it. There was no movement and they could hear him straining. He swore loudly and then there was a sharp metallic screech and the whole vertical bar juddered out six inches, spitting rusty fragments. There was a spontaneous 'whoop' of satisfaction from both men, followed by hastily suppressed giggling. Takk tutted nervously, casting anxious looks along the shore line towards Wapping Old Stairs, but there was no-one to be seen.

In the space of about twenty minutes, and sometimes by working together on a single bar, Marik and Joycey – with enthusiastic help from Takk - managed to open a break in the bottom of the grille about two foot square. One of the bars had snapped off, however, leaving a sharp dagger of metal which they managed to beat to the side using a muffled hammer. Once they had cleared this, Takk didn't wait. She dropped to her stomach and crawled through the gap before anyone could protest. Once inside she asked for the torch and they saw her make her way into the tunnel. Almost immediately Marik began forcing himself through the gap, to follow.

Inside the tunnel, Takk turned on the torch and moved forward cautiously, inspecting the masonry all round her as she did so. Under her feet fragments of glass, gravel and weed crunched loudly and each step released a powerful odour. Where the tunnel bent round to the left she stopped, and retraced her steps. Joycey saw her coming back, the light from the torch picking up the wet rubble beneath her feet.

'Ok,' she said to Marik. 'Let's go.'

Outside the tunnel Joycey went to drop to his knees, then hesitated.

'Perhaps I should wait out here…and keep watch.'

There was a moment of ambiguous silence and then Takk

spoke.

'Well someone's got to keep a lookout.'

Marik nodded in agreement. 'Yes boss. No need for three here.'

In the darkness they looked at one another. Marik feeling awkward, Takk impatient and Joycey secretly relieved. He didn't like confined spaces. So he nodded and told them to be careful. Then, almost as an afterthought, he asked, 'How long have we got?'

It was Takk who answered. 'An hour and a half at the most, but the weather might change all that. Oh, and keep an eye out for the wake of any passing boats. I don't think there will be anything large in the river at this time of night, but it might be worth watching.'

Joycey nodded, feeling from the authoritive tone of the young woman's voice that he suddenly had something important to do. He pushed the remaining equipment through the gap in the bars, and Marik and Takk put on the safety helmets.

'I have bag,' Marik murmured, hoisting the heavier bag onto his shoulder. The tools within it gave a clink. Then, with both torches lit, they turned into the tunnel.

Joycey watched their silhouettes receding. The surprisingly broad-shouldered and stooping Marik, preceded by the shorter form of Takk, made shapeless in her huge waterproof. Almost as soon as they disappeared round the curve in the tunnel, Joycey felt desperately in need of a cigarette. He tried to push the idea out of his mind, but the need grew. To keep his mind occupied, he found his tobacco and papers, and crouching close to the tunnel mouth he rolled a limp looking cigarette. Then, casting a long and careful look around, he found his lighter, but nothing that he could do would make it work. Finally, in a quiet fury he stood and hurled both items towards the river. The lighter gave a little splash about a yard from the water's edge, but the roll-up was picked up by the wind and span up and away into the darkness.

Takk led the way into the tunnel. The interior was small. The highest point of the smoothly arched roof was probably about five feet above the ground, but this was hard to tell because over the centuries the river had washed in a carpet of silt and debris; and she guessed it hadn't been flushed through since the London Dock itself closed forty years before – if it had still been in use then. The masonry of the tunnel seemed to be a greenish coloured granite, smoothly jointed, but blackened and weed-hung in many places. In several places the stone had been replaced by patches of red and yellow brickwork, presumably from later repairs. As she walked forward this time Takk had the uncomfortable sensation that they were being swallowed by some enormous beast. From the gas detector slung over Marik's shoulder came a regular, quiet beep and a flicker of green light.

They made their way to the bend in the tunnel and, as they reached it, the floor began to rise gradually and they were walking on finer shingle and then sand. Plastic bottles, polystyrene chunks and shards of soft grey wood littered the floor. The air was thick with the smell of decaying weed.

Ahead of them there came again the echoing 'plok' 'plok' of water dripping onto water. Takk stopped abruptly, uttering a short exclamation, and Marik blundered into her from behind. The tunnel was not as long as they had thought it might be. It wound its way round smooth curves twice and then, after little more than a hundred feet it came to an end. They found themselves in a small circular, domed chamber. The roof was slightly higher than the rest of the tunnel and the walls extended out in a smooth circle of perfectly worked masonry. In the centre of the sandy floor was a pool of water, and into it, water dropped at regular intervals from the roof, sending circular ripples outwards like a pulse.

On the far side of the chamber the surface of the wall was punctured by three circular holes, each about eighteen inches in diameter. The perfectly dressed stonework had been cut to lead in to these three shafts, so that the jointing formed the most beautiful geometric design. Marik gave a little whistle.

'This good work.'

Takk nodded, 'Yes, isn't that just amazing. For something that was probably never going to be seen, they still took so much trouble over it.'

Marik was silent. In the beam of the torches they could see that the three shafts continued on in the same direction, though the lower third of them seemed to have become clogged with sand and small pebbles.

'This is end then?' Marik sounded disappointed. He lowered the black sack to the floor. 'So, where go to from here?'

Takk was inspecting the walls around them with the torch. After a few moments she spoke, her voice sending little whispering echoes back along the tunnel and her breath turning to clouds of steam as she spoke.

'Well, according to the dock company records, they built this conduit alongside the water company's conduits. The question is whether the records refer to this main tunnel or the smaller pipes there.' She pointed her torch to illuminate the three circular pipes behind him.

Marik nodded solemnly.

'But I don't know how we are going to tell.'

For a moment they stood there shining their torches this way and that, then Takk stopped, fumbled inside the sack and extracted the hammer.

'This is just a hunch,' she half explained, holding up the hammer. Before Marik could frame a question she stepped close to the side of the chamber and tapped the stonework with the hammer. There was a loud, dull metallic thud. It sounded worryingly loud and Marik grimaced, but Takk took another few steps round the chamber and repeated the blow. Gradually she worked her way round the chamber, but everywhere the hammer blow resounded from solid wall. Once she had completed the circle she gave a sigh.

'Come on,' she said flatly and led the way back down the tunnel. Every few paces, almost with a growing sense of frustration she struck out to either side, and always there came back the dull clunk of the steel hitting the stone. The crunch of their footsteps was accompanied by the steady, but increasingly annoying bleep of the gas detector. As they reached the second bend, the air freshened noticeably and they could sense Joycey fidgeting anxiously outside the grille.

Takk was just about to tell Marik off for not switching off the pointless and now downright infuriating gas detector, when a hollow clang rang out from the wall beside her. She froze and swung the hammer again. Both torches span to the wall and they saw there a patch of crumbling yellow brickwork.

'There's a difference here.' She tapped again and the sound that came back repeated its hollow ring. 'There's definitely something different about this section.'

Marik put his ear to the wall and she tapped again. The brickwork resonated and vibrated.

'That sounds hollow,' she said patting the brickwork. 'I think there's some form of cavity behind this.'

Marik was looking at the bricks carefully under the light of his torch. Takk spoke again.

'This doesn't look as old as the rest. My guess is that this brickwork is Victorian, a repair of some sort.'

'Oh, yes?'

Marik too was carefully examining the brick surface. It had worn badly, the craftsmanship being poorer than the original masonry. Then he gave a little exclamation and shone the light by Takk's boots. At the base of the wall, where the brickwork met the floor, the rubble had given way to a sandy streak over which ran a small stream of water. He dropped the sack again, pulled out the bar and began digging at the bottom of the wall. Within a few minutes he had revealed a small irregular opening and, dropping down onto his stomach, he pushed his hand into the cavity until his shoulder was against the wall. He grunted several times and then withdrew his arm.

'Here, something. Big space, maybe.' He gave a broad grin.

From the tunnel entrance, Joycey's voice came with a nervous quaver. 'You found anything?'

'Ssshh. Yes, maybe.' Takk grinned back at Marik. Hope renewing excitement.

'How much longer have you got?' Joycey called.

Marik pushed back the sleeve of his jacket and showed the watch to Takk. She was shocked to see that half an hour had elapsed.

'Depends on the tide.' She called back to Joycey. 'What's

it doing?'

'Well it ain't standing still,' Joycey called back grumpily. He was cold, wet and miserable, and the thought of finding pirate treasure was beginning to lose its appeal.

'What shall we do?' Takk asked Marik.

'We look, perhaps? For a minute?'

She nodded and as he dropped to his knees again with the bar, she called back to Joycey. 'Just keep a good look-out, we won't be long.'

Kneeling on the floor, Marik paused, put the bar down and pushed the gas detector into the cavity at the bottom of the wall. The machine gave a happy little beep, and then another. Then, giving Takk his torch, he pulled a lump hammer and cold chisel from the bag and began chipping at the brickwork around the cavity. To their surprise it seemed to crumble easily. First a shard of brick, and then a lump.

'It wet,' he explained to Takk. 'Very soft, so!'

He lined the chisel up against the pointing and gave a heavy blow with the hammer. The chisel drove in and the brick itself shifted. He hit the brick itself. It collapsed inwards. He struck again and again until half a dozen bricks lay on the sandy floor of the cavity. Takk knelt and scooped them clear and Marik lay on his stomach to point the torch inside. Then he beckoned to her. Lying on her stomach Takk could see into the gap. Behind the wall was a gap and then another wall, perhaps three feet behind it. She considered the hole carefully for a moment and then taking the hammer, she began knocking out the bricks at the top of the hole until she had created a pointed arch just over two feet in height. She looked at Marik for a moment and then thrust her head and shoulders inside.

Standing in the tunnel. Marik could hear some muffled exclamations and then, in a series of ungainly jerks, the rest of Takk's body was swallowed by the hole.

33. The Hidden space

Back at the entrance to the tunnel Joycey was leaning against the river wall, watching the river slowly passing in a glittering slide. Every now and again a cloud of rain swept down past Tower Bridge, which he could just see, obscuring it in a curtain of iridescent mist. There appeared to be very little traffic on the river now, and the only boat that he had seen for some time was a police launch which idled its way past before turning down stream. Its wake came ashore in gentle ripples, and Joycey found himself staring at them to see what would happen. But all the little waves did was to bring ashore a distinctive looking piece of driftwood, and he decided that he might be able to use this as a gauge to measure the tide's advance. Something like an hour had passed now. He had heard the laboured sounds made by Marik as he broke through the side wall of the tunnel, and then some muffled sounds. And then nothing for some time. Every now and again he took a few paces up and down, his arms wrapped around him to stave off the cold. His curiosity and misery seemed to be growing in equal measures. But he felt that he had been given something important to do and so he waited. The time would come when he would have to tell them that the tide was rising. But for now he waited.

When Takk pulled herself through the hole in the tunnel wall she found herself kneeling in a narrow cavity between what appeared to be two brick walls. The gap into which she had inserted herself was little more than two and a half feet wide, so that getting to her feet hadn't been easy. She bent down and called Marik, helping him as he struggled through, lugging the sack in after him. There was a pause while he got his breath back and then he checked the gas detector again, but it kept up its reassuring little bleep without any hesitation. If anything, the air smelt of wet earth, and there was nothing unpleasant about it, though heavy drops of icy water fell on their heads and faces perpetually and unpredictably, so that each one made them jump.

By the light of their torches, they could see that they appeared to be in some form of cavity or conduit. Facing them was a wall of rough brick. The ceiling of this area was some fifteen feet above them and appeared to be made up of rough concrete beams interspersed with roots and clumps of rubble. Beneath their feet was a surface of very wet sand or muddy silt, and this rose to either side of them. It was as though the space had been flushed through with water for a considerable period.

Takk shone her torch to their left. Some twenty or twenty five feet further on was a narrow wall of green granite masonry. Takk sidled along the space until she reached the end. Her torch swung backwards and forwards up and down, and then Marik saw her returning.

'Nothing there. A dead end,' she said. 'Have a look the other way.'

She saw Marik twist and he began sidling along, his back towards what she guessed was the tunnel. Then it occurred to her that the tunnel actually curved away from them at this point.

Marik came to a halt some fifteen feet to the right, where the cavity ended in rough cut stone. He turned his torch up and she heard him give a little exclamation. She began working her way towards him and at the end of the tunnel she looked up to where Marik's torch was shining. At first all she could see was what she took to be an uneven shadow on the wall in front of him, but then she realised it was something else entirely. Moving closer to Marik she realised that they were looking at a section of collapsing brickwork. It sagged heavily like a boxer folding at the knees. She put an exploratory hand to it and with a startling rumble, a section of brickwork collapsed away from her. Instinctively they covered their faces, but nothing fell in their direction. Marik shone his torch into the dusty space beyond and an excited cry burst from his lips. In the light of the torch was a flight of old stone steps rising up away from them to the left. They were standing beside what appeared to be a set of stairs.

Moving carefully, they both climbed into the cavity and stopped in astonishment, for they were indeed standing near the foot of a flight of ancient stone stairs. These had been truncated, so that the lowest step was level with Takk's waist. But from there they rose towards the uneven concretion of the ceiling. The steps themselves were narrow and badly worn but, with the exception of the lower three or four which were dark with dampness, they appeared to be dry and coated with a carpet of dust.

On the far side, the steps were set against an ancient looking brick wall. At the base were the remains of what looked like large timbers and, set in the wall, about four steps up, a heavy looking iron ring.

Marik was looking at Takk expectantly.

'This is good yes? You think?' he asked at last.

Takk was thinking hard, chewing her lower lip as she did so. Marik turned the flashlight into her face, as a friendly nudge. She smiled.

'I know what I *think,*' she said, with emphasis, 'I'm just not sure what I believe.'

'Ok,' he nodded, adding assertively. 'This very old.'

'Well,' said Takk, shining the light up the worn stairs, 'This looks like one of the old stairways to the river. My guess is that, somehow, presumably when the docks were built or even before then, this was covered over. Perhaps the Pierhead houses were built over the top. Perhaps they filled it with rubble or earth and…,' she flashed the torch to the ceiling, '…and covered it with concrete.'

'Yes,' said Marik quietly.

'The steps must have gone down to the foreshore originally, but the river wall was extended outwards when they built Pierhead, which is why they end here.' She shone the torch against the side wall.

Marik was now examining the brick wall on the other side of the steps.

'And the iron ring was probably used for tying up boats,' she continued. The ring hung against the wall, a brown stain of rust dribbling from it down the dusky red of the ancient brickwork.

'What is the time?' Takk asked suddenly.

Marik consulted his watch for several long seconds. Then he looked across the stairs to the old wall. 'Half an hour. Not long.' There was a slightly disappointed note to his voice. 'Then water come.' He raised his hand to his chin.

'Well, let's just look up the steps, check that wall. There's not much else we can do anyway.'

Marik shook his head. 'No. It dangerous I think. Best go and come back tomorrow. Yes?'

'It'll probably mean getting here even earlier. Which means more chance of being seen.'

Marik nodded and hissed. 'Yessss, but tomorrow quicker I think.'

There was a long pause and then, with obvious reluctance, they began to sidle back along the cavity and as they did the light from Marik's torch turned a sickly orange colour. He pulled one of the head lamps from a pocket and pulled the elasticised band over the top of his helmet. It was efficient, but actually harder to use than the torch.

Back at the entrance to the tunnel, Joycey had been watching the piece of driftwood lift and swing several times. Lulled into a reverie he had not realised the significance for ten or fifteen minutes, but then he seemed to wake with a start, the tide was rising fast. And just as he turned to warn the others, he heard the sound of their exertion as they climbed back through the cavity, and then their feet crunching on the gravel.

Marik and Takk spent several minutes pushing bricks roughly back into place in an attempt to disguise the hole, then scraping shingle and sand against them before walking back to the tunnel mouth. Joycey was stamping his feet impatiently.

Well...?' he asked.

Takk was staring at the rising water, which was now beginning to lap within a couple of yards of the river wall. 'The tide has risen a lot hasn't it,' she hissed, darting a venomous look at Joycey in the darkness. 'Let's get out of here while we can.'

'Yeh, but what…?' Joycey persisted.

'In a minute,' Takk snapped.

Joycey grumbled quietly, but helped Marik pull the tools through the grille.

'What to do about this?' Marik asked pointing downwards.

'All we can do is push the bars roughly back into their original position, and hope no-one comes down here looking too closely tomorrow,' Takk sighed. 'I can't imagine many people coming down here in this weather anyway.'

Marik made a half-hearted attempt to push a bar back into place, but it snapped in his hands, and Takk just shrugged at him. Then they set off back towards the van.

There was one awkward moment as they walked alongside the pub, when they heard the sound of somebody moving around inside. Instinctively the three of them froze. A curtain twitched ominously, but after a minute or two the lights in the bar went out, plunging them into more or less complete shadow. Six minutes later, they were rolling through Limehouse, on their way back home, talking hurriedly and all too aware of a rank smell that was beginning to fill the van. None of them looked out of the rear window, so none of them saw the large black Audi that was snaking along just fifty yards behind them, never quite catching up and never quite falling behind.

34. Interlude

With Marik hunched over the wheel, Takk began explaining what they had found. Joycey, listened in silence, a newly rolled cigarette hanging unlit from his lips.

Finally he grunted.   'No gold then?'

'Not yet, but I think we've found the location of the Sugar Loaf.'

Marik gave her a sideways glance and Joycey's roll-up gave a quick jerk.

'You reckon?'

'It's a buried stairway, and an old one. It has to have been one that led down to the river up until the end of the eighteenth century. I think we are in the right spot.'

'Oh?'

'Look riverside pubs have always been adjacent to Watermen's stairs or landing places. Everyone moved about by the river in the old days, so it was good for business. All that rowing made watermen thirsty, and many of the pubs had cellars with direct access from the river.' She gave a grin. 'It was good for smuggling.'

Joycey gave a laugh. 'Ok I get it. So what's the plan now?'

'We have to go back. Tomorrow night. Now we know what we are dealing with. We go straight in to the steps and this time we check around there to see if we can find any evidence of a cellar.'

Half an hour later Marik parked the van in a quiet backstreet in East Greenwich and they made their way to his flat. Marik and Takk were busy in the kitchen, and Joycey sat trying to reassure himself by reading through the notes on Takk's tablet. It took him a little while to work out how to turn pages but once he got the hang of it, he felt quite jubilant. He even offered to help throw together some sort of meal, but Takk pointed out that Marik's tiny kitchen made that impracticable. Joycey didn't argue, but continued gleefully looking at Takk's notes.

By the time Takk pushed a plate of toasted cheese sandwiches under his nose, he had thought of a question.

'The thing is..,' he started ponderously, 'although Captain Kidd was executed, he wasn't the only person that knew the treasure was there, was he?'

'No-o,' admitted Takk cautiously.

'There was this Sarah Hawkins and the man she was with.'

' 'H'. Yes that's true.'

'So what was there to stop them taking the treasure for themselves? After all, it was hidden in their cellar wasn't it?'

Takk looked thoughtful. 'Well the strange thing is that apart from being with her when she visited Kidd in prison, he seems to have had little to do with this. It's always Sarah who gets mentioned. My guess is that she's the one with the brains.' Takk grinned. 'Believe me, a woman recognises that sort of thing.'

Joycey's expression was one of perplexity, even outrage. But he could think of no adequate retort. He swallowed several mouthfuls of food, then spoke with his mouth half full.

'Yeah, well then, what was to stop her making off with everything after the pirate was executed?'

Takk shrugged. 'Don't know. Except as far as we know she drowned a few months later. She hardly had time to make much use of it and presumably she would have had to convert it into cash anyway, before she could use it. And from the report you found, it doesn't sound as though she had suddenly become a very wealthy woman.'

'Well I bet there were plenty of people in Wapping who could have helped her launder the stuff in some way.' Joycey sniggered.

'Yes but that might have aroused some suspicion, mightn't it? After all, she was known to be the relative of a famous pirate who had hidden his loot somewhere. And suddenly, shortly after he is executed, she turns up with a lot of money. It doesn't take too much to put two and two together there does it? I think she may have been much cannier than that. Planned and bided her time. After all, what would have been the hurry? Everyone else thought the treasure was hidden in the Caribbean, or perhaps on the coast of New York.'

Joycey nodded slowly.

'Added to which,' Takk continued. 'We shouldn't underestimate the effect of Kidd's execution. They presumably had a fairly close relationship, and she had to watch him hung on the foreshore near her home. And by all accounts it was pretty horrific. According to eyewitness accounts, Kidd was really drunk when he arrived at the gibbet and as they put the rope around his neck, instead of asking forgiveness, he swore and warned all seamen not to be taken in by the rich and powerful. Then when they went to hang him, the rope broke and he fell through the trap onto the foreshore. By the time they had dragged him back to the scaffold, he was dead sober and very confused.'

The temperature in the room seemed to have turned cold again and she shivered. Even Joycey pulled his jacket closer around his body.

'I know people were supposed to be much more hardened to violence and death in those days,' she commented quietly. 'But even so, it might have taken her months to recover. And his body was still hung up in a gibbet down river for years. She wasn't likely to get over that easily.'

Mickey sprang suddenly from under the table and landed on Joycey's lap. Joycey began stroking him automatically.

'I'm knackered,' he said after a while.

Despite Marik's noble offer of the sole use of his bed, Takk insisted she needed to change her clothes and freshen up in her room in the Halls, so Marik walked her back along the main road into central Greenwich. Left on his own, Joycey pulled the sofa and easy chair close together and made himself comfortable with a pile of cushions around his back and Mickey clinging warmly to his stomach. It was some time before Marik reappeared, his face red and his eyes bright with cold. He blew on his fingers and shivered in front of the fire.

'It turned very cold, boss.'

Joycey snorted. 'Serves you right. Should have persuaded her to stay.' He thought for a moment, then decided against adding further comment.

Marik shrugged. 'You want drink boss?'

'You got any whisky?'

Takk arrived shortly after breakfast, clutching her tablet and several files. Joycey was chewing the hard crust of a pasty from a nearby shop, a dismal expression on his face, and Marik was in the kitchen washing dishes in a bowl. He appeared when he heard Takk's voice.

'You need to open the window,' she scowled, sniffing pointedly.

Joycey grumbled and Marik sprang forward to push open one of the fanlights looking out onto the road. A police car was parked outside the hardware shop opposite. He glanced at it briefly and then turned away. A cold breeze swept into the room.

Joycey glanced at Takk's files as she dropped them on the table. 'Homework?'

She nodded. 'It's going to be a long day and I have work to catch up on.'

'I was going to spend it watching the tv!' Joycey mumbled.

The two stared at each other for a moment.

'Can work in the bedroom,' Marik intervened with a smile. 'Small desk is good, yes?'

Takk nodded and followed him out of the room.

Chuckling to himself Joycey located the remote and turned on the television, then adjusted the volume to a provocative level.

And that, more or less, was how they spent most of the next day.

They left the flat very much as they had on the previous evening. The main difference was the temperature. The wind had swung round to the north-east and a cold, blustering wind was driving itself up the Thames. The strength and temperature of this could only really be appreciated once they had crept their way past the glowing windows of the Town of Ramsgate. Then, standing at the top of Wapping Old Stairs, they found themselves being buffeted by a strong wind which seemed to be sending large waves rolling up the amber and ink surface of the river. Takk was looking at these pensively and then she spoke.

'What time is high tide?'

Joycey looked at his watch. 'A few hours yet. It's still falling. The wind's blowing those waves against it, so it looks like they're coming in.'

Takk stared at him incredulously.

'On my Life!' he protested. 'Marik. Tell her. We checked it, didn't we?'

'Sure. We did.' Marik nodded beside Takk.

She glanced up at him and then stared at the water again

for a moment.   'Ok, come on then.'

And with that she led them down the steps to the foreshore. There they paused momentarily in the hissing darkness, beside the gurgling waves as they surged on the shingle, to make sure they didn't have company. Then they made their way along to the tunnel.

35. The tunnel gives up its secrets

Ten minutes later they were standing inside the grille, breathing heavily after the exertion of squeezing through the gap in the bars. This time, Joycey had insisted on waiting inside the tunnel. His very reasonable excuse was that it was far too cold to stand there on the exposed foreshore while they were inside in the shelter of the tunnel. He could see the river just as easily from inside the grille, and if he needed to warn them of anything, it made more sense if he was inside the grille rather than outside it. He might also have added that it would enable him to light the odd roll-up now and again, but this seemed an unnecessary detail. Takk and Marik had accepted his argument, so now they all stood in the pungent reek of the tunnel while Marik sorted out the tools and torches. He had still brought the gas detector, but he had abandoned some of the items of the previous evening. Once the gas detector gave its irritating little cheep, Takk and Marik began making their way along the tunnel.

Joycey heard their steps crunching on the gravel and glass, and saw them switch on their torch. Then they stopped just by the elbow of the tunnel and he saw them stooping towards the ground. There came the sound of bricks being moved, of gravel being pulled aside, and then one after the other, they disappeared into the wall, as though performing some Victorian music-hall trick.

Behind the wall, Marik and Takk were standing in the narrow cavity, shining their torches about them. Once again they saw the heavy ceiling of concrete and earth encrusted with what looked like tree roots. The space felt different, and Takk was wondering about this when Marik nudged her with his elbow. The light of his torch was glistening on the wall opposite them, at about waist height. He sniffed.

'This not good.'

'What?' she whispered.

'Smell.' He sniffed again, almost theatrically.

She took a gentle sniff and understood. The air was wetter, and the brickwork in front of them looked dark with a dampness that hadn't been noticeable before. She shook her head.

'Come on.'

Marik hesitated, but she sidled to the right until she reached the cavity created by the collapsed brickwork. Without waiting, she climbed through and hauled herself up onto the steps in front of her. This time she noticed how ancient and worn the steps were. Their surfaces hollowed into deep dips and mellow curves from the tread of ancient feet. Rising from her knees, she experienced a strange sensation, as though she had suddenly materialised in a different world, a different time. In some inexplicable, even indescribable way, the space around her felt different, alienated from the world she had just left.

Behind her heels, the gas detector gave a quiet bleep, and Marik began hauling himself onto the lowest step. Takk climbed ahead of him, shining her torch on the ancient brick wall to her right. The bricks were smaller than usual, thinner and soft looking, the mortar light and sandy to the touch. She ran her hands exploratively over the dusty surface and then remembered something.

'Marik.' She hissed. 'Give me the hammer.'

The Pole put his bag down and pulled out the hammer she had used on the previous night. Then, once again, she began striking the surface in front of her, gradually and carefully making her way up the steps to the accompaniment of what sounded like a small, broken bell. About half way up she paused, continued, and then took several steps back. Watching from several yards below, Marik heard the note of the blows changing subtly. His torch caught her expression as she grinned at him.

Marik climbed quickly, dropped the bag and pulled out a solid-looking chisel and a heavier hammer. Kneeling beside her, he placed the broad blade of the chisel against a line of mortar and struck the end with a solid blow. To their surprise, the chisel drove deep through the brickwork. Takk gave a little exclamation and grinned, but Marik was busy working the chisel free. He aimed and took another blow. This time the brick above crumbled into pink shards. He smacked it with a hammer and the brick disappeared leaving a rectangular black hole. This time they exchanged meaningful looks. She nodded and he struck the wall again and again until four or five bricks had disappeared. Takk crouched forward, thrust the torch into the hole and pushed her face to the cavity.

'Jesus!' she shrieked suddenly. 'It's here! There's a cellar behind the wall.'

She sat back and Marik squatted forward. Then he nodded in a serious manner and thrust the gas detector into the cavity. It gave a cheerful little cheep and the little needle on the gauge on the top remained static.

'OK,' Marik muttered quietly. 'No gas here.'

Takk squatted down again and took a good look at the space beyond the wall. Sweeping the beam of the torch round slowly, she could see a large chamber, the far wall of which appeared to be about thirty feet away. The ceiling seemed to be made up of barrel-vaulting constructed of the same sort of brick that they had just broken through, and she could see that the hole that they had just created was up near that ceiling. There was a drop below her, but she wasn't sure how far below the floor lay. It looked like seven or eight feet, but it was hard to be sure. In the middle of the chamber there were some large shapes which were casting shadows around the far wall as her torch moved. They were encrusted in thick grey sheets which moved very slightly and it suddenly occurred to her that these were cobwebs. She was also aware of a strange odour. A dry, musty, mouldy smell which was familiar yet hard to identify. She mentioned it to Marik, who frowned and put his face to the cavity for several long moments.

When he looked up he was frowning, but after a few moments he shook his head. Then he took up the hammer again and gently began knocking the bricks away so that they dropped into the dark cavity, each one falling with an alarming thud. The mortar was soft and crumbling and in very little time they had created a hole, just large enough for Marik to get his shoulders through.

They exchanged glances in the light of the torch and then Marik turned and slid his legs into the hole. He turned over onto his stomach and then giving Takk a broad grin, he lowered himself easily into the void. She watched as his fingers flexed for a moment on the edge of the brickwork and then he dropped.

There was a soft crump as his feet hit the floor and, leaning in herself, Takk found herself looking down at his upturned face. His torch quickly swept round the darkness and from her elevated position she could see that he was standing on a grey flagstone flooring about eight feet below. Great grey swathes of cobweb were strewn in the air, waving eerily in the torchlight. Over towards the far side of the vault, there were humped shadows. The heap of shapes which were still hard to interpret.

'I'm coming in,' she hissed.

Marik said something in reply, but she had already rolled over onto her stomach and thrust her legs into the space. His words were lost and all she could hear were her own excited heartbeats and the coarse rasping of her breath in the enclosed space. She dropped awkwardly, aware of Marik's hands attempting to break her fall, and they both staggered back a few steps. The torch flickered and then it went out. For a few brief seconds they were in thick, cloying darkness – an atmosphere so dense that Takk felt a moment of unparalleled fear. Then her hands found her headlight and pressing its switch she illuminated Marik wrestling with his torch. At that moment its bright beam shot out across the space and they found themselves laughing quietly.

Looking around they could see now that they were in an underground chamber about thirty feet in depth and extending further to the left, where there seemed to be several alcoves in the wall. Overhead, the ancient brick-vaulting arched on to two stone columns standing in a line in the middle of the floor. Between the columns stood what they could now see was a very old oak table, its legs black with age. Thick dusty sheets of cobweb were strewn over it and across large bulky shapes scattered around and on top of it. Takk and Marik stood for a moment staring, conscious of the sound of their breathing in the heavy atmosphere around them, as they sucked in the thick musty air. Takk coughed, feeling phlegm thickening in her throat, dust settling in her nostrils.

'Should have masks,' Marik moaned.

'Too late now, we left them up there in the bag.'

Then without waiting for a response she stepped forward and, extending a hand gingerly, began wiping away the cobwebs over the table. It wasn't easy. They clung like sticky strings to her fingers, attaching themselves in long skeins to the sleeves of her waterproof. Marik moved closer and without speaking they began working on one of the objects on the table. Then they began flapping quickly at the flying webs, because what they had begun to reveal was a small chest.

The cobwebs left a thick, sticky pale coating over it, but they had soon cleared enough to see that they were looking at a very old chest bound with iron strapping. Marik glanced sideways at Takk. She nodded and he put his hands to the sides of the lid and gave an experimental pull. The whole chest shifted and then with a sharp metallic screech the lid opened.

36. The resident

Standing in the dank darkness, Joycey had smoked four roll-ups, taking his time on each occasion to extract the strands of tobacco from a plastic wallet, carefully distribute it in the fold of a paper, and then roll it with considerable care into a thin, neat tube before applying a flame. The problem was that with each successive cigarette he became less satisfied, and the gap between them grew shorter. It was not just that the tobacco didn't seem to be effective in the rank and chill atmosphere of the tunnel, it was also that he was bored. He had watched the river intently for a while, and then he became distracted by the lights on the far bank. They shivered and blinked as the wind outside increased in strength, and the growing distortion of the reflections on the river's surface became tiresome after a while. Then there was the incessant 'swash, 'swash' of the waves as they ran up the muddy gravel of the foreshore. They too had been growing in intensity so that now, every third or fourth wave flung itself up the incline with impatient energy.

It occurred to him that the water seemed to be getting much closer, but then he checked his watch and reassured himself that it was ages before the tide would be high enough to pose any threat whatsoever. Then the rain began. It fell suddenly, as though someone had opened the sluice of a great overhead tank. One moment the air was clear and then it was full of a grey hissing wall that made the surface of the river boil. The lights on the far bank were extinguished seconds later, and the temperature plummeted.

Joycey greeted this development with a string of his choicest exclamations and then, feeling cheated, he turned in to the tunnel and called out, 'You're havin' a fuckin laugh aren't you. What's the point of this?'

He emphasised the last word by kicking the toe of one shoe into the sand and gravel, sending a clump of stinking weed and a sliver of wood into the darkness. Almost unconsciously, he pulled out the tobacco pouch again. Then he discovered that he had run out of papers. With chilled fingers he pulled the little card packet to shreds, but there was no doubt of it. He had no cigarette papers.

'Oh fuckin' bollocks!'

It was at this moment that a strange sound came ringing along the tunnel towards him. It was a sharp metallic screech, almost of wood shearing under pressure, almost of rusty iron. With his head on one side, listening intently, Joycey flicked the switch on his torch and began walking into the tunnel.

Inside the cellar, Takk and Marik were standing in silence. The chest was empty. Sure, there was dust, some of it spread in a shallow wave across the bottom of the chest, some of it rolled into feathery strands. But there was nothing else. They exchanged glum glances, sharing the disappointment. Then, without speaking, they quickly cleared a second similar chest and forced open the lid. This had taken more effort, as it seemed to be jammed with rust and the accumulation of age. Marik had prized a length of iron from the first chest and used it as a lever. The lid of the second chest opened with a frightful screech, a sound which set their teeth on edge and, for a moment, shocked them into silent immobility. Then they peered inside, and for several long seconds gazed at yet more thick layers of dust. Marik ran his fingers through it, and shook his head in response to the enquiring glint in Takk's eyes.

Pushing through the thick webs they circled the table and stumbled into other shapes lying on the floor. They were of varying sizes. Marik set about clearing one of them and Takk watched, her jaw set in an indecipherable mask. Then she knelt beside him impatiently and, together, they quickly cleared away some of the sticky web. This chest was plainer, made of wood that had darkened with age but had much less in the way of iron strapping. The lid was slightly domed and Marik gripped this with his fingers and began to pull. At that moment a voice made them both leap to their feet in fear.

'Blimey, wotcher found here then?'

It was Joycey.

Before they could speak, he had rolled himself into the gap in the wall, and despite their sudden protests he dropped down to join them on the cellar floor.

'What. Didn't expect me to stay out there all night did you? It's pissing it down now. And cold too.'

'But you're supposed to be keeping a look out!' Takk snapped angrily.

For an instant Joycey looked sheepish. 'Yeah, well. There won't be anyone out on a night like this. You should see it out there.'

Takk's annoyance flared in the semi–darkness, but Joycey

was too excited by his surroundings to notice.

'Bugger me, so this is it. It does exist. The cellar.' He kicked one of the chests experimentally. 'And have you found the treasure?'

There was a hollow silence as Marik looked at Takk.

'Not yet,' she hissed. 'There are chests here, but so far they have been empty.'

'Oh. But there are more boxes and things. What are you waiting for? Let's get on and look some more.'

Marik bent to the chest he had started work on and Joycey eagerly pushed his way forward, elbowing Takk to one side. She gave an angry exclamation and Joycey backed away again looking apologetic in the flickering semi-darkness. Giving him a furious sideways look she resumed her place beside Marik. Joycey stood over them both, peering eagerly over their shoulders, and pointing his light in what he thought was a helpful fashion.

Again, Marik wrenched at the lid and again they found themselves peering into an empty space. The chest contained nothing but the dried corpses of long dead spiders and dust. Disappointed, Marik lifted the box to test its weight. Then with a grim glance at Takk he rose and strode to another shape. This time he didn't bother trying to clear the webs, he simply bent and lifted the entire thing. There was comparatively little weight to it, the chest was empty.

Takk knelt watching him as he moved from chest to chest, his shadow looming over the brick vaulting of the ceiling, sending dark shapes reeling around the space. Her initial excitement had given way to dreadful disappointment and now her heart felt like a cold ball in the pit of her stomach. While

Marik continued with the shapes on the floor, she rose and turned her attention to the table itself. There was another rectangular shape, another chest. She went to lift it and then paused. It might contain something small and fragile, papers even, which could be brittle with age and dampness and easily damaged. She carefully wiped away the clinging webs and opened the box. Surprisingly there was no sound, but neither was there anything inside. It was another empty chest. She put her hand down onto the table top and felt something soft which made her start suddenly. Cautiously she brushed with her finger tips and found what appeared to be a low heap of rotten material. It had the texture of long damp newspaper and was black or grey in colour. She picked at it with her finger tips and it disintegrated into clumps.

'Look at this!' she called softly.

Marik rose quickly to his feet and stepped over to the table.

'Is it the treasure?' Joycey asked eagerly.

'Not exactly.'

'What is it?'

'I'm not certain, but I think it must have been packets of textiles of some sort.'

'Textiles?' Joycey sounded puzzled.

'Yes. Packets of silk were mentioned in the inventory of Kidd's treasure. They must have been left here and have just rotted away, to this.' She thought for a moment. 'And the letter to Sarah Hawkins said she was to take the silk and sell it.'

Joycey picked up some of the stuff and crumbled it between his fingers.

'Won't be worth much now then. I s'pose it means we are

looking in the right place though, doesn't it? I mean if it was really part of Kidd's treasure?' He turned away then turned back. 'Hang on a mo. If this is where Kidd's treasure was, how come the silk is still here?'

'I don't know.'

'Yeah but...' Joycey gabbled hastily, 'if no-one got the silk, doesn't it seem more likely no-one got to the treasure either.'

Takk stared at the dark outline of Joycey's face, silhouetted against the beam of a torch, and thought for a moment. There was, she realised a certain logic to what he was suggesting.

'Well, maybe,' she shrugged.

Marik and Joycey turned quickly towards the other large chests sitting in their soft, mysterious shrouds. Within seconds the air was full of floating shreds and rags of web. Takk turned away, holding a gritty hand across her face as she tried not to inhale the sticky clouds of dust. Turning, the light from her headlight swept up to the cavity through which they had entered the cellar, and illuminated a stream of tiny dust motes flowing like a silver stream into the cellar from the stairs outside. The sight made her more aware of the dust. It was drifting in the air in thick clouds now and her throat felt clogged and sticky. She coughed quietly, becoming increasingly conscious of the strange smell in the air, of something she could not quite identify. She moved to the far end of the table where other, shapeless heaps lay piled in their antique anonymity. Exploring carefully with her hands, she detected more heaps of rotting fabric. At the far end of the table a larger, more promising heap rose from the table in curves, heavily swathed in thick webs. Encouraged she swept her hand across the lowest part of it and lifted it.

Takk didn't scream, but she expressed a sound that was a

combination of compressed horror and shock. For there in her fingers sat a blackened, shrivelled human hand. Joycey and Marik were springing towards her even as she let it fall with a light thump onto the surface of the table. Marik put his own hand on her shoulder protectively as they stared down at the shape on the table. Joycey stopped, peering around Marik.

There on the table lay not just a hand, but an arm. Marik eased Takk to one side and began swiping his way along the shape. Strips of grey and black floated lazily in the air, stuck in their noses and clung to the clamminess on their faces, for the temperature seemed to be rising and they were sweating. When Marik had finished, they could see that they were not alone in the cellar. Had never been. For there, slumped forward across the table, was the body of a man. It was a man, yet not a man, no longer completely human.

It lay with its left cheek pressed to the table. Long, dark, ragged hair spread untidily. The face, blackened and leathery looking. The eyes and mouth were large black hollows in the torchlight, and as Marik brought the light closer, they saw that the mouth was open in a dark scream, blackened lips drawn back from jagged teeth. The eye sockets were ugly and vacant. He was sitting in a chair, though the chair had been pushed backwards from the table. His arms were thrust out in front of him, stiff with age. He appeared to be wearing a black or brown leather apron over a shirt that may once have been a cream colour, but was now stained by damp and age and something darker, because protruding from his back was the curved blade of a cutlass.

It took several minutes for all of this detail to register. When it finally did so, Takk found that her breathing was more controlled, though her throat hurt from the tension or the supressed cry. It was Joycey who spoke first.

'Jes-us. Is that Captain Kidd.'

The question set Takk's mind working rapidly. 'Well it isn't Sarah Hawkins.'

Marik found himself supressing a grin.

'Perhaps they brought his corpse here after they hung him.' Joycey suggested.

Takk frowned in the torchlight. 'What and stabbed him with a sword just to make sure he was dead?'

Marik was kneeling beside the corpse, examining the neck where it protruded from the filthy cloth.

'No rope here.' He gestured delicately with a finger-tip.

Takk knelt beside him and shone a torch, wondering just what it was that made her so able to be this close to a corpse. She looked closely to where Marik pointed. The blackened skin was leathery but smooth. There appeared to be no signs of scarring or a wound from a rope. She shook her head.

'It doesn't look as though he was hung, whoever he was. Besides, according to the records, Kidd's body was tarred and hung at Tilbury for years. And this guy hasn't been covered in tar.

Joycey's laugh was sudden and vaguely inappropriate. 'Bloody pirates, eh. What do you expect? Some sort of argument over the treasure's my guess.'

Marik sighed suddenly, looking at his watch. 'We have to go soon.'

'Nah hang on,' Joycey protested, 'we haven't checked all the boxes yet.'

With sudden haste, the two men began tearing at the remaining shapes crowding the centre of the cellar. Shuddering at the thickening clouds of dust and web, Takk made her way to the far side of the vault, where the air still seemed a little clearer, though the stone-flagged floor was soft with dust and her every footfall kicked up a little cloud of the stuff. The walls were a mixture of grey granite and old red brick, now spalling with age and ancient dampness. Unnoticed when they first entered, she now found that the back wall of the cellar consisted of three alcoves or recesses. She made her way towards them, conscious of Joycey's exasperated grunts as he opened another empty trunk. The alcoves were partially concealed by grey sheets of web that hung heavily under rounded brick arches. As she approached the first one it shimmered slightly as though her very movement had caused a ripple in the air. Little shreds of fibre separated and drifted away, swirling slowly in the beam of her torch. She hesitated for a moment in front of it and then cautiously extending a hand, she pushed her fingers into the thick grey sheet. The web resisted her touch but bent inwards under her fingers, and then suddenly it seemed to collapse, folding down like a fallen cloak and sending thick dust rolling up in a wave that made her cough and sneeze.

Shining her torch inside, she could see that the recess was little more than two foot in depth and about three in width. Against the back wall was a small black dresser. One of the shelves had collapsed and hung down at a drunken angle. On some of them stood dusty bottles and some blackened pewter tankards. She picked one up, feeling its weight unexpectedly heavy in her hands. If nothing else, they had found these, she thought to herself. She glanced back at Marik and Joycey but they were engrossed in clearing another trunk.

Apart from the coarse rasping of their breathing, the air was heavy and silent. She moved to the next alcove, and putting her hand forward hesitated and then dropped it slowly. An involuntary shudder had slipped down between her shoulder blades. The thick grey sheet in front of her shifted inwards slowly and then billowed outwards, and then it sucked in again. With a shocked start, she recognised the movement - it was like the working of a lung. She stood fascinated and repelled at the same time, wondering whether perhaps the movement was an echo of their own breathing, as if their breath was causing waves in the air. She took a few steps to one side and approached the third alcove. The web here was much thinner. She wiped it away with a sudden movement to reveal a blank brick wall. As she stood contemplating this, a thought occurred to her. Before she could speak, Joycey gave a loud groan.

'Nothing. Empty. Every bloody one of them.'

Marik stood in the centre of the cellar, his arms by his side. On his face was an expression that spoke failure. He looked at Takk. She shrugged and then turned to the wall again. 'If the chests are all empty, is it possible the treasure was hidden behind one of these walls?'

Joycey joined her first, being already bored and disillusioned with the search. Marik appeared grasping the piece of iron he had prized from the chest. He tapped the wall in front of them. The metal gave a solid ring.

'Not here.' He shook his head.

'Well this was a right waste of time.' Joycey whined.

Takk gazed at him as he stood despondently in the torchlight his arms hanging limply at his sides. His own torch cast a pool of light around his feet, and Takk thought for a moment how ironic it looked, as though he was standing on a platter of gold leaf. But then something caught her eye, something under the table. It was the tiniest glint of a deep, rich red light. She scrambled forward and knelt, her hands delving in the dust that lay there by the extended legs of the corpse. Her fingers closed over something small and hard. She picked it up and turned it in the beam of her head lamp.

'Look.' She exclaimed.

Between finger and thumb she held a stone about the size of a small sugar cube. It glowed with the ruby red of a fine wine glowing in the sunshine, and as her hand moved, brilliant red light flashed across the cellar. They too scrambled towards the table, and all three were suddenly on their knees, groping on the floor, but it was Takk who found it. A small leather bag, lying torn and open between the man's feet. She scooped it up carefully and put it on the table. Bending over to peer intently, the two men watched as she carefully prized open the split in the leather and tilted it towards the light. The interior of the purse sparkled and glowed with light. It was half full of rubies.

'Bloody hell'. It was Joycey who broke the long silence.

'Pirate treasure.' Marik was smiling quietly.

'Kidd's treasure certainly contained rubies,' Takk's eyes were shining. 'Rubies from the East Indies. They're just…amazing.'

'I wonder what rubies are worth?' Joycey said, a broad grin splitting his face.

Takk shrugged.

'Quite a bit I guess. And with this provenance, even more.'

'What's that then, 'provenance'?'

Takk closed the bag carefully and laid it carefully on the table.

'The fact that it could be…is part of Captain Kidd's lost treasure. It would add to the value.'

'So we could be talking a lot of money then?'

'Too fucking right,' said a harsh voice. They span round just as a dark shape dropped lightly into the vault behind them.

37. Intruders

There was little time for shock or reaction. Instinctively their torch beams swung onto the one spot, where a crouching figure was rising to its feet, and as it did so, they saw the dull black glint of the gun. Then a flash of light in the aperture caught their attention and they saw a familiar face twisted into a jubilant smile – a man wearing a leather jacket over a grey hoody.

'Oh...I know you,' Joycey half-sneered. 'You're that copper.'

'Detective Sergeant if you don't mind.' The policeman sniggered.

It was indeed Detective Sergeant Martin. There was more scuffling in the cavity beside him and the face of a third man appeared. Then suddenly they were blinded by the stark glare of a brilliant white light. It was so intense, the brilliance hurt their eyes and they recoiled, blinking and shielding their faces with pink, translucent fingers.

'What d'you want?' Joycey's voice was not welcoming. But then, neither was Martin's. 'What are you doing here anyway?'

The question was rhetorical and it met with a long silence

while the powerful beam swept round the cellar. Instinctively they refused to follow it, and kept their eyes from the surface of the table. The light passed over the mummified corpse at the end of the table, then swept back to illuminate it for several long moments. There were muffled exclamations from the aperture.

Martin's face was illuminated from the side. He was grinning broadly.

'Well I suppose you could say we're following up on enquiries aren't we.'

Joycey snorted. 'What d'yer mean?'

'Following you lot, that's what. Honestly talk about bleedin amateurs. All that driving round and round the East End. Who was that supposed to fool?'

There was silence in the chamber. The man with the gun leaned back against the wall watching them warily. His expression was hard like flint. He looked wiry and strongly built, the sort of man that Joycey would have described as 'trouble.' Looking at him Takk felt fear stirring deep within.

The bright light shifted and Joycey covered his eyes, squinting in the direction of DS Martin.

'So what's this then? You working for Keeley?' The question was addressed generally to the three men but he knew that it would be Martin who responded.

'Keeley! No, he's got what he wanted. We're here on our own account.'

'Oh yeah, so who are your friends then?'

There was a momentary silence and then Martin answered, 'Just friends.'

'Oh right, yeah, I get it. Bent coppers.'

The man with the gun shifted uneasily and glanced up at Martin. Martin spoke again.

'Just using our initiative, that's all. We helped out Christopher Keeley, and now we're following up on an independent basis. What's wrong with that?'

'I don't follow. Does Keeley know what you're up to?'

Martin smiled slowly.

'You haven't got a clue have you? You really don't know.'

'What?'

Martin was grinning again.

'All Christopher Keeley was interested in was getting his letter back. He asked us for help, and we helped him. What any public servant would do. It was just stolen property after all.'

'You mean he isn't interested in the treasure?'

Martin shrugged. 'As far as I know he doesn't know about it. Bootham didn't say anything to him. He was too scared after we spoke to him.'

'How's that?'

Martin eased himself into a slightly more comfortable position on the steps. 'It was Bootham who reported the theft of the letter from his car. When he told us it belonged to Christopher Keeley we felt a certain obligation to help, as you can imagine. After all, the Keeley Corporation has a reputation for being, how shall we say, generous when it wants to show its gratitude.'

'Oh yeah, backhanders is it?' Joycey sneered.

Martin shrugged again. 'If you like. Anyway, we told Keeley who had stolen the letter. Even gave him Gavin Douglas's address. Some of Keeley's employees went round there to find out what he'd done with it and persuaded him that it would be in his best interest to get it back again.'

'Oh!' Joycey exclaimed. 'So it was Douglas who broke into me shop!'

Martin nodded.

Joycey's mouth hung open for a moment. 'And then they killed him. Keeley's blokes killed him anyway.

'Oh no.' The policeman was shaking his head, giving a superior smile. 'You got that all wrong. Douglas' murder had nothing to do with this. We thought it had initially. Made things a bit awkward for us, having helped Mr Keeley out and all. But no, turns out Douglas wasn't killed by Keeley at all. The little shit was killed by some Eastern Europeans. Turns out they were running drugs in through Ramsgate and Douglas's brother did the dirty on them and then did a runner. They couldn't find him but they did fund Douglas, so they did him instead. Nasty business though.'

There was a lengthy pause and then Joycey suddenly blurted out, accusingly, 'So it was you who took me to Rainham fucking marshes then was it?'

The man next to Martin in the aperture, guffawed suddenly and nodded, his eyes sparkling. 'Twat!' he spat out. 'Had you shitting yourself there, didn't we.'

Martin raised a hand sharply, shutting the man up.

'Then it was you who planted my tablet back in Joycey's

house?' Takk asked, finding her voice.

Martin gazed at her for a moment. 'Yes. Bootham grabbed it from you in the tube. He told us what was on it and changed some of it to try and put you off. Then when he had explained all about Kidd's treasure, we threatened to charge him with attempted murder. Scared him shitless.' He laughed.

'Attempted murder?'

'Yeah. CCTV's everywhere you know. You made such a fuss after he snatched your bag on the tube, we had a look at the film. He nearly pushed you under that train. You were lucky.'

'I know.' Takk snorted angrily.

There was a lengthy silence again which was disturbed only by the sound of their breathing which, to Takk, seemed to be getting louder, coarser.

'So, what now?' Joycey asked.

'Well, as I said, we all know why we're here.'

Joycey was thinking fast, and perhaps harder than he had ever done before. He hadn't a clue what to do next and could only think that asking questions might eventually throw some light on the options available to them, some clue on how to act. For a moment he wondered whether to feign ignorance about Kidd's treasure, but it was obvious that this might be just too provocative under the circumstances.

'So you're after Captain Kidd's treasure.'

Martin nodded. 'Clever aren't you.'

'And Keeley really isn't interested in it? Find that hard to believe.'

'As I said, s'far as I know he doesn't know about it, so

why should he be?'

'You sure about that?' Joycey smiled.

The expression on Martin's face changed subtly and the man with the gun gave a sudden glance upwards. Suddenly, Joycey realised that he had hit upon something. Something which might turn to their advantage. What little he knew about Christopher Keeley he had got from DI Walker – but the Detective Sergeant might not know this. Without thinking it through he decided to bluff his way into unsettling Martin.

'Only,' Joycey continued, 'I can't believe that someone like Christopher Keeley wouldn't be interested in pirate treasure. Especially if he thought he had any claim on it.'

Martin was silent.

'If you found it easy enough to follow us around, surely his blokes would too. You sure they ain't watching you? Your governor told me they were pretty mean too.'

The man with the gun looked up suddenly. In the aperture there was a sudden whispered conversation. Then it stopped. There was a pause and Martin spoke in a steady, controlled voice.

'Let's just get to the point again, shall we? What have you found?'

Joycey laughed suddenly. 'Nothing. Hate to disappoint you after all this. But there's nothing here. It's all gone.'

There were exclamations of dismay, disbelief from the two unidentified policeman. But Martin appeared unperturbed.

'What do you mean?'

It was Takk who spoke. 'It's all gone. It was here, once.

But now it's gone.'

She stepped forward to the table, ignoring the threatening gesture from the man with the gun and scooped up a handful of the rotting fabric. 'This is all there is. It was probably silk, once.' She let the soft shreds slip through her fingers.

'What are these chests then?'

'Empty,' Joycey grunted. 'All of 'em. We checked.'

One of the policemen groaned. Martin shifted his position and reached down to the man in the chamber.

'Check them.'

The gun was handed up to Martin and the man moved forward warily. Grasping one of the web shrouded chests, he lifted the lid and turned it towards the light.

Martin's face seemed to darken. 'Check the others. Quickly.'

The man set to his task, keeping a careful eye on Marik who stepped back, himself wary of the gun now aimed in his direction. Suddenly, there came the sound of another voice from beyond the aperture. Someone unseen was speaking to Martin in low, urgent tones. A rapid, tense conversation followed. Words exchanged in monosyllabic haste. When Martin spoke again he was clearly agitated.

'Get on with it, for fuck's sake. Get the Pole to do it.'

The powerful beam of light focussed on Marik. He looked at Joycey, who nodded quickly, and then stooped and opened another of the chests. He tilted it towards the beam and swept the bottom with his fingers, leaving dusty trails across the base of the chest.

'Kick the base in,' Walker snarled. 'Quickly.'

Marik pushed the chest onto its side and lifting a foot, drove the heel of his boot into the damp timber of its base. It splintered into soft dark shards.

'Another.'

Marik complied, smashing one chest after another under the solemn gaze of Takk and Joycey. When he had finished the policeman checked the table, sweeping the dust aside. He paused in front of the corpse, and then roughly kicked the leg of the chair. Wood scraped on the floor and the corpse slid backwards and collapsed to the floor with an unpleasant crackling sound. 'There's nothing else here.' His voice croaked with disappointment. 'Fucking nothing.'

'See,' Joycey ventured, 'empty.'

Martin gave a long sigh. 'So it seems. Pity. Well we'll just have to make do with the rubies.'

'What!' Takk's wail seemed to add another layer to the tension.

'What rubies?' Joycey's bluff sounded weak even to him.

Martin snarled with sudden ferocity. 'Don't fuck with me. I heard you talking about them. Just hand them over and do it fucking quickly.'

Takk glanced at Joycey and he nodded resignedly. She crouched down and scooped up the tattered leather purse from where she had dropped it in the shadow of the table and placed it on the table top. The policeman snatched it up and passed it up to Martin who grinned, feeling the weight of the stones in his palm.

'Well that's something, anyway. Now,' he said addressing the man below him, 'get the fuck out of there.'

The policeman made a sudden agile leap for the aperture and, with toes kicking at the crumbling brickwork, hands hauled him quickly up and out of sight leaving a trickle of dust and brick fragments.

Joycey, Marik and Takk watched, silent, unmoving. There was another muffled and urgent discussion up on the steps. As Takk strained unsuccessfully to hear what was being said, she became more conscious of the thick white swirls in the air around them. The powerful lamp was picking up far more of the dust motes than their small torches had done, and now they seemed to be standing in a white mist, which curled round them and then swept back past their heads in little pulses.

'So what now?' Joycey asked uneasily.

38. A fall

High in the wall there was scurried movement behind the aperture. A strange face appeared, thrust a torch into the cellar and stared about with obvious curiosity. Behind this new body an angry exchange was taking place. The men on the steps were in a clear state of agitation and whispers of their dispute echoed around the cellar. The word 'time' was repeated again and again, and someone was making a loud protest about something. Lights were flashing in a confused fashion. Suddenly Martin's face reappeared.

'Sorry to leave you like this.'

'What do you mean?' Joycey's question sounded strangely unconvincing.

There was a movement and a heavy roll of duct tape bounced onto the floor of the cellar.

'You.' Martin gesticulated at Takk. 'Tie them up with that.'

She hesitated.

'It's either that or I shoot you. Take your pick'

Again Takk hesitated, and then there was a flash of light and a loud, sharp detonation. Marik gave a cry and suddenly wheeled round, his right arm flying in a wide circle before he fell to his knees.

'No.' Takk yelled. She leapt to the young Pole's side and threw herself in front of him. 'Don't shoot again. I'll do it.'

'Would have been better if you'd done it in the first place,' Martin snarled.

Takk picked up the roll of tape.

'Feet together. Wrap it round his ankles.'

Marik groaned. He was clutching his arm with bloodied fingers, but he still helped by putting his legs together for her.

'I'm sorry Marik,' she said quietly, shocked by the sight of several large drops of blood on the dusty floor. The tape rasped off the roll and she bit through it when done.

'Now his wrists. Behind the back. And make it snappy otherwise we'll have to take the quicker solution.'

Takk tore more tape and gently eased the wounded arm back. Marik bit his lips as she wrapped the tape round his wrists. She stared at the paleness of his face and felt sick.

'Now the other,' Martin instructed, his voice shaking.

Beyond the aperture there were hurried sounds of movement, then a heavy metallic crash.

'Fucking wait!' Martin yelled suddenly over his shoulder, his voice becoming ragged with what almost seemed to be a note of panic.

Takk finished tying Joycey, who rolled over onto his side, grumbling to himself.

'Now sit down,' Martin said to her, the barrel of the gun pointing directly at her face. 'Wrap all the rest of the roll round your legs.'

Takk began rolling the roll round and round her legs.

'This won't stop me,' she snapped defiantly up at the policeman's face.

'No, but it will slow you down.'

Suddenly a frightened face appeared beside Martin's.

'Come on Martin, it's coming in fast.'

'I'm coming.'

The second face disappeared and there came the sound of someone scrambling down the steps. There was a sudden silence. And Takk sat looking up at the policeman.

'Why are you doing this?'

'Why do you think?'

'What are we going to tell anyone, who would believe us anyway?'

Martin smiled. 'Maybe. But it's just simpler this way. I like simplicity. Fewer loose ends. Know what I mean.' He backed away from the hole, but hesitated when Takk spoke again.

'So, that's it, is it?'

Martin laughed his voice turning malicious. 'You know, you thought you were so fucking clever, didn't you. So clever. Smart arsed student! But you and your dumb friends just couldn't get anything right.'

'Couldn't we?'

'No. Sadly for you.'

'What do you mean?'

'Who checked the tides. You? Him?' he pointed the gun towards Marik, ignoring Joycey. 'Didn't check it properly though did you. Got it badly wrong. Forgot about the Spring Tides.'

'Martin!' An almost hysterical yell came echoing up from the stairs. The Detective Sergeant's face disappeared. There was a confusion of flashing lamplight and shadows. Then his face appeared again.

'I'll say goodbye then. Hope you can swim.'

At that moment, somebody outside the chamber began shouting loudly. First one voice, then another. Martin's expression changed to one of alarm. He glanced down at them quickly, then disappeared abruptly.

For several moments there was silence and then the shouting began again. Takk, grabbed the edge of the table and hauled herself upright. Turning towards the aperture she heard a voice which she recognised as Martin's, crying out as if in pain. There were other voices now, angry sounds. The nature of the noise made her shuffle backwards instinctively. Whatever was going on, it was not pleasant. There was a scream, then silence.

By chance, one of the policemen's' powerful torches had been left lying on the stairs and its beam illuminated the cellar brightly. Takk looked round at the pale, worried faces behind her. Joycey shook his head, his eyes staring at the aperture, his mouth hanging open. Takk turned and leaning forward gently touched Marik on the leg.

'Marik?'

'I'm ok. I think it not bad.'

Blood was spreading slowly down his arm to join the thin stream on the floor. Takk glanced up at the aperture again, then with urgent fingers, she began tearing the tape from her legs. Joycey rolled over suddenly on the floor and began complaining.

'Hurry up. Get this off us.'

Marik gave him a reproving glance and he shut up suddenly.

Takk released her legs and crawled behind Marik to unbind his arms. For several minutes the chamber had been silent but for the sound of their own breathing and the ripping of the tape. But suddenly they became aware of a distant sound. Of water splashing, of feet kicking noisily as if in a pool. Takk stopped what she was doing to listen. There was a long silence and then, just as she turned to tear the tape from Marik's legs, a sudden, deafening sound filled the cellar. She was thrown forward on top of Marik as the air boomed and shuddered with a force that stunned them, numbing their heads and making their eardrums ring. The bright light went out and the cellar itself shook violently. The sound was immediately followed by a terrifying rumble and the sound of stone and earth falling. There were heavy splashes. Chunks of masonry crashed through the aperture, some hitting Joycey where he lay, and some bounding noisily across the chamber floor. Joycey turned his face away but could move little with his arms tied behind his back as they were.

Takk had buried her face in Marik's chest, simply because there was nowhere else close enough to shelter. When she looked up, the air, where it was caught by the thin light of their remaining lamps, was full of dust clouds so dense, it was hard to see more than a few feet. Cascades of mortar, sand and brick dust were falling in streams and trickles from the roof of the vault where large, terrifying cracks had appeared.

Takk began to cough, then realised that she was deafened, and beyond this there seemed to be a heavy, ominous stillness. When she finally managed to control the tickle in her throat she looked across to the others. Marik was sitting up rubbing his face but Joycey, who had been nearest the aperture wall, was partly covered in rubble. She quickly helped Marik free the tape from his legs, and then both crawled over to Joycey and began lifting lumps of stone and brick from his legs. By the time they had done this, the deep numbness in their ears had begun to pass, enough for them to hear Joycey groaning. Takk began tearing the tape from his wrists and he sat up, whining feebly. He had had a gash over one eye and the stream of blood which ran into his eye socket looked rather like an eye patch, which, ironically, made him look like a pirate. However, in response to Takk's enquiries he admitted with some reluctance that, apart from some other cuts and bruises, he was ok.

'What happened?' she asked the inevitable question.

'That explosion,' Marik asserted quietly. 'Like bomb.'

'Why…who?' she looked from one to the other.

It was Joycey who came up with a suggestion. 'Keeley?'

They looked at one another for a moment and then Takk began tearing the rest of the tape from his legs.

'Keeley?' she asked, her voice shaking.

'Yeah, my guess. Perhaps he was more interested after all.'

They exchanged solemn looks in the semi-darkness.

When all three were free of the tape, Takk picked up one of their torches and inspected the cellar around them. The aperture was completely blocked by a fall of rock, rubble and soil which had not only filled the aperture but had also poured through onto the floor of the cellar itself. Other large cracks had appeared in the walls as well as the ceiling.

She and Marik began climbing the landslide of rubble in the direction of the former aperture. But when they reached the unstable top of the slope they found that the way was completely barred by huge slabs of concrete. Takk tugged frantically at several of the jagged lumps, assisted ineffectively by Marik. But the more they pulled, the more loose material scattered under their feet, and more trickles of earth and sand spilled through in its place. After five minutes exertion, it was clear that the debris was wedged completely. There was no way out. They were trapped. Entombed.

Takk looked at Marik and shook her head. 'This is useless.'

Marik wiped a sweating brow on his sleeve and nodded miserably. The cellar had suddenly become very warm. Takk slipped down the scree and sat down next to Joycey on the littered floor of the cellar.

'Spring Tides?' Joycey asked suddenly.

Marik pulled an unhappy face. 'This my fault. Spring is...' he hesitated. 'Highest than usual.'

'What?'

'He means that Spring tides are higher than usual,' Takk intervened. 'It happens every month According to the phase of the moon. It affects the height of the tides.'

'I forget.' The young Pole groaned. He was now cradling his right arm and was clearly in pain. Takk insistently helped ease off his jacket and inspected the bloody hole in his shirt with an anxious expression. Then she removed her own waterproof and jumper and tore her shirt to create a sling and a bandage which she tied tightly round Marik's arm. Then feeling suddenly exhausted, she slumped to the floor beside Marik.

'Now what?' Joycey asked.

Marik stared round them and shook his head slowly, his face expressing a combination of pain and misery.

Takk was sitting staring at the corpse on the floor. Its blackened face, with its evil grin and empty eye sockets, seemed to be deliberately mocking them. She shuddered.

'Well we can't stay here.' Joycey mumbled.

'Sure. Well you lead the way and we'll follow.' Takk snapped angrily.

Joycey pulled a sour face. 'Then I suppose we'll just have to wait till help comes,' he mumbled without conviction. But then added. 'Thing is, no-one else knows we're here. Do they?'

There was a silence, during which a sudden cascade of brick fragments clattered onto the floor.

'I don't know.' Takk said bluntly. 'Something must have happened on the surface as a result of this. They're bound to want to find out the cause.'

'A big hole was reported in Wapping,' Joycey snorted with dark humour, 'and council workmen are looking into it.'

She gave a short unconvincing laugh and leaned back against the table.

'Even if they do, we could be here for some time. And if a hole has appeared in the gardens or even the road, no-one's going to be able to do much until the morning.' On an instinct, Takk suddenly looked at her watch and was surprised to find that it was nearly 1am.

'Maybe we should think about conserving the lights,' she suggested. 'We don't know how long we are going to be down here and it won't be much fun in total darkness.'

'It's hardly a bundle of laughs now,' Joycey gave a sick grin in the soft light.

Marik nodded in agreement, a half smile flickering across his face too.

'How's your arm?' she asked with sudden gentleness.

He nodded and looked down at the bloody bandage. 'Is ok I think. Sure it hurt, but no bone broken I think.' He gave a brave smile and Takk returned a grateful grin.

'Let's hope so.'

39. Under Wapping

With most of their lights turned out, the cellar seemed to become hotter and, gradually, the air in the chamber seemed to grow heavier. All three were suddenly weary and without consultation they sat in a row facing the blocked aperture as though wanting to be the first to recognise any sound from the outside world. As time passed they fell silent, and Marik and Takk were half-dozing when a thought suddenly occurred to Joycey as he sat hugging his knees.

'How high do you reckon this Spring Tide comes then?'

Takk looked at him and shrugged.

'Well,' Joycey licked his lips. 'The Thames rises and falls by about twenty feet normally. So....' His voice tailed away.

Takk gave him a sideways look. 'You think it might get in here?'

He shrugged and looked unhappy. 'Well, I don't know, do I? I'm merely speculating. It comes pretty high up the river wall, even flows over it at Greenwich when the tide is very high. I just wondered how far below the top of the wall we are...."

'But the cellar was fairly dry when we came in.'

'Steps', Marik stirred. They both stared at him. 'Water on the stairs. When we came in. It had water. Last night.'

A grim realisation suddenly settled over them.

'Marik, are you saying you think it could get in here?' Takk asked in a strained voice.

The young Pole looked dazed. 'Maybe. I think. Yes.'

'Oh Jees-us!' Joycey swore quietly. 'That's all we fuckin need now. First buried alive then drowned.'

'If we don't suffocate first,' Takk added in a sober tone.

'Yeah, well, if we can still breathe perhaps we can get on the table and float out of here.'

Takk gave another quiet laugh, but her humour sounded hollow. The heavy silence cloaked them once again. The atmosphere was oppressive, but after some time they gradually became aware that the silence around them was not complete. There were other sounds. Trickles of falling earth and stones, the sound of water dripping and even a gentle washing sound, as though they were deep inside the hull of a great ship which was pushing its way through waves. She tried to avoid thinking about the river. That huge dark presence only yards away, pushing its enlarged might against the river wall, seeking for the gaps and the chinks in the stonework, finding the tunnels and broken walls and pushing its way inexorably up the ancient stairs. It was hard not to stare through the gloom at the jagged debris that hung in the aperture.

Beside her, the two men were silent, though, worryingly, she could feel Marik beginning to shiver. They were being brave, she knew that. No-one had said anything about what would happen if the water level rose too high. But in her imagination she could see the debris in the aperture turning suddenly to slurry and then a wave of water bursting through – or perhaps it would be fingers of water trickling through at first, growing in their dark volume as they began to run into the scree and make their way across the cellar floor. Would they end up standing in a murky soup, perhaps on the table with the dark evil smelling brew up to their lips as the lights went out?

Yes, they were being very brave. And the corpse just grinned at them, as though enjoying their plight, or perhaps enjoying the company that had come at long last to share its tomb. Tomb. Strange word. So Gothic. But who was he? Who was he, and why was he here? Kidd's treasure must have been here. The chests, mouldering fabric and rubies all indicated that. But who had removed it, and when? If someone from the Admiralty had come to recover it, why was there no official record of it? And why had someone been killed in the process? Or had Kidd been hideously betrayed before his execution as he had feared? Had someone else come to take the treasure, and was the corpse that of somebody loyal to Kidd, someone who had tried to defend the pirate's interests? In the hollowness of that tomb, the loud plunking of water was accompanied only by a strange sighing in the air. It could have been the woeful lament of Kidd's ghost. She woke from this reverie with a start. She must have fallen asleep, for the shadows in the chamber were deeper. Joycey was snoring with a regular, peaceful buzzing sound and Marik too was asleep, though he stirred momentarily and then became still again.

It was darker because the torch was giving out. She found one of the spares and tested it. After the faint ambience of the failing lamp, it glowed brightly, picking out the swaying curtains of web to her left, and throwing the long shadows of the chests across the flagged floor. She sat for a moment, trying to gather

her thoughts. There was still no sound from above. No sound of tools, of digging, of any form of rescue. She sighed, feeling her lungs moving stiffly as though caked in dust, and her head rolled back, eyes sweeping over the dark stone of the vaulting, and then across to the webby alcoves. The pale shreds of web waved lifted and curled, fluttering like little pennants in a light air. In the centre, the grey sheet which was still largely intact filled and collapsed slowly, a barely perceptible movement in the gloom.

She sat up suddenly, the words of a question crystalizing in her brain. Why were they moving like that? Why was any of it moving? Easing her stiff legs, she rolled onto her side and crawled over to the alcoves. Then, rising to her feet unsteadily, one hand on the back of the corpse's chair, she extended an arm and pushed her hand into the thick sheet of web. It collapsed suddenly, tearing unpleasantly under its own ancient weight. Behind it was another alcove identical to the other two, with a semi-circular brick arch at the top. It was perhaps three feet in depth and a little more in width. The walls were black as though it had once been whitewashed and had darkened with age and dirt. There were faint marks on the wall as though a piece of furniture had once stood in position there. She ran her palms over the surface of the wall. It was crumbling, damp, even wet to the touch. And there was a smell too, a familiar damp, mouldering unpleasant smell. It was the odour which they had first noticed on entering the cellar. As she stood there the smell seemed to grow stronger for a moment and then fade. It seemed to ebb and flow, like some obscene corrupt hand stroking her face. She lifted the torch, and saw in the top right hand corner of the alcove, a deep crack where the wall and ceiling met. She lifted her hand to it and a cool waft of air ran through her fingers, as tactile as running water. It took some moments for the significance to register, and then she gave an excited yell.

40. The Alcove

Takk's yell brought the two men scrambling to their feet. Joycey swearing out of alarm, and Marik groaning as he put pressure on his injured arm. For a moment there was a confused babble of voices and then Takk gave a powerful, commanding yell from the pit of her stomach.

'Listen!'

There was a sudden hush.

'There's a draught. Here. In this alcove.' She waved her hand excitedly towards the wall. Joycey's eyes followed her hand, a look of incomprehension on his face.

'A what?'

Marik though was suddenly wide awake. He pushed into the alcove and raised his good hand to the wall. Then he put his face to the crack and sniffed for several long seconds. When he turned, there was a smile on his face.

'Don't you see what this means?' Takk challenged Joycey. He looked confused.

'What?'

'It means that there is air getting through here somewhere.'

Marik nodded. 'Air. Could be tunnel. Maybe?'

With sudden interest, Joycey pushed in beside Marik and began patting at the wall. Within minutes he had found another crack, and was digging his fingers into what appeared to be wet mortar, as though trying to claw his way through the wall. After several minutes he stopped, panting.

'This is no bloody good. It might be for mice.'

Marik turned quickly, glanced around among the debris of stonework and shattered chests and located the piece of iron strapping. Then he turned to the alcove, and using his good arm, began attacking the back wall vigorously, forcing the others to back away, shielding their eyes from flying fragments of plaster, brick and stone. Starting at one side, he hammered and chiselled for what seemed an age but it wasn't long before the blows were less frequent, and he was gasping for breath. Finally he stopped altogether, leaning against the side of the alcove, the piece of iron hanging limply at his side.

While Marik had been at work, Joycey had found a handy lump of masonry. And now as Takk pulled the young Pole away, Joycey took over, raining a series of furious blows on the brickwork until, from the sound of the iron and the little pieces of brickwork flicking violently out past him, it was clear that something was giving.

When he finally stopped, Takk and Marik closed in again to stare. The surface brickwork had smashed at the top, but behind it seemed to be another wall of solid stonework, interspersed with dark chinks where mortar had disintegrated in the distant past.

'Let me have a go,' Takk insisted.

Joycey nodded reluctantly and relinquished the chunk of stone.

Takk massaged the stone to find a comfortable grip and then stood surveying the surface brickwork and the stonework behind it. She dropped to her knees inspecting the angle at the floor, testing with her finger tips, pressing her cheek to the brickwork, sniffing.

At that moment there was an ominous crash from beyond the cellar, as though something had fallen on the stairs outside. They swung to look at the aperture, and Takk covered it with the beam of the good torch. Marik clambered forward up the slope of debris and stared at it for a moment. Then he pushed his left hand into it and extracted a handful of soil. He cast it aside and thrust his hand in again. It sank in to the elbow. Then he turned and slithered back down into the cellar. Without speaking he raised his palm to the light. It was covered it wet mud.

'It very wet now.' He said sombrely.

'The river...?' Joycey asked quietly.

'I think. Must be.'

'Let's have a look.'

The two men clambered up the slope again. Behind them Takk turned back to the alcove wall and began hammering and levering against the chinks in the bricks, bracing her shoulder against the wall and using the iron to prise off chunks again and again.

On the debris pile, Marik helped support Joycey as he climbed higher on the rubble, finding another small hole into which he could insert his arm. The expression on his face changed abruptly.

'Water,' he hissed. 'There's water there.' He pulled out his hand and stuck two fingers into his mouth. Then he spat. 'It's fucking salt, isn't it. It's the river.'

The two men exchanged grim looks.

On the other side of the cellar, Takk's insistent hammering and scraping stopped.

'I think you ought to have a look at this,' she said after a long pause.

With sudden haste, the two men slid down the slope, crossed to where Takk was kneeling and peered in over her shoulder. At the bottom of the alcove wall was a pile of crumbled brick and plaster. Behind it there was a dark cavity. In a welter of protests, she was elbowed out of the way by Joycey, and even Marik seemed suddenly impervious to her anger.

Takk's well-directed labour had revealed a hole at the bottom of the stone wall about a foot in width and eight inches in height. Joycey flung himself to the ground and with his cheek grinding against the sharp fragments of stone on the floor, he thrust an arm into the cavity and then rolled onto his back. A gust of unpleasant air was blowing on his face but after a few seconds he gave Marik and Takk a broad grin.

'It's bigger. Behind this wall. It's bigger. It may be another tunnel.'

Picking up the chunk of stone he began thumping away at the brickwork around the hole. Takk gently pushed Marik to one side and began scooping away the fragments of brick and stone.

Marik stood behind them, stooping to watch in anxious fascination. He had been given the torch now, to give Joycey the best possible light. But some instinct made him turn suddenly back towards the aperture, and so it was they paused in their efforts and all saw what had attracted his attention. A trickle of slurry had penetrated the debris at the base of the aperture. Even as they watched a handful of sandy soil to the right of it suddenly fell softly onto the slope, and a small black stream washed down the brickwork onto the slope.

Without speaking, Marik turned the torch back into the alcove and Joycey, with frantic energy, began levering out chunks of brick and mortar. Then, with a sudden crash, he levered a large square of brick from its position. A larger portion above it suddenly collapsed, leaving a cavity about two feet high and a little more in width. Marik passed him the torch and they watched as the light disappeared from the cellar.

'It's a tunnel or something all right.' Joycey cried, his voice slightly muffled.

Beyond the wall was the entrance to what looked like an older culvert or drain constructed of smooth green stonework which seemed to glisten with damp. It was arched at the top and little more than two foot wide and high, and as Joycey peered into it, his nostrils twitched with the damp, musty subterranean odour. The floor of the culvert was actually wet, and he could see that a thin stream of water lay along it in a shiny dark line, fed by drops from the ceiling. Like the other tunnel, it curved to one side. There was no way of telling where it led.

Joycey crawled backwards, and one by one Takk and Marik took turns to peer into the tunnel. It was Takk who noticed the dangerous peculiarity about this tunnel.

'It slopes down,' she muttered, her head thrust into the entrance. 'It slopes down away from the cellar.'

'So?' Joycey asked cautiously.

Marik pulled a worried face, but it was Takk who explained.

'We don't know where this goes. It could be a dead end. If we go in there and the cellar fills with water, it'll be a death trap.'

Joycey thought about this. 'What. More than this place, you mean.'

Takk was peering into the tunnel again. 'Tell you one thing though, there is a much stronger draught here. It has to be getting in somewhere.'

'And out too I guess.' Joycey mumbled. 'Must mean there's some way to the outside'.

Takk nodded. 'Perhaps. It makes sense.'

'So, what do you reckon?' Joycey asked. 'Do we try it?'

'Do we have any choice? There isn't much room though. Not enough the crawl properly.'

With a sudden chill, Takk thought of Marik. He had the broadest shoulders, and with his wounded arm, it wasn't going to be easy. She made a decision.

'I'm going to give it a go.'

'No,' Marik grabbed her arm. 'I go first.'

Takk glared at him suddenly and the young Pole blanched suddenly in the lamplight.

'Wait a minute,' said Joycey with unusual authority. 'Let's just think about this. Marik's the biggest of us, but he's also handicapped by that arm. You're the smallest,' he nodded at Takk, 'but if you go first that doesn't mean we'll get through. If I can get through, you will, and it will mean we can both try and pull him through.'

Takk thought about it and saw the logic. 'How will we pull him?'

Joycey thought for a moment. Then pulled his shirt out of his jeans. 'I got a leather belt. Maybe we can use a jacket too.'

Takk nodded, and without further discussion, handed Joycey one of the head lamps. Then, he rolled onto his stomach and pushed his head and shoulders into the culvert.

41. Like a rat up a drainpipe

Joycey wasn't really an activity sort of person, and the only time he had ever had to practice crawling in a confined space was years before at Snidey Johnson's thirtieth birthday party at Camber Sands when things had got a little out of hand. Now he found that the only way to make any progress was to push himself along with his elbows and toes. It was a painful and uncomfortable mode of travel, and within seconds he was hating it. He was also quick to realise that a hat might have been useful. His head banged perpetually on the roof of the tunnel, so every exertion was rapidly accompanied by a grumbling chorus of dissatisfaction.

Back in the cellar, Takk watched his awkward progress and grimaced at Marik. The young Pole gave a brave smile and nodded. 'Good. Yes?'

Takk returned the smile. 'Maybe.'

After several yards, Joycey began to feel claustrophobic. The tunnel closed about him and as his limbs and joints began to ache, he was reminded how constricted he actually was. The sound of his laboured breathing was amplified, and the roughness of the sound was discomforting. Quickly out of breath he paused for a few moments and the thought occurred to him that the slope of the tunnel was probably making the crawl forward easier than it would be to reverse. For several long moments he entertained the idea of simply backing up and saying that there was no way through, but some innate and long forgotten sense of honour set that thought aside. He inched forward again, conscious that the strain of holding his head up was giving him a chronic pain in the neck and shoulders. He closed his eyes, laid his cheek to the wet floor and moved forward blindly, groping with his finger tips to make sure the way was clear. He was also increasingly conscious that the front of his clothing was soaking up the wet stream on the tunnel floor. It didn't improve his temper.

The atmosphere wasn't encouraging either. The air reeked with the smell of earth and decay. His fingertips, already roughened by his earlier activity, became sore and cracked, and his fingernails splintered. Unseen, tiny fragments dug into his knees causing disproportionate levels of pain and his elbows were soon rubbed raw on the sides of the shaft. But he pressed on. Whenever he looked up, the bobbing light from his headlamp just seemed to illuminate an endless narrow prison of smooth stone, and after a while he gave up looking.

An age seemed to pass in this slow labour and, remembering that he was actually wearing a wristwatch, he paused to check the time and estimated that he had been crawling for about ten minutes. With a heavy sigh he pushed himself forwards again and found himself convinced that he could feel the heat of Takk and Marik's watchful gaze at his back, though in truth he was long out of their sight. He was wondering just how far he had managed to crawl when his hand plunged into cold, soupy water.

The coldness and the surprise shocked him out of the reverie into which he had slipped. His fingers dipped down and he realised that the stone floor of the culvert simply disappeared under the water. He inched forward, straining to look ahead, and saw a black surface stretching ahead for at least six feet. Some sort of small flooded chamber had opened up in front of him. On the far side of the black water he could see the tunnel continuing, but his way seemed to be barred.

He pushed his arm forward and thrust his hand down. The pool was deep, deeper than he could reach. And the water stank. His hand stirred it and a whirling black mass of what seemed to be rotting vegetable matter rose in front of his face. He pulled a face and grinned in spite of himself. Methane. Bad farts. His weird chuckle echoed back along the culvert and reached Takk and Marik shortly before the stench. Takk rapidly backed away from the tunnel entrance, a hand clamped across her nostrils.

Joycey was perplexed. This looked like the end, the end of their escape route, and the end of their hopes. He sighed heavily, watching the stinking black water as it slurried around just under his face. But something also made him curious. He wasn't the adventurous type, not by any means, but the situation was so unique, that he just succumbed to an unusual impulse to know more. He crept forward until his chin was just over the foul water, and then turned his head from side to side so that the beam from the head lamp swept around the space in front of him. Doing this he saw that secondary culverts converged on this chamber from either side at an oblique angle. Much smaller, they offered no form of escape route and he had no idea what purpose they might serve, other than as some form of drainage system. But for what, he had no idea. The only possibility for escape would be in crossing the pool to reach the continuation of his tunnel. Looking up he could see that the roof over the pool seemed to be much higher than any of the culverts. He rolled awkwardly onto his back, so that the beam shone vertically. But it simply illuminated another brick arched vault, some six feet over the water. He guessed he was on the edge of a flooded shaft of some sort.

For a moment he lay there, uncertain and unhappy. He had no idea how deep the shaft was, only that it was deeper than his arms could reach. This wasn't very reassuring. He either had to go back or try and get across the water. And it seemed as though the only possibility would be to swim. It wasn't far, but there was precious little room. And Joycey had stopped going to the local baths when he was fourteen. He hadn't enjoyed the water then. He had no reason for thinking he would like it any more now or that he would show any more competence about keeping himself afloat. Furthermore, if he got it wrong and he dropped head first into the flooded shaft, he might not be able to get back out again. The prospect made him feel sick.

He rolled back over onto his stomach and looked ahead. Then, gritting his teeth, he determined to try and achieve something. He pushed with his toes against the side of the culvert, braced his knees and stretched his hands to either side to support himself on the edges of the side culverts. So far so good. His chest and face hovered inches above the water, and his stomach muscles screamed with unusual exertion. He was panting heavily, feeling his arms and legs trembling with the strain. Then he launched himself forward pushing his hands ahead like a demented diver. The water sploshed up over his head, filling his mouth and nostrils. Then he surfaced and began laughing. The shaft may have been deep, and the pool may have been six feet wide – but under that black surface, the shaft was much narrower. He groped under the water and soon confirmed the truth. The water from the lateral culverts ran in a deep gully across his path and crossed through the chamber, but the shaft below him was little more than three feet in circumference. Reaching forward, he groped just a few inches under water, and touched the floor of the opposite tunnel. Grinning with relief, he scooped up some of the cool, foul water and splashed it on his sweating face. Then, taking his weight on his hands, he began sliding forward again, his body trailing through the gully and emerging like a black, slime-covered beast on the far side.

Back in the chamber, Takk and Marik listened intently to the mystifying range of sounds echoing back up the culvert. In the distance they could see the glow of Joycey's lamp, and see the shadow of his body distorted into a dark writhing mass. There were sounds of exertion, water, and laughter. They exchanged worried glances and at last Takk was unable to resist calling out, to see if everything was all right. But Joycey's muffled reply was unintelligible. Marik stood up, unsettled, and picked up the spare headlamp. He pushed it over his brows and while Takk continued her anxious watch in the tunnel, he stole quietly across the chamber to climb the debris slope again. It took some effort to clamber up and locate the small breach that they had made earlier. But once he had found a steady foothold, he pressed his face to the hole, ready to put his hand through and then stopped. The light from the headlamp had flashed momentarily into that small shaft and what he saw chilled him suddenly. Black water glinted evilly just in front of his face. A gust of cold air swept in against his forehead and even as he watched, horrified, a finger of water pushed forward and sprang in a thin pattering arc onto the soft pile below.

He skidded quickly and recklessly down the slope, attracting a startled look from Takk, and scrambled across to her. He said nothing in response to her enquiring glance, but nodded to her in false reassurance. Then, from the far end of the shaft, they both heard an exclamation.

42. A black torrent

As Joycey dragged himself into the opposite culvert he became aware that the angle of the floor was different. It began to rise, and as his toes splashed in the water and found purchase on the edge of the gully, he gave himself a sharp thrust forward. Some fifteen feet further along, the roof of the culvert rose suddenly and he found himself in a taller tunnel. He pushed himself upright, easing the pain in his cramped limbs and curling his toes to try and diminish the pins-and-needles.

The stonework here seemed older, of a slightly different hue. He began edging along sideways, relieved now that he could move almost upright again. He was walking up a sharp incline, and then, without warning he stepped into an open space. It was another chamber, this time lined with narrow, crudely-set yellow bricks. For some reason it felt older than the cellar of the Sugar Loaf, but he had no way of knowing for sure. Not that it really mattered. The space itself was rectangular. The floor consisted of earth and what seemed to be sticks and fragments of wood that crunched under his feet. The roof was made up of a series of curved brick barrel vaults with two narrow columns along the centre of the floor. The space was empty and devoid of any features. But at the far end, the wall appeared to have sagged slightly, and a small cascade of dark earth lay heaped in a line across the floor. He moved quickly across and began to climb. The earth was soft and wet to the touch. His feet sank in a little but he climbed quickly to the top, and saw that the wall had collapsed outwards. Beyond there was another cavity, stone lined. A vertical shaft. He began clawing with his hands like a dog, pawing away the loose earth until he had cleared enough room to enter.

The shaft was about six foot by three foot, and the floor was again a mixture of wood, earth and soft sticks. He looked up and with a start, realised where he was. Now the crunching sound underfoot made him uncomfortable, but he was suddenly excited too. Seven feet above his head was a smooth stone slab, and the top of the shaft was lined with matching stone. He was standing in the base of some form of box tomb. Reaching up, he found a broken piece of stone and pushed it. It fell out and a rush of cold air flooded in. He pushed his hand through the hole and felt water dropping onto his skin. The scent of rain slipped into the tomb and he knew that he, Joycey, had found their way out. With sudden haste and hope, he scrambled back to the culvert crawled to the place where the roof dropped. Then he stopped and let out a yell.

Back in the cellar, Takk and Marik had become increasingly anxious since Joycey's light had disappeared and the tunnel had fallen into darkness. They had heard his voice once, and then nothing. They had called, but the only response had been the repeated cold swirl of stench from the darkness.

Now, crouching together in the alcove, they strained to hear as Joycey shouted to them, explaining what he had found and what they needed to do. Takk had to come first and bring the iron bar with her. There was some argument about this. Takk resisted the idea with some heat and was slightly shocked when

Marik responded with unexpected firmness. She had not seen or heard the water springing into the chamber, and he realised it would only be a short time before the water began streaming across the floor towards them. And then, as pressure built up outside, there had to be the possibility that it would burst through suddenly, giving them no time to crawl through the tunnel.

'It better.' He argued. 'You carry this. I...' he waved a hand at his arm apologetically, '...you see.'

Takk glared at him in the semi-darkness and saw the logic of what he was trying to say all too clearly. With an injured arm it was going to be difficult for him to crawl, let alone manoeuvre the iron bar as well.

'All right.' She said decisively. Then, she quickly pulled off her waterproof smock and pushed it into his hands. 'You must bring this, push it in front of you, see? With the belt.'

Marik looked at her quizzically.

'We may need both. We can use them to pull you forward if we need to. Ok?'

He looked doubtful, but nodded obediently. She squeezed his good arm and then said, 'OK, come on then.'

Dropping on to her stomach, Takk crawled into the tunnel. Like Joycey before her, she was quickly aware of every sharp stone that lay on the damp floor as it ground itself into her hands and knees. Before every push forward she thrust the iron bar ahead of her. It wasn't heavy, it was just that after a while having to lift and push it at arms-length was tiring. She had one advantage in that she was smaller and fitter than Joycey, so altogether her progress was no slower. But she was also spurred on by the fact that Marik had to wait for her before he too could begin his journey. However, she soon had a different problem altogether. Five or six minutes after she had begun her crawl, the lamp on her headlight suddenly dimmed and began to flicker. She swore and tore the light from her head with her fingertips. She shook it. It flickered several times and then the tunnel went black.

This time when she swore there were anxious enquiries from ahead and behind. She shouted that her lamp had died and within a few moments she was aware of a glow from behind as Marik directed his torch down the tunnel. Ahead, the light of Joycey's head lamp also appeared in the distance and she had the strangest feeling that she was looking vertically down a very deep well and that he was somewhere at the bottom of it looking up. She began crawling forward again, this time shouting back to Marik to encourage him to begin making his own way. In the virtual darkness around her, she felt damp and cold. And then, with a sudden shock she realised that there was water running past her. It was cold, spilling gently down past her, gradually soaking into the front of her jeans and sweater.

'Marik?' she called, suddenly afraid. 'What's going on?'

There was a long pause and then his response came from some way behind her.

'Is ok.'

The Pole's voice seemed cheerful, reassuringly close behind. She stopped her own uncomfortable movement for a few moments, listening hard. Behind, she could hear the heavy scraping of Marik's boots as he pushed forward, his breathing, strong and urgent, and just a hint of a groan.

'What do you mean, its ok? Where is this water coming from?'

'No worry.' He gasped from behind. 'Keep going, yes?'

There was another sound now, one she did not like at all. It was the sound of water trickling into water, somewhere ahead. Then suddenly she came to the pool of water, to the black gulley, and gave an exclamation of dismay. In response, a light appeared in the tunnel opposite, and Joycey's face appeared. He pushed the torch into the small chamber and for the first time she could see the water running quickly past her from behind, finding its way down into the black pool.

Panting for breath suddenly, she lifted the iron bar and held it out. Joycey grabbed it quickly before it could fall into the unknown depth of the gulley. When he looked at her again she was staring at the pool of water, her eyes dark and wide in the shifting light of his headlamp.

'It's ok,' he reassured her. 'It's only a few feet wide. Put your hands out on either side and push yourself forward.' He pointed with the light to the lips of the side tunnels. A nervous sound escaped from her throat, but she did as directed. 'Now, when I say reach out and grab my hand.'

She nodded and when he said 'Now', she threw her hands forward and grasped his extended arm. Gripping one of her wrists, Joycey pulled until she slid across the cold pool, her face pressing close to his. Then, panting heavily he began backing up the tunnel.

As soon as she felt her knees on the safe side of the tunnel, Takk called back to Marik, urging him forward. But his reply seemed distant, uncertain. Ahead of her Joycey was backing slowly uphill – realising for the first time just how much steeper this tunnel was than the first. He saw Takk hesitating and stopped, staring at her.

'If you stop, Marik won't be able to get through. You have to keep moving.'

Still not completely in the tunnel, Takk could twist enough to see back to where Marik's light was moving in the tunnel behind her The sounds of his movements were slow and heavy, but there was another sound too, that of rushing water, and even as Takk stared, a low wave of water flashed down the tunnel.

'Marik!' she shrieked. 'Hurry.'

There were shouts. Both Marik and Joycey were shouting to her. She kicked wildly at the tunnel floor and began crawling upwards, following Joycey as he backed up the slope. Her breath sounded loud in her ears and she thought it was possible she might even be whimpering in her hurry to get through the tunnel.

Joycey was ahead, the headlamp shining in her eyes, calling her forward, counting off the distance in feet. Then she was suddenly in a more open space. Hands grabbed her and lifted her up. Despite herself she was sobbing. The air was full of strange noises. Crashes, thuds and groans. The ground seemed to shake slightly. Immediately she dropped to her knees and peered down the tunnel. She had thought that Marik would be close behind. But the tunnel was empty and it wasn't possible to see back to the pool, though a light was moving erratically some distance back.

'Marik!' She yelled.

There was no reply. Before Joycey realised what was happening she threw herself down and crawled back into the tunnel. Again she had the advantage of the slope, but now as she advanced there came a sound that filled her with horror. It was the sound of water, pouring in strength and volume, cascading and crashing with sudden violence. Frantic, she crawled forward, ignoring the way her nails splintered painfully on the hard floor, gritting her teeth as sharp stones tore at her palms and thighs.

The light from Marik's head lamp grew gradually brighter, but its effect was distorted, reflected and refracted by splashing water. She was almost crying when she came in sight of the pool, and there she paused as terror finally overwhelmed her. For Marik was lying inside the mouth of the first tunnel, waving one arm, beating it in front of his face as thick jets of water boiled around his body. Somehow the light of his torch was casting his face into shadow so she could not see his expression, but she could tell from his painful, jerky movements that something was badly wrong.

Pushing herself further forward, she could see that the water was pouring thickly around his body, spilling into the dark pool and churning its surface into a violent frenzy. The sound filled the little vault with a terrible cascade of noise. For some reason the water in the shaft hadn't risen, but it heaved and shuddered, and bubbles erupted into the surface like some hideous submarine volcano. The smell was terrible, and she began retching uncontrollably.

On the other side of the pool Marik was struggling, his body twisting and jerking in the confined space as though shocked by sudden volts of electricity. The sounds inside the tunnels began increasing to a frightening volume. Takk screamed Marik's name and reached out a hand.

'Give me the end of the jacket,' she shrieked above the noise.

Marik's eyes met hers and he became still for a moment, the water jetting past his face. He shouted something but it was unintelligible. She screamed again and his face turned towards her, eyes screwed tightly. He shook his head and blinked.

'Leg…stuck,' he yelled. 'Something, caught.'

'The jacket,' she screamed 'I can reach it, pull you…'

There was a sudden crash. A wall of black water exploded into the chamber, as though somewhere above them a waterfall had suddenly opened up. Marik's pale face disappeared for a moment. The light flickered, went dim. Under her face, the black pool heave and boiled and then it began to rise like some irresistible aquatic monster it filled and heaved upwards. There was a loud splash as something heavy fell into the pool.

'Go…Go!' Marik was yelling his good hand waving her backwards.

The air was filled with spray, and clods of what looked like soil were tumbling into the pool and disintegrating into powdery bombs. Suddenly Marik's light went out and he disappeared behind a wall of water and stonework. She screamed his name, unable to believe what was happening in front of her, petrified despite the water that was now rising up around her neck. Suddenly she was under water. She opened her mouth, desperately trying to breathe. Her lungs sucked in water, she vomited painfully and saw blackness. Then suddenly, hands grasped her ankles. She was jerked backwards violently. The water on her face felt like a slurry of soil and weed and rotting decay. She arched her back, pushing her face up and sideways, gagging and gasping for air. Then she was then jerked back again. She spat water and wretched, feeling her lungs vibrating and churning. Another sudden movement and the water swept back past her, like a wave washing up and then back down a beach. She drew a deep breath, coughing and choking as another wave seemed to charge up the slope of the tunnel floor into her face, throwing itself over her shoulders, soaking her clothing, streaming though her hair. Another long pull, and then another. The violent sound in the tunnel seemed to reach a crescendo, the banging of stones and debris echoing loudly in the larger space.

She was still gasping for breath when hands grabbed the

waistband of her jeans and pulled her back into a crouching position. She knelt, her face pressed to the floor, coughing, spitting and breathing as though through shredded lungs. The taste in her mouth was indescribable and her nose seemed full of slime.

'Marik?' Joycey knelt beside her.

She looked up at him and then stared at the tunnel, as though expecting the young Pole to appear there. Joycey read her expression with a mixture of disbelief and horror. Then he threw himself down and crawled into the tunnel again. As soon as he did, he knew the worst. He didn't have to see it, he could feel it.

Then, with a suddenness that was almost as violent, the terrible maelstrom subsided. There were several isolated crashes, things splashing in the darkness, and then a stillness that was as harsh as his own fearful breathing. Ahead of him the tunnel was full of water. The light of his lamp turned the surface into a distorted mirror of brown and gold. It shimmered, rippled and then convulsed. And as it did so it began to ebb away, as though flowing down some gigantic drain. He crawled forward several feet, following it as it began to subside.

Behind him came Takk's tremulous enquiry. He called back, telling her to wait, trying to sound in some way reassuring. Then the water stopped. It convulsed again, filling the tunnel in front of him as though someone somewhere was maliciously stirring a great tank of water. It had stopped receding. The tunnel ahead was completely flooded.

'Marik?' Joycey shouted once, desperately. His voice echoed back at him from the walls and the surface of the water. Nothing moved, nothing spoke. And after a long moment, he began the painful crawl backwards up the slope of the tunnel to where Takk was waiting.

She was sat, hunched in a corner of the vault, fists wrapped in the cuffs of her dirty, sodden jumper. Her eyes were darker than usual, her face blacked and grimed, with white streaks down the cheeks. Her eyes caught Joycey's as he turned and rose from the tunnel and she gave a quiet, trembling wail.

'No.'

Joycey shook his head.

'I don't know, girl. Can't see anything.' Words struggled to find an order in his mind, fought to attach themselves to something meaningful, and failed. He sat down next to her and slid an arm round her shoulders. She was rigid with emotion, angry and distraught, confused and yet determined in some way that she couldn't resolve. After several minutes she spoke.

'He can't be...,' her voice tailed off.

'I don't know,' Joycey shook his head. 'I...just don't know. Perhaps he managed to escape the other way.' He rubbed his face with gritty hands and then sighed resignedly. Even he knew that he didn't sound convincing. 'We'd better get out of here anyway.'

Takk was sniffing. Controlling emotion. She cleared her throat and swallowed heavily.

'Is there a way?'

Climbing stiffly to his feet, Joycey helped her up and, picking up the iron bar, led the way to the top of the earth slide and the base of the tomb. For several long moments they stood, staring up towards the slab over their head, and then down at the splinters of wood and bone beneath their feet. Then, at last Joycey took the bar and tried to strike a blow against the wall of the tomb. The effort was too much and in the end, Takk had to climb onto his back and poke away at the broken stone. Then, as more and more fragments of the stone fell way, the shaft around her head was lightened by grey light infused with sweeping, flashing blue and yellow lights, and there came the occasional and strangely welcoming sound of sirens.

43. A view from the river

Out on the black swirl of the river the police launch *John Harriott* was rocking gently. In the stuffy warmth of the cabin, PC Jane Roscoe was staring intently at the twisting brown water, watching it as glittering gold and red flecks twisted and scattered and span across the surface of the river. It always amazed her that people would pay so much money for fireworks and yet, had they bothered to look, they could see the most astonishing light show of all for free, on the surface of the Thames. Of course, it was really only best seen from a boat out in the middle of it, and knowing where on the river to be was also pretty important. Upriver of the Thames Barrier was always a good position, especially when the barrier was closing, when the warning lights started to flash and the frustrated waters of the falling river surged and writhed in frustration. Mind you, the barrier wasn't closed that often, so it was a rare treat to watch – and Jane made sure she was there when possible - as she was now, in the early hours, with the other members of the crew dozing in the fug of the cabin.

Below her feet, the powerful engines of the launch throbbed quietly, puttering every now and again as the stern rose, lifting the exhaust from the water. She turned the wheel, slowly nudging the bows up into the falling current of the river. The Barrier might hold back the incoming tide, but the Thames still tried to find its inexorable way to the sea. At the steel walls of the barrier it was forced to turn in a turmoil of eddies and rippling currents. The launch lurched through these and began an idle movement up Bugsby's Reach. Jane ducked her head to see the second great light show, the towers and floodlights of the O2 Dome. On good nights the towers pulsated with different coloured lights. At first she had mocked them as gaudy barbecue skewers, but over time she had become fond of the sight. Now the blue lights of the towers rippled along the surface, throwing into deeper shadow the black edges of the river where the few older industrial yards lay silent. As they neared the dome, the riverside began to rise and glow with the more recently built apartment blocks. The syringe shaped Edwardian Hotel, built on the site of the old East India Docks. She often wondered whether the people who stayed there or who occupied the more expensive upper apartments, realised the history that lay beneath their feet. The launch swung around Blackwall Point, passing under the looming hump of the O2.

'Blackwall Point.' Jane mused quietly. Every member of the river police was told about the history of the river, and of the gibbet cages that were used to hang felons and pirates. And there had been one there on Blackwall Point, clearly visible for ages as ships worked their way up or down the river. Jane was not unimaginative. She could recreate the dark shape of the cage with its gruesome contents silhouetted against the glittering amber walls of the O2.

For a moment her reverie was distracted by the low crackling of voices on the radio. Communications had been steady but comparatively quiet all night. She preferred it that way. The occasional message from the base at Wapping; some small boat-to-boat chatter, but very little of that as there was virtually nothing on the river now. Occasional banter with the up-river launch. She listened idly, the oval reflection of her face and the green and orange lights of the launch's console reflecting in the glass windshield in front of her. Her face a ghostly impression on the riverscape. Streaks of rain suddenly wrapped themselves across the glass in front of her, shattering themselves with a sound like shingle on the cabin roof. She switched on the wipers and watched as orange clouds of rain began sweeping across the river.

In the distance now, the elegant white colonnades and facades of the old Royal Naval College, still and ethereal in the light. The night's Conditions Briefing had warned them that the tide would be unusually high. And they weren't kidding. The river was already over the riverside walk in front of the naval college, and as the launch passed slowly, the ripples of its wake sent flickers of light running across the wide lawns of the College itself. Jane turned the launch in a slow arc to get a better view. She had never seen the river this high. There was surely going to be flooding somewhere?

At that moment, there was a louder burst of static on the radio and a heavily distorted voice. She listened, shook her head, and picked up the handset.

'This is the duty boat *John Harriott*. Could you repeat please?. Over.'

Again there was a buzz of static, irritating and unintelligible. Jane frowned and shook her head.

'Wapping, I'm getting too much interference. Must be unusual atmospherics. I'll motor up towards Convoy's Wharf, reception is usually better there.'

The radio was silent. Then it buzzed again angrily and a voice cut in.

'Jane, we have a report of someone in the water near Wapping Old Stairs. Unconfirmed but...,' the voice broke off suddenly and then there was a buzz of voices. 'Jane, it's all kicking off by the sound of it. Better make your way up towards Limehouse as fast as you can. Over.'

'Understood. Over.'

Jane turned towards the dark slumbering forms of her colleagues and shouted,

'Ok you lazy sods, work to do. Going Forward!'

She pushed forward on the launch's throttles and beneath her feet, the powerful engines rumbled into life. As Charlie White and Hamish Davis grabbed suddenly at anything to stop themselves sliding to the floor, the bows rose sharply, the launch dug its stern in the water and accelerated into the wind and waves.

Charlie White appeared beside her...a little too close beside her, rubbing his face and blinking. 'What's happening?'

Jane shrugged, allowing her elbow to dig him slightly in the ribs. 'Don't know. Possibly a body in the river at Wapping. Perhaps more.'

The launch bounced and twisted its way up past the ever glittering towers of Canary Wharf, and swung round Cuckold's Point, past Rotherhithe, and slowly bringing the distant lights of Tower Bridge into view. As they ran up towards the Lower Pool they saw lights flashing on the north bank. Blue lights, yellow lights.

'That's Pier Head,' Jane called out, her voice sharp above the thunder of the engines and the vibration of the launch's panelling. She began to edge the boat away from the calmer waters near the south bank, moving out into the greater turbulence in the centre. Above their heads the radio was crackling and a several voices were conversing in urgent tones.

Charlie White pulled some binoculars from a rack and began focussing them on the far riverside. After a few moments he whistled quietly.

What is it?' Hamish Davis appeared, clutching at the console.

'We-ell,' the older man began, 'it looks to me as though part of the river wall has collapsed.'

As the boat drew nearer they could see, through the increasingly driving rain, the shapes of fire tenders, and other construction vehicles manoeuvring into position. Someone was also shining a powerful lamp onto the surface of the river.

The radio crackled again.

'*John Harriott, John Harriott*, are you receiving, over?'

Jane picked up the hand-mike and pressed its transmit button. 'This is the *John Harriott*, receiving you. Over.'

'Jane, we've had a garbled message that there may be two men in the water. Urm, it's possible they are both police officers. And they may have been in the water some time.'

Jane and Charlie White exchanged grim glances. In these conditions and at this time of the year, survival times were going to be severely shortened.

'Understood. Any other information you can gave us? Over.'

The radio crackled and clicked several times and then the voice came back with a slightly apologetic tone.

'Sorry, all we know is that someone has reported two

police officers being trapped on the river's edge and then being washed into the river near Pier Head. Over.'

'What river's edge?' Hamish snorted.

And indeed, the river was washing slowly close to the high embankment. The foreshore was somewhere deep under the curling darkness and had been for hours. And as they moved closer to Pier Head they could indeed see that the heavy masonry of the wall had collapsed and water had poured into the breach in front of the Georgian houses, creating a gently heaving lagoon of shrubbery, tree branches and twisted iron railings. Figures in bright yellow waterproof suits were milling around in what seemed, from the river, to be total confusion.

Jane swung the launch past the chaos and began a slow motor past several heavy iron lighters, lifting and falling with threateningly heavy movements on the water, clanking ominously as they did so. A searing beam of light suddenly swept across the surface of the water in front of them. Hamish was on deck, and the Sergeant bellowed to him to make sure he was clipped-on. Hamish's reply was swept away in the scudding wind and rain, and Jane peered carefully around, watching the swinging iron monsters and the spattered yellow surface of the river, but knowing that in reality, there was not a hope.

44. A face on the screen

They drove back in heavy silence. Joycey had found some tobacco in the clutter on the dashboard and managed to roll a cigarette. He had offered it to Takk, but she had pulled a face and then turned away to press her forehead against the side window. Now, she was at least grateful for the stale fragrance of the smoke, for the reek of their clothes as they began to warm inside the van was almost too much to bear, as was the terrible aching anguish inside her chest.

Dawn was breaking as they cleared the Blackwall Tunnel and turned off towards East Greenwich. Joycey felt miserable and inadequate in the presence of the young woman in the seat next to him. Despite the time they had spent together, he realised now that he hardly knew her, and because of this, he didn't know how to reach out to her, to bridge that terrible gap between them. She was obviously silently distraught, her body wracked every now and again by fiercely restrained sobs. He didn't know what to say, how to break that awful silence. He hadn't even begun to face his own emotional turmoil. In such a short time, so much had happened. But a few hours before, the hunt for Kidd's treasure had seemed comparatively harmless, innocent in spite of all the apparent threats fired in their direction. Now all that had changed. And Marik...

Joycey found that he was biting his lip, searching deep within for that tough old shell that had served him for so long. He kept trying to recall Joycey Becket, the Greenwich wheeler dealer, fly boy of the Deptford Market, scourge of the scavenger sellers. But somehow all he could feel was a weakened, shattered wraith of his former self.

Without speaking or even looking to the side, he drove straight past Marik's flat. He really wanted to pick up Mickey, to literally bury his nose in the cat's fur and feel him purring quietly in that innocent reassurance that cats have. But he couldn't go there yet. And he couldn't just abandon Takk either.

He managed to find a vacant parking space in Straightsmouth and located one of several parking permits that he had acquired over the past few years. Then he helped Takk from the van and putting an arm round her shoulders, led her to his house. It struck him how strange this was. Under his arm she felt frail, insubstantial, as though the strong spring that had kept her so taut had snapped. They were still without words as he let her settle on his sofa while he went to make a hot drink. It had to be black coffee, there was no milk. But at least there was sugar, and Joycey always had a good coffee in the house.

When he took the mug in to her, he put the television on and watched as she gazed at it momentarily, as though stupefied, before turning to face the back of the sofa and curling into a tight ball. Sometime later he checked on her again and found that she was asleep. He put a fleecy blanket over her and turned the volume low on the television. Then he climbed the stairs with stiff, aching limbs, showered and threw himself onto his bed. There would be time later to talk or do whatever was necessary. Now there was only the need for sleep.

But sleep was a reluctant partner. It kept disappearing into a dark void. And in the imagery that filled his thoughts as he lay there, black water and dark subterranean passages turned round and round as though twisted by a child's kaleidoscope in a malignant hand. And gradually the true horror crept over him. His ability to resist his feelings about Marik disappeared, as though the dark waters of the Thames had dissolved the barriers like evil sugar. And in the bleak space that was created there, he saw Marik trapped as the waters engulfed him. Reaching out for help with his one good arm. Gasping as the waters filled his eyes and ears and mouth and nostrils. And then Marik was crying, quietly, sadly, alone and abandoned, while the waters full of black rags and shreds of weed swept over him, and erased him. Joycey awoke, and he was crying.

For a long time he lay there, unable to move, but the demands of his tired body had their way in the end. He fell into a deep slumber, so deep that no thoughts or images could penetrate it. It lasted so long and was so profound that he was completely unaware that the bedroom door opened and Takk's stained and scratched face appeared for several moments, surveying him as he lay there. Then she nodded silently to herself and silently made her way back down the stairs.

When Joycey woke, it was not because he was refreshed. Far from it. He woke because Takk was shrieking in a voice that he imagined must have been the closest she got to hysterical. He leapt from the bed fearful of the state of mind to which she must have plummeted in her grief to make such a noise. But, bursting into the front room, he found her pointing excitedly at the television and jigging up and down like a demented rubber puppet. He looked at the screen and stopped dead. For there on the screen. Sitting in an ambulance, swathed in red blankets, was

Marik. He gaped and looked again. There was no doubt about it. The man in the ambulance was definitely Marik.

'Quick,' Takk screeched. 'Where's the remote? Turn the volume up.'

By the time Joycey had fumbled through the mess of newspapers, CD's and other items still homeless after the break-in, the news story had moved on. Hunched side-by-side in front of the television they peered at the screen as Joycey searched channel after channel for the latest news. And at last they found what they were looking for. A morning newsflash.

'Reports have been coming in for the past two hours of a major flooding alert here in the centre of London.'

The prim, carefully made-up early-morning face of the newscaster disappeared to be replaced by dark film work showing the Thames and lots of flashing lights. The newscaster's voice continued.

'London emergency services were put on standby in the early hours of this morning after reports were received of a breach in the river wall at Wapping in East London. Our reporter Elizabeth England is there on the spot.'

A bedraggled looking young woman in a bright yellow hi-visibility jacket appeared on the screen, her blonde hair whipping violently to one side as she stood in front of the grey river.

'Yes thank you Susan. I'm here at Pier Head, just downstream from Tower Bridge where, at about two o'clock this morning, an off-duty police officer witnessed the collapse of the river wall.'

The screen changed abruptly to show a massive pile of rubble and stonework, now lapped by the gradually receding river. The camera turned to show the old Georgian terraces beside the old dock entrance. The iron-railed garden in front of them had gone. A great hollow of fallen trees, shrubs and rubble lay there instead, as though the ground had opened up in an attempt to swallow what was there before. The reporter appeared on screen again.

'Local residents reported hearing a loud bang and at first thought there had been a terrorist attack. The Fire Service were called immediately, and on their arrival found this scene of devastation. It is now believed that the river must have undermined the more recent structure installed after the closure of the entrance to the London Docks in the 1980s.'

The face of the newscaster appeared.

'And of course, last night saw exceptional weather conditions. That must have contributed to the damage?'

The reporter appeared again.

'Well yes. Last night there was one of the North Sea's rare tidal surges, similar to the one that devastated Canvey Island over fifty years ago. You may remember that these surges are caused by the coincidence of wind and tide forcing a particularly high flood back into the bottleneck of the Thames Estuary – and on this occasion, that flood met the waters of the Thames heavily swollen by heavy rainfall. The Thames Barrier was raised to defend the city, but it obviously proved just too much here at Wapping.'

The newscaster was seen frowning.

'And I understand that there may have been casualties?'

'Yes, it is thought that two police officers who went to the aid of another man who may have fallen in to the river, are missing. We have yet to receive confirmation of this, but there is at least one known survivor who was rescued from the collapsed river wall just a few hours ago.'

The view switched to the back of an ambulance, and there, sure enough was Marik, wrapped in a red blanket and grinning sheepishly as the doors were closed. The Newscaster's serious expression appeared again. 'Has anything been said about the reported explosion?'

'Not officially, though a Senior Fire Officer has said that they are keeping an open mind about the possible detonation of a Second World War bomb, of which many are thought to still lie undetected under the streets of East London.'

The newscaster appeared again looking serious.

'This will presumably encourage further criticism of the Mayor of London for his failure to commit funding to the renewal of flood defences for the capital?'

'Yes indeed. In fact environmental campaigners are already issuing calls this morning for a public enquiry, and this can only add to the growing pressure on the Mayor to take action on behalf of Londoners.'

'Thank you Elizabeth. And we will hear more about that situation later. And now lets' get an update on the weather situation.'

Takk turned to look at Joycey and was moved to see that tears were streaming down his face. She beamed at him.

'How....?'

He shrugged, beginning to feel embarrassed.

'I got no idea. The tricky little bastard. Just wait til I see him.'

Then they both began to laugh.

45. The story so far

The media had a story and they were happy with it: London's aging flood defences, so often criticised, had been proved to be inadequate. The Mayor of London was challenged and then castigated for spending all his energy on another proposal for a new airport, when the real need lay in controlling not the airways but the seaway. London's ancient river wall was bound to weaken over time. Little attention had been given to it. The various authorities protested, argued and fell-out out very publicly. Insurance companies prevaricated and angry local residents formed campaign groups and lobbied parliament.

There was considerable interest in the role of the off-duty policeman who had witnessed the collapse of the river wall, and it was confirmed that two officers were missing, presumably drowned in an attempt to rescue a man who had been asleep in the little park at the time of the incident. A body recovered from the river at Erith several days later was identified as a Detective Sergeant Martin.

The off-duty officer who had reported the incident initially was found to be in a state of deep shock. He was admitted for medical treatment but was unable to give any further information or explanation of the events.

The man the doomed policemen had been attempting to rescue, and who was pulled from the river later, was a Mr Marik Makowski. Mr Makowski was interviewed by the police but all he could tell them was that he had been drinking in a pub somewhere in the East End – he couldn't remember which one – and that he had gone to sleep on a bench in the park. Several television crews attempted to film interviews with him, but they gave up in the face of his more than hesitant grasp of English.

A week later the third page of the East End Advertiser carried a story questioning the coincidental vandalism of one of the ancient tombs in the old St. John's churchyard at Wapping. It was astonishing, the paper noted, that such vandalism should occur on the same night as the collapse of the river wall, and within two hundred yards of both Pierhead and the Wapping police station. This story soon faded from public interest for everyone except Joycey, Takk and Marik.

On discovering Marik's escape, Takk and Joycey had quickly discovered that he had been taken to the nearby Royal London Hospital, with cuts and bruises and a puncture wound to his right arm. They arrived there just as Marik was being discharged by a concerned looking nurse. For a moment the three of them had stood in silence, glancing from one to another to see who would speak first while a suspicious looking uniformed police officer watched them. Then Takk had broken the impasse by punching the young Pole very hard on his uninjured arm, Marik yelped, the nurse protested loudly and the policeman laughed. Then the three of them hurried out of the building as fast as they could – partly to get away from the police scrutiny and partly because Joycey had left the van on double yellow lines.

That evening, back in Marik's flat, the three met again to

eat, picking their way through an Indian take-away meal laid out in front of them in silver foil trays. Joycey was unusually silent. He had kept away all afternoon, reasonably sensing that they wanted time together after the ordeal underground. When he saw their faces that evening he knew he had been right and he felt an unusual satisfaction in his own judgement in this unfamiliar territory. He was, however, on tenterhooks with regard to one issue, and eventually he reached the point where he could no longer contain the vital question.

'So how did you get out of that tunnel then?'

Marik stopped chewing for a moment and glanced quickly at Takk. Then he blushed and shrugged. 'I get out.'

'Yeah, well I can see that. But you're not telling me you just walked out of there! There has to be more to it than that.'

Marik was looking disconcerted now. His mouth worked and he looked distinctly sheepish. But it was Takk who spoke.

'What he isn't telling you,' she laughed, '…though I don't know why he's so coy about it, is that he did his national service in an engineer battalion in the Polish Army. His specialism was working underwater on bridge building and demolition.'

Marik nodded enthusiastically, giving Takk a long and grateful look.

'Blimey,' Joycey had put his fork down. 'I didn't know they did National Service in Poland.'

'They don't any more. Marik was among the last to be called-up for it.'

Joycey grinned at the young Pole. 'Dark horse, isn't he. Just as well though. Given the circumstances.'

There was silence for a moment and then Joycey asked,

with his mouth full, 'So how'd he get out with that arm then?'

Marik nodded again. 'Ok, Ok,' he sighed, 'this I can tell you.'

They waited while he took a sip from a glass of water.

'I wait till water fill space, then I swim.'

'But I thought you were trapped?' Joycey murmured. 'Your legs were trapped.'

'Yes, but water lifted weight. Concrete. Weight come off and I swim.'

Takk was frowning doubtfully. So was Joycey.

'But how did you swim? Where?'

Here the Pole looked confused. 'To left like this.' He wiggled his left arm to the side like a fish.

'But where…how?'

Again the Pole shrugged. 'Water came. Boom. Like big wave. And then, wood, water, and at last I breathe, yes?'

'You telling me you were holding your breath?' Joycey grunted, unconsciously rolling a cigarette.

'Yes. I learn this. Good eh?'

They laughed, nodding at what was clearly something of an understatement.

Later they also tried to piece together the sequence of events of the previous night. Their interpretation – the most likely that they could agree upon, was that somebody had detonated some sort of explosive charge in the tunnel. Joycey thought that it had been the policemen's plan to blow up the tunnel to hide all evidence of the chamber or anything which might help incriminate them and prevent anyone escaping. However, something had gone wrong. He suggested that perhaps Martin and his colleagues had been in such a panic to get back into the main tunnel, they had placed the charge in the wrong place. It had gone off but instead of bringing down just the roof over the old steps, it had brought down part of the tunnel too. The policemen had probably found that they too were trapped, or at least unable to escape as quickly as they had planned. By the time they had got out of the wrecked tunnel, the river was much higher and they had either tried to swim for it, or they were literally swept away as they tried to wade along the river's edge. One of Martin's accomplices had apparently survived, and all that he had been able to suggest was that they had come across the collapse by chance and had tried to investigate it, with disastrous consequences.

Takk and Marik thought about this for a while. But then Takk pointed out that the alarmed shouts they had heard while they were lying in the chamber had occurred before the explosion. Something else had happened which DS Martin and the other men had not anticipated. Perhaps Christopher Keeley had intervened after all.

Several days later it was reported that during their work to repair the damage to the site, Council engineers had discovered a disused cellar, and it was widely believed that this had contributed to the collapse of the river wall. There was no mention of an ancient corpse, nor was there anything said about treasure, rubies or anything else. As Joycey noted with his usual cynicism, the London newspapers were far more interested in the potential insurance liability on the Georgian houses than a seventeenth century cellar.

With nothing to show for their experiences but cuts and bruises – slightly more serious in Marik's case - and the photocopy of Kidd's manuscript, Marik and Joycey soon returned to the much more reliable routine of the little book shop in East Greenwich. Takk, on the other hand wanted understanding. She returned to her formal studies, but spent all her spare time poring over the known details of the Kidd episode and the mystery surrounding the manuscript and cellar – much of which she did either at Marik's flat or the bookshop, where Joycey had, with some pleasure, installed a desk for her to use.

Christmas came and passed. Takk came and went, sometimes disappearing for days on research projects – for which she was now being paid on a free-lance basis by different London universities. Then one afternoon in early May, she arrived at the shop looking unspeakably pleased with herself. She sat herself down in the shop and waited until Joycey was visibly beside himself with frustrated curiosity.

'I know what happened to Captain Kidd's treasure.' She announced at last.

They stared at her for a moment. Joycey felt a sudden deflation.

'Someone nicked it.'

Takk's grin didn't falter, but she shook her head, slowly, knowingly.

'How do you two boys fancy a day trip out to the country?'

46. The Suffolk Connection

Marik was driving. Takk was in the passenger seat and Joycey was sitting in the back where he could open a window so that the smoke from his roll-ups could cause less offence. They weren't in the battered old van either. For the slightly longer trip that Takk had planned, she had insisted they borrow or hire something both a little more reliable and lot more reputable. So it was that less than a week later, the three of them were enjoying the comfort of a borrowed and rather aged BMW as it rumbled its way up the uneven road surface of the A13 towards Ipswich.

Takk had remained tight lipped about the reason for the trip and even once the journey was underway she refused point blank to give away any information.

'Wait, wait and see. It'll prove more interesting. You'll see,' was all she would offer.

Clutching a large road map she gave a series of directions and just over two hours after they had left Greenwich, Marik turned right at a small roundabout and drove up hill into a neat looking little market town.

'Bungay.' Joycey read as they passed the sign beside the

road. 'This looks fun,' he said drily.

Takk just laughed quietly and gave further directions to a car park just outside the centre of the little town. Then they walked the hundred yards back into what appeared to have been a small market place, where a triangle of buildings enclosed a domed Georgian shelter that Takk thought had once been a corn market. A steady flow of traffic streamed through the town despite its small size and they found themselves walking in single file along a narrow pavement until Joycey stopped resolutely outside an old-looking pub on the high street.

'The Fleece,' he called out meaningfully. 'Looks as good a place to eat as any.'

Takk gave Marik a sideways grin and they followed Joycey as he ducked under the low doorway, stepping down into the dark, beamed interior. The bar was decorated with old agricultural tools, and shelves of books lined a large chimney breast in which a wood fire was quietly popping sparks. They ordered food and drinks and then Takk waited patiently while Joycey stood at the bar thirstily swigging back a whole point before sitting down with a fresh one. Then she took the ubiquitous tablet from her bag, gave them both a broad grin, and said:

'I think that I have now solved the mystery of Kidd's treasure. And I think I also know what happened to Captain Kidd.'

'Is that why you brought us all the way up here?' Joycey interrupted. 'And are you going to tell us Captain Kidd wasn't hung after all?'

Takk grinned and held up a stern finger. 'Just you wait. All will be revealed in due course.'

Joycey grumbled and settled himself more comfortably on the bench cushion. More discomforted by the obvious enjoyment which Takk was getting out of this than by the distance they had travelled.

'Well at least the beer is good,' he mumbled

'Good. Are you ready?'

'Yeah, alright.'

Takk laughed quietly to herself. 'Ok, well, to get the gist of this, we need to do a quick recap on what is already known. Ok?'

The two men nodded obediently. And Takk's face became serious.

'We know that having plundered several ships, Captain Kidd arrived back in the Caribbean with his treasure in April 1699 and, as he later claimed, he left it there in a secret location, on board the *Quedah Merchant*. Yes?'

Joycey and Marik frowned, trying to recall the story, then nodded.

'But realising that he might be betrayed by the syndicate, he really brought the treasure back to London and hid it in the cellar of the Sugar Loaf. That voyage, which he never admitted to, explained the missing ten months in his story, between June 1698 and April 1699.'

The two men were now concentrating closely.

Takk continued. 'Kidd's plan was to try and do a deal with the Tories to save his own life. But as we know that failed and he was sentenced to death. However, I think there was a Plan B.'

'Go on.' Joycey selected a match and started nibbling the end.

'We know that Kidd had relatives in London - Sarah and Matthew Hawkins - and that they had been turned away when they tried to visit him in prison. I think they may have been involved in some sort of attempt to get him out. Then the trial took place and Kidd was sentenced to death. But, as I said, Kidd may have had a Plan B. And that is where the letter comes in.'

Joycey nodded slowly in encouragement.

'But before we look at that, let's just consider what we do know. Kidd's attempt to do a deal with the Tories failed and he was executed and his body was gibbeted at Tilbury. And according to the information you found at the Local History Library, some months later Sarah Hawkins disappeared and was presumed drowned.'

Again Joycey nodded. Marik was gazing at Takk intently.

'The critical thing about Sarah Hawkins is that since it was presumed that she had drowned, there was an air of uncertainty. So,' she paused thoughtfully. 'Sarah certainly disappeared, a body may have been found, but no-one knew anything for certain. However, we know that the treasure had been stashed away in the cellar of the Sugar Loaf and a man, not Kidd, had been murdered there.'

'Ok,' Joycey was looking slightly bewildered.

'So. The cellar of the Sugar Loaf was chosen because it was convenient, being close to the river. But is that the only reason it was chosen?'

'How do you mean?' Joycey frowned.

'Ok let's look at the letter again.' Takk pulled out the

tablet and pulled up the image of the letter. Joycey, squinting through his glasses, read it aloud.

'*Cous*

Since it must be I am condemned to dye, I have writ his ldship this day and told him of what is to be offered if he will secure what I wish I am assured he will bee honble to this but as I doubt not some trickery might befall from other honble gentlemen known to you Whereof do you beg our friend H remove that we bt from the Old Mrcht in the woes If he cavilles show him this He will know all as we spoke thereof Doe not trust ye Dowgat man The silks you may take to the mercer in Cheapside the value thereof to have unto yrslf Wm

April 29th *1701'*

Joycey shook his head and looked at Marik. 'Nah. Still don't get it. Do you?'

Marik shook his head slowly.

Takk sighed with suppressed impatience. 'Ok, who is the letter addressed to?'

'His Cousin.'

'Exactly. Now 'cousin' was used as an affectionate term. If the letter had been written to Matthew Hawkins, it would have been written 'Sir'. So it wasn't written to Matthew Hawkins. In fact I think the 'H' referred to is Matthew Hawkins. And since the letter refers to Matthew Hawkins as 'H' it must have been obvious to the recipient who 'H' was. Therefore It must have been written to Sarah.

And the implication is also that H, that is Matthew, may have been in some way be reluctant to help. So, why was it Kidd trusted Sarah and not her husband?'

The two men looked blank.

Takk groaned. 'Think about it guys! What was going on?'

There was a bleak silence in response. Takk groaned again.

'When Kidd first arrived in London he stayed with Matthew and Sarah Hawkins. But a year or so later when he is looking for somewhere to stash his treasure, somewhere where he can trust someone to look after it, he thinks of Sarah and the Sugar Loaf. Why? Because they were having an affair.' Takk's voice had risen in excitement. 'Don't you get it? It fits.'

Joycey was looking unconvinced.

'I think that when the attempt to do a deal with the Tories failed, and Sarah failed to spring him from Newgate, she and Kidd came up with another plan. But whatever they were going to try and do depended on Hawkins co-operation. And it may be that Hawkins suspected or found out about Sarah's infidelity. The letter was meant to initiate the plan. If Matthew failed to cooperate, she was meant to show him the letter to make him realise that he was implicated anyway.'

'Blackmail!' Joycey exclaimed. 'It was blackmail then. But in the end he was hung and she drowned. So it don't really matter.' Joycey finished his pint and sat looking wistfully at the empty glass.

Takk was grinning provocatively and fell silent, so that slowly Marik and Joycey started to feel uncomfortable as though they had missed something important, like the punchline of a joke. Finally it was Marik who broke the spell.

'This not so? This...um, not truth of what happened?'

Takk shook her head very slowly, her eyes fixing them in their seats. She took a slow, irritating drink from her glass.

'Do you remember,' she said at last, 'the account of Kidd's execution?'

'Yeh, kind of.' Joycey nodded

'Remember there was something unusual about it?'

'Um' Joycey looked frantically at Marik. Marik frowned and then spoke hesitatingly.

'He fell. The rope it broke.'

Takk nodded.

'Hmmm, yes. According to the records Kidd was carried on a cart from Newgate in the early afternoon and paraded through the streets all the way down to Wapping. Apparently a large number of people turned out to see him, and there was a massive crowd milling around on the Thames foreshore. It was low tide and the gallows would have been set up on the shingle.

The river was wider then than it is today, but Wapping High Street was already built up, with buildings and structures all along the river wall. There would not have been a huge amount of space. Things probably got crowded, chaotic. Hundreds, possibly thousands of excited people milling round. The London mob. But this crowd was very different to the sort who normally turned out for a hanging at Tyburn. This was Wapping. And many of those who turned out here were seafarers or their families.'

Joycey and Marik were listening intently.

'There were two contemporary accounts of the execution, both printed within hours of the event and according to both, Kidd was roaring drunk by the time he arrived at the gallows.

Now, the official account was written and printed by the Chaplain of Newgate prison, and printing and selling accounts of the last hours of convicted criminals was one of the perks of his job. The more famous or infamous the victim, the more money he stood to make. However, because he was a State official, his printed narrative of the execution also had to reinforce the authority of the State. So, no matter who the victim was, at the last minute he or she had to recant, renounce their evil ways, and urge all right thinking people to live a lawful and righteous life.'

'Fuck me.' Joycey muttered under his breath. Takk ignored him.

'The point was that the State didn't want any folk heroes being created. But in both of the printed accounts of his execution, Kidd was angry and refused to repent. He used his final speech to condemn the corrupt and wealthy and to denounce the Whig Lords. The crowd themselves were drunk, excited and were probably whipped-up by what was tantamount to an inflammatory speech.'

The two men nodded, imagining the scene. Takk continued.

'Now, remember that several other men were being executed at the same time. The Admiralty Officers were probably getting worried about the state of the crowd by this time, so they hurried though the usual formality and opened the trap door.' Takk took a drink. 'And as we know, the rope round Kidd's neck broke and he fell though the trap door onto the mud beneath, probably falling in front of the huge crowd of onlookers.' She paused for effect. 'Doesn't it strike you as odd that of all the ropes that were being used in the execution it should be the one round Kidd's neck that broke?'

Marik and Joycey exchanged glances.

'And there is something else. According to the Chaplain's account - the official account - Kidd was so shocked when the rope broke that he sobered up immediately, became placid and compliant, and appeared to be on his knees praying before finally being turned off for the second time. The unofficial account actually seems to concur at this point that Kidd finally died quietly.'

Joycey sat back in his chair looking puzzled.

'You could almost say,' Takk said with quiet emphasis, 'that he was a different man when they finally hung him.'

There was a moment of silence, then an exclamation exploded from Joycey's lips, bringing disapproving looks from various parts of the bar.

'You think they switched him!' he gasped. 'When he fell. They had the rope cut through and then when he fell, they smuggled him away.'

Takk nodded. 'Probably used some of the opium from the treasure to drug some poor innocent, and substituted him during the commotion.'

Joycey swore again, his eyes glinting with admiration. And at that point their food arrived.

47. Captain Kidd

'I still don't get why we've come all the way here.' Said Joycey, dabbing bread onto a smear of pickle.

'Well, if you've finished,' Takk rose eagerly, 'I'll explain why.'

The two men rose obediently and followed Takk from the bar, blinking into what had turned out to be a bright, sunlit afternoon. From the pub she led them straight across the road and into a churchyard. It was dominated by an impressive grey and white flint tower. But she didn't stop there. Instead she led them on through the back of the churchyard to another, quiet road on the edge of an escarpment. There she stopped, letting them admire the view over the eastern side of the little town.

'In 1688 there was a serious fire here which destroyed much of the town and it took years for the place to be rebuilt. Fortunately, Bungay was quite wealthy. The town benefited from the corn trade with London. Boats took the stuff downriver from here to Lowestoft, and from there it was shipped round to the Thames. Even so, it wasn't until about 1710 that the place was fully restored.'

Joycey nodded, his interest clearly beginning to wane.

'Anyway, a large part of the cost of the rebuilding of the town came from the local corn merchants, so the townspeople thought quite highly of them.' She turned and began walking southwards along the road. 'But Bungay had another church at that time. Holy Trinity. In fact, it's not far from this one, and it's older and, I think a lot more interesting.'

They followed rather meekly until they saw through a clump of trees beside the road ahead, a round stone tower of mellow stone which was glowing gold in the sunlight. Behind it the roof of the nave provided a soft terracotta backdrop.

'So what is this, a guided tour?' Joycey grumbled quietly, to be quickly silenced by one of Takk's fierce looks.

Without speaking she led them round the church and into the cool white-washed interior. Inside, shafts of sunlight bathed the bleached timber of old wooden box pews and, as they entered, there was a fragrance of freshly cut flowers. Takk grinned conspiratorially and slid into one of the pews in the side aisle. Marik slid onto the pew next to her, and Joycey took the one in front, sitting sideways to face the young woman's grin.

'I like this church,' she said. 'It survived the fire. Wasn't touched at all. And I came here quite by chance one day several months ago. A guy doing research into the East Anglian Corn Trade sent me some information about the merchants of this town. And there was something in it which struck me as very curious. So I did a bit more digging and then I found something interesting. Something very interesting.'

She produced the tablet again and, with evident relish, found an image and held it up for them to see. It was an image of a printed page from an old newspaper. It was enlarged so the lettering looked blotched and clumsy. At the top someone had annotated in a modern hand:

'*The Ipswich Journal July 7th 1715.*'

Joycey put one hand on the corner of the tablet, tilted his head back slightly to see better through his glasses, and began to read.

'*On Monday last was buried at Bungay Captain William Hawkins, merchant of that town aged sixty nine years. His corpse was interred at the Holy Trinity Church with a most unusual memorial in the south aisle. His interment was attended by many of that place and the chief mourners were Dundee, his truly lamenting servant, a Negro, and his wife etc.*'

Joycey frowned. His mouth opened and he made a soft grunting noise, then he read on.

'*Captain Hawkins, being a person of known probity and integrity was mourned by many of that place, it being said he arrived there the year preceding the death of his late Majesty King William, and that he brought a great fortune from the Indies.*'

There was a moment of silence and then Joycey asked quietly. 'King William, when did he die then?'

Takk was grinning broadly. '1702'.

There was a long silence and somewhere above their heads one of the timbers of the roof creaked in the heat of the afternoon sun.

'Jesus Christ!' Joycey blurted out. 'Are you telling me what I think I'm hearing?'

Marik looked from one to the other, puzzled.

'I don't know, I'm not a mind reader.' Takk was still grinning.

'Are you saying that this Captain Hawkins was Captain Kidd?'

There was a barely perceptible nod. 'It seems to me the evidence is pretty conclusive. Hawkins – he adopted Sarah's name. Dundee, the Negro – also the name of one of Captain Kidd's African cabin boys. He arrives here in 1701, the same year Kidd was supposed to be executed; and then there's the great fortune from the Indies. It all fits. And of course,' she nodded, 'it fits with our theory. He was rescued by Sarah Hawkins, the woman who loved him. They collected the treasure from Wapping and disappeared to the depths of East Anglia.'

'But, why here. I mean Suffolk, it's not far from London! Why didn't they go the Caribbean or somewhere like that? Not here, surely? Wouldn't people here suspect…catch him?' Joycey's face was a mask of disbelief.

Takk shrugged. 'Why? As far as the authorities knew he was dead, and his corpse was hanging in chains by the River Thames at Tilbury. And remember, Henry Avery came back to England and they never caught him either. He simply 'disappeared.''

Marik was nodding, smiling to himself. Joycey was shaking his head, looking down at the tablet, overwhelmed by what seemed an inescapable conclusion. Then he began to laugh. 'So the old bastard got away with it in the end. You know, I really like that.'

'So it seems.' Takk rose, and Marik slid from the pew allowing her to step out into the aisle.

'Captain Kidd's treasure in Bungay…..Captain Kidd in Bungay', Joycey was chuckling gleefully. 'And do you know, there were times when I thought he had to be laughing at us, from the past. Now I know what he was laughing at. And it wasn't us!'

'Well I think our Captain Kidd had a sense of humour.' Takk had taken several paces back down the aisle and was beaming with pleasure. 'Remember what I said about how he disappeared for ten months before reappearing in the Caribbean?'

'Yeah.'

'About how he must have had time to sail from Madagascar into the Thames and then back across to the Caribbean.'

'Yeah.'

'Well, it would have required a very fast passage, and only a very good seaman and navigator could have achieved that.'

Joycey nodded. 'Yeah probably.'

'And you'd have thought a man would have wanted to make something of that?'

Joycey nodded. 'Yeah, why not. '

Takk beamed at both of them. 'Well then, look down!'

She pointed down, and at their feet lay a large red marble slab set flush into the floor, polished by the shoes of centuries. And clearly cut into it was an inscription.

'*Here Underneath this marble lyeth interned the body Of Capt. William Hawkins formerly Commander of the Good ship Merchant Quest from the East Indies who by his indefatigable industry made ye voyage from Surat and thence to London and Jamaica in ten months, the like not done by any since. In his returne he fought & beat a French pyrat & brought hys trade (to his never Dying fame) safe into the River Thames. He departed this life at Bungay the 25th June 1715 in the 69th year of his age, here also being intered ye body of Sarah his beloved wife. Rest* *here in hopes of a joyful Resurrection. Vivant in Aeturnum.'*

And at the top of the slab, neatly carved in an oval cartouche, was a skull and cross bones.

The Kidd Conspiracy – Background note.

The Kidd Conspiracy is a work of fiction, but the historical background is true. The career of Captain William Kidd is as represented by Takk in the story. Kidd was eventually hung at Execution Dock at Wapping. According to the records, the rope around his neck did break at the first attempt, though it succeeded on the second, and his body was subsequently coated in pitch or tar, and hung on the north bank of the Thames at Tilbury for several years.

All of the historical characters in the story were real people though I have taken one or two small liberties here and there. Kidd was related to a Mrs Hawkins in Wapping. He stayed with her during his visit to London in 1695 – 1696, and she does appear to have tried to help him during his imprisonment in Newgate. However, there is no evidence that she owned an alehouse nor that she disappeared.

Kidd's treasure has been the source of endless speculation. Kidd himself claimed that it was worth £100,000 in

1700. The current value of that is difficult to compute though if compared with earnings, it would equate to around £241 million pounds today. The value of some of the components of the treasure would vary, e.g. current price of gold and uncut gems, opium etc. Some have argued that Kidd vastly inflated the value of the treasure to increase his negotiating power with the Admiralty. However, since no complete manifest has been assembled it would be difficult to know for sure, a situation made more complicated because Kidd certainly gave away valuable pieces of the treasure as he made his way northwards from the Caribbean.

Whatever the true value of the treasure, the question of its whereabouts still remains and the mystery of what Kidd did with it has obsessed many people ever since. Countless hours have been spent by enthusiasts trying to work out where it is, and there are people hunting for it even today. Speculation about the location of Kidd's plunder features places stretching from the East Indies to the Caribbean to the eastern seaboard of the United States. Though, no-one, as far as I am aware, has suggested it could have been brought to London.

The fact is however, that Kidd's whereabouts between May 1698 and April 1699 are unaccounted for. He did eventually arrive in the West Indies with the *Quedah Merchant* though whether it still held the treasure is unknown. The ship was 'hidden' on the coast of Hispaniola (now the Dominican Republic) and was last seen ablaze and adrift by several unconnected witnesses. Amazingly, the wreck of the *Quedah Merchant* was discovered off the coast of Dominica in 2008 by the Indiana University's Academic Diving and Underwater Science Program, directed by Charles Beeker. At the time of writing it is still being assessed, though there is no suggestion that there might be treasure on board.

Hubert Palmer, the undiscriminating collector of pirate relics, was a real person, as were the people who feature in his part of the story. Anyone wanting to follow up this extraordinary tale should get hold of *Captain Kidd and his Skeleton Island* by Harold T Wilkins. (New York. 1937). This very eccentric and scarce book is worth hunting down in its own right.

Gavin Douglas's letter is fictional but the other original documents mentioned in the book all exist in either The National Archive or the British Library, in London. Cordelia Wainwright's book on Wapping is fictitious, though it and the author were suggested by real sources. The Tower Hamlets Local History Library and Archive is a real place, and its staff are as helpful as indicated in the book. The archives of the London Dock Company (and the other dock companies) are held at the Museum of London Docklands at canary Wharf.

The locations in this book are all real – with the obvious exception of the underground chamber. Wapping is much as described in the story, and the Captain Kidd pub makes a fine location for a pint on either a sunny afternoon, or a storm-wracked winter's evening.

The Shadwell Waterworks' conduits did exist at the time of the building of the London Dock, because that company launched a bid for compensation for the loss of them when the dock entrance was built. Furthermore, during the building of docks in the early 19th century, it was not unusual for unplanned drainage conduits to have to be inserted so that water seeping into the excavations could be drawn off by steam powered pumps.

For further reading, I would strongly recommend the book mentioned by Takk, *Captain Kidd and the War Against the Pirates* by Robert Ritchie (Harvard University Press. 1986). This is without doubt the best academic study so far of Kidd's career, and still loses none of the excitement and mystery of the tale. *Honour Among Thieves* by Jan Rogozinski is particularly good on Avery and the other Indian Ocean pirates. Richard Zack's *The Pirate Hunter – the True Story of Captain Kidd* (Review. 2002) is also a valuable study and a very lively read, revealing additional material. Barry Clifford's *Return to Treasure Island and the Search for Captain Kidd* (Perennial . 2003) recounts that investigator's attempt to explore the pirate base of Ile St Marie on Madagascar. Graham Harris's *Treasure and Intrigue: The Legacy of Captain Kidd* (Dundurn Press. 2002) focuses on the treasure and the hunt for it but not everyone will agree with some of his assertions. The story of Captain Henry Avery or Every is given in a good detail in E T Fox's *King of the Pirates: The Swashbuckling Life of Henry Every* (History Press. 2008). Anyone with a general interest in pirates is recommended to read David Cordingly's *Under the Black Flag: The Romance and Reality of Life Among the Pirates* (Random House. 2006) – though this has also been published with a different title. Finally, no-one writing about pirates would fail to recommend *A General History of the Pyrates* by Captain Charles Johnson. Originally published in 1724, it was attributed to Daniel Defoe for many years though is now generally recognised to be the work of a real sea captain – the enigmatic Charles Johnson. The book is still in print.

Finally any visitors to the Church of Holy Trinity in Bungay would earn my eternal gratitude if they would convey my apologies to the shade of Captain Thomas Stanton. They will realise why.

ABOUT THE AUTHOR

Tom Wareham is a historian and researcher, and former museum curator. He was awarded a PhD for his research into naval frigate commanders during the Napoleonic Wars, and is the author of *The Star Captains*, *Frigate Commander*, and *Frigate Commander: A Supplement*, all of which have been enthusiastically received. He originally began researching the Captain Kidd story for a museum exhibition and simply carried on. He lives in South East London.

Printed in Great Britain
by Amazon